THE DARK ANGEL

THE DARK ANGEL

A RUTH GALLOWAY MYSTERY

Elly Griffiths

MARINER BOOKS
HOUGHTON MIFFLIN HARCOURT
BOSTON • NEW YORK

For Andy

———

First Mariner Books edition 2019

hmhco.com

First published in Great Britain in 2018 by Quercus

Library of Congress Cataloging-in-Publication Data
Names: Griffiths, Elly, author.
Title: The dark angel / Elly Griffiths.
Description: First U.S. edition. | Boston ; New York :
Houghton Mifflin Harcourt, 2018. | Series: A Ruth Galloway Mystery ; 10
Identifiers: LCCN 2017057874 | ISBN 9780544750326 (hardback)
ISBN 9781328585202 (paperback)
Subjects: LCSH: Galloway, Ruth (Fictitious character) – Fiction. | Women
forensic anthropologists – Fiction. | BISAC: FICTION / Mystery & Detective
/ Women Sleuths. | FICTION / Mystery & Detective / General. |
GSAFD: Mystery fiction.
Classification: LCC PR6107.R534 D37 2018 | DDC 823/.92 – dc23
LC record available at https://lccn.loc.gov/2017057874

Printed in the United States of America
DOC 10 9 8 7 6 5 4 3 2
4500808417

Thou wast not born for death, immortal Bird!
No hungry generations tread thee down;
The voice I hear this passing night was heard
In ancient days by emperor and clown:
Perhaps the self-same song that found a path
Through the sad heart of Ruth, when, sick for home,
She stood in tears amid the alien corn;
The same that oft-times hath
Charm'd magic casements, opening on the foam
Of perilous seas, in faery lands forlorn.

— JOHN KEATS, "ODE TO A NIGHTINGALE"

AUTHOR'S NOTE

Ruth and other archaeologists in this book use the phrase 'before Common Era', or BCE. This refers to the time before the birth of Christ, previously depicted as BC. 'Common Era' describes the time after Christ's birth, or AD. Most universities and museums now use this terminology so I thought that Ruth would do the same.

PROLOGUE

'This grave has lain undisturbed for over two thousand years.'
Professor Angelo Morelli speaks directly to the camera. 'This
countryside has been the scene of invasion and battle from
the Neolithic times until the Second World War, when the
German troops fought Italian partisans in the Liri Valley. In
all that time, this body has lain under the earth. Now, we
are going to exhume it.'

He pauses and smiles into the lens, knowing that his
boyish charm – dark curls lifting slightly in the breeze – is
the real reason why so many viewers tune in to his show
'The Secrets of the Past' (*I Segreti del Passato*) every week. And
it is a magical moment. The whole production team seems
to hold its breath, even the birds are silent and the Italian
sky is high and blue and still. The camera swoops into the
trench in front of the professor, showing the layers, sharply
defined: topsoil, subsoil, bedrock. The site has been the
focus of intense archaeological attention for weeks, but the
skeleton at the bottom of the trench is still covered with
a fine layer of earth because Angelo Morelli is determined

that the final moment of excavation should be shown live on television. He is therefore extremely irritated to hear the shrill tones of a mobile phone shattering the tense silence.

'Someone answer that,' he snaps.

The ringing continues. Then, the production assistant says, timidly, 'I think it's your phone, Professore.'

Embarrassed, Angelo digs in his pocket for his iPhone. He is too vain to wear his glasses on television so he holds it at arm's length. Then he brings it closer. The team watch as he stares, rubs his eyes and stares again. The word on the screen is 'Toni', the name archaeologists have given to the skeleton (presumed, rather typically, to be a man) because he was found on Saint Anthony's day. The phone stops ringing and, in a daze, Angelo swipes the notification to return the call. And, to his amazement, he hears a phone ringing beneath his feet. Seizing a trowel, Angelo jumps into the trench and starts to scrape away soil. The skeleton emerges, bones embedded in the earth, lying face down. The ringing continues. Someone says, 'It's under the earth.' And there it is. Next to the skeletal hand, an iPhone 6. Slowly, almost fearfully, Angelo picks it up. 'Professor Morelli', reads the incoming call alert on the screen.

He cancels the call, then his phone beeps loudly. It's a text message – from Toni.

'Surprise!' it says.

1

The confetti is still blowing in the street. Ruth watches as Clough and Cassandra get into the white Rolls-Royce – Cassandra laughing as she shakes the pink and yellow hearts from her hair – and drive away. They're an unlikely pair, no-nonsense policeman DS Dave Clough and beautiful actress and daughter of local aristocrats Cassandra Blackstock – but they met in the course of work and fell in love. And to prove it, they're getting married. Bully for them, thinks Ruth, although that sounds bitter even to her own ears.

Mr and Mrs Blackstock-Clough are on their way to a reception at Blackstock Hall. Ruth should be on her way there too – next to her, Kate is positively hopping with excitement and anticipation – but all she wants is to get back to her little house on the salt marsh, shut her door and sleep for a week. But Cathbad and Judy are approaching, with Michael and Miranda skipping between them, like an advertisement for family values. Ruth plasters on a cheerful, I-love-weddings smile.

'Have you got your car?' says Judy. 'If not, there's space in ours.'

'It's OK,' says Ruth. 'I've got my car.' There's no way she's going to risk being stuck at Blackstock Hall, a crumbling stately home in the middle of the Norfolk marshes, without her own transport. 'I'll see you there,' she says, keeping on the smile. Her cheeks are hurting now.

The car park is full so she has to wait before she can get her car out. As she stands, holding Kate by the hand, Nelson drives past in his Mercedes, Michelle at his side. Nelson is frowning at the other cars and doesn't seem to notice her, but Michelle smiles and waves. Ruth waves back. With any luck, Michelle won't want to stay at the reception long. She is pregnant, after all.

Within a remarkably short time, most of the guests have left. Ruth's red Renault and a sporty black jeep affair are almost the only cars left.

'Hurry up,' says Kate. 'We might miss the cake. Uncle Dave is going to cut it with a sword.' Uncle Dave is what Kate calls Clough, who is quite a favourite with her. Ruth dreads to think what might happen if Uncle Dave gets his hands on a ceremonial sword.

'They won't cut the cake for ages yet,' she says. 'There'll be other food first.'

'Will there be prawns?' asks Kate suspiciously.

Almost certainly, thinks Ruth. She is sure that Cassandra will have put together a sophisticated menu, in defiance of Clough's often-stated preference for pie and chips. But she knows that Kate dislikes prawns 'because they have whiskers'.

'The food will be lovely,' she says. 'Let's go now.'

As Kate climbs into her car seat, a voice behind them says, 'Ruth.'

Ruth turns. It's Tim Heathfield, the detective sergeant who used to be on Nelson's team but has now moved back to Essex. Ruth has always liked Tim, who is both intelligent and sensitive, but she wants to talk to him about as much as Kate wants to eat a prawn vol-au-vent. Because she knows the reason Tim left Norfolk. Tim was in love with Michelle, and what with Ruth being in love with Nelson, it all makes things rather tricky.

She forces herself to turn and smile. 'Hello, Tim. How are you?'

'I'm fine,' he says. 'How are you? Kate's growing up fast.'

'I'm six,' says Kate from the car, determined not to be left out of the conversation.

'Are you going to the reception?' says Ruth. The jeep must belong to Tim, she thinks. It's like him, handsome in an understated way and tougher than it looks.

'No,' says Tim. 'I promised Cloughie that I'd come to the wedding but I couldn't really face the reception. Blackstock Hall doesn't hold the best memories for me.'

Ruth can understand that. Tim once shot a man at Blackstock Hall, saving Nelson's life and probably Ruth's as well. She can see why he wouldn't want to go back there. She's not exactly looking forward to it herself.

'I'm staying in King's Lynn overnight,' Tim is saying.

'And I wondered if we might be able to meet up for coffee tomorrow. I'd like to ask your advice about something.'

Ruth wonders how long it takes to emigrate. There is nothing she wants less than to have a cosy chat with Tim.

'That would be great,' she says. 'Why don't you come to the house? It might be difficult to get a babysitter. Say eleven o'clock?'

The reception is in full swing by the time Ruth arrives at Blackstock Hall. The austere grey house has been transformed into a glittery bower full of fairy lights and flowers. There is a marquee on the lawn and a string quartet playing in the entrance hall. Ruth compliments Sally, Cassandra's mother, on the décor.

'Oh, it was all Cassie's idea,' says Sally, in her vague way. 'But we're planning to open the hall as a wedding venue, so if you know anyone who's getting married . . .'

But Ruth's friends are all mired in domesticity or getting divorced. Only her gay friends are still getting married. She smiles and moves on into the marquee where she sees tables laid with a multitude of glass and cutlery, all signs that a long and formal meal is expected. This means hours of eating and drinking and speeches and little chance of a quick getaway. At least she is at a table with Cathbad and Judy and their kids, miles from Nelson. She sees place cards for Tanya, another DS on Nelson's team, and her partner, Petra, too. Tanya will not be pleased to be seated at a table full of children.

Kate is delighted to be next to Michael, who is younger than her and perfect for indoctrination. She immediately regales him with a description of prawns. 'They have little black eyes and long, long whiskers.'

Michael's face crumbles. 'I don't want . . .'

'It's all right, Michael,' says Cathbad. 'There won't be prawns. I've looked at the menu. Anyway, we've both got the vegetarian option.'

Ruth looks at the menu in the middle of the table and feels slightly sick. All those courses. When will she be able to escape? She can't even drink because she's driving. She takes a sip of her water and discovers that it's elderflower, musty and slightly perfumed. She puts her glass down.

'Are you all right?' asks Cathbad, who is sitting next to her.

Ruth doesn't want to have a heart-to-heart with Cathbad because there's a danger that she will actually tell him what's in her heart. Luckily, at that moment, Cassandra and Clough come into the tent, to a chorus of 'Congratulations' from the band and the cheers of the guests.

Kate stands on her chair and Ruth doesn't have the energy to tell her not to.

'Cassie looks like a fairy princess,' she tells Ruth.

'She really does,' says Ruth. She has failed to pass on her republican principles to her daughter.

It's past nine by the time Ruth finally drives away across the marshes. It's still light, the sky all soft pinks and blues, the sea an azure line against the horizon. Kate is quiet in the back and Ruth thinks that she'll be asleep before long.

It hadn't been too bad really. Cassandra's father made a heartfelt, though mercifully brief, speech and Clough had surprised them all with a witty and emotional tribute to his bride. For Ruth, the best – and worst – moment had been when he had thanked, 'the boss, the one and only DCI Nelson.' Nelson had raised his hand, looking embarrassed, but all the police officers in the room had cheered lustily. Ruth thinks that Nelson is in danger of becoming popular, partly because he is known to be at loggerheads with *his* boss, Superintendent Jo Archer. Super Jo herself, stunning in a bright red dress, had watched serenely from the table she shared with sundry Blackstock relatives. When Ruth left the marquee she had been dancing rather suggestively with cousin Roger.

At least Nelson and Michelle hadn't danced together. After Clough and Cassandra had circled romantically to Ed Sheeran's 'Thinking Out Loud', various other couples had taken the floor, including Cathbad and Judy and Tanya and Petra. Ed sang about people finding love in mysterious ways and Ruth watched as Nelson leant forward and whispered something to Michelle. She smiled and shook her head. Ruth had turned away, not wanting to be caught staring at them.

Cathbad was a surprisingly good dancer and also did turns with all the children. He asked Ruth, too, but didn't object when she said no, thank you. Ruth was rather touched that Clough also came over to ask for a dance. 'Thanks, Dave,' she said, 'but I'm quite happy watching. Go and dance with your wife.'

Clough looked over to where Cassandra was dancing with PC 'Rocky' Taylor, holding her long skirt out of the reach of his size twelves. Sally was holding Clough and Cassandra's baby son, Spencer, who stretched out his arms to his mother as she passed.

'I've got a wife,' he said. 'How about that?'

'Congratulations,' said Ruth. 'You're a lucky man. And she's a lucky woman, of course.'

She has never wanted to be a wife. Just as well really.

They are home now. Kate has fallen asleep and is very grumpy at being woken. 'Look,' says Ruth cajolingly, 'there's Flint waiting for us.' Flint, their ginger cat, is sitting in the window, looking at them accusingly, but his spell is strong enough to get Kate out of the car and into the house. Inside, the answerphone is flashing. For a moment, Ruth thinks it is her mother, whose barbed messages have punctuated all her adult life. But her mother died six weeks ago. Ruth presses play. A deep, sexily accented voice fills the room.

'Hello Ruth. This is Angelo Morelli . . .'

2

Angelo Morelli. Ruth remembers a conference twelve years ago. A hotel in Rome looking out on Trastevere: terracotta rooftops, Vespas roaring over the cobbles, a floodlit fountain. Ruth had just split up with her live-in boyfriend, Peter, and had been giddy with freedom and with the miracle of having wrested this overseas trip from under Phil's nose. Angelo was an archaeologist from Rome University, an expert on the Romans. He had studied in America, she remembered, and spoke perfect English, though with that heartbreakingly sexy accent. And one evening, after a seminar on the Etruscans, the fountains and the frescoes had got too much for them and they'd ended up in bed. It had only been one night and Ruth remembered that, in the morning, she hadn't even felt embarrassed. They'd had a civilised breakfast in the Piazza de Santa Maria and gone on to a lecture on dating ceramics. She didn't even know if Angelo had a girlfriend or not. He hadn't been married, though. She'd checked that much. She had always vowed never to sleep with a married man, until she met Nelson and all the rules changed. She and Angelo had kept in touch for a while – those were the days of postcards and letters – but Ruth hasn't heard from him in eight years. And now there's a message from him on the phone.

'Mum.' Kate is holding a long-suffering Flint in her arms. 'Can I take Flint to bed with me?

'You can take him upstairs,' says Ruth, 'but he won't stay.'

After falling asleep in the car, Kate is annoyingly wakeful. She puts Flint on her bed, he gets off immediately and Kate chases him around the room until he takes refuge on top of her wardrobe. She then demands a Josie Smith story. All this time Ruth is longing to get downstairs, have a glass of wine and listen to Angelo's message again.

Eventually, Kate lets her go and snuggles down with her cuddly chimpanzee and a story tape. Ruth pours herself a glass of red so quickly that it spills on the floor, then goes into the sitting room and presses 'play messages'.

'Hello, Ruth. This is Angelo Morelli. Do you remember me? So long since I've seen you and you've become famous. I have a proposition for you. Call me.' And he leaves a number. Ruth stays in the dark, drinking her wine and thinking about Italy.

Tim arrives promptly at eleven the next day. Ruth is glad that she asked him to come to the cottage: it's a beautiful morning, the tide is out and the salt marsh is a magical place of purple sea lavender interspersed with glittering streams and the occasional limpid, blue pool. Ruth and Tim sit on the bench in the front garden, watching Kate construct a 'summer house' for Flint out of old Amazon boxes.

'He's upwardly mobile,' says Tim, 'now that he's got a second home. It'll be surfing holidays in Cornwall next.'

'Our next-door neighbours are weekenders,' says Ruth. 'This is their summer house. I think that's where Kate got it from – they babysit sometimes. And I don't think Flint has any intention of moving into his new home.'

Flint is watching Kate from his vantage point on the roof, and when she tries to tempt him down he simply moves further up.

'He's stuck, Mum,' says Kate.

'No, he isn't,' says Ruth. 'Cats never get stuck.'

'She's growing up fast,' says Tim.

'Yes. It doesn't seem possible that she'll be going into year two in September.'

They are silent for a few minutes, drinking their coffee. It all seems very relaxed and friendly – the sunshine, the child playing at their feet – but Ruth feels tense and unsettled. She feels sure that Tim hasn't come round to discuss Kate's growth spurt. And, eventually, Tim speaks, looking out towards the marshes and avoiding eye contact.

'Have you heard that Michelle's pregnant?'

'Yes,' says Ruth.

'The thing is,' says Tim, and falls silent again.

Ruth bears it as long as she can, then prompts, 'The thing is?'

'The thing is, Ruth,' says Tim, speaking in a rush now, 'there's a chance that the baby could be mine. I don't know who else to tell. I thought you might understand because . . .'

There's another silence. Ruth takes a gulp of coffee but her mouth remains dry.

'Because Michelle told you about Nelson and me,' she says.

'Yes,' says Tim. 'I'm sorry, Ruth, but I feel like I'm going mad here. There's no one I can talk to about this.'

'Have you talked to Michelle?'

'Yes. But she says that she wants to give their marriage another go. Things haven't been good since Kate ... well, since Kate was born, and she says this is their last chance.'

Ruth has a flashback to the days when they first found the henge on the beach. When the authorities had wanted to remove the timbers, local druids (led by Cathbad) had clung desperately to the wooden posts as the sea surged around them. Michelle is clinging just as desperately to her marriage. Ruth respects her for it.

'I thought your affair with Michelle was over,' she says.

'It was,' says Tim. 'It was over before it began, really. I moved away so that we wouldn't be tempted any more. Then, I don't know, we got in contact again. Just emails and WhatsApp messages at first. But then, in May, I came to Norwich and we met at a hotel and ...'

What had Ruth been doing in May? Teaching at the university, trying to juggle work and motherhood, trying not to think about Nelson. Then, in June, she had been drawn into one of Nelson's cases as he hunted a killer in the tunnels below Norwich. In June, Ruth's mother had died. And, in June, Ruth and Nelson had rekindled their affair, just once, in the bedroom a few metres from where she and Tim are sitting.

When she speaks, it sounds as if her voice is coming from a long way away. 'And you think the baby might be yours?'

'Well, the dates add up but, then again, she was sleeping with Nelson too. She never made any secret about that.'

Ruth has, over the years, tried to convince herself that Nelson and Michelle don't have sex any more. But, deep down, she has always known that this isn't true. Something keeps that marriage together, something besides being the parents of grown-up children, because, apart from that, they seem to have little in common. She rather fears that this something is intense physical attraction.

'What are you going to do now?'

'What can I do except wait? After all, I'll know pretty quickly if the baby is mine.'

Ruth looks at Tim, who often used to describe himself as the only black policeman in Norfolk. While this isn't quite true, there's no doubt that Tim's ethnicity will make a DNA test unnecessary. What must Michelle be thinking now? Ruth remembers her looking rather pale and wan when she saw her in July, but she'd put it down to morning sickness. What must it feel like to have this uncertainty hanging over her for nine months? And Nelson? Does he suspect? He's suspicious by nature – he's a policeman, after all – and it is unlikely that his thoughts haven't strayed towards Tim. Then again, Nelson has a pretty strong belief in his own potency. He has fathered three children and has probably never doubted the paternity of this fourth baby.

'I've always wanted children,' Tim is saying. 'People talk about women feeling broody but never about men.'

Time to bring the conversation to an end if Tim's going to start one of those 'men have feelings too' speeches. Ruth stands up. 'Sorry, Tim, but I have to get going soon. We're meeting some friends for lunch.'

Kate looks up from her boxes. 'Are we?' she says in surprise. 'Can we go to Pizza Express?'

Nelson has never really got the hang of Sundays. When he was a child, it was a day dominated by church. His mother, Maureen, was (and is) a devout Catholic, and Nelson passed through all the religious staging posts – first holy communion, altar boy, confirmation – without ever really asking himself whether he believed in the holy Catholic church, the forgiveness of sins, the communion of the saints and life everlasting amen. He doesn't go to Mass now but he thinks that he probably does believe in God, if only because it would be just like Maureen to be right all along. But Sunday remains a day when you feel that you should be doing something special, something *else*. In Nelson's twenties and thirties, Sunday football had filled the gap, but he thinks he's too old now and doesn't want to end up with dodgy knees like all his footballing contemporaries. Michelle and the girls have always seen the day as a chance to worship their own god, that of conspicuous consumption, but Nelson hates shopping and visits to places like garden centres bore him rigid. Michelle always makes time to cook the traditional Sunday roast, although usually for supper rather than lunch. Nelson usually ends up walking the dog, doing some vaguely penitential work in the garden, eating a huge meal and falling asleep in front of the TV. He supposes that that's honouring the Sabbath, in its way.

Today, Michelle says she feels tired after the wedding and wants to stay in bed. Not that they had stayed late at the reception. Nelson had left as soon as he decently could, but not before he'd seen Ruth and Katie making their way out of the marquee, Katie hanging back but Ruth looking as if it was only politeness that stopped her from running. He'd wanted to go after them, to ask if they were all right, but he knew that he couldn't. He'd been forced to stay for another hour, watching his junior officers make fools of themselves on the dance floor. He'd asked Michelle if she wanted to dance but she'd said no. This pregnancy is more draining than the others – not surprising, as she's twenty years older. Laura, their eldest daughter, is twenty-four. She studied marine biology at Plymouth (a mystery to Nelson) and then seemed to have an extended holiday, working as a travel rep in Ibiza. To her parents' relief, Laura has now decided to train as a teacher. She is living at home before starting a PGCE at the University of East Anglia in September. Rebecca is twenty-two. She did media studies at the University of Brighton and still lives there. Katie is six and, although Michelle knows that she is his daughter, Laura and Rebecca do not. For this reason, although Michelle very generously allows him to have contact with Katie, she cannot really be part of the family. Nelson knows that this state of affairs can't continue for ever.

Nelson decides to take Bruno out for a long walk. The dog, a young German Shepherd, needs a lot of exercise and neither Laura nor Michelle are very keen on this aspect of dog ownership. But Nelson enjoys it. He thinks of Bruno as *his* dog and he can tell that the animal feels the same way. 'German Shepherds are one man dogs,' the famous police-dog handler Jan Adams once told him, 'one person dogs anyway.' It's nice to know that he's popular with someone anyway.

He drives to Sandringham, the queen's country house, which is set in miles of woodland and heath, open to everyone. Nelson doesn't have strong views about the monarchy: he's glad they're there, he supposes (he had been quite shocked to find that Ruth was an anti-monarchist), but he can't be bothered with all the stuff in the papers about the little princes and princesses and what some duchess was wearing when she opened a factory. But he does like walking on the estate. It's not as lonely as the sea or the salt marsh – at least this is a place where people live, albeit very grand people who only helicopter in once or twice a year. There are signs of human habitation – notices, fences and so on – but, if you come early enough, you can have the place to yourself. People are always going on about the bluebells and rhododendrons but, to Nelson, flowers are just flowers. It's the peace he likes and the chance to think, the only sounds his feet on the forest path and Bruno scuffling madly in the undergrowth.

The trouble is, he doesn't want to think today. Because, if he starts thinking, he will go back to the expression that he saw on Tim's face yesterday. He knows that Tim was in love with Michelle and that they had an affair which included everything except sex. Michelle told him this and he believed her. But yesterday there was just something in the look on Tim's face, something both troubled and slightly smug, that is proving impossible to forget, no matter how many miles he walks. Could Michelle and Tim have consummated their relationship? Could the baby be Tim's? Michelle has been behaving very oddly since the announcement: distant and short-tempered, very unlike the serene nesting of her earlier pregnancies. Is this just because she's older now and this baby is such a shock? He could ask her straight out, he supposes, but that might lead them onto dangerous ground. Nelson has an illegitimate child and Michelle has, ostensibly, forgiven him. Nelson owes Michelle, that much is certain. But if Michelle is in love with Tim, does that leave Nelson free to be with Ruth? Is this what he wants? Is this what she wants?

That's the trouble with questions, he thinks, throwing a stick for Bruno and watching him jump joyfully into the air to catch it. Questions need answers and he hasn't got any. He strides through the queen's trees, trying not to think.

Ruth ends up taking Kate to Pizza Express in King's Lynn after all. Kate enjoys herself hugely and doesn't ask when the mythical friends are turning up. Afterwards, they walk by the quay and eat ice creams. Although it's still August, there's almost an autumnal feeling in the air, thinks Ruth. The sun is warm, but when they walked through the park earlier there were leaves on the ground, and the shops are full of cheerful 'Back to School' posters. Ruth always slightly dreads giving Kate back to the alien world of school, but there is no doubt that Kate is looking forward to it. She has already drawn up a shortlist of people she wants to sit next to her.

'Ruth!' Someone is walking towards her. Someone effortlessly elegant in a stripy top and narrow blue trousers, burnished hair gleaming. Someone pulling a disgruntled-looking toddler by the hand.

'Shona! What are you doing here?'

Shona sits on the bench next to her, and Louis, her four-year-old, makes a beeline for Kate, who ignores him. 'I'm escaping from Phil for a bit,' says Shona. 'He's working on spreadsheets for the new term.'

Phil is Ruth's boss at the university, where she's a lecturer. She has no doubt that on the spreadsheets she will be taking all her tutorials at 8 a.m.

'I was just thinking that summer is nearly over.'

'No, it's not,' says Shona. 'It's mid-August. It was the Feast of the Assumption yesterday.'

Shona, like Nelson, was brought up a Catholic and always remembers the saints' days. Her interest is more cultural than religious these days though. Shona teaches English at the University of North Norfolk and specialises in T. S. Eliot.

'It was Clough's wedding too.'

'So it was! How did it go? I bet Cassandra looked lovely.'

Shona is always generous about other women's looks, perhaps because she is so beautiful herself.

'She did,' says Ruth. 'It was OK, as weddings go.'

'You sound a bit down.'

'I'm all right,' says Ruth. 'The wedding was a bit difficult, you know . . .'

She doesn't have to say more. Shona knows about Nelson and Ruth and, although fascinated by the situation, usually manages not to talk about it.

'You need a holiday,' she says now.

'That would be lovely,' says Ruth. 'Do you remember when we went to Florence and Siena? It's been over ten years since I went abroad.'

'I'd love to go again,' says Shona. 'Not with Phil though. He keeps moaning about the exchange rate. Glad I didn't know him when Italy had the lira and everything was in millions.'

Ruth and Kate are just settling down to watch a Disney film when the phone rings. Somehow she's not surprised when a voice says, 'Hello, Ruth. It's Angelo.'

'Angelo. Hi.'

'Long time no see. That's what they say in England, yes?'

'Yes,' says Ruth, thinking that Angelo's English is as good as ever, though still with that gorgeously lilting accent.

'How are you, Ruth? I see you're still working at North Norfolk.'

'Yes,' says Ruth, wishing that this was North Norfolk College, Cambridge. Still, it's flattering that Angelo has looked her up. 'What about you?' she says. 'Still in Rome?'

'Yes, I'm head of department now. And . . .' He gives a self-deprecating laugh. 'I have my own TV show.'

'Really?'

'Yes, it's called *I Segreti del Passato*. It's about archaeology. These programmes are very popular in Italy.'

'It's the same here. There's a programme called *Time Team* that always seems to be on television.'

'And you, Ruth. You've been on television. You're a media star.'

Ruth has been on television twice. Once in a series called *Women Who Kill* and once on a programme about American air-bases in Norfolk. She doesn't look back on either experience with great fondness, not least because the camera seemed to add about two stone. She wonders where Angelo got this information. She hopes there aren't any clips on YouTube.

'And I've read your book,' says Angelo, 'about the excavations in Lancashire.' He seems to give this last word ten syllables.

This is better. She's proud of the book.

'The thing is, Ruth,' says Angelo, 'I'm digging in the Liri Valley, not far from Rome, and we've found some bones. We think they're Roman but we've found some . . . what is the word? Anomalies.'

'What sort of anomalies?'

There's a pause. 'The thing is,' says Angelo again, 'I'd like you to see them for yourself.'

'You could send me some photographs,' says Ruth.

'Is there any chance you could come to Italy?' says Angelo. 'Just for a few days? I've got an apartment you can use. It's in a remote hilltop village, a really beautiful part of the country. You could have a holiday there.'

3

'Italy?' says Ruth's father, Arthur, standing among the graves as if turned to stone. 'Why would you want to go to Italy?'

It's a genuine question and Ruth considers and rejects a variety of answers. Because Italy is beautiful, because it has a wealth of history and culture, because I haven't had a foreign holiday in ten years, because my married lover's wife is expecting a baby. Instead she says, 'It's a real opportunity for me, professionally. This archaeologist, Angelo Morelli, is very well known. He presents a TV programme in Italy. And he wants my advice on some bones he has discovered. I met him years ago at a conference and he's followed my career. He's read my book.'

This mollifies her father, as she had known it would. Though both her parents officially took the position that being a wife and mother was the highest role to which a woman could aspire, they were both very proud of her career. When Ruth had her first book published, her mother had actually *told* her she was proud, an almost unprecedented

occurrence. Ruth knows that her father wouldn't understand going to Italy for pleasure, but he can accept it as a
work trip. And that's what it is, she tells herself. In a way.

'What would your mother say?' says Arthur, as if he would
really like to know. As he speaks, he turns to the tombstone,
white and stark among the older graves, like a false tooth
in a mouth full of decaying molars.

Jean Galloway
Beloved wife and mother
At rest with the angels
1938–2015

There is a space underneath for Arthur's name. He'd
explained this quite matter-of-factly to Ruth as they walked
from his south London house to Eltham Cemetery.

'I'm going to be buried with her,' he'd said, 'so I've asked
them to leave some space on the stone.'

Kate, who had been skipping alongside them, said, 'Will
your body go on top of Grandma's?'

'Yes,' said Arthur, 'they've left space for my coffin.'

Husbands and wives were often buried together in Roman
times, Ruth thinks now. She remembers two skeletons excavated inside the walls of Modena. The tomb was believed
to date from the fifth century, but it was the skeletons
who had attracted interest because they had been buried
together holding hands. The woman is looking at the man,
whose head is turned away, but archaeologists believe
that his skull rolled after death. Originally the two bodies

may have been placed so that they were looking into each other's eyes.

Ruth looks again at her mother's grave. The stone was put up only recently and this is the first time that she has seen it. There's a faint whiff of censure that it has taken her so long. Her brother, Simon, and his family came as soon as the stone was erected. They brought a lovely bouquet, according to Arthur. Ruth looks at the remains of Simon's flowers lying on the grass in their cellophane wrapping, and feels that her own offering is distinctly inadequate. She brought sunflowers because these were Jean's favourite flowers (and, as such, figured prominently in her interior decorating schemes). Ruth and Kate carried one flower each and they placed them next to the white stone.

'Nice,' Arthur had said. 'Cheerful. Shall we say a prayer?'

He's always making suggestions like that, although he must know that Ruth hasn't prayed aloud since losing her faith in her teens.

'Go ahead,' she'd said, hearing herself sounding like a sulky fifteen-year-old.

'Father God,' Arthur began briskly, 'we pray that your servant Jean is this day with you in paradise. We ask you to look down on her loved ones, on Ruth and Katie, on Simon, Cathy, George and Jack. We ask you to comfort us in our sorrow. In Jesus' name.'

'Amen,' said Kate unexpectedly.

'Amen,' muttered Ruth.

Arthur had fussed over the grave, tidying the flowers,

giving the granite a polish with his handkerchief. It was then that Ruth had dropped the bombshell about Italy.

'When are you going?' asks Arthur now, turning away from the gravestone and back to Ruth.

'Wednesday,' says Ruth.

Her father is aghast. 'But that's the day after tomorrow.'

'I know,' says Ruth, who has had the same panicky thought all day. 'But there's not much planning to do. I've already bought the plane tickets online.'

'Where will you stay?' says Arthur.

'Dr Morelli is lending us an apartment,' says Ruth. 'It's in a little town called Castello degli Angeli, about an hour away from Rome. It's a very beautiful area, apparently.'

'What will Katie do when you're busy with these bones?' says Arthur.

Ruth sighs, and not just because her father seems to have picked up Nelson's annoying habit of always adding an '—ie' onto Kate's name.

'My friend Shona is coming with us,' she says. 'You remember Shona? She's got a little boy called Louis. He'll be company for Kate.'

'I know Shona.' Arthur brightens a little. He likes Shona despite the fact that she, like Ruth, is what he would call 'an unmarried mother'. But at least Shona lives with her child's father and besides, like most men, Arthur is prepared to make allowances because Shona is so pretty. Also, she sent a lavish wreath to Jean's funeral.

'I hate Louis,' says Kate, who is walking carefully between the gravestones.

'No, you don't,' says Ruth. 'You liked him when we saw him in Lynn that day.' She has been afraid of this. Louis is two years younger than Kate and sometimes it seems a lot more than that. When they were toddlers he often used to hit Kate, so much so that Ruth stopped arranging play dates for a while. Louis does seem to have improved since starting school though, and he actually admires Kate greatly. Ruth hopes that this will make up for his shortcomings as a playfellow.

'I wish Tasha was coming,' says Kate. 'Or Holly.'

'Come on, Kate,' says Ruth, with false brightness. 'Let's see if we can find the pilot.'

When she was younger she often used to walk in Eltham Cemetery. It's not grand and gothic like Highgate, or quirky, like Ruth's favourite urban cemetery in Hammersmith, where she used to eat her sandwiches while doing a holiday job at the Apollo. Eltham is more of a sober, utilitarian space, with rows and rows of uniformly shaped stones and a brown-brick chapel at the end. But it has its own charm, picturesquely overgrown in places and, at the end of a row of ivy-covered graves, there's a half-size statue of a pilot, a monument to an airman killed in 1938. Ruth used to visit the statue as a teenager and invent sentimental stories about the dead hero. She would pick daisies and put them at his feet, and once, with her school friend Alison, she had drunk half a bottle of Blue Nun and attempted to commune with his spirit. She realises now that the airman died in the year that her mother was born.

After several wrong turns, they find the right address. The pilot is still there, a little more lichen on his uniform now, his features softer and more weathered. Ruth is ridiculously pleased to have found him again.

'Why's he so small?' asks Kate.

'Maybe they couldn't afford a bigger statue,' says Arthur. He's not keen on images of the dead, Ruth knows. He thinks they're sinister or – worse – Catholic.

'Why's he wearing those clothes?' says Kate.

'It's his uniform,' says Ruth. 'What he wore to fly planes.'

'How did he die?'

'An accident, I expect. Shall we pick some daisies for him?'

'All right,' says Kate, obviously humouring her mother. They pick the flowers and place them at the pilot's booted feet. Arthur sits on a nearby bench, watching them. He gets tired more easily these days, Ruth has noticed, and often has a little nap after lunch. Is he all right, living on his own? She pushes the thought away. Simon and Cathy live nearby and Arthur has his church and all his friends there. He's just tired after the walk and the emotion of the grave.

Kate approaches her grandfather now. 'Shall we pick some daisies for Grandma?' she says.

'No, love, she's fine. She's got her beautiful sunflowers.'

Ruth thinks her father sounds sad, but he takes Kate's hand and as they walk back through the serried ranks of the dead he recites a comic poem about a boy being eaten by a lion. It's a rather ghoulish choice, but 'The Lion and Albert' is always a sign that Arthur is in a good mood.

*

They stay the night at Ruth's childhood home. It still feels wrong to be in the house without her mother. Arthur doesn't fill it; he spends most of his time in the kitchen and he's even moved a small television in there. The rest of the house reverberates with the loss of Jean. She should be there, hoovering noisily, commenting on the neighbours' behaviour, laying the dining-room table even if there were only two of them eating, hanging out her washing in the narrow garden (she regarded tumble dryers as sinful). But Ruth finds that she doesn't mind it so much if Kate is with her, sleeping on a camp bed pushed close to Ruth's old single bed. She cooks Arthur the sort of supper he likes, eggs and bacon, and they watch a DVD thoughtfully supplied by Simon. It's a film about spies and explosions and stunts involving travelling on the roofs of trains and the undercarriages of planes. Ruth finds it rather tedious, and Kate covers her ears when the shooting gets too loud, but Arthur enjoys it hugely. He's always liked James Bond, and action films in general. An odd choice for a quiet, deeply religious man. Perhaps there's a secret agent in him, longing to be let out.

The next morning they drive back to Norfolk, Ruth's head buzzing with all that still needs to be done:

Check that Bob can still look after Flint.
Packing. Swimming costumes? Does Kate's still fit? Digging clothes. Sun hat?
Book a taxi to Shona's for Wednesday morning. Phil has kindly offered to drive them to Heathrow, but she

doesn't want to push her luck by asking him to drive all the way out here to collect them.

Check that she's got enough sun protection cream, Calpol and mosquito repellent. Oh, and plasters. What else does the conscientious mother need? Antiseptic cream? Nit comb? Gin?

It's a relief to be back in Norfolk. London had been overcast but it's a beautiful afternoon on the salt marsh, warm with a gentle, salty breeze. Ruth and Kate go to call on their neighbour Bob, an Indigenous Australian who teaches poetry at the University of East Anglia. He's a slow-moving, reassuring sort of man and Flint likes him as much as he likes anyone who isn't Ruth. Bob offers Ruth herbal tea and they sit in the garden drinking it while Kate plays with a set of wooden tribal figures.

'I was wondering if you would look after Flint for a bit while we're in Italy,' says Ruth. 'He hates going to the cattery.'

'I'll be happy to look after the little fella,' says Bob. 'Are you going away for long?'

'Two weeks,' says Ruth. It still doesn't seem possible. When Angelo had rung on Sunday night, it had been the words 'you could have a holiday' that had swung it. She needed a holiday, she decided. She needed to get away from Norfolk, get some distance and put things in perspective: Michelle's pregnancy, her mother dying, her own recently revived relationship with Nelson. It will all seem different in a different country, she told herself. The fact that the trip came with accompanying archaeology was a bonus. And she'd like to see Angelo again. He was fun, she remembers, although he had been serious about his archaeology. And now, it seems, he's rather famous. He'd sent her some clips from his show, *I Segreti del Passato*, with helpful English subtitles. It's a standard documentary, really. Every week Angelo explores a different archaeological site, strolling through ruins, chatting with experts and looking at relics under microscopes in space-age glass-walled laboratories. There's usually some sort of fake suspense. Will they excavate this skeleton before the self-imposed deadline? Will isotope analysis show that the Iron Age bodies were native to the area? Did the child in the well die naturally or were they some sort of sacrifice? For Ruth's taste, the programme makers concentrate rather too much on Angelo's aquiline profile as he strides along the Appian Way or delves into Etruscan tombs, but there's no doubt that it's effective television. She looks forward to being involved, as long as she doesn't have to appear on camera.

She tries not to dwell too much on the night in Trastevere with the Vespas roaring outside. When she has thought about Angelo over the years it's been with a quiet satisfaction that, for once, she had behaved like a sophisticated, modern woman. She had had a one-night stand and there had been no drama, no recriminations, just a satisfying professional friendship. All the same, she has a faint hope that spending some time with an attractive, single man might take her mind off Nelson. And Angelo is still single. She has checked.

In June, Ruth had another one-night stand, if anything about her relationship with Nelson can be described in such a frivolous way. They had slept together and this time the whole thing had been fraught with wonderful, terrible emotions. Ruth had even thought that Nelson might leave Michelle and move in with her and Kate. But then Michelle announced that she was pregnant and everything changed. For a while, Ruth had half-dreaded, half-hoped that she would be pregnant too. But miracles like Kate don't happen twice. Ruth's period had come and with it a sense of acceptance. Nelson isn't going to leave Michelle. Ruth is left with Kate, Flint and her career. Not a bad trinity, all things considered.

She must concentrate on the bones. After all, that's why Angelo has invited her to Italy. There's obviously some mystery there. Why couldn't Angelo explain over the phone? Ruth hopes she will be able to offer enough insight to justify her air fare. But Angelo had been insistent that only her expertise would do. 'I need a real bones expert,' he had said. 'Someone to raise the profile of the project. I need you, Ruth.' And Ruth, battered by the storms of the last few weeks, takes comfort from the thought that there is still something she is good at.

Back at the cottage, she explains to Flint that Bob will be looking after him. Flint closes his eyes at her. In the sitting room, Kate is sorting out which Sylvanians and books she will be taking with her. Ruth adds 'find large travel bag' to her mental checklist.

'Shall we tell Dad that we're going?' says Kate, putting the rabbit family in height order. Kate doesn't ever ask why her dad doesn't live with them. Sometimes this self-restraint makes Ruth want to cry.

'Not just yet,' says Ruth.

4

Angelo Morelli is in his office at the University of Rome, looking at pictures of dead bodies. They are long dead, from the early days of the Roman Empire, but there is still something shocking about the images, the skeletal shapes, the sightless eyes. Some of the pictures show bodies buried in stone coffins, others contorted shapes from Pompeii, impressions of the place where a human body had once stood or lain. Angelo gets out a file marked 'Toni' and takes out some more photographs, this time showing a skeleton lying face down. When he hears a knock on the door, he instinctively hides these images.

'Come in.'

'You wanted to see me, Professore.'

It's Marta, one of his graduate students. She's a serious girl, short-haired and fresh-faced. She came to archaeology late but she's a good worker, painstaking and thorough. Angelo never feels very comfortable with her, though. You can't really share a joke with Marta or quiz her about her love life. In fact, Angelo suspects her of being a practising Catholic.

'Yes, sit down, Marta. I was wondering – are you planning to go home this summer? To your mother's house?'

Marta opens her eyes wide. 'Yes. I usually go for some of August. It's quiet. I can get some reading done.'

Reading. As a professor, Angelo is all in favour of studying but shouldn't Marta be out partying and taking drugs? Sometimes he despairs of the younger generation.

'I'm going to be in the area too,' says Angelo. 'Staying with *my* mother.' He attempts a comradely smile. 'And I want to carry on the excavation work in the Liri Valley. I was wondering if you would like to be involved.'

'But I thought . . .' Marta stops. Angelo looks at her encouragingly.

'I thought that we'd stopped work on the dig. After the phone was found in the grave. It must mean that the site is contaminated.'

'It means nothing of the sort,' says Angelo. 'It was just some silly joke. It's still an important site. It'll make good television.'

'But I thought the television company weren't interested any more.'

'They will be,' says Angelo. 'I've got a bones expert coming over from England. You know how Italians love a British expert.'

'What's his name?'

Angelo smiles. It's rare that he can catch his students out in casual sexism. '*Her* name is Dr Ruth Galloway, from the University of North Norfolk.'

'I've read her book,' says Marta. '*The Tomb of the Raven King.*'

'Yes. She's an old friend, and she's getting quite a reputation for her work on skeletal remains. I hope she'll be able to cast some light on Toni. She's going to stay in Castello. In my grandfather's apartment.'

'My mother told me that Pompeo had died. I'm sorry.'

Angelo spreads out his hands. 'He was an old man and he lived a full life. I was with him a lot towards the end. He was a remarkable man. They gave him a full military funeral in Casserta. Flag on the coffin, marching band, the lot.'

'He's with my great-grandfather now.'

Marta's great-grandfather, Giorgio, was a close friend of Angelo's grandfather. Even so, he's surprised at the way she mentions it now. 'Yes,' he says. 'I suppose he is.' He hopes they aren't going to get onto any of that life after death stuff. But then Marta says, as if this is what she wanted to discuss all along, 'What about the other dig? The one at the church?'

'Oh, you've heard about that, have you?'

'My mother says that Don Tomaso wants you to look for the foundations of the original church.'

'That was just some mad idea that he had. You know what the old man's like. He gets these obsessions.'

'My mother says he's a saint.'

'Very likely. Now, are you interested in the Liri Valley dig? I'm going to ask Roberto too. Roberto Esposito. He's from the area, isn't he?'

'His family live in Cassino.'

'That's right. So, Marta, are you in?' He tries to imply that he is offering her a wonderful adventure, rather than a summer brushing dust off old bones.

'Yes, of course,' says Marta. 'Thank you very much for thinking of me.'

When the door shuts behind Marta, Angelo doesn't immediately go back to his work. He picks up his phone, ignoring the two Post-it notes on his desk telling him to call Don Tomaso in Castello degli Angeli and keying in a different number.

'Commissario Valenti.'

'Flavio,' says Angelo, 'I think someone is trying to kill me.'

5

Nelson is in his office when he gets the message that human bones have been found at a building site near King's Lynn. He immediately pushes aside the spreadsheet he is half-heartedly studying ('Crime reduction targets 2015') and puts on his jacket. He knows that he should send Judy or Tanya. A DCI has no business rushing around looking at bodies that could turn out to be from the Stone Age or suchlike (despite knowing Ruth for almost eight years, Nelson remains vague on prehistory). This is a job for a DC or a DS. His job is strategy, public relations, budget management . . .

'Leah!' he calls.

His PA appears at the door. 'You don't have to shout,' she says mildly.

'Can you call Dr Galloway and ask her to meet me here?' He pushes the address towards her.

'You've got a meeting with Superintendent Archer at two.'

'Make my apologies,' says Nelson. 'This looks urgent.'

Leah takes the address and leaves the room. Nelson

wonders how she can make even her back look reproachful. Michelle can do it too. Perhaps it's a woman thing.

The bones were found near Castle Rising, where Judy used to live before she left her decent, dull husband and set up with Cathbad, a development that stunned many in the force but which Nelson understands perfectly. Judy and Cathbad have nothing in common: she's a hard-headed police officer; he's a druid who believes that he might have been a tree in a former life. But in Nelson's view, human relationships defy rational explanation. At any rate, Judy and Cathbad have three children between them and seem very happy.

A sign at the entrance to the site says that twenty luxury townhouses are being built by Edward Spens and Co. Nelson looks dubiously at the muddy field. To fit twenty houses on here they will have to be very small and close together – not his definition of luxury. And what's all this with townhouses anyway? They are miles away from anywhere that he considers a town.

The foreman is waiting for him by the gate, wearing a hard hat and a gloomy expression. Human bones are bad news for builders; even at the most conservative estimate, they will hold up the construction work for weeks. If the bones are relatively modern, that means a full-blown police investigation, which could take months. Nelson is surprised that Edward Spens himself isn't there – he usually likes to get involved in everything that happens on his sites. Having encountered Spens on several previous investigations, Nelson is glad that he has stayed away.

'Where are these bones then?' he asks, accepting a hard hat but not putting it on. 'The forensic archaeologist, Dr Ruth Galloway, should be joining us in a minute.'

The foreman stares at him. 'The archaeologist is already here.'

Nelson follows the pointing finger. The ground has been churned into an alien landscape of craters and hillocks, but the actual building work doesn't seem to have started yet. The field is empty apart from an abandoned JCB, a portaloo and a man standing beside one of the biggest craters. When he sees Nelson, the man comes forward, grinning wildly.

'DCI Nelson. Fancy seeing you here.'

'Phil. Why are you here? Where's Ruth?'

'Oh, didn't you know?' Phil grins even more broadly. 'Ruth's away. She's gone to Italy. I took her and Shona to the airport this morning.'

Ruth and Shona are currently in mid-air. It's odd, thinks Ruth, how quickly you get used to this strange form of travel, held apparently stationary in the sky, yet travelling hundreds of miles an hour. This is Kate's first flight and she had been quite mesmerised by the take-off, not scared at all, watching the earth disappear with frank enjoyment. It was Ruth who had felt nervous. She has flown before, of course, but never with this precious cargo, this child whose safety overrides everything else. While Kate had squealed as if she were on a roller coaster, Ruth had been reduced to muttering one of Cathbad's calming mantras under her breath ('Goddess bless, Goddess keep'). Louis had cried because his ears hurt. Ruth had been sympathetic, but also relieved that they were sitting two rows away from him.

But now the children are sitting together, poring over an iPad game, and Ruth and Shona are managing a few minutes of whispered conversation.

'Where are we staying again?' says Shona. 'It's all a bit mad, isn't it? Running away like this at a moment's notice.'

Running away, thinks Ruth. Is that what they're doing? And it is a bit mad, she can't deny it. Now that they are in the air she can't quite believe that she has left everything – her home, her cat, her last-minute lesson planning – to assist on a dig in a remote part of Italy. But she tries not to show any of this to Shona.

'Castello degli Angeli,' she says. 'It's in Lazio. Apparently it's about an hour away from the airport. Angelo said that his friend Graziano would come and collect us. I've got his mobile number.'

'Graziano,' says Shona. 'That's a great name.'

'I suppose it is.'

'Do you know what the house is like?'

'It's an apartment, really,' says Ruth. 'I've seen some pictures but it's hard to get much sense of it. There are three bedrooms though, so we should be fine.'

'Is it near the sea?' says Shona. 'Louis would love to go to the beach.'

'Not far,' says Ruth. At least, it doesn't look far on the map, but it's hard to tell with those winding mountain roads. Castello degli Angeli seems to be on the very top of a hill, looking down on the valley. Ruth thinks of Italy, the long thin boot with its spine of mountains. Mountains on one side and sea on the other, like a fairy-tale world.

'It'll be great just to chill. Eat pasta, drink wine, sunbathe,' says Shona. 'I'm looking forward to turning up at UNN in September with a tan.'

Despite being a redhead, Ruth is sure that Shona goes a beautiful, even brown in the sun. She is pretty sure that she will return to UNN bright red and peeling gently.

'I'll be working some of the time,' she says.

'How long will it take you to look at a couple of bones?' says Shona. 'No, we'll have plenty of time to enjoy ourselves in the sun.'

Ruth thinks of this when they have landed and battled through customs and baggage reclaim to find themselves in a car park with white-hot heat pouring down on their heads. She had forgotten what August in Italy was like. She had got used to thinking of sunny days in Norfolk as hot, but those benevolent rays are nothing compared to this killer heat, which seems to skewer them to the spot, leaving them unable to move or even speak. Kate and Louis, who have, during the flight, moved from being best friends to hating each other, now stand side by side, transfixed. In front of them, two men argue volubly over a taxi and an armed policeman lights a cigarette. There is no sign of Angelo's friend, Graziano.

'Why's it so hot?' says Kate.

'That's what it's like in Italy,' says Ruth.

'Where's Italy?' says Louis.

'Italy is here,' says Kate crushingly.

Louis starts to cry and Shona picks him up. The sun shines on her red-gold hair and the two arguing men break off to look at her appreciatively. One says something about the Madonna.

'I'd forgotten what it's like,' she says. 'All that attention. You never get a moment's peace.'

Ruth doesn't answer. She's starting to worry all over again. What if Graziano never appears? What if it's all a scam – the dig, the apartment, Castello degli Angeli, everything? She searches on her travel documents for Graziano's phone number. Are you supposed to add a zero for calls inside Italy?

'Signora Galloway?'

Ruth turns. The heat has fried her brains so much that she can't even remember the Italian for 'yes'. A youngish man with a dark beard is standing in front of her. He has parked his car, a red Alfa, in the space clearly meant for police cars.

'I am Graziano. The friend of Angelo. I'm taking you to the apartment.'

'Oh, hello,' says Ruth. 'It's great to see you.'

'I have child seats.' Graziano gestures to Kate and Louis. 'And air conditioning.'

Ruth doesn't think she's ever heard two such beautiful words. Almost before she can reply, Shona is shaking Graziano's hand and installing the children in the back seats of the car. Ruth doesn't even mind when Shona gets in the front and leaves her to sit between the children.

It's disconcerting being in a left-hand drive car, especially as Graziano seems to move very fast through several lanes of hooting traffic without indicating. Italy slides past them, suburbs giving way to sun-bleached grass, cypress trees and villages clinging to the side of mountains. Shona tries to chat to Graziano, but as her Italian is extremely limited, and, in an effort to be understood, Graziano often takes both hands off the wheel, Ruth is glad when they lapse into silence. Graziano's road skills remind her of Nelson, who always drives as if he is pursuing suspects. But the one thing she is not going to do is think about Nelson.

They leave the motorway and drive through an industrial area. Ruth thinks that she's never seen a grimmer place: litter on the verges, empty buildings, abandoned cars. By the side of the road stand several young women in short skirts and high heels, their attempts at glamour all the more tragic because of the squalid setting.

'What are those ladies selling?' asks Kate.

'Fruit,' says Ruth, not wanting to introduce her daughter to the concept of women being forced to sell their bodies. For a moment, she wishes she was back in Norfolk, beside the grey–green marshes. She thought that Italy was supposed to be scenic. But then they start to climb, up and up, away from the rubbish and the fruit sellers, up into the hills. They pass roadside shrines and farm buildings, olive groves and fields of sunflowers. They have to stop once to let a wild boar across the road. Higher and higher. Louis starts crying because his ears hurt again, but Kate is entranced, pressing her face to the window.

Then they see it, on the top of the highest hill: turrets and towers, crenellated walls, rooftop upon rooftop. It's a terracotta fortress, every shade from dark orange to palest pink and, above, the sky is a perfect azure.

'Castello degli Angeli,' says Graziano.

A few more turns of the road and the Alfa seems to drive straight at a wall. Ruth shuts her eyes. When she opens them again they are in a cobbled square with a fountain playing in the centre. Behind them are the walls of the castle and in the foreground there is a church, so beautiful and symmetrical that it looks like a stage set. A group of old men sitting outside a café turn to stare at them; not hostile, but not exactly welcoming either.

When they get out of the car, the heat hits them again. Ruth thinks that she actually staggers under the weight of the sunlight. And it's five o'clock, well past the hottest part of the day.

'We have to walk.' Graziano gestures apologetically at one of the narrow lanes leading off from the square. He takes Ruth's suitcase in one hand and Shona's in the other and sets off. Ruth follows, still feeling pretty weighed down by her hand luggage and by Kate pulling on her arm. At least the narrow street is shady, a cool stone passage rising steeply in front of them; in fact, it feels as if it never gets the sun. Ruth looks around at the doorways and arches, hears a caged bird singing, a child laughing from a balcony, inhales the scent of Italian cooking. They continue to climb until, just when Ruth thinks that she must ask to stop for a rest,

Graziano comes to a halt by a green door which seems to lead into the castle wall itself.

'Is the apartment actually in the castle?' she asks.

But Graziano, key in hand, is staring at the door. He makes a sign for Ruth to keep back, but she has already seen. Scrawled in chalk across the stone architrave are the words, '*Stranieri andate a casa.*'

Ruth doesn't know what it means, but she's pretty sure that it's not a welcome banner.

6

'What do you mean, she's gone to Italy?'

Nelson sounds so ferocious that Phil takes a step back.

'Some professor at Rome University invited her,' he says. 'He wanted her help dating some bones apparently. UNN is getting quite an international reputation.' He manages to sound both proud and resentful as he says this.

'Has she taken Katie?'

'Katie? Oh, Kate. Yes, of course. Shona's taken Louis too. A regular mother and baby outing.' He laughs, then stops when he sees Nelson's face.

'Do you know when they're coming back?'

'In two weeks' time. It's cutting it a bit fine for the start of the term, but I told Ruth that it would be all right in the circumstances. I think she's feeling a bit low. You know, losing her mum and all that.'

'*Two weeks?*' Nelson practically shouts the words.

Phil looks around nervously. 'Well, they want to have a holiday. Apparently it's a beautiful part of . . .'

But Nelson has already turned away. He has to call Ruth.

How could she have taken Katie out of the country without telling him? His hands are shaking as he gets out his phone.

'DCI Nelson?'

Phil is hovering at his elbow. Nelson has to resist the temptation to push him away. Super Jo would just love to have him up on a charge of assaulting the public.

'Don't you want to see the bones?'

'The bones? Oh . . . yes.' Nelson puts his phone away and reluctantly follows Phil to the edge of a muddy hole. At the bottom, half-submerged in water, are several long bones, broken and discoloured.

'They look human,' Phil is saying. 'Of course, to be sure—'

'Are you going to excavate?' Nelson interrupts him. 'How long will you need for the digging?'

Phil looks shocked. 'I'm not going to *dig*. First, I thought, we'd get a drone—'

'A drone?'

'Yes, they're the latest thing in archaeology. They allow you to get measurements in double quick time with remarkable precision, not just in terms of surveying. I'm just dying to try my hand with a drone.'

Nelson stares at him stonily.

'Funnily enough,' continues Phil, 'the Italians are the leaders in this sort of technology.'

Nelson is breathing heavily. 'Let's get this straight,' he says. 'I want you to excavate this site using a shovel – not a bloody drone that's probably going to cost me a fortune and bring down a few passenger planes for good measure. I want you to dig up these bones and tell me how old they are. I don't want a lecture on surveying. I just want to know if this is a crime scene or not. Got it?'

'Can I do some geophysics, just for good measure?'

'No. Just dig up the bloody bones. Liaise with DS Johnson at the station.'

And he's gone, before Phil can ask if there's any chance of television coverage.

'What does that say?' says Kate.

'It says hello,' says Ruth. 'In Italian. Shall we go in? Isn't it exciting to be living inside a real-life castle?'

'It's a lot of words,' mutters Kate, but she allows herself to be ushered over the threshold. Inside, it's pitch black after the brightness of the day. Graziano uses the torch on his phone to light the way up two flights of stairs. By the time they get to the top they are all out of breath and Shona is carrying Louis. Graziano finds another key and opens another door. Stepping inside, Ruth is immediately struck by a sudden sense of space. They are in a high-ceilinged room, shadowy and cool with shuttered doors at one end. Ruth opens the shutters and steps out onto a small balcony. They are far higher than she imagined, above the rooftops of the town. There are mountains in the distance, wooded and wild, and, far below them, the valley, silver with olive trees and golden in the late afternoon sun. On the opposite hill there is a single ruined tower, somehow ominous, like a sentinel. The photographs she'd seen, which mostly showed empty white-walled rooms, had given no hint of what was in store.

Kate comes to join her. 'Are we on the top of the castle?' she asks.

'I think so,' says Ruth. 'You must never come out on this balcony on your own. It's too dangerous.'

She looks around for Shona to corroborate this, but Shona has collapsed onto a sofa with her eyes shut. Louis sits beside her, too tired even to whine. Graziano is speaking into his phone, but looks up when Ruth comes back into the room.

'Beautiful view, yes?'

'Yes,' says Ruth.

'I speak with Angelo.' He waves his phone. 'He will meet you in the piazza at nine. At the bar. Yes?'

No, Ruth wants to say. Both children are exhausted and Kate usually goes to bed at half past seven. She doesn't want to drag her out to a bar in the middle of a strange town. She wants them both to sit down, watch CBeebies for an hour, eat undemanding nursery food and go to bed. But how can she say any of this to Graziano? Shona, who still has her eyes shut, clearly isn't going to be any help.

'OK,' she says.

'I show you the rest of the apartment,' says Graziano, clearly relieved that his duties will soon be at an end.

The apartment is grand but somehow rather cheerless. The rooms are all large, with moulded cornices and double doors, but they are sparsely furnished: beds, sofas and tables marooned in a sea of polished marble. The bathrooms are beautiful, though, tiled from floor to ceiling, with windows looking out over the valley. The kitchen is bristling with modern devices. Ruth, who had been expecting a rustic galley, is pleasantly surprised.

'Some food.' Graziano opens the vast fridge to reveal cheese, milk, salami, tomatoes, grapes, mineral water and orange juice. There's also pasta, coffee and two bottles of wine. Ruth feels her spirits rising.

'That's very kind,' she says.

'Also,' Graziano opens a cupboard door with the air of a magician, 'Nutella.'

'Nutella, Mum,' says Kate, in the voice of one who has seen a vision.

'And bread.' Graziano flourishes a loaf.

'Thank you,' says Ruth. She's not sure if it's Angelo or Graziano who has provided for them, but she's very grateful, all the same. At least they'll be able to make supper for the children. Graziano starts explaining about the recycling, which sounds incredibly complicated, with different coloured containers for glass, plastic, paper and something called 'mixed materials'. There is a refuse collection every day and a special calendar shows which recycling is collected on which day. Ruth looks at the calendar, trying to make sense of the romantically named days: lunedi . . . mercoledì . . . domenica. She is impressed that a little town on top of a mountain has a rubbish collection every day though. Why is it so hard to get her recycling collected in Norfolk?

Shona is already opening the wine.

'Will you have some?' she twinkles at Graziano.

Ruth prays that Graziano will say no, and he does, saying

that he needs to be at work. What does he do, wonders Ruth, that demands his presence at half past five in the afternoon? Graziano says '*ci vediamo*', one of the few Italian phrases that Ruth remembers. *See you soon.* Then they hear him running down the stone steps. The apartment suddenly seems very big, very old and very silent.

'Have some wine,' says Shona, pushing a glass towards Ruth.

Nelson drives back to the station in a foul mood. How dare Ruth take Katie out of the country without consulting him? How could she go swanning off to Italy with that flaky Shona? Anything could happen to them. To his child. To Ruth. He shoots a red light, narrowly avoiding oncoming traffic. Super Jo sent him on a speed awareness course a few months ago but it hasn't taken.

By the time he reaches King's Lynn, he is calmer, if no less angry. He knows that Ruth has been feeling low, to use that idiot Phil's phrase. The news of Michelle's pregnancy, coming so soon after her mother's death, must have hit her hard. Not that she has said anything to him, beyond formal congratulations on his impending fatherhood. But they both know that, moments before Michelle's bomb-shell announcement, they had been on the verge of moving towards a new stage in their relationship, one that might have involved forsaking all others. But now things are back where they were, only with added tensions. On balance, Nelson thinks that he won't ring Ruth today.

The CID rooms are quiet. Judy has gone home and Tanya is investigating a possible malicious wounding in Swaffham.

They all miss Clough: his stream of un-PC consciousness accompanied by hearty snacks allows little time for intro-spection or boredom. But none of them are willing to admit this. Nelson reads through some case notes and adds a com-ment on a circular from head office ('What does this mean in English?'), wondering if he should head home. Michelle is still feeling very tired and Laura is often out in the evenings. Someone needs to cook dinner and walk Bruno. He starts to gather up his things.

'Leaving already, DCI Nelson?'

It's Jo Archer, wearing what he recognises from his daugh-ters' wardrobes as exercise clothes: leggings and a crop top, giant fluorescent trainers, hoodie tied around her waist. Nelson considers the outfit unsuitable for a woman of her age and position. Not that he knows her exact age, which is a closely kept secret. Clough once organised a competition to find Jo's date of birth but no one was able to come up with a definitive answer. Jo often implies that she's nearing 'the big Four-O' but Nelson suspects that it's actually the big Five-O.

'Yes,' he says, not wanting to demean himself by saying that it's past five and he has been in the office since seven that morning. 'Are you off to do aerobics?'

'Aerobics? You're out of date, Harry. Hello?' She mimes answering a phone. 'Hello? It's for you. The eighties are calling.' Nelson waits for her to come to the point – some-times Jo's little jokes go on for ever. Eventually Jo says, jogging slightly on the spot, 'Actually I'm off for a run. I just wanted to have a word with you before I go.'

'Oh yes?'

Jo sits on the visitor's chair, which forces Nelson to sit back behind his desk. Jo says, in a voice from which all traces of banter have vanished, 'Micky Webb has been released.'

'Micky Webb.' Nelson leans back in his chair. 'How come he's out already?'

'He's out on licence. He served ten years.'

'Ten years! For killing his wife and kids.'

'He pleaded diminished responsibility, if you remember.'

'He set their house on fire.'

'I know. I've been reading the case notes. The point is that he might still be holding a grudge against you, as the officer who put him away. That's why the probation service have alerted us.'

'Has he said that he's coming after me?'

'No, he got religion in prison. A changed character, apparently.'

Nelson laughs hollowly. 'I'll believe that when I see it. I still remember his kids' bodies being brought out of that house. While Micky was planning to go on holiday with his girlfriend, paid for by the insurance.'

'He sounds a wrong-un all right.' Jo has never quite got the hang of police slang. 'Anyway, Micky claims to be completely reformed, heartbroken by the deaths of his kids, that sort of thing. I just wanted you to know that he was on the loose, that's all.'

'I'm not scared of Micky Webb.'

'I know you're not,' says Jo, 'but you've got some holiday owing. It might not hurt to go away for a week or two.'

'We're too busy with Clough away,' says Nelson. He loathes holidays.

Jo waves a hand at the silent suite of rooms. 'We'll manage, Nelson. Think about it. *Ciao*.'

After Jo has jogged away, Nelson sits at his desk, remembering that summer, ten years ago, when he'd been called to a house fire on the outskirts of Lynn. All coppers dread a fire – the injuries are terrible and there are often children involved. And this case was especially harrowing, three little bodies brought out of the house: Tammy, aged eight, Petey, six, and Chelsea, two. The mother, Marie, was actually found with Chelsea in her arms, lying in the hallway where they had both been overcome by smoke. Micky Webb had been two miles away, drinking with friends in a snooker club, but witnesses saw another man, Todd Larkin, pushing what turned out to be petrol-soaked rags through the letterbox. Todd was arrested and claimed to be acting on Micky's instructions. CCTV cameras placed the two men together and money changing hands. Nelson had interviewed Micky over twenty-four hours and, at the end of this, Micky admitted paying Larkin to burn down the house, saying that he thought his wife and children would be away at the time. Later he claimed that Nelson had intimidated him to get this confession. In court he pleaded diminished responsibility and was sentenced to fifteen years. As he was led out he spat at Nelson, who was sitting with Marie's family, and vowed to get even with him. And now Micky Webb is free, having served ten years 'with good behaviour'.

Driving home, Nelson wonders whether Jo, reading through the notes, thought that he might have been guilty of intimidation. He'd played it by the book, as he remembered, but there's no doubt that he'd played the hard cop to ... what was the name of the sergeant he'd had then? Freddie Burnett, that was it, a tough copper of the old school who also knew how to offer spurious man-to-man sympathy when he thought it would get him a conviction. He'd better warn Freddie that Webb is on the loose. Not that Freddie will care; he's happy in his retirement bungalow in Cromer, playing golf all day and having the occasional holiday with his wife in Tenerife. Is that what lies in wait for him? Retirement in a Norfolk seaside town? But, by the time Nelson is sixty, this new child will only be twelve, just starting secondary school. Nelson sighs heavily as he pulls up outside his house. He can already hear Bruno barking.

7

In the end, Ruth walks down to the bar on her own. Shona, revived by the wine and a meal of pasta, bread and cheese, offers to stay behind with the children. 'We can snuggle on the sofa and watch *The Lion King.*' Ruth has prudently brought a stack of DVDs from home, and the sight of the crypto-Shakespearean cartoon appearing on the television screen in the vast, echoing sitting room is curiously comforting. The children are in their pyjamas and Shona is finishing the wine. Ruth suddenly feels very tired and wishes that she could join them on the sofa, even though it is white leather and extremely uncomfortable. But she has to go to the bar – braving the stares of the old men who are probably still sitting at the same table – and see Angelo.

It's still warm, but at least the murderous heat has gone out of the sun. She's able to appreciate the beauty of the evening, the glimpses of the valley through archways and across rooftops, the scent of lemon trees and wild garlic, so deliciously un-English. Although it's not yet dark, the shadows are lengthening and the moon is up, a white disc in the purplish sky. It's hard to get much sense of the town: the houses seem to have been built on top of each other, some with elaborate balconies and grand, pillared entrances, others with little wooden doors like Hobbit holes. The narrow street is empty, but from inside one of the shuttered houses, she can hear a piano playing, from another the sound of cooking pots clattering. The caged bird is still singing and she hears a child's voice raised in complaint: 'Mam-*ma*'. She recognises the tone immediately. Some of the houses seem to have been abandoned, with trees growing out of roofs and feral cats sleeping in the doorways. Near the bottom of the hill, she passes a large house that looks half-ruined – the upper windows are boarded up and some roof tiles are missing, revealing the wooden rafters below. Through the open downstairs window, she sees a man cooking over a camping stove. There's a camp bed too and clothes hanging on a rail. Is he a squatter? Do they even have squatters in picturesque Italian towns? The man looks up as she passes and says, '*Buonasera.*' Ruth says it back to him, embarrassed by her English accent and by the uncomfortable feeling that she had been spying on him.

If the streets are empty, the square seems very full. Children are running about, flicking water from the fountain at each other and squealing with excitement. There are several youths on mopeds exchanging backchat and the old men are still there, now playing an intense game of cards. The other tables are full of people, some of whom look alarmingly smart, like extras from Italian *Vogue*, others in overalls and working clothes. A young woman with a chic haircut glides between them, dispensing lemon sodas and tiny glasses of wine. On the other side of the square is a church, white-brick and classical, with sweeping steps at the front and rows of columns and arches above. At the very top is a stone pediment with two winged figures on either side, silhouetted against the purple twilight. One has a sword and one holds what looks like a scroll. They must be angels. Is this how the town got its name? It seems a very grand building for such a small place. As Ruth stands, looking about her, a man rises from one of the *Vogue* tables. 'Ruth?'

At first she thinks that she wouldn't have recognised him. The Angelo she remembers had a mane of black hair, dressed in bright colours and was given to wild hand gestures and violent laughter. This man has greying hair, still curly but cut rather short, and is soberly dressed in a black shirt and dark trousers. But as he approaches, she sees that her old Angelo is still there; he still walks as if he owns the place and, when he comes closer, his eyes are the same – dark brown yet full of light.

'Ruth. How good to see you.'

He kisses her on both cheeks. Ruth feels rather embarrassed at this very public reunion. She wonders how she appears to Angelo. She's not grey yet, but she's twelve years older and a lot fatter. And, in the last eight years, she's had a baby and has been almost constantly involved with violent death. She's pretty sure that this shows in her face, if not in her hair.

'Did you have a good journey?' says Angelo, smiling down at her. She had forgotten how tall he was.

'Yes, thank you. Graziano met us at the airport. He was very kind.'

'He is an old friend of the family,' says Angelo. 'And the apartment? Is all as it should be?'

'It's lovely,' says Ruth. 'Thanks for getting the food in.'

'It was OK? I thought you might not want to go out to eat on your first night.'

'It was perfect. Thank you.'

'But there are some excellent restaurants around here. I'll take you another time.'

Ruth doesn't quite know how to answer this. She intends to keep their relationship entirely professional this time. But she still feels rather dizzy and disorientated. In the evening light, the square looks more like a stage set than ever, the steps of the church just perfect for a soprano belting out a dying aria, the moon hanging overhead like a backcloth. Now Angelo is steering her towards an empty table and asking her what she'd like to drink.

'Coffee, please.' She has already had two glasses of wine and feels that she should keep her wits about her. But when the coffee arrives it is so strong as to be almost solid, served in a tiny gold cup. Drinking it makes her feel headier than ever. Too late, Ruth remembers that coffee in Italy is always espresso, unless otherwise specified. And no self-respecting Italian would drink cappuccino after lunchtime.

'It is very good of you to come,' says Angelo.

'That's OK,' says Ruth. 'It's great to be back in Italy.'

'You haven't been to any more conferences here?' Angelo is smiling in a way that she doesn't quite like.

'No,' she says evenly, 'but I've been on holiday a few times.'

'Tell me about your life, Ruth,' says Angelo, leaning back in his chair. 'Are you married? I know you have your daughter with you.'

Ruth would much rather be talking about archaeology, but she supposes they have to get through the social stuff first. She had ascertained Angelo's marital status from Facebook, but she isn't on social media, something Phil (or @archaeoman) often bemoans.

'I'm not married,' she says, 'but, as you know, I have a daughter, Kate. She's six.'

'I have a daughter of fifteen,' says Angelo unexpectedly.

Ruth looks surprised. Angelo hadn't mentioned his daughter all those years ago at the conference, but then they hadn't talked very much about their personal lives.

'I got married when I was at the University of Columbia,' says Angelo. 'The marriage broke up and I came back to Italy. It's hard to be so far away from Poppy.'

'Poppy?' It seems an odd choice for an Italian.

Angelo laughs. 'My mother still thinks it's not a real name. But Shelly wanted to call her Boadicea so we had to compromise. She is an archaeologist too, specialising in Roman Britain.'

Ruth hopes he isn't going to ask about Kate's father. She says, rather hurriedly, 'It must be difficult, but I'm sure Poppy loves coming here for holidays.'

'She does,' says Angelo, 'and now she's older, she can come on her own. I'm hoping she'll come for a long stretch next summer, even work with me on a dig. My mother loves having her to stay.'

'Does your mother still live in Castello degli Angeli? It's where you're from, isn't it?'

'Yes,' says Angelo. 'I was born here. My parents used to live in Castello but, when my father died, my mother moved to a flat in Arpino. It's more convenient. My grandfather lived here all his life though. It's his apartment that you're staying in.'

'Is your grandfather . . .?' She doesn't know how to phrase the question without using the D word.

'He died two years ago,' says Angelo, 'aged ninety-six. He was a big resistance hero in the war. He won the gold medal of valour. People still talk about his exploits. He had a state funeral, at the church in Cassino. Four priests officiating, two senators, a marching band, the choir from the abbey at Monte Cassino.' He lapses into silence.

'I'm sorry,' says Ruth. 'He must have been a wonderful person.'

Angelo laughs, but his eyes are bright with what could be tears. 'Yes,' he says, 'he had some amazing stories. This area was occupied by the Germans, you know. The resistance fighters had to hide in the hills. The Nazis carried out terrible reprisals if you were caught communicating with the partisans. They must have been terrifying times.'

'I don't think we British can imagine what it must have been like to have your country occupied,' says Ruth. 'I mean, Britain suffered terrible bombing raids, but at least the Nazis weren't walking the streets. Except in Jersey, of course.'

'They used to sit here at this café, my grandfather said. With their boots on the table, calling for beer.'

Ruth looks round the square, the café full of laughing, gesticulating people. It's nearly dark now and the fountain is illuminated in blue and green. It's hard to imagine jackboots on the tables. She wonders if it was the final insult to call for beer rather than wine.

Angelo says, cutting into her thoughts, 'I'm very glad that you were able to come to give your opinion on the bones.'

Ruth is grateful to get back to archaeology. 'I'm looking forward to seeing them,' she says. 'It'll be interesting to be involved in an Italian research project.'

'It's not exactly a research project,' says Angelo, looking slightly gloomy again. 'I did get a research grant to begin with, but the excavation only went ahead because Cielo Blu, the TV production company, backed it. Then we found a body, a fully articulated skeleton, so that was even better. I wanted to film the excavation live on TV.' He pauses. 'Do you want another drink? A glass of wine? Limoncello? Grappa?'

'A glass of red wine, please,' says Ruth. She is on holiday, after all.

Angelo speaks rapidly to the waitress as she passes, then turns back to Ruth. 'It was all set. The TV people were all in place. Lights, cameras, action. I was just about to dig through the final layer when a telephone rang. Turned out to be mine.'

'God, how embarrassing,' says Ruth. 'That happened to me in a lecture once.' It had been Nelson, ringing to check that Kate's swimming teacher had been CRB checked.

'Embarrassing,' says Angelo, 'yes. But, when I looked at my phone, the caller came up as "Toni". That was the name we had given the skeleton.'

'Goodness,' says Ruth. Her wine has arrived and she takes a gulp.

'Exactly. I thought I was going mad. I started digging away in the trench, and when I got to the bones, there was the phone. In his hand. In Toni's hand. At that exact moment, I got a text. "Surprise", is all it said.'

'How could that happen?'

'Apparently it's fairly easy with new smartphone technology,' says Angelo. 'It's the same application you use in Find My iPhone. All you have to do is link both devices. A clever trick, eh?' He grins at Ruth but this time there is no humour in the smile. His white teeth flash in what is almost a snarl.

'But what about the layers?' says Ruth. 'Surely you'd know if the grave had been disturbed recently.'

'The layers were intact,' says Angelo. 'We had just left a thin covering of soil over the bones. That could easily have been dug up and replaced.'

'Have you any idea who did it?' says Ruth.

'Lots of ideas,' says Angelo, 'each more ridiculous that the last. The problem is that the TV company have lost interest now. They were furious to have wasted a day's filming. And I need their money if I want to continue.' He lapses into a rather morose silence, draining his glass of wine.

'Angelo!' calls a voice. Ruth looks round and sees a figure approaching, grey-haired and vigorous-looking. He's wearing a black robe, which reminds her of Cathbad and his cloak. What's Cathbad doing now, she wonders. She only had time to leave a voice message for Judy before she left. Will they think she's gone mad, disappearing to Italy at a moment's notice?

'Don Tomaso,' says Angelo. Of course. It's a priest, and that's a cassock, not a cloak.

Angelo's voice is expressionless but the priest seems delighted to see him, kissing him on both cheeks and turning to Ruth with a broad smile.

'This is Doctor Ruth Galloway from the University of North Norfolk.'

'Delighted to meet you.' Don Tomaso takes her hand in both of his.

As if by magic, the waitress appears at their table. Angelo orders grappa. Ruth, only halfway through her glass of wine, asks for water.

'Water?' says Don Tomaso. 'You should have limoncello. It is a speciality of the region.' He speaks good English, but with a heavy accent.

Ruth is rather confused that a priest seems to be urging her to drink alcohol. Aren't they meant to be in favour of abstinence and bread and water? But as her only priestly friend, Father Hennessey, would say, 'Catholics. That's different.'

'Another glass of wine then,' she says. 'You must let me pay this time. And some water, please.'

'Never mix water and wine,' says Don Tomaso. 'Our Good Lord turned water into wine for a reason.'

'To please his mother,' says Angelo. He seems curiously subdued by the arrival of the priest.

'Are you here on holiday?' Don Tomaso asks Ruth. 'We don't get many tourists here.'

'I'm helping Angelo with some bones that he's discovered.'

'Bones!' The priest throws up his hands in mock horror. 'Why all this talk of the dead, Angelo?'

'That's what archaeology is all about.'

'Beware of waking the dead,' says Don Tomaso, patting him on the shoulder. 'Concentrate on the living. That is my advice.'

The waitress is still hovering. She asks the priest a question in Italian and he answers, smiling and shaking his head. Ruth guesses this means that he's not about to join them. Sure enough, Don Tomaso takes his leave, bowing courteously to Ruth. 'Maybe I'll see you on Sunday,' he says.

'I don't think so.' Ruth feels that she should be honest about this, but the priest does not seem to have heard. He moves off, calling out greetings to his friends.

'He seems nice,' says Ruth.

'All priests are charlatans,' says Angelo. 'I'm like you, I won't be going to Mass on Sunday.'

Their drinks arrive. Angelo drains his grappa in one gulp. Ruth takes a sip of her mineral water. It tastes odd, she thinks, almost sulphuric.

'Can I ask you something?' she says.

'Ask away.'

'There was some writing above the door of your

apartment. Graffiti. It said *"Stranieri andate a casa"*. I looked it up on Google Translate. It means "foreigners go home". Why would someone write that? Was it aimed at us?'

Angelo is silent for a moment, then he says, 'In a small town like this, there are resentments. People go away and come back rich and successful. Sometimes it's hard for those left behind.'

'So the writing was aimed at you? But you're not a foreigner.'

Angelo shrugs. 'Round here, people from the next village are foreigners.'

Ruth understands this. It's the same in Norfolk.

'I thought your grandfather was a war hero,' she says. 'He had a state funeral. I would have thought that would make you popular.'

This time she thinks there's something almost demonic about Angelo's smile. Like the water, it has a whiff of sulphur.

'Being a hero doesn't make you popular,' he says. 'Not in Italy anyway.'

8

'Micky Webb hasn't got the guts to kill someone. Not face-to-face anyway. Paying someone to torch his wife and kids when he's miles away, that's different.'

'My thoughts entirely. I just thought you'd want to know.'

Nelson and Freddie Burnett are sitting on a bench, looking down on Cromer pier and esplanade. It's a sunny day and the beach is full of families building sandcastles, eating ice creams, venturing into the freezing North Sea. On the smooth lawn behind, a group of elderly men are playing bowls. It seems wrong to be talking about murder and arson, and yet, thinks Nelson, a passer-by would probably assume that the two men – one white-haired but still vigorous, wind-tanned and fit, the other heavyset and greying – are simply a father and son enjoying the view. On second thought, maybe that's giving him too much credit. He and Freddie probably look like brothers, and there is a similarity in the way they are sitting, relaxed yet still alert, eyes constantly scanning the innocuous surroundings for signs of trouble. Any self-respecting criminal would be able to spot them as a pair of coppers from a mile off.

'Ten years,' says Freddie. 'It's laughable.'

'He found God when he was inside,' says Nelson. 'Changed character, apparently.'

Freddie grunts sceptically. 'First thing you learn to say to the parole board. "Please, sir, I'm very sorry. I've found Jesus and he's taught me to be a good boy." God help us.'

Nelson thinks the mention of God is probably not meant to be ironic. As he remembers, Freddie is short on irony and on any sort of religious belief. He also clearly thinks that criminals are all male.

Nelson looks out over the storybook seaside town in front of them. The tide is out and the sands stretch for miles, dotted with tiny figures. From this distance, you could be in the last century, he thinks. Even the pier is devoid of flashing lights and amusement arcades. It's a leggy Victorian creature striding out into the shallow sea. Nelson suspects that Freddie would probably prefer to be living in a different time, when policing was both simpler and more brutal.

'I'll never forget seeing those little kiddies being brought out of the house,' says Freddie. 'Hanging was too good for him, in my opinion.'

'There's a lot you don't forget,' says Nelson. 'That's why the job gets to you in the end.'

Freddie looks at him curiously. 'Is it getting to you? You're too young to retire though.'

'I'm forty-eight,' says Nelson.

'I retired at fifty-five,' says Freddie. 'Best thing I ever did.'

'I can't retire,' says Nelson. 'Michelle's pregnant again.'

'Bloody hell.' Freddie's laugh sends two seagulls, who are fighting over a chip on the grass in front of them, squawking into the air. 'You old devil.'

'Old is right,' says Nelson. 'I feel a hundred. Far too old for all that nappy changing.'

'Michelle must be happy though.' Freddie has two children, both grown up now, but Nelson bets that nappy changing didn't feature much in his experience of fatherhood.

'She is happy,' says Nelson, 'but it was a bit of a shock to both of us.'

'I bet,' says Freddie. 'How are things at Lynn? I hear you've got a woman boss now.'

'Terrible,' says Nelson. 'She's one of the PC brigade, all yoga and quinoa salad and talking about your feelings. Going into the station these days is like being on the set of *Loose Women*.' He's aware, as he says this, that he's not being entirely fair to Jo. True, she does sit on a balance ball to conduct interviews, but, during the course of their last investigation, he learnt that she's also a hands-on police officer who enjoys driving fast and interrogating suspects. But today he craves some male chauvinist sympathy. Perhaps because he still hasn't heard from Ruth.

'Bloody hell,' says Freddie. 'Things have changed since our day. Remember the super we had back then? Chubby Brown? You wouldn't be able to call someone chubby today. They'd have you up in front of the employment tribunal before you could say—'

'You're right,' Nelson cuts in, before Freddie can say

something unsayable. He remembers Roy 'Chubby' Brown, the super when he'd first moved to Norfolk. He'd been a good boss, even if he had been rather prone to calling women officers 'love' and doing most of his briefings in the pub, next to the dartboard. It was Chubby who had first promoted Nelson to detective inspector. His career had only stalled with the arrival of the new superintendent, Gerald Whitcliffe, a perma-tanned graduate with a passion for appearing on television. That and his failure to solve the Lucy Downey case, of course.

'Dave Clough is a DS now,' he says. 'You remember Dave?'

'I certainly do,' says Freddie. 'I arrested his brother a few times. A DS, eh? Who would have thought it?'

'He's a good copper,' says Nelson. 'And he's just married a rich actress. They've got a baby, too.'

'Bloody hell,' says Freddie. 'Cloughie has landed on his feet all right. Give him my best, won't you?'

'I will,' says Nelson. He remembers that Freddie had always taken an interest in Clough, perhaps because of the link to the ne'er-do-well brother. Sometimes an early brush with the law can stimulate an interest in policing as well as in the criminal life. It can go both ways. Tim, he remembers, also has a brother who has been in prison. But he doesn't want to think about Tim.

Freddie cuts into this line of thought. 'Where's Micky living now?' he says. 'Hope it's got a fire escape.'

'Spalding,' says Nelson. 'He's out on licence, has to sign in at the local nick every day.'

'Did he marry that bird?' says Freddie. 'The one he was planning to run away with?'

'Wendy Markham,' says Nelson. 'No, she didn't wait for him. But he met another woman when he was inside. She wrote to him, apparently, and they got married last year. Had the wedding ceremony in the open prison.'

'Why do women do that?' says Freddie. 'Marry prisoners. Seems like the worse the villain, the more women want to marry him.'

'A psychologist once told me it's because women are attracted to alpha males,' says Nelson. 'Apparently killing someone makes you an alpha male.' Nelson never had that much time for the psychologist in question, Madge Hudson, known to him as Queen of the Bleeding Obvious. But there's no doubt that women are sometimes attracted to villains. He's not sure if it works the other way, though, with female killers deluged with letters from admiring men.

'Nothing alpha about most murderers,' says Freddie, standing up. 'Pathetic specimens, most of them.'

Nelson stands up too, realising that the conversation is at an end. It's certainly true that a lot of criminals are inadequate people who take out their frustrations on those they consider even lower than them in the food chain. Micky Webb had certainly fallen into this category.

'Fancy a pint?' says Freddie. 'There are a couple of nice pubs in Cromer.'

'I've got to get back to work,' says Nelson. 'My boss would just love to get me done for drunk driving. She's already had me on a speed awareness course.'

Freddie's laughter follows him all the way back to the car park.

Angelo is at the apartment bright and early. Shona, still in her silky kimono, gives him the full hair tossing, eyes twinkling treatment. Angelo seems appreciative, if slightly amused. Ruth is dressed and ready to go. She's wearing dark trousers to seem more businesslike, but already feels too hot. Angelo, in black jeans and a black shirt, seems oblivious to the heat.

'Bye, Kate,' says Ruth, kissing her. 'Be good. Have fun with Shona and Louis.'

Graziano is going to take Shona and the children to a nearby swimming pool. Graziano is an old friend of the family, Angelo had said, but that doesn't quite explain why he's at their beck and call like this. Still, there's no denying that he is being very useful. The pool is apparently only a mile away but it would be a gruelling walk over the hills. Shona seems delighted at the chance to get to know Graziano better. Ruth prays that she won't become so distracted that she forgets to put on Kate's factor 50.

Angelo drives fast and well down the switchback road and across the flat valley, between fields of sunflowers, their heads rising up towards the sun.

'There must be some interesting prehistory around here,' says Ruth. 'It looks the right sort of landscape.'

'Yes,' says Angelo. 'The valley used to be a huge lake and there have been some very old bones found there. There was a fossilised skull found near Ceprano that was approximately half a million years old. Homo heidelbergensis. And there are Bronze Age and Iron Age remains too.'

The bones are being held in a laboratory at the University of Cassino. As they approach the town they see the abbey, gleaming white on the very top of the highest mountain.

'What a vantage point,' says Ruth. 'It was bombed in the war, wasn't it?'

'Yes,' says Angelo. 'There's almost nothing left of the ancient monastery. The new building is very beautiful though. I'll take you one day.'

'Was it bombed by the Allies?' says Ruth, wishing she knew more about recent history. She's fine on the Battle of Tollense in the Bronze Age, but the Second World War is linked in her mind to the sort of films her father used to watch on Sunday afternoons. She wonders what her dad is doing now.

'Yes,' says Angelo. 'Cassino was in a very important position defensively, the lynchpin of the Gustav line, but, of course, it was also important as a lookout. The Germans told the Vatican they wouldn't use the monastery as a base because of its historical significance, but the British bombed it anyway. The church was full of monks and Italian civilians seeking sanctuary. They were all killed. Apparently it was a mistake in translation from a British Intelligence officer. He intercepted a message saying that the abbey was full of monks, but he mistook the German word "monk" for a similar word meaning "battalion".'

'How terrible,' says Ruth. 'The more I read about historical wars and battles, the more they seem to be full of mistakes.'

'Except the Romans,' says Angelo. 'The Romans were experts on battle strategy.'

This is partly why Ruth prefers prehistory, the dark and mysterious years before the Romans. Battle strategy is all very well but there's something cold and inhuman about it.

'The monastery was fourteenth century,' says Angelo, 'but the order was founded by St Benedict in the fifth century. The hilltop site was originally a pagan temple dedicated to Jupiter with an altar to Apollo. When St Benedict arrived, the local people were still worshipping the old gods in the sacred grove. St Benedict was a pragmatist though – he simply turned the Temple of Jupiter into a church, dedicated to St Martin of Tours. '

'Who first settled this area?' says Ruth. 'Was it the Romans?'

'The Volsci,' says Angelo. 'Do you know about the Volsci? They were one of the Italic tribes. Rivals and enemies of Rome. The Volsci inhabited all of the Liri Valley and the Pomentine plains. Very interesting people. One of my students is doing a dissertation on them.'

After all this history, Ruth is rather disappointed with the university. It's a modern building in the middle of a traffic intersection, all glass and concrete blocks. Angelo lets them in with his pass key. They ascend an open-plan staircase, the glass balustrade cracked in places, the walls pock-marked where posters have been taken down. The building seems empty – but then it is August. UNN would be the same.

Ruth is panting by the time they reach the third floor. Angelo, who has been talking constantly about the Romans and the Volsci, is hardly out of breath.

'Now here,' he says, flourishing another key, 'is Toni.'

They are in a laboratory, familiar the world over, with microscopes and gas taps and test tubes in racks. The bones are laid out on one of the work surfaces. They are complete, fully articulated in Angelo's phrase, laid out in anatomically correct order and remarkably well preserved.

Angelo hands Ruth a lab coat and gloves and she approaches the skeleton, feeling the thrill that she always experiences at seeing old bones, knowing that they will have secrets that she can uncover.

'Is it unusual to find a skeletal burial from this era?' she says. 'Wasn't cremation more common?'

'Before the first century, cremation was more common,' says Angelo, 'but articulated burials are often found afterwards. We think the site is about 500 Common Era but we won't know about the bones until we have the carbon-14 results.'

Waiting for test results is obviously an international problem. She walks slowly around the table. From the pelvic bones, she thinks that she is looking at a male, not very tall. The skull isn't complete, but it looks as though it has been broken up by ploughing rather than brute force.

'And the body was face down?' she says.

'Yes. That could have some cultural significance, but he could just have been buried in a hurry.'

'The position is always important though,' says Ruth. She realises that she is echoing her old archaeology professor, Erik Anderssen: 'Look which way the bones lie. The position tells you everything. In Christian burials, bodies are usually buried facing east, supposedly towards heaven. Sometimes priests and religious leaders are buried facing west, so that they can rise facing their people. Facing downwards, you are looking at something else altogether.'

'One strange thing,' says Angelo, 'we found something between his teeth.'

'What?' Ruth straightens up.

'This.' Angelo proffers an object in a transparent evidence bag. It looks like a flat, grey stone.

'A stone?'

'Yes, it looks like it may have been lodged between his teeth.'

Ruth leans closer. 'I wonder . . .'

'What?'

'I wonder if the tongue was removed. It's hard to see because the soft tissue will have rotted away. But, if so, it could have been some kind of punishment. Have you ever seen anything like that before?'

'No. It sounds more Germanic than Roman.'

'If the tongue was cut out,' says Ruth, 'there could be traces of infection in the bones. The mouth is full of bacteria.' She circles the bones once more and comes to a halt by one of the leg bones. She takes a magnifying glass from her bag and trains it on the left tibia.

'What is it?' says Angelo.

'That mark there,' says Ruth. 'It could be the sign of a periosteal reaction in the bone.'

'Reaction to what?' says Angelo. 'An infection?'

'Perhaps,' says Ruth. 'Where I've seen it before it was caused by a tattoo that had become infected.' That was in Bosnia and the tattoo had helped them identify the corpse. But Ruth doesn't intend to tell Angelo about her work in the Bosnian war graves. It's a subject she rarely mentions and tries not to think about.

'A tattoo,' says Angelo. 'That's not very Roman either.'

'It could be an infection caused by a leg shackle,' says Ruth. 'Perhaps Toni was a slave.'

'Perhaps,' says Angelo, but Ruth thinks he sounds rather distracted. Perhaps this isn't what he wants to hear. Maybe he'd rather hear that Toni was a rich Roman with a villa and underfloor heating, not a slave who wore a shackle, or some unfortunate who had their tongue cut out.

'Was there anything buried with the body?' says Ruth. 'Any grave goods?'

'No,' says Angelo. 'That's unusual, isn't it?'

'It is in a high-ranking grave,' says Ruth. 'I'll need some time to do a proper examination.'

'Go ahead,' says Angelo. 'When you've finished, let's have a *spremuta limone* in the café next door. Bones make me depressed.'

An odd remark for an archaeologist, thinks Ruth. She loves bones, personally, the older the better. She wonders why Angelo brought her all the way to Italy if he is going to rush her through her examination. But, then again, it is quite hot in the lab, especially with the overhead lights on, and the lemon drink sounds rather nice.

'All right,' she says, and then turns back to the bones.

Outside, the heat is intense. Ruth feels as if the sun is focussing its rays directly onto the top of her head. Even the short walk to the café makes her feel exhausted and sweaty, her cotton trousers sticking to her legs. Angelo's only concession to the sun is to put on dark glasses.

The café, which has tables in the shade, is an oasis. *Spremuta limone*, which turns out to be lemon juice and water, is delicious and refreshing. Ruth adds sugar to hers but Angelo drinks his neat, rather as he disposed of the grappa last night.

They sit in silence for a while, watching the cars going past. The air smells of lemon trees and petrol. Ruth starts to count Fiats but gives up after twenty. A pack of racing bikes streaks past, all spokes and neon Lycra. Who on earth would want to go cycling in this heat? She is just about to suggest going to join Shona at the pool when Angelo says, 'The thing is, Ruth, there are people who want to destroy the work I'm doing.'

It sounds so dramatic and incongruous, sitting under a café awning in the white heat of the midday sun, that Ruth almost wants to laugh. Instead she says, rather weakly, 'Why?'

'People are jealous,' says Angelo. It strikes Ruth that she's heard him say this before. 'And there are some people who are against another Roman excavation.'

'Why?' says Ruth again.

'There are too many Roman sites in Italy,' says Angelo. 'There are only two metro lines in Rome, because whenever they start digging, they come up against another damn amphitheatre. The Romans are everywhere. Some historians think that we should be spending our time learning more about the other Italic peoples.'

'Like the Volsci?'

'Yes, exactly like the Volsci.' He stares into space for a moment and then seems to come to a decision.

'Ruth, I asked you to come here because I respect your work. You're a leading expert on bones. I hoped you'd find something new about Toni, something that would get the TV people interested again.'

'The shackle marks . . .' begins Ruth.

'Yes, I will tell them that. About the possible tattoo, too. That might be enough. The thing is . . .'

There's another long pause.

'What is it, Angelo?' says Ruth. 'I've come all this way. You might as well tell me.'

'I think someone's trying to kill me.'

9

'He said that someone was trying to kill him?'

'Yes,' says Ruth. 'And he seems to think that I can help him find out who it is. I think he's confused me with Miss Marple.'

Ruth and Shona are sitting on the balcony. Although it's past nine o'clock, it's not yet dark, the shadows in the valley just deepening to violet, and the air is still warm. The children, worn out by their day by the pool, are asleep. They are sharing a room and Ruth is pleased that, by just tilting her chair back, she can see Kate's sleeping silhouette. Something about the apartment, beautiful though it is, makes her unwilling to let Kate out of her sight. She has the room next door to the children and does not begrudge the fact that they wake her up at 6 a.m., playing sliding games on the marble floors. Shona has a smaller room by the entrance hall, which is darker but quieter. 'I need my eight hours,' she says.

It has been a good day though. After their *spremata limone*, Angelo had driven Ruth to the swimming pool, which turned

out to be an idyllic spot at the top of one of the neigh-
bouring hills. When Ruth heard 'public swimming pool' she
had pictured somewhere full of chlorine and shouting children, with corn plasters floating in puddles, but this was an
imitation Greek temple, set in an olive grove, with statues
and vine-covered terraces. The shallow end of the pool had
plastic mushrooms that sprayed out water, and Kate and
Louis had run between these all afternoon, laughing hysterically. Ruth had even ventured into the water herself,
although she was slightly intimidated by the presence of
Graziano and by the sight of Shona sunbathing in a tiny
yellow bikini. Thank goodness Angelo had only dropped her
off outside. Ruth didn't think she was ready for a poolside
encounter, it would bring back too many memories of the
last time she had seen him without clothes on. But Angelo
had headed back to the excavation site, saying that he had
work to do. Ruth is going to visit the dig tomorrow.

'Do you believe him?' says Shona now. She's drinking
white wine and has her legs up on the stone parapet. Her
skin is the colour of weak tea and her hair has acquired
golden streaks. Ruth knows that she herself, despite slath-
ering on the factor 50, is slowly turning London-bus red.

'I don't know,' she says, 'but why would he make it up?'

'What makes him think someone's trying to kill him?'
says Shona. 'You told me about the mobile phone thing, but
that could just be someone's idea of a joke.'

'Apparently someone has been texting him pictures of
graves and skeletons,' says Ruth. 'It's an unknown number,
probably pay as you go, so they can't trace it. And he got a

message on his answerphone, no words, just laughter. You know those laugh boxes you used to get?'

'That's quite spooky,' says Shona.

'Yes, but apparently the police aren't interested. They say it's just someone playing a prank. There are abusive messages on Angelo's Facebook page, too, but the police say that's just free speech. Angelo says the police chief here doesn't like him – he's a fascist, according to Angelo. And someone cut the brake cables on his car.'

'Bloody hell. That does sound serious.'

'But then again, his mechanic said it could have been an animal chewing through the wires. They have a lot of wild animals around here. Remember the wild boar yesterday?'

'Was it only yesterday? Seems like we've been here for weeks.'

'I know what you mean,' says Ruth. She looks out over the valley, watching a car zigzagging up the hill. Now it's hidden by the olive trees; now she can see it again. She couldn't say why, but the car makes her nervous.

'Why would anyone want to kill Angelo?' says Shona. 'He seems really nice.'

Ruth looks at her friend. Does she really think that only nasty people get murdered?

'He says that there are people who want to stop him excavating the Roman site,' she says. 'They think he should be concentrating on the Italic tribes, like the Volsci.'

'The Volsci,' says Shona. 'Don't they come into *Coriolanus*? He became by famous by fighting the Volsci, then, when he was exiled, he joined the Volsci to besiege Rome.'

Ruth has only the vaguest idea of the plot of *Coriolanus*. She did *Macbeth* for O level and *King Lear* for A Level. Both tragic, doom-laden plays. *The sleeping and the dead are but as pictures . . . Nothing will come of nothing.*

'I'd like to see the Roman dig,' says Shona. 'It sounds really interesting.'

'Come with us tomorrow. I warn you that it might not look very exciting. I think most of the site is still below ground.'

'I don't mind,' says Shona. 'The kids will love it, lots of muddy holes everywhere. Then we can take them to the sea afterwards.'

Angelo has promised to take them to the beach tomorrow. Ruth will have to steel herself to see him in bathing trunks. Please, God, don't let him wear speedos.

Ruth's phone starts buzzing, vibrating furiously on the stone parapet. She picks it up. 'Nelson', says the screen. Even his name looks accusatory.

'I'd better get this,' she says. 'Sorry.' She goes back into the sitting room, which seems very dark now and somehow oppressive. She answers the call, feeling apprehensive.

'Ruth,' says a familiar voice, loud enough to reach Italy without the need of radio waves. 'What the hell are you doing?'

'Hi, Nelson. Nice to speak to you, too.'

'Don't give me that. What are you doing in Italy?'

'I was asked to advise on a dig. I'm an archaeologist, remember? That's my job.'

'Why didn't you tell me?'

'Why should I tell you? You don't tell me everything.'

There is a short, charged, trans-European silence. Then Nelson says, in a slightly different voice, 'I had to hear about it from Phil. Made me feel a right goon.'

'Phil?'

'Yes, some bones were found on a building site near Castle Rising. Phil came to look at them.'

'But he's not a forensic archaeologist.'

'No,' says Nelson, 'but he was the only archaeologist available. He told me that you and Shona were in Italy.'

Ruth wants to ask about the bones in Castle Rising, but she knows that this would not be wise. 'I felt like I needed a holiday,' she says, her tone more conciliatory. 'After Mum and everything. This Italian archaeologist, he's lending us an apartment in a hilltop village. It's really beautiful here, very peaceful.' As she says this, she thinks of *Stranieri andate a casa* and of the apparent plot to kill Angelo. But these are not thoughts that she can share with Nelson.

'Just let me know next time,' he is saying. 'I was worried.'

'About Kate?'

'About both of you.'

'How's Michelle?' says Ruth.

'She's fine,' says Nelson, after a pause. 'A bit tired, but that's only to be expected. Everything's much the same here. Very quiet at work without Cloughie.'

'I bet. Where did they go on honeymoon again?'

'Some Greek island. Seems that I'm the only person left in bloody Norfolk.'

'You hate holidays, Nelson.'

'You're right. I do. Wish Jo would go on one though.'

'Where would she go?' says Ruth. Speculating about Jo is one of their few shared jokes.

'New York.'

'Hong Kong.'

'The Amazon rainforest.'

'Dubai.'

'You're right,' says Nelson, 'she'd go to Dubai, on one of those God-awful man-made islands that looks like a palm tree.' There is a faint bark in the distance.

'I'd better go,' says Nelson, 'I'm walking Bruno. Take care of yourself and keep in touch.'

And he's gone. Of course, he would have to call her when Michelle is not in earshot, but the thought of Nelson tramping through the streets or the park with Bruno at his heels suddenly makes Ruth feel tearful and rather lonely. Get a grip, she tells herself. You're in a beautiful Italian village with your daughter and your best friend. How many people get a break like this?

Then there's a gunshot outside.

Nelson puts away his phone. Bruno looks up at him as if he understands. And he probably does. Nelson has told Bruno so much about Ruth and Katie that it's a wonder the dog isn't charging him consultancy fees.

'They're fine,' he tells Bruno. 'Fine and enjoying Italy.' He realises that he forgot to ask which part of Italy boasted the beautiful and peaceful hilltop village. Nelson has only been to Italy once, for a family holiday in Sorrento. He hadn't liked the hotel much. It had been full of Brits who were either intimidated or too interested when they found out that he was a policeman. The only thing he had enjoyed was a day trip to Pompeii. Michelle and the girls had got tired walking through the ruins in the heat, but Nelson could have stayed there all day. He remembers being mesmerised by the grooves in the stones, grooves put there by actual Roman chariots. And that was before he'd met Ruth, who could probably have told him the make and vehicle registration number of the chariots.

Who is this archaeologist who is lending Ruth an apartment? He didn't find that out either. Calls himself a detective. He knows that it's none of his business, but he doesn't like the idea of Ruth and Shona in Italy, surrounded by unknown and probably smouldering Italians. What was it that Michelle had said about Marco, her colleague at the salon? 'He's very good-looking, but then he *is* Italian.' Marco is gay, though, and Nelson has a sneaking suspicion that Ruth's archaeology friend isn't.

They are nearly home now. Bruno whines and pulls on his lead, impatient for supper. But Nelson stops, pulling the dog into the shade of a hedge. His house is in a cul-de-sac, so there is no need for anyone to pass by unless they are calling on one of the residents. But, as Nelson watches, a man is walking slowly around the half-moon of houses. He is slightly built, probably in his forties, wearing a heavy coat despite the warmth of the evening. He has glasses and thinning dark hair, ineffectual looking, carrying a local paper under his arm.

'Shh,' Nelson tells Bruno, but the animal is already quiet, listening intently with his head tilted to one side. He came from a litter of police dogs, so maybe this sort of thing is inbuilt.

The man completes his circuit and walks on briskly, towards the town centre and the station. He's on the other side of the road so Nelson doesn't get a good look at his face. He thinks he recognises him though. He thinks that the last time he saw that man, he was swearing and shouting that he would get even with Nelson, if it was the last thing he did.

'Was that a gun?' Shona stands framed in the doorway.

'It sounded like it,' says Ruth. She steps out onto the balcony.

'Be careful,' says Shona. They stand side-by-side, listening. Miraculously, the children haven't woken up. The night is silent apart from a faint croaking that could be frogs or cicadas. Ruth leans over the edge of the parapet. Is that a figure moving quickly through the lemon grove? It's too dark to see now but the night doesn't seem peaceful any more, it's as if the trees below them are seething with life. Even the warm air on her face feels like some great animal is breathing on her. She's about to go back into the house when a ghastly howl rents the air.

'What the hell was that?' says Shona.

'Probably a wolf,' says Ruth. 'They still have wolves in Italy. Angelo told me. There's a wolf sanctuary near here.'

'For God's sake, come in and let's shut the door,' says Shona. 'I don't want to meet a wolf or a gunman.'

They shut and bolt the door. Shona turns on the overhead lights and Ruth switches on the television, wanting to hear human voices. A quiz show is in progress, with a spinning wheel and contestants apparently miming their answers. They watch in silence for a few minutes, comforted, despite not being able to understand a word of the proceedings.

'Shall I make us a cup of tea?' says Ruth, when the ad break comes up.

'Let's have a proper drink,' says Shona.

10

Angelo rings the entry phone while they are still eating breakfast. Ruth has no option but to buzz him up, acutely conscious of the crumbs that the children have spread all over his space-age kitchen and of the fact that Louis has just broken a heavy, expensive-looking glass. She hastily wraps the shards in a three-day-old copy of the *Guardian* and reminds the children to keep their shoes on.

Angelo, though, doesn't seem in the mood to notice crumbs or broken glass. He greets Ruth cheerfully, waves at the children and accepts a cup of coffee from Shona.

'So kind of you to take us all to the dig today,' says Shona, placing a coffee cup in front of Angelo. This is rather embarrassing, as Ruth hasn't mentioned this change of plan yet. But Angelo takes it in his stride.

'Of course,' he says. 'The more the merrier, as you say in England. I will take you to the beach afterwards. Do you like the beach?' he asks Kate and Louis, both of whom are staring at him.

'Sometimes,' says Kate judiciously.

'If there's sand,' says Louis.

'There's sand at Formia,' says Angelo. 'Miles of sand. Not like Brighton beach. I went there once and I thought I was going to die. And the sea was so cold. Like ice.'

'There's sand in Norfolk,' says Ruth, feeling an obscure loyalty to her adopted county.

'But the sea is always freezing,' says Shona, less loyal.

Kate chooses this moment to fix Angelo with one of her Paddington hard stares. 'Are you a policeman?'

Angelo laughs. 'No. Why?'

'My dad's a policeman.'

Angelo shoots a glance at Ruth, who concentrates on her coffee.

'That's a very fine thing to be,' says Angelo.

Kate seems satisfies with this answer. Louis says, staring into his Coco Pops (brought from England), 'My dad isn't anything.'

'He's an archaeologist,' says Shona quickly. Hair toss, eye flash. Ruth thinks that Louis has a point though. There is something rather null about Phil. But she thinks she should bring an end to this talk of fathers.

'We had a bit of a shock last night,' she says to Angelo. 'We thought we heard a gunshot outside.'

'We were terrified,' says Shona. 'Clinging on to each other in the dark.'

Ruth shoots her a look. She doesn't want to frighten the children and, besides, she doesn't want Angelo to think of them as two pathetic women, screaming and having the vapours.

But Angelo doesn't look too concerned. He certainly doesn't seem to think that this is part of the supposed plot against him.

'Probably hunters,' he says. 'You get a lot of hunters around here. Shall we get going? You'll want to see the site before it gets too hot.'

The house in Spalding is the definition of inoffensive. It's on a housing estate, a maze of tiny houses with neat front gardens and contrasting front doors. Although the houses are much smaller, it's not a million miles away from Nelson's cul-de-sac. True, there are more satellite dishes here and fewer four-by-fours, but it has the same smug, safe feeling. Two children are playing tennis in the street and a postman is delivering letters. Maybe Micky Webb really has become respectable at last. There's no parking on Micky's street and the houses don't have garages, so the road is full of cars, including a white van outside Micky's house. Nelson parks two streets away. It'll be good to have an element of surprise. The Mercedes would be a bit of a giveaway.

Micky's house is one of the neatest: paved front garden, plants in tubs, a sign that says 'The Nook'. The Crook might be more appropriate, thinks Nelson. He raps loudly on the door.

The door is opened by a woman wearing jeans and a pink jumper. She's probably in her mid forties, slim and not unattractive, with shoulder-length brown hair. If this is the prison-visiting wife, then Micky has done quite well for himself.

'DCI Nelson.' He shows his warrant card. 'Is Micky in?'

'Yes.' The woman looks rather scared, but the sight of Nelson on the doorstep would do that to anyone. Her voice is composed, though. 'Yes, he's here. Do come in.'

She ushers Nelson into a small but extremely tidy room that is obviously both sitting room and dining area. Micky Webb is sitting at the table, reading a newspaper. He jumps up when his wife comes in, and when he sees Nelson his mouth falls open in surprise.

'Hello, Micky. Long time no see.'

'DI Nelson.' Micky looks older: receding hair, glasses, a slight sagging of the chin. He's in his stockinged feet, which makes him look smaller than Nelson remembers. Nelson is pretty sure that this is a house where people take their shoes off when they come in.

'It's DCI now,' he says. 'Can we have a chat?'

'Is anything wrong?' says Micky. 'I signed in at the station this morning.'

'Glad to hear it,' says Nelson. 'No, this is just a friendly chat. Sit down,' he tells Micky, hoping to wrong-foot the man by telling him to sit down in his own house.

Nelson sits on the sofa and Micky resumes his seat at the table. The woman remains standing in the doorway.

'This is my wife, Louise,' says Micky. 'We've got no secrets.'

'That's nice for you,' says Nelson.

'Can I get you a cup of tea or coffee?' says Louise.

'No thanks,' says Nelson. Louise sits at the table next to her husband. Nelson notes the discreet gold cross round her neck. Maybe it's religion that has brought these two together. He can't see any other signs of God-bothering in the house. None of the pictures and holy water stoups and palms fashioned into crosses that he remembers from home.

'Is that your van outside?' he asks Micky.

'Yes,' says Micky. 'I'm doing some painting and decorating. Trying to get myself back on my feet, you know.'

Work can't be going very well if Micky's home at 10 a.m. reading the newspaper, thinks Nelson. But, then again, who would want Micky Webb in their house?

'Congratulations on your release,' says Nelson. 'That was a bit of a result for you, wasn't it?'

'I'm a changed man,' says Micky. 'I know you find that hard to believe, DI Nelson.'

'I do,' says Nelson. 'And it's DCI Nelson, remember?'

Louise leans forward now. She speaks in a low, pleasant voice, with just a trace of a Norfolk accent.

'Micky has given his life to God now. We both have. Isn't there more joy in heaven over one sinner that repents than over ninety-nine righteous persons?'

'If you say so,' says Nelson. 'The maths seems wrong to me. I'm just concerned with your husband. You see, I know Micky of old and I find it hard to believe in Saint Francis here.'

'Just give me a chance,' says Micky, fixing him with an earnest stare, magnified by the glasses. 'That's all I ask.'

'All right,' says Nelson. 'I'll give you a chance to explain what you were doing outside my house yesterday evening.'

He looks at Louise as he says this, wondering if this

information will come as a surprise to her. But Louise is smiling at Micky with unwavering affection and encouragement.

'Tell him, love.'

Micky takes off his glasses and wipes them. Buying time, thinks Nelson.

'I came to apologise,' says Micky at last.

'To apologise?'

'Yes, last time we spoke, I said some hard things to you. I wanted to take them back. To assure you of my goodwill.'

'You came to my house to assure me of your goodwill?'

'It's a programme, you see.' Micky looks at his wife for support. 'It's organised by our church. You go to see the people you've wronged and ask for their forgiveness. I went to your house yesterday, but I didn't have the nerve to knock on your door.'

'You might have had a shock if you did,' says Nelson. 'I've got a very fierce guard dog.' He feels the need to tell Micky that his house is protected, even though Bruno is more likely to greet a new arrival with tail-wagging and affectionate, slobbery kisses.

'I was scared to face you,' says Micky. 'That's why I'm glad God sent you here today.'

This, Nelson remembers, is what he has always disliked about evangelicals. The way they talk about God as if he's God Smith who lives next door. At least Catholics have a bit of awe and respect.

'God didn't send me anywhere,' says Nelson. 'And isn't it your ex-wife and your children that you should be apologising to? But you can't, because they're dead. You had them killed.'

He expects this to cause a reaction – anger, tears, perhaps even violence. Instead, Micky puts his head in his hands. Louise pats his shoulder.

'Offer it up to God,' she says. 'Offer your suffering up to God.'

Her voice is low and calm and it seems to have an effect. Micky looks up. 'I wish I could. They're dead and it's my fault. My fault, as surely as if I'd set the house on fire myself. I'll suffer for that every day of my life. My kids . . .' He wipes his eyes. 'So often I wished I was dead,' he says. 'But God has kept me alive. It has to be for some purpose. I have to believe that. So I'm speaking at schools and colleges. Trying to stop youngsters from taking the path I took. And I'm trying to apologise to people I've wronged. That's all.'

Micky looks straight at Nelson and, despite everything, there's a strange dignity to him at this moment.

'If you want to get things straight between you and me,' says Nelson, 'you'll never come near my house again. Do you understand?'

'I understand,' says Micky. 'God bless you, DCI Nelson.'

At least he's got the rank right this time, thinks Nelson.

The archaeological site is on farmland about a mile outside a town called Arce. Although Angelo's car is air-conditioned and comfortable, after half an hour of descending hairpin bends and ten minutes of juddering over unmade roads, both children are complaining of feeling sick and Ruth isn't feeling too good herself.

'We ought to stop,' says Ruth nervously, looking at the car's smart red interior.

'Nearly there,' says Angelo. Over his shoulder, he says, 'You know, kids, you can't be sick if you sing. It's a scientific fact.' And he launches into a version of 'Old MacDonald Had a Farm'. After a few minutes of animal noises, the children join in. Shona is laughing in the back seat (Ruth was rather pleased to ride shotgun this time).

'Old MacDonald had a pig . . .'

'Sing, Mum,' says Kate.

Ruth oinks half-heartedly. She is rather worried about the car's brake cables.

They stop in what seems to be the middle of a field. Kate, looking around critically, says, 'Where's the pool?'

'What pool?' says Ruth. 'We're going to the seaside after this.'

'The pool,' says Kate. 'The Roman pool. Like in Bath.'

'Ah, Aquae Sulis,' says Angelo. 'You're an archaeologist already, Kate.'

'I'm not,' says Kate. 'I want to be an actor.'

Ruth groans inwardly. She has a secret hope that Kate will be a scientist or a doctor. Certainly not an actor. Nevertheless, she can share Kate's disappointment with the site. Even to her expert eye there are no recognisable archaeological features, just grass, yellowed by the sun, and a few stunted-looking olive trees. Scaling rods in the middle of the field are the only signs that a dig is taking place.

Angelo, who is watching her, says, 'There's nothing to see on the surface, but geophysics shows that this was quite a significant settlement, about twenty-five hectares. We've found a marketplace and a theatre, as well as some sizable dwellings. And some of them have pools,' he says, turning back to Kate.

'Where are they, then?' says Kate.

'Under the earth,' says Angelo. 'But I've got a special camera that can show me pictures of what goes on underground.'

'What techniques did you use?' says Ruth. Having recently been involved in a case featuring bodies buried in tunnels, she doesn't much like to think about what goes on deep underground.

'Magnetometry and GPR,' says Angelo. 'Absolutely fascinating.'

'What's GPR?' says Shona. She is looking rather hot and bored. Louis looks on the verge of a tantrum. He has the sensitive skin (and bad temper) that often goes with red hair.

'Ground penetrating radar,' says Ruth. 'Phil's a big fan.'

'Can I see the pictures of the underground pool?' says Kate.

'Later on,' says Angelo. 'There's a well here too.'

'Did they have wells?' says Shona. 'You think of the Romans as being all viaducts and hypocausts.'

'Wells had ritual as well as practical significance to the Romans,' says Angelo. 'You often find objects placed in Roman wells as sacrifices, perhaps to do with the cycle of the seasons or even fertility.' He turns to Ruth. 'Do you want to see where we found Toni?'

Shona asks if she and Louis can wait in the car with the air conditioning on, but Ruth is keen to see the trench, even though it's so hot that her T-shirt is sticking to her back. She follows Angelo across the field, Kate holding her hand.

'As I said, the settlement dates from about 500 CE,' Angelo is saying. 'We think it was abandoned and then the building materials were scavenged.'

'Do you have any idea why it was abandoned?'

'No, but there was a lot of fighting around that time. Lots of these little towns were centres of resistance against the Romans. Have you heard of Fregellae?'

'No, I don't think so.'

'It was a town near here, established by the Volsci. This was Volsci territory at one time, until they were pushed further south. Initially, Fragellae was on friendly terms with the Romans and stopped Hannibal's advance by burning the bridges across the Liris. Later on, though, they rebelled and the Romans razed the place to the ground.'

'And you think the same may have happened here?'

'Maybe. It's a similar set up to Fregellae and quite close to the Via Latina, which was the main road to Rome. It could be a really significant site, if only . . .'

'What?'

'There are people who don't want money spent here,' says Angelo. He's silent for a minute, and Ruth wonders if he's going to mention jealousy again, or the plot to kill him. But then she realises that he's looking past her. A black Fiat

500 has left the main road and is bumping over the grass towards them. Angelo says something in Italian – Ruth can't tell if it's an expletive or an expression of pleasure.

'What is it?' says Ruth.

'My team,' says Angelo, and strides off towards the car, which has parked next to Angelo's jeep. Ruth doesn't follow him. Angelo will introduce her if he wants to. She also thinks that he didn't sound too keen to see his teammates.

She and Kate walk over to the trench, which is roped off with police tape. A slightly melodramatic touch, thinks Ruth, but it's probably for the TV cameras. The trench is neat though, its edges perfectly straight. Ruth approves. She bends down to examine the grave cut. Kate copies her.

'Ruth!'

Ruth straightens up and sees Angelo coming towards them with a man and a woman, both young and dressed in shorts. Angelo is now grinning broadly.

'Ruth, I want you to meet Marta and Roberto, my graduate students and colleagues. This is Dr Ruth Galloway from the University of North Norfolk, and this is Katie, who is going to be a famous actor one day.'

Handshakes all round; Roberto even bends down to shakes hands with Kate. Ruth is rather impressed that Angelo remembered about Kate wanting to be an actor, even though it makes her cringe to hear this particular ambition out loud. She imagines people thinking she's a pushy showbiz mother.

'Good news, Ruth,' he says. 'Marta took a call from Cielo Blu, the TV people. They want to start filming again. They're really excited that I've brought in an expert from England. They want to interview you tomorrow.'

'Interview?' says Ruth, with a feeling of dread.

'Film you,' says Angelo. 'We can do it at Mamma's house. That's scenic enough.'

Ruth opens her mouth to say that she doesn't want to appear on TV, but she knows how much this means to Angelo so she just smiles and says, 'That's great.'

'It's more than great,' says Angelo. 'It means that we can carry on with our work here.'

And you'll be back on television, thinks Ruth. Sometimes, in spite of the tan and the designer black shirts, Angelo reminds her of Phil.

'What do you think of the site?' asks Marta. She speaks perfect English too. She's very slim, with short, dark hair and narrow, intimidating-looking glasses. Despite the glasses, Ruth warms to her.

'It's interesting,' she says. 'I've just been looking at the trench where the bones were found. The bones were well preserved but the soil is quite chalky. Do you think that there may have been a coffin?'

'You sometimes get wooden coffins from this era,' says Angelo, 'but stone is more usual. There's no sign that this body was enclosed in anything though. No marks on the soil indicating decayed vegetable matter.'

'No grave goods either,' says Marta. 'That's unusual. Romans were usually buried with something for the after-life. Pottery, say, or glass beads.'

'And the grave wasn't within a house?' says Ruth. 'Romans were sometimes buried in the home, weren't they?'

'Yes,' says Angelo, 'in early Roman houses it's quite common to find dead family members buried under the house. They were called *dii manes*, the spirits of the good. No, the body was buried a little outside the main town. That, and the fact that he was buried face down, makes us think that Toni was an outsider.'

Stranieri andate a casa, thinks Ruth. She remembers Angelo saying that, here, even people from the next village are foreigners.

'If he did have a tattoo on his leg, or the marks of shackles, maybe he wasn't Roman at all,' she says. 'Maybe he came from overseas.'

'You could be a Roman citizen even if you were born overseas,' says Angelo. 'There were black Romans – even a black emperor, some say.'

'I know,' says Ruth, 'but it's unlikely that a high-status Roman was buried face down without any grave goods.'

They are all looking into the trench now. Roberto and Marta hang back respectfully. Ruth kneels down to look more closely at the soil. 'The topsoil's broken up by ploughing,' she says, 'but the layers are preserved lower down. I don't think our man was buried in a hurry. I think he was left here, quite deliberately, face down, with a stone between his teeth.'

She has almost forgotten Kate's presence but, as usual, her daughter is listening hard.

'That's horrible,' she says.

'Come, Katie,' says Roberto. 'You want to see what I found in another trench? Is the skin of a snake.'

Ruth is grateful to Roberto for the distraction, even though she's rather scared of the thought that there must be snakes in the vicinity. When Kate is out of earshot, she says, 'I've been looking up cases of bodies buried with stones in their teeth.'

'Really?' says Angelo. 'What did you find?'

'There was a recent case in Ireland where skeletons were found in a church cemetery with stones in their mouths. Researchers thought it had been done because they believed that it would prevent the bodies returning to haunt the earth.'

'Like vampires being buried with stakes through their hearts?' suggests Angelo. Ruth thinks his tone sounds rather frivolous.

'Vampires are a sixteenth-century construct,' she says. 'This church was eighth century. It was more like a belief in zombies. Revenants, they're sometimes called, dead bodies that return to life.'

'I've never heard of that happening with a Roman burial,' says Angelo.

'Maybe not,' says Ruth, 'but there was a Roman British skeleton found in Stanwick in England, dating from the third or fourth century. The body had been buried face down with a stone replacing its tongue.'

Marta, who has been listening intently, says, 'Like Toni?'

'There are some features which sound similar,' says Ruth. 'Sometimes you do get body parts replaced by stones in

Roman British burials. A rock in place of the skull is most usual. But this did seem to imply some sort of punishment.'

'Punishment for what?' says Marta.

'Maybe for spreading malicious lies,' says Ruth. 'Maybe for treachery.'

'Or maybe the poor man was epileptic,' says Angelo, 'or mentally ill, and bit his own tongue off. The stone could be a way of replacing it for the afterlife.'

'That's possible,' says Ruth. 'But the fact that the body was buried face down does seem to indicate a deviant burial. Either the dead person was a felon or some sort of outcast, or people were genuinely afraid that he would rise from the dead.'

To her surprise, Marta crosses herself. Angelo looks over to where Roberto is helping Kate dig in the dry earth.

'Come on,' he says. 'The place for digging is at the seaside.' He bounds over and sweeps Kate off her feet, whirling her round. She squeals with excitement, rather as she did on the plane.

'Come on, Katie,' he says. 'Let's go to the beach now.'

He strides ahead with Kate. Marta and Roberto follow, talking intently, heads together. Ruth walks slowly back across the parched grass. It hasn't escaped her notice that Angelo is now calling Kate 'Katie'.

11

Formia turns out to be perfect. At first Ruth is quite worried, as Angelo drives them past ancient walls and a rocky harbour.

'This was a famous port in Roman times,' he tells them. 'Formia is from the Greek word for landing place. It was a fashionable resort, even then.'

That's as may be, thinks Ruth, but the children want sand and shallow water and ice creams. She starts moodily at the harbour with its multicoloured boats and picturesque tower. A huge grey shape that looks like a warship looms in the background.

'Cicero was assassinated outside the town in 43 BCE,' Angelo is saying. 'There's a monument to him here. And, after the fall of the Western Roman Empire, the town was sacked by the barbarians.'

Louis starts to whine softly, like a plane coming in to land.

But, as Angelo drives along what he calls the *lungomare*, the rocks give way to sand and colourful umbrellas and families carrying beach towels. Kate and Louis perk up and start singing, 'Old MacDonald had a beach'.

'Life's a beach,' mutters Ruth. She doesn't like seaside resorts that much – she prefers her coastlines wild and lonely – but there's no denying that this looks like the children's idea of heaven. And they do deserve a break, she thinks, after following her to an archaeological dig in the middle of a field, not to mention staying in an apartment that the locals daub with graffiti and use as target practice.

Angelo parks the car near a café with a red and white awning. There's a deck, too, with chairs and tables.

'This is my friend Stefano's beach,' explains Angelo. 'He'll look after us.'

Ruth, getting the beach bag out of the car, is rather confused. How can a beach belong to anyone? It's just there, part of the sea and sky, as Cathbad would say. But, when they get to the café, everything becomes clear. This is a private beach, owned by Stefano. For a daily fee, visitors get their own umbrella and sun loungers, use of showers, Wi-Fi and their choice from what looks like a bewildering array of food, including *spaghetti alle vongole* and squid ink risotto.

Stefano waves away Ruth's offer of money and they make their way to their umbrella along a path of wooden planks. 'It's because the sand gets so hot,' Angelo explains. Ruth thinks of the sand on the beach where the henge was found, firm and cold beneath her feet; she can't remember it becoming even warm. Kate and Louis are in their swimming things in no time and Kate nags Ruth to get in the water. Ruth hesitates. She has her swimming costume underneath her clothes, but it seems rather uncouth to get undressed surrounded by these bronzed and beautiful strangers.

Angelo comes to her aid. 'There are changing rooms,' he gestures. 'I will watch the children while you and Shona change.'

'It's a bit different from Cromer beach, isn't it?' says Shona, as they walk along the wooden planks to the changing rooms.

'Yes,' says Ruth. Though she still thinks she might actually prefer Cromer.

She's also slightly embarrassed by her black one-piece. Every other woman on the beach, including the grand-mothers, is in a bikini. Also, her body is so white and – there's no getting away from it – there's far too much of it. Pull yourself together, she tells herself, fat is a feminist issue. Just because she doesn't conform to society's ideal of what a woman should look like, it doesn't mean she should feel ashamed, she should celebrate her curves. All the same, she wishes she'd brought a wrap of some kind.

'I'm ready,' shouts Shona, and Ruth watches her sashay along the planks in a white bikini with a multi-coloured sarong tied round her waist. Ruth sighs and follows in her M&S one-piece, grimly aware that the top half is reinforced by what feel like steel girders.

Nelson is in a slightly less scenic location, a Lincolnshire town, grey with summer rain. He is here to see Micky Webb's probation officer. Policemen often distrust proba-tion officers. They are part of a breed, along with social workers, categorised as 'do-gooders'. But Nelson is a fair man, most of the time. He realises that it's better to do good than do evil. It's just that probation officers have a tendency to see things from the criminal's perspective (or, as they would put it, 'my client's perspective'), which is galling, to say the least, when you're the one who put the villain inside. But Nelson likes Derek Hobson on sight. He's nearing retirement age, a heavyset man with a drinker's nose who looks like he may have played rugby once. He welcomes Nelson into his untidy cubbyhole of an office and offers him black coffee from a flask. 'I can't abide all that messed-up stuff. Cinnamon lattes and the like.'

Nelson registers something familiar and comforting about the vowels.

'Are you from Lancashire?'

'Salford,' says Derek with a grin. 'The jewel of the north.'

'I'm from Blackpool,' says Nelson, accepting a cup of viscous-looking coffee. 'Whatever brought you to this god-forsaken part of the world?'

'The love of a good woman,' says Derek. 'I met Mary on holiday in Greece. When she said that she was from the east coast, I thought it might be something like Santorini. Then I saw Spalding.'

'I came here for the job,' says Nelson. 'Now my daughters have ended up saying "barth" instead of "bath".'

'My kids are the same,' says Derek. 'Lincolnshire lasses, both of them.'

So Derek has two daughters too, which is another bond between them. Of course, Nelson actually has three daughters and (maybe) another on the way, but he doesn't think this is a conversation he should get into.

'I came to talk about Micky Webb,' says Nelson. 'He claims to be a changed man. Got married, got religion and all that. But I saw him skulking around my house the other evening. I went to see him this morning and he says that he came to apologise, to set things straight. I wondered what your take on it was.'

Derek is silent for a few minutes, drinking his coffee. Then he says, 'I've seen a lot of ex-cons find religion. A few of them meant it. I think Micky's one of the rare people who actually has had a change of heart. He's a weak man. I've always thought that he was under the thumb of his previous girlfriend, Wendy Markham. Micky once told me that she was the one who'd had the idea of torching the house and then, when you came knocking on his door, she scarpered, leaving him to take the rap. Micky didn't testify against her in court because he was still in love with her. A man like that, he can go either way, depending on who's pulling the strings. Micky's biggest stroke of luck was meeting Louise Martin. She converted him to Christianity and she's made him a better person. It's as simple as that.'

'Is it ever as simple as that?' says Nelson. 'Micky Webb killed his wife and children. Can he really be one of the good guys now?'

'It's not about good and bad,' says Derek. 'It's opportunity and environment that creates criminals. That's one thing I've learnt after nearly forty years in the probation system. The qualities that make you a good policeman – courage, risk-taking, single-mindedness – would probably have made you a good armed robber if you'd been brought up in the Kray family. Micky mixed with criminal types, that's all in the files. Wendy Markham, too. Her dad had a history of fraudulent insurance claims. It's possible that she thought that was the only way to make money. Of course, Micky was greedy and stupid, but, in a different life, he'd probably be an investment banker.'

Nelson thinks about Clough. Freddie Burnett had arrested Clough's brother; the family were known to the police. It would have been easy for Cloughie to follow in his brother's footprints but, for some reason, he had sided with the angels.

'Other people grow up in criminal families,' he says, 'but it takes a particularly nasty person to burn a house with people living inside.'

'Micky didn't know that his wife and children were there that night,' says Derek. 'I believe that. I think he's suffered agonies of guilt.'

'Good,' says Nelson. 'But do you really believe that Micky's new wife has enough influence to turn him into a law-abiding citizen?'

'Never underestimate the influence of wives,' says Derek. 'Why else would I have ended up in Spalding?'

Nelson thinks about this conversation as he drives back to the station. Was it really as simple as that? If you're brought up in a criminal environment, you become a criminal? It would make his job simpler, if so. But Nelson has met many law-abiding people from so-called problem families, and many hardened criminals with unimpeachably middle-class credentials. There's good and bad in all of us, that's what he thinks. He's pretty sure that he could commit a crime, given the right circumstances – driving too fast doesn't count, in his book. But he's been tempted to violence a few times. When he first found out about Tim and Michelle, for example.

As he drives along the A17, fuming when he gets stuck behind a slow-moving vehicle, Nelson can't stop himself thinking about Tim. He was the one who had brought Tim to Norfolk. He'd worked with him on a case in Blackpool and admired the younger officer's intelligence and self-possession. Tim had joined the Serious Crimes Unit, facing some hostility at first, especially from Clough, but quickly establishing himself as one of the team. Nelson had worked hard to make Tim feel at home, even inviting him to Sunday lunch, which is where he met Michelle. And this is how Nelson has been repaid. Tim had an affair with his wife, un-consummated according to Michelle, but an affair nonetheless. And now Michelle is pregnant. Could Tim be the father? Did they consummate their affair some time in May? Nelson has done the maths. He saw Tim at Clough's wedding, and he thought that he read something on his face, something that went beyond the pain of seeing Michelle and his colleagues again. Well, come February they will know for certain.

This train of thought lasts all the way to King's Lynn, through the traffic by the city gates and into the station car park. Nelson is so preoccupied that, when Leah tells him that someone from UNN is on the phone, Nelson momentarily thinks it's Ruth. But Ruth is sunning herself in Italy and a far less congenial archaeologist is on the case.

'DCI Nelson? It's Phil Trent here from UNN. It's about the bones.'

'What bones?'

'The ones found at Castle Rising. Well, I've got the carbon-14 results back. I got them to expedite the testing, said it was an emergency.'

Phil sounds extremely pleased with himself, but Nelson doesn't give him the satisfaction of congratulating him on his efficiency.

'Well?' he says.

'Well, it looks as if the skeleton might be Roman. The results show that the bones are about two thousand years old, and we know there was a Roman settlement in the area. Of course, the context has become contaminated, probably through farming and building work, but it might be worth doing more excavation in the area.'

'Fine,' says Nelson. 'You tell that to Edward Spens.' Edward Spens runs the building company and, though superficially charming, he is not a man to take kindly to a suggestion that his site become the focus of an archaeological project.

Phil obviously senses this. 'Can you speak to him?'

'It's not police business any more.'

'No,' says Phil, sounding disappointed. 'I just thought you might be interested.'

You thought wrong, thinks Nelson. Aloud he says, 'Have you heard from Shona?'

'Yes,' says Phil, 'sounds as if they're having a whale of a time. They're going to the beach today, apparently.'

'I hope it stays fine for them.'

'No doubt of that.' Phil gives a little laugh. 'It was nearly ninety degrees in the shade yesterday.'

'What the name of the town they're staying in again?'

'Castello degli Angeli. It's in Lazio, near Monte Cassino. You know, where they had that battle in World War Two.'

'I've seen the movie,' says Nelson. 'I have to go and do some policing now. Thanks for calling.'

But, when Phil rings off, Nelson finds Google Earth on his computer and starts to float through the medieval streets of Castello degli Angeli.

Maybe resorts aren't so bad after all, thinks Ruth, as they finally leave the beach, trailing towels and mats and an inflatable beach ball bought by Angelo. Kate has had a wonderful day, and Ruth has to admit that there is something very pleasant about swimming in the sea and not freezing to death when you come out. She has swum several times and played with Kate in the shallows. Angelo emerged from the changing rooms in black trunks (not Speedos), dived into the sea and set off with a flashy front crawl, apparently aiming for Tunisia. But, when he came back, he seemed happy to play on the sand with the children, allowing Ruth – who hates sunbathing – a few minutes in the shade with her book. Then they had eaten squid ink risotto at Stefano's café (even though Kate had stated that food should not be black, 'it's the law') and returned for more sun, swimming and sand. It's been a long time since I've had a day like this, she thinks, feeling the grittiness of sand between her toes and the not unpleasant dampness of her costume under her clothes. Her skin, too, feels tingly and tight, despite liberal application of factor 50. That's not unpleasant either; there's something sensuous about the beach, it makes you aware of your body and its possibilities, which is why all the pop songs go on about sun, sea and sex. There was a particularly silly, sexy song playing at the café at lunchtime. 'Hey hey, fun in the sun, hey hey. Down on the beach, hey hey. Fun in the sun.'

Doing nothing makes you tired, too. Both children fall asleep on the drive home and Ruth feels her head nodding. She is in the back this time and she can hear Shona and Angelo laughing and talking. Their voices blend with the pop song and with the jumbled emotions of the past few days. The sun-baked countryside flashes past: cypresses, olive groves, churches, mountain villages. *Fun in the sun . . . went backpacking in Greece once . . . used to swim for my university . . .* stranieri andate a casa . . . *they have wolves in Italy . . . concentrate on the living . . . hey hey, fun in the sun . . .*

When she wakes, they are parking in the square at Castello degli Angeli.

'Sleep little three eyes,' says Angelo. Where did he get *that* one from?

'You must have been tired,' says Shona. 'All three of you fast asleep in the back, like babies.'

Ruth feels rather stupid and hopes that she hasn't been snoring. She wakes Kate, who is also distinctly grumpy.

'I don't want to walk up the hill,' she says.

'I'll put you on my shoulders,' says Angelo.

'Me,' says Louis, waking up with his mouth already open in protest. 'I want a piggyback.'

'Katie as far as the first lamp post,' says Angelo. 'Then Louis.' The children accept this, though they wouldn't from their mothers. The square is quiet, just the old men at the café table, the water trickling lethargically from the fountain. It's six o'clock, early in Italy, where it seems that the children never go to bed, and still hot. They walk up the hill, Angelo with Kate on his shoulders, Shona hand in hand with a recalcitrant Louis, Ruth following behind. The same cooking smells, the piano playing, the bird singing in its cage. It's funny how quickly you get used to a place, thinks Ruth. This almost feels like home now. Well, if not home, then somewhere familiar. At the lamp post, Angelo puts Kate down and lifts Louis up. Kate skips along next to Ruth, singing 'Old MacDonald had a beach'. They reach the green front door, and Ruth, like every English tourist, thinks longingly of a cup of tea.

'Home sweet home,' says Angelo, putting Louis down. Then he gives an exclamation, something that sounds like '*Dio*'. He bends down to look at something on the doorstep.

'What's that?' says Shona.

'Nothing,' says Angelo. 'Some animal must have left it.' He pushes the object behind the recycling bins.

But Ruth has seen what it is.

It's a skull.

12

When Nelson gets home, Michelle's car isn't in the driveway. He pauses for a minute, wondering what this means. Either Michelle is working late, or has gone out, or she has lent the car to Laura. If it's the latter, then he and Michelle are in for an evening alone together, something that hasn't happened since Clough's wedding. As he parks his car, Nelson reflects that there was a time when an evening alone with his wife was a treat. When the girls were little, for example, or when they were teenagers and always demanding lifts everywhere. Now, he almost hopes that both his wife and daughter have gone out, leaving him to an evening with the dog and a can of beer. He can already hear Bruno barking excitedly inside the house.

Michelle is in the sitting room. She is watching one of those programmes where people buy rubbish at car boot sales and then seem surprised that it isn't worth anything.

'Hello, love,' says Nelson, stooping to kiss her. 'How are you feeling?'

'Not bad.' Michelle looks pale, and she hasn't changed out of her work clothes, a sure sign that all isn't well. 'I still feel a bit sick though. I couldn't face starting supper. Sorry.'

'That's OK. I can put some chops on. Master Chef, that's me.'

'You hate *MasterChef*,' says Michelle, but she manages a faint smile. 'I don't think I could manage a chop. I'll just have toast or something.'

'You should eat properly,' says Nelson, fending off Bruno, who has brought him his lead as a hint. 'When's your next check-up?'

'It's the scan next week,' says Michelle. 'I told you.'

'So you did. Exciting stuff.' He remembers the thrill of seeing Laura and Rebecca on the screen, tiny shapes that, hard as he tried, he was never able to assemble into a baby. This time, though, he feels nervous. It's not a concrete fear. They have already had the dating scan and the screening for Down's Syndrome. As an older mother, Michelle is receiving extra care and attention. 'A geriatric mother,' she told him after her first visit to the midwife, 'that's what they're calling me.' Nelson had sympathised, but he does feel that there is something odd about having a baby at their time of life. He'll be eligible for a Saga holiday in two years. And he feels nervous about this scan because he has the ridiculous notion that they will be able to tell, from the cloudy shape on the ultrasound, whether the baby is his or Tim's.

He immediately feels disloyal and, to cover it up, kisses Michelle again. 'Good to have the place to ourselves, isn't it?'

Michelle smiles, a stronger effort this time. 'Yes, though Laura's really good. She's done all the shopping this week.'

'She does it all on the computer.'

'Yes, but it still takes some thinking about. I can't even think about food at the moment.'

'What about some tea and ginger biscuits?' That worked with Michelle's previous pregnancies. Nelson has a sinking feeling about Laura doing the internet shopping. That means that the groceries will be high on quinoa and brown rice, and low on biscuits.

'That would be lovely,' says Michelle. 'Thanks, Harry.'

Nelson goes to the door, accompanied by Bruno, still carrying his lead in his mouth. In the doorway, he pauses, 'You haven't seen anyone hanging around outside the house today, have you?'

Michelle looks up. 'What do you mean?'

'Probably nothing,' says Nelson. 'Just that I saw someone in the street the other day. A stranger. I wondered what he was doing here.'

'Honestly, Harry,' says Michelle. 'You're so suspicious of everyone. It was probably just somebody who was lost.'

'Yes,' says Nelson, 'you're probably right.' Louise Webb, née Martin, would probably say that her husband is a lost sheep who has been gathered into the Christian fold. The jury is out as far as Nelson is concerned.

'Ginger biscuits coming up,' he says. Bruno gives a staccato bark of encouragement. He understands the word 'biscuit'.

*

Ruth doesn't mention the skull in front of Shona. She waits until the children are settled in front of another Disney classic and Shona has gone off to ring Phil. Angelo seems to be hanging around, so Ruth asks if he'd like a cup of tea.

'Ah, this English obsession with tea.'

'Is that a yes then?'

'No, thank you. I should be going. I'll pick you up at nine tomorrow.'

'You will?'

'For the TV interview.' Ruth has forgotten all about the interview. 'We'll meet at my mother's apartment in Arpino. You'll like my mother. She's very interested in history. And in everything, really.'

Ruth can't really imagine Angelo with a mother. She's probably a little woman swathed in black who adores her only son. Ruth follows Angelo to the door.

'What was that skull doing on our doorstep?' she says.

'So you saw that, did you?'

'Yes,' says Ruth.

'I don't know,' says Angelo. 'It was an animal's. A dog's, I think. Another animal must have left it there.'

'Come on,' says Ruth. 'Someone writes a message on our door, telling us to go home, and now there's a skull on our doorstep. And what about the gunshot in the night? There's something you're not telling me.'

Angelo regards her for a moment, one hand on the door, then he says, 'These things aren't aimed at you.'

'Who are they aimed at? You?'

'Maybe,' says Angelo.

'Maybe? Who else is there?'

'Maybe . . .' Angelo pauses again. 'Maybe my grandfather.'

'Your grandfather? I thought he was a war hero?'

'To some, yes. But not everyone sided with the resistance.'

'You mean . . . fascists?' This is an alien word to Ruth, an extremist's word. She knows about the far right – there's a strong UKIP vote in Norfolk, after all – but the word fascist conjures up images of goose-stepping troops, swastikas, pictures from a grainy newsreel.

Angelo grimaces. Perhaps the word is alien to him too. 'Not fascists,' he says. 'People who supported Mussolini.'

What's the difference, thinks Ruth. 'You think some passing blackshirts left the skull on our doorstep?' she says. She is doing sums in her head. Surely any surviving Mussolini supporter must be at least ninety years old. Are they being targeted by some lunatic nonagenarian?

'Not everyone agrees with armed rebellion,' says Angelo. 'Look at Fregellae. I'm sure there were some people there who thought it might be politic to side with the Romans. And they would probably have been right.'

That was two thousand years ago, thinks Ruth. But she says nothing. She is beginning to think that time is a relative concept in Italy.

'I'll take the skull back to the lab,' says Angelo in a conciliatory tone.

'Maybe you should take it to the police.'

'I know the police chief here,' says Angelo. 'And he's a fascist if I ever saw one. I'll see you tomorrow.' And he's gone.

Ruth is still staring at the door when Shona appears, phone in hand. 'Phil says hello. He's been working closely with Nelson, he says. He thinks those bones on the building site were probably Roman.'

'Then it's not a police matter,' says Ruth. She wonders whether Phil's bones were buried face down. She longs to see them.

'No. Phil's trying to get funding for an excavation,' says Shona. 'He's got the press involved.'

I bet he has, thinks Ruth. 'Don't talk to me about the press,' she says. 'I've got to be interviewed for Italian television tomorrow.'

'How exciting,' says Shona. She managed to get herself on screen for *Women Who Kill*, and very fetching she had looked too.

'It'll all be in Italian,' says Ruth, aware that she is sounding grudging and ungrateful.

'Don't worry,' says Shona. 'Angelo will translate. He speaks brilliant English, doesn't he?'

'Yes,' says Ruth. 'He seems to be brilliant at everything. Languages, archaeology, swimming.'

Shona looks at her curiously. 'Don't you like him? I thought you were old friends.'

Ruth feels ashamed of her snarky tone. 'I do like him,' she says. 'I'm just feeling a bit tired. Too much sun.'

'Poor you,' says Shona. 'Why don't I give the kids their bath and you can have a rest? Have a glass of wine and watch Italian TV. You might see that weird game show again.'

Shona is being so nice, thinks Ruth. After all, she didn't

have a sleep in the car. She should be the one resting. But she appreciates the peace, as she sits in the space-age kitchen under the ancient beams, drinking her tea. She doesn't know why she feels so unsettled. It's almost as if she's homesick, but she hadn't thought that she could feel homesick if Kate was with her. Maybe she misses Flint. That's it. She will ring Bob later and get an update on Flint's progress. After all, there's no one else she could be missing, is there?

13

As soon as she sees Angelo's mother, Ruth feels ashamed of her cultural preconceptions, because Elsa Morelli is slim and extremely attractive, with short, streaky hair. Angelo told Ruth yesterday that he was forty-five, which must make Elsa at least in her mid-sixties, but she bounds up the stairs to her apartment like a teenager. Ruth follows at a slower rate, feeling fat and unfit.

'We are top floor,' says Elsa. 'Nice view but boring.'

She speaks good English, though with a tendency to leave out the articles.

'You park car?' she says, over her shoulder.

'Yes,' says Angelo, 'by the piazza.'

'That car is too big,' says Elsa. 'Me, I drive small car.'

'Me too,' pants Ruth. She hopes they are nearly at the top floor.

But the view is certainly wonderful. Arpino is another picturesque hilltop town, allegedly the birthplace of Cicero, and Elsa's balcony looks out over the valley; the now familiar olive groves, the winding road, the glimpses of the river.

Elsa ushers Ruth into a sitting room that is comfortable and over-furnished, glittering with sunlight reflecting on orna-ments and silver picture frames. It has none of the starkness of the apartment where Ruth is staying in Castello degli Angeli. Ruth has often wondered what happened to all of Angelo's grandfather's belongings. She is sure that he can't have lived in minimalist splendour, surrounded by gleaming marble and state-of-the-art appliances.

'Coffee?' says Elsa, plumping up cushions and fiddling with flower arrangements. 'Or tea? Tea for two? I make special cakes for TV people.'

'Don't bother about them,' says Angelo. 'They probably had a nice juicy plate of cocaine for breakfast.'

'Oh, you.' Elsa aims a playful swipe at him. 'What would you like, Ruth? Tea?'

'Coffee, please,' says Ruth. She doesn't want to seem like the sort of English person who has to be given tea wherever they go. She sits on a gold brocade sofa, enjoying the air conditioning and the faded glamour of the room: bookcases, velvet curtains, etchings of Rome, a plethora of photographs. Is that Angelo on the piano, scowling in a graduation gown? Or is he the little boy in a sailor suit, in pride of place on the mantelpiece? On the table next to her there's a faded photograph of two young men, arm in arm, with rifles slung on their backs.

Angelo sees her looking. 'My grandfather, Pompeo,' he says, 'with his best friend, Giorgio. This was them out hunting before the war.'

'What happened to Giorgio?'

'He died in the war,' says Angelo. 'Shot by the Nazis. They never found his body. It broke my grandfather's heart. I was very close to Nonno. I saw a lot of him in his last years.'

That's a long time to live with a broken heart, thinks Ruth. It also slightly changes her view of Angelo, that he was close to his grandfather and visited him in his old age. Maybe that's why he was left the apartment and why he changed everything in it, so he wouldn't be reminded of his nonno. She looks more closely at the picture. The black and white image gives little away: two dark heads, two grins, two swaggering poses. The background is more informative – she recognises the valley immediately, and the ruined tower that she can see from her balcony.

Elsa comes back into the room, carrying a tray. '*Caro Papa*,' she says, but cheerfully and without sentiment. 'That was his best friend. Granddaughter still lives in Castello.'

'Great-granddaughter,' says Angelo. He seems nervous, constantly looking out of the window that opens onto the town square. 'They're due at ten,' he says. 'It's nearly ten now.'

'Who's coming again?' asks Ruth. She is becoming more nervous by the second. At least when she filmed *Women Who Kill* she'd been able to cover up with an anorak because it was outdoors. But in the Italian summer there is nowhere to hide. She's wearing cotton trousers and a loose blue top. She thinks she'll look like a Smurf beside Angelo in his white shirt and jeans.

'Daniella di Martile,' says Angelo. 'She's the producer and the director. You used to get a whole crew of people filming these things but now there's only one or two. Daniella edits, as well. She'll probably bring her researcher with her.'

Elsa says something in Italian, and Angelo answers with a laugh. Ruth thinks she catches the word '*inglese*'.

'I write about the interview on the Castello website,' Elsa tells Ruth, putting a tiny gold cup next to her. 'I am hot shot reporter.' Elsa seems to know a lot of slightly outdated colloquial phrases. This one reminds Ruth of Lois Lane in childhood comics. Now Elsa is asking if she takes sugar, 'one lump or two?'

'No, thank you.'

'Nor me,' says Elsa. 'I never take sugar. I have to watch my figure.' Since Elsa is approximately the width of a stick insect, Ruth rather doubts this.

'Mamma looks after the town website,' says Angelo, from his position by the window. 'She writes a blog and she knows everything about everyone.'

'That's true,' says Elsa comfortably, sitting beside Ruth on the sofa. 'I know all about you, Ruth.'

'Really?' Ruth looks at Angelo, who gives her one of his sardonic smiles.

'I know you have beautiful little daughter,' says Elsa. 'Are you married?' Angelo gives a stifled groan.

'No,' says Ruth.

'Angelo was married once,' says Elsa. 'Pretty girl, but not . . .' She searches for a word.

'Faithful?' suggests Angelo.

'Happy,' says Elsa at last.

'Angelo has beautiful daughter,' says Elsa. 'I miss her. Next year she comes to me for the whole of summer.'

'That's not decided yet,' Angelo begins. Then he breaks off, leaning out of the window. 'That's Daniella,' says Angelo, leaning out of the window. 'I'll go down.'

In the silence that follows his departure, Elsa looks encouragingly at Ruth. 'Angelo is good man,' she says. 'But he needs someone.'

Don't we all, thinks Ruth.

Daniella di Martile is another scarily slim, attractive woman. She's wearing a sleeveless yellow dress and looks not unlike Audrey Hepburn. Why are all Italian women so thin, thinks Ruth. You'd think all that pasta would be fattening, but maybe they don't have thirds plus whatever their children leave on their plates too. Ruth has plenty of time to admire Daniella's figure as she prowls around the room, looking for camera angles.

'Ricco!' She gestures at her assistant. 'Try here. No too tight.' She looks at Ruth with her eyes narrowed.

'We film you greeting Angelo,' she says. 'Let's go to the hall.' They troop into the hall, Elsa excitedly videoing everything on her mobile phone. What's happened to older people, thinks Ruth. She's sure that her father thinks using a TV remote is high-tech, but here's Elsa talking about live blogging, Snapchat and Instagram. It's just not right.

'Ruth, you climb the stairs,' says Daniella. 'Angelo, you greet her at the top. Not too fast, Ruth, and not too slow. Ricco, you film her from underneath.'

Oh please, God, no, thinks Ruth.

She climbs the stairs, trying to keep a friendly yet intelligent smile on her face. At the top, Angelo kisses her on both cheeks.

'Ruth,' he says, sounding completely natural. 'How good of you to come.'

'Cut,' says Daniella. 'Let's do it again. Less out of breath this time, Ruth.'

By lunchtime they have only managed to film the greeting (Ruth kept getting the kiss wrong and once, embarrassingly, fell up the last two stairs) and a brief conversation on the landing. Now Ruth is meant to be discussing the sorts of deductions she will be able to make about the Roman skeleton. 'Don't tell us too much,' says Daniella, peering into her viewfinder, 'leave that for the outdoor scene.'

Ruth and Angelo are sitting on Elsa's sofa. Ruth is sure that she is sweating. She tries to breathe normally and pull her stomach in at the same time.

'What will you be able to tell us about the bones?' Angelo says, once again sounding exactly right, warm and interested.

'Well,' says Ruth, feeling herself going red and trying to ignore the furry microphone that Ricco is waving under her nose. 'You can tell all sorts of things from bones. Isotope can tell us where someone has been living before their death. But bones renew themselves every seven years. To find out where a person grew up you need to examine their teeth.'

She looks at Daniella, who makes a 'keep going' gesture.

'It is true,' says Angelo, 'that you can tell from bones whether someone has had a tattoo?'

'Well,' says Ruth, 'the ink used in tattoos can migrate to the lymph nodes so, if you had the relevant lymph nodes, you could tell if a person had a tattoo, and even where it was, even if you didn't have the limb itself. Tattoos don't show on bones, but a tattoo that has gone septic can leave a periosteal infection and signs of this may be visible.'

'Are you excited to see Toni?' says Angelo.

'Yes,' says Ruth, thinking that she has never sounded less excited in her life. 'It'll be fascinating to see a fully articulated skeleton from this era.'

'Cut,' says Daniella, while Elsa repeats the word 'fascinating' as if it's the funniest thing in the world.

'I film you at the site tomorrow,' she says to Ruth. 'Then you tell us what you find about the bones.'

'It's good stuff,' says Angelo. 'You won't be disappointed.'

Daniella says something in Italian which may well be 'I'll be the judge of that'.

'I should go,' says Ruth. 'I promised Shona I'd be back by lunchtime. We're going to eat at the café.'

'I'll drive you back,' says Angelo.

'Thanks,' says Ruth. 'And thanks for the coffee,' she says to Elsa. 'And for your hospitality'

'Is no problem,' says Elsa, kissing her on both cheeks. 'I see you later.'

Ruth looks enquiringly at Angelo.

'It's the cultural association dinner tonight,' he says. 'In the square at Castello. You're invited. And Shona and the children, of course.'

Ruth is struck dumb. The dinner sounds terrifying. Unfortunately, Elsa takes her silence for assent. '*Ci vediamo*', she says. 'See you later. I die to meet Katie.'

The cats make Nelson think of Ruth. He's never quite got the measure of her ginger tabby cat, Flint. The animal often chooses to sit on him, leaving behind copious amounts of orange fur, but, when Ruth is out of the room, it stares at him rather disconcertingly. *I know*, those round, unblinking eyes seem to say. *I know all about you and Ruth, and I don't approve.* Flint wants to be the only male in the cottage on the edge of the marshes, that much is clear. And, on the infrequent occasions that Nelson imagines himself living with Ruth in that house, he has to admit that Flint isn't in evidence.

But today Nelson is in a cattery and so there are not one, but about ten pairs of cats' eyes staring at him. The animals are in pens, each with a basket and a scratching post, and they look quite content, but they are staring. The nearest animal, a grey furry cat with one of those squashed-in faces, lets out a staccato meow, as if warning the others. 'Chill out, cat,' mutters Nelson. The cat continues to stare.

Late last night, intel came up with an address for Wendy Markham, Micky Webb's ex-girlfriend. She is running a cattery near Downham Market, about twelve miles from King's Lynn, and so, on Saturday morning, Nelson is knocking on the gate of Happy Cats, posing as an anxious pet owner keen to see the facilities for himself. He is shown into the garden of a suburban house, lined on both sides by cat pens. The assistant, a nervous-looking girl in a plastic apron, has gone into the house to fetch Wendy because, of course, Nelson wants a word with the boss before he can entrust – what's the name of his fantasy cat? What was that thing he used to watch as child? *Bagpuss*, that's it, a fat, cloth cat that lived in a junk shop – before he can entrust Bagpuss to her care.

Wendy emerges from the house. Nelson remembers her as rather mousy looking, an unlikely femme fatale, but the years have sharpened and polished her. She now has ash-blonde hair, cut short, and a tan that looks more sunbed than Tuscany. She's smiling, not a look that he remembers from the old days, and displaying rather of lot of orange gum.

'Can I take you on a tour?' she says, wiping her hands on her tight jeans before extending one to shake. 'All our moggies are very happy here. I'm sure yours will be too.'

Nelson shows his warrant card. 'Is there somewhere we can talk in private?'

They sit in the conservatory. The business obviously doesn't extend into the house; there's a prefabricated shed where Wendy takes bookings and checks vets' certificates, and inside it's all wicker furniture and chintz cushions. A photograph on a side table shows Wendy and a perma-tanned man standing beside a pool.

'I haven't seen Micky since he went into prison,' she says, tapping on the arm of her chair with long, coral nails. How can she look after animals with nails like that?

'Did you know he was out?' asks Nelson.

'Yes, the probation office got in touch. They told me that he was out on licence. And they said he'd married again.'

Wendy had once declared undying love for Micky and, in court, he had sworn blind that she hadn't known of the plot to burn down the house and claim the insurance. But Derek Hobson had thought that she was the brains behind the whole business. Wendy certainly looks pretty formidable, sitting at the centre of her cat empire, but Nelson is wary of putting Micky's crimes at her door. He's seen it before – a man kills and the armchair pundits say, 'Of course, I blame *her*,' meaning the wife or the mistress. In Nelson's opinion, the person to blame is usually the person who committed the crime.

'I've been married to Terry for eight years now,' Wendy is saying. 'We've got a good life. We go to the Canaries every winter, that's the slow time for the business, and we've got an active social life. Terry's got his golf and I do amateur dramatics.'

I bet you do, thinks Nelson. Eight years of marriage means that Wendy must have met Terry quite soon after Micky went to prison. Are there any children? There is no evidence of them in the house or in the photographs, all of which seem to show Wendy and Terry on holiday.

'Micky's found God,' says Nelson. 'Did you hear that?'

Wendy laughs. Not a particularly happy sound. 'Really? That'll be the new wife, I expect.'

'Is Micky the sort of man to be influenced by his wife?'

'Of course he is,' says Wendy. 'Weak as water, Micky.' Then she stops, realising what she has said.

'Do you think that Micky is still dangerous?' asks Nelson.

'No,' says Wendy. 'A neutered cat, that's what he is.'

It's an uncomfortable image. They had Bruno neutered and Nelson still feels obscurely guilty about it, even though all the animal charities insist on it. Castrated is another word for it, of course. Has Micky Webb been castrated by his marriage?

'Will you let me know if Micky tries to get in touch?' says Nelson, giving Wendy his card.

'He won't try and contact me,' says Wendy, with another laugh. 'It'll be all about the new woman now. That's what Micky's like. When he was with me he forgot all about Marie. It'll be the same with whatshername.'

Nelson doesn't supply the name. There doesn't seem any point in continuing the conversation with Wendy Markham. She accompanies Nelson to the door, and he asks her if she has any pets herself.

'No.' She looks quite shocked at the question. 'Terry's allergic and I couldn't stand the fur in the house.'

Outside, a young couple are waiting with a cat in a basket. Nelson wants to tell them to run for the hills.

14

'What does one wear to a cultural association dinner?' says Shona. 'It's not something you get in King's Lynn.'

'I've no idea,' says Ruth. She is still wearing her cotton trousers, now with a vaguely smart top. She imagines all the other women – including Elsa – in Versace or Prada or any one of those designers who would faint if asked to create clothes for normal-sized women. She thinks that Shona, in a pale blue dress that shows off her tan, will fit in nicely.

They have spent a quiet afternoon at the apartment, the children watching DVDs, the adults catching up with emails and phone calls. Ruth took the opportunity to ring Bob Woonunga to ask about Flint. 'He's fine,' Bob had said, 'eating well and spending a lot of time asleep on your bed.' She'd asked what the weather was like in Norfolk. 'A bit changeable,' said Bob, who has become fluent in British weather-speak. 'But it's nice today, the weekenders are down and have been kayaking.' Bob had been for a long walk along the coastal path, renewing his astral energies. He'd met Cathbad for a drink the other day; they had discussed

Halloween and the coming of autumn. When Ruth said goodbye, she'd found herself feeling acutely homesick for Flint, Norfolk, Cathbad and the coastal path.

Now, Kate and Louis are sliding around the apartment, getting thoroughly overexcited at the thought of a grown-up dinner.

'Does Louis look smart enough?' says Shona to Ruth. 'I didn't bring any of his party clothes.'

Louis is wearing beige shorts and a blue T-shirt; Kate is in her only dress, white with embroidered pink roses.

'I think they look lovely,' says Ruth. 'And they're children, everyone will love them. We're the ones who need to worry.'

'Oh, everyone will love us,' says Shona, shaking out her mane of hair. 'We're new blood.'

Walking down the hill, Ruth wishes that Shona had put this differently. Not everyone appreciates new blood.

When they reach the corner by the lamp post, they can see the lights twinkling in the trees.

'Is it a birthday party?' says Kate, skipping with anticipation.

'I think it's sort of a party for the town,' says Ruth. She has no idea what a cultural association does.

As they pass the abandoned house at the bottom of the hill, Ruth sees a movement in one of the downstairs rooms. Is the squatter still there, cooking over his camp stove? She wishes that she had thought to ask Angelo about him.

The square has been transformed. Trestle tables stretch from the café to the church, decorated with ivy and red, white and green tablecloths. A stage has been erected by the pine trees and, on the church steps, cauldrons are being stirred by men in chef's hats.

'Ruth! *Bambini!*' Elsa comes towards them, elegant in tight-fitting black trousers and a lacy top. Ruth immediately feels scruffy and underdressed.

'This is Shona,' she says, hoping her friend's beauty will make up for her own poor showing.

'*Bella*,' breathes Elsa. 'Like Titian.'

'This?' Shona pats her hair. 'In England we call it ginger.'

'And the little ginger.' Elsa pinches Louis's cheek. 'And is this Katie? *Che carina.*'

Ruth does think Kate looks rather pretty, with her dark hair and bright, dark eyes. Kate behaves nicely too, saying hello to Elsa and not minding too much about having her cheek pinched.

'Angelo!' Elsa calls across the square to where Angelo is helping arrange lights around the columns of the church porch. 'Ruth is here.'

Ruth is touched to see Angelo leave his work and come over immediately. At least they have one friend in Castello degli Angeli. Angelo greets Ruth and Shona and fetches them red wine in paper cups and orange juice for the children. The square is filling up now and Ruth sees Roberto and Marta from the dig as well as several other faces that have become vaguely familiar over the last few days. One such figure, massive in clerical garb, comes towards Ruth with a bottle of wine in each hand. Don Tomaso, hell-bent on hospitality.

'Dr Galloway. More wine? I make it myself.'

'Just a little,' says Ruth. The wine is strong and she's already feeling slightly light-headed. She introduces Shona. Kate and Louis are already running around with the other children.

'*Piacere.*' The priest beams at Shona, and looks as though it is only fear of spilling the wine that stops him kissing her on both cheeks. Shona twinkles and tosses her hair and manages to get in the fact that she is a Catholic.

'You must both come to my church for Mass tomorrow,' says Don Tomaso. 'Is a beautiful church. The church of San Michele e Santi Angeli.'

'Does it date from the Renaissance?' says Ruth, only too glad to admire the building, if not what goes on inside.

'Fifteenth century,' says Don Tomaso, 'but was on the site of a really old church. One of the oldest churches in Christianity. Fourth century. Angelo was going to excavate but then he got distracted by the Romans in the valley.'

'I never agreed to do the excavation,' says Angelo. 'And the Roman site is very important. We might have found another Fregellae.'

'What about my church?' says Don Tomaso. 'What do the English say? Charity begins at home? Which is why they cannot help with the European refugee crisis.'

He smiles at Ruth, who feels unequal to defending Britain's stance on refugees, especially as she didn't vote for the present government. Luckily, at that moment, Elsa arrives to tell them that the food is ready.

Ruth and Shona join the line on the church steps and are given generous helpings of pasta and a rich, meaty sauce.

'What's the vegetarian option?' whispers Shona.

'Pasta on its own,' says Ruth. 'Good job Cathbad isn't here.'

Ruth fills her bowl and takes a bowl for Kate, hoping she can persuade her to stop playing for moment and eat something. She and Shona sit at a table under a canopy of vines and, after a few minutes, Angelo joins them. He is accompanied by Graziano, who seems delighted to see Shona again. The three of them talk animatedly in Italian-peppered English about universities (it turns out that Graziano teaches computer science at Cassino University), books, films and whether British women are repressed. Ruth gives up trying to follow the conversation and gives her undivided attention to the food, which is delicious. She also tries to keep her eye on Kate, who is darting about like a pink and white fish, followed by a trail of adoring Italian boys. Not for the first time, Ruth reflects that Kate is far cooler than her.

'A penny for them? That's what they say in England, isn't it?' It's Don Tomaso again, bearing a plate piled high with pasta and what looks like half a cow.

'You know a lot of English phrases,' says Ruth.

'I had an English nanny,' says the priest. 'She was just like Mary Poppins.'

Ruth has an image of Julie Andrews floating over the rooftops of the town, singing about a spoonful of sugar. The sky is dark blue now and she sees shapes that could be bats circling the angels on the roof of the church.

'Are you from this area?' she asks Don Tomaso, who is tucking a napkin into his collar.

'Yes,' he says. 'I've lived here since I was a child. I'm an old man now, over eighty, but there are no new priests. Once, every big family gave a boy to God. Not now. *Che peccato.*'

Giving your son to God sounds sinister somehow. Ruth once found the body of an Iron Age girl who had been tied down and left on the marshes to die, an offering to some faceless, nameless deity. She thinks of Isaac carrying the wood on which he is going to be sacrificed by his father, a story that pops up quite often in her parents' church, where it seems to be held up as an example of good parenting. Don Tomaso seems harmless enough, but she's quite glad that the desire to become a priest is dying out.

'I knew Angelo's grandfather, Pompeo,' the priest is saying, 'and his great friend Giorgio Bianchi. I remember when the Nazis took over this town and the hills were full of resistance fighters. They were dark days. At first the Germans soldiers were gentlemen. They sat in this square and ate food from the café. Potatoes! They ate potatoes like we eat bread. I was a young boy and I used to help in the kitchen. We were peeling potatoes morning, noon and night. But then those Germans left and the SS came in. Then it was very different.'

'It must have been awful,' says Ruth. 'I was saying to Angelo, I don't think British people can imagine what it was like to live under an occupation.'

'Our blessed Lord lived in an occupied land,' says Don Tomaso. 'Sometimes grace lies in unexpected places. And now we are sitting here with Pompeo's grandson and Giorgio's great-granddaughter.'

Ruth looks around the table at the laughing and gesticulating townspeople. Which one is Giorgio's great-granddaughter?

'Martyr,' says Don Tomaso.

'I suppose he was.'

'No. Marta. Angelo's student. She is the great-granddaughter of Giorgio. So all things come full circle.'

Ruth sees Marta and Roberto sitting slightly apart, talking earnestly. Are they discussing the dig? It seems incredible that this slight young girl is linked to the dark days of the Second World War. But then the war is only a few generations away; Angelo's grandfather fought in the resistance, as did Marta's great-grandfather, Don Tomaso was actually there. As Ruth watches, a man approaches the tables on the church steps. Compared to the dinner guests, he is shabbily dressed in tracksuit bottoms and a stained football shirt. He is unshaven and has greasy-looking brown hair tied back in a ponytail. The chefs give him a generous helping of food, but the man does not join one of the dining tables. He sits on the church steps, eating hungrily.

Don Tomaso is looking too. 'Samir,' he says quietly. 'He is a Syrian refugee.'

'Does he live in the ruined house at the bottom of the hill?' says Ruth. 'I think I saw him the other day.'

'Yes,' says Don Tomaso. 'The commune lets him live here, but they don't give him any kindness.'

'They gave him food just now,' says Ruth.

'Food!' Don Tomaso makes a contemptuous gesture. 'Food is not love.'

There's no denying that, but all the same, Ruth thinks, food is pretty valuable. As if reading her mind, Angelo leans across the table and asks if Ruth wants another helping of pasta.

'No, thank you,' says Ruth. 'It was delicious though.'

'You must eat,' says Don Tomaso. 'You young women are too thin.'

It's almost enough to make Ruth become a Catholic. She gives Angelo her bowl to be refilled and she lets Don Tomaso fill her glass too.

'Angelo is a clever man,' says Don Tomaso. 'I know his mother very well. We were brought up together. She was so sad when he went to live in America. I am happy that he's home now.'

'I thought he lived in Rome,' says Ruth, looking over to where Angelo is offering some wine to Samir the refugee. She can't hear what they're saying, but she thinks Samir is refusing.

'Rome is not far,' says Don Tomaso. 'And who knows, perhaps one day he'll settle in Castello again. Perhaps he will remarry. We are relaxed about such things in the church now. Are you married, Ruth?'

'No,' says Ruth. 'I had an affair with a married man and now I have a daughter.'

She has no idea why she, always so careful to maintain her privacy, comes out with this. It's as if Don Tomaso has some strange power over her. Perhaps this is why Catholics go to confession. She wonders how relaxed the priest will be about this revelation.

But Don Tomaso doesn't react at all. He simply says, 'Your daughter is a lovely girl. Already she makes friends here.' From across the square, Ruth can hear her daughter's voice: 'No, I'm the leader.' Sometimes Kate reminds her painfully of Nelson.

'Yes,' she says, 'she's good at making friends.'

'And that's a good thing to be good at,' says the priest comfortably. He might be about to say more but, at that moment, the band strikes up with a crash of brass and drums. The first tune is greeted by applause from the crowd and, almost immediately, people are pushing their way to the front to dance. What's wrong with them? Although she likes grooving gently to Bruce Springsteen in private, Ruth can't imagine cavorting in public like this.

Ruth checks that she can see Kate and leans back to enjoy the spectacle. But, at that moment, Angelo materialises in front of her. 'May I have this dance?'

It's past ten o'clock by the time Ruth, Shona and the children make their way up the hill. Ruth has danced with Angelo, with Graziano, even with Don Tomaso. Shona has danced with half the town. Kate has had two proposals of marriage from smitten six-year-olds and has been given a cap saying 'I ♥ Italy'. Now they are all tired and Louis is dragging his feet.

'Come on,' says Shona, 'just a little bit further. There's a good boy.'

Kate mutters darkly under her cap.

The music is still playing – pop songs now. Ruth can hear a version of 'Uptown Funk' echoing incongruously around the medieval buildings. Both Angelo and Graziano offered to accompany them home, but it seemed unfair to take them away from the party. But now, walking through the high, dark buildings, Ruth suddenly wishes that they had company. An owl hoots somewhere very close and the blank windows of Samir's ruined house seem to gape at them. Ruth starts to walk faster.

'Wait for us,' says Shona.

Ruth and Kate wait by the lamppost, its light now extinguished. They can still see the glow from the square, but it seems very far away. Behind them, the castle is a looming presence, not threatening, exactly, but somehow watchful. *I have withstood sieges and battles*, it seems to say. *I have no compassion to spare on you.*

As Shona and Louis approach, Ruth sees a movement in the bushes behind them. Kate sees it too.

'What's that?'

'Nothing,' says Ruth. 'A stray cat, perhaps. Here's Louis. Let's see who can get to the top of the hill first.'

But when she looks back, the figure is still there, moving silently in the shadows, following them at a discreet distance.

She can't be sure but she thinks it's Angelo's student, Roberto.

15

Ruth dreams of dancing, of Kate running around the fountain in Castello degli Angeli followed by a pack of wolves, of her mother trying and failing to pass on an important message, of Mary Poppins floating high above the church of San Michele e Santi Angeli. Then a thunderous crash sends the dream smashing into smithereens. She sits up and reaches for the light. The room remains in darkness.

'Ruth! Did you hear that?'

Shona is standing in her doorway. It's too dark to see her face but her voice is trembling.

'I couldn't help hearing it,' says Ruth. 'What was it?'

'I don't know.'

'The electricity doesn't seem to be working.'

Ruth follows Shona into the sitting room just as Kate calls, 'Mum!' Ruth rushes into the children's room. They are both awake and Louis is crying.

'It's all right,' says Ruth. 'Probably just thunder or something.'

'My room moved,' says Kate. 'I felt it.'

Shona is cuddling Louis. Suddenly she says, 'Ruth! The picture.'

Ruth looks at the wall opposite the children's bed, where a strange picture, a modernist blur of shapes and colours, had hung. When she first saw it, Kate had been convinced that it showed elephants in a sandstorm, but Louis was sure that it was ships at sea. Now the picture is on the floor, the glass smashed into pieces.

Ruth tries Kate's bedside light. Nothing.

'What's happening, Mum?' Kate's voice is unsteady.

'Probably just a power cut. Wait here with Shona. Don't tread on the floor in your bare feet.' Ruth goes into the sitting room and out onto the balcony. The valley looks much the same as before, the full moon turning the trees to silver. Far below, a dog is barking hysterically.

She turns to see Shona, her face illuminated by her iPhone screen.

'I can't get a signal,' she says. 'Try yours.'

Ruth retrieves her phone. The display tells her that it's 2 a.m., and she has a faint signal. As she looks at the screen, it flashes into life. *Angelo.*

'Hello,' she says, hoping that she doesn't sound as scared as she feels.

'Ruth,' says Angelo, 'don't be alarmed, but there's been a small earthquake.'

'An *earthquake*?'

She didn't mean to say it so loudly. In the background, Shona gives a scream and both children start crying.

'It's OK, it's OK,' she tells them. At the same time, Angelo is telling her, 'Nothing to worry about. No one hurt. Just some structural damage to the church and a couple of houses. Graziano has been on the phone. Best thing for you to do is just stay where you are.'

'There's no electricity,' says Ruth, trying not to sound pathetic. 'Is there a trip switch here?'

'Power lines must be down. It often happens in these mountain villages. Don't worry. I'll come up and see you in the morning.'

Ruth wishes that she could tell him not to bother, that they'll be all right on their own. Instead she says, 'Good. See you then. Bye.' Then she turns to Shona and the children. 'Everything's OK,' she tells them. 'I'm going to try to switch the lights back on.'

By the light of her iPhone torch she searches the hall and kitchen, looking for a fuse box. Even though it won't help if the power lines are down flicking the trip switch is something she can do – she often has to do it in her isolated cottage – so she is determined to show this much initiative, at least. Eventually, she finds a small wooden door in the kitchen which opens onto a cupboard full of empty wine bottles. And, at the back, she sees the familiar black and red levers. Ruth reaches through the dusty bottles and flicks the switch. Nothing. Angelo was right.

Shona appears behind her. 'Shall we make a cup of tea?'

'How can we?' says Ruth.

'The cooker is gas,' says Shona, 'and I think I saw an old kettle somewhere.'

Shona uses her torch app to locate the old-fashioned kettle at the back of the cupboard, fills it with water and puts it on the hob. This action calms both of them. They stand looking at the rusty kettle as if it has magic powers, waiting for the steam to blow its whistle. Shona makes tea for all of them, even the children, and they sit on the sofa in the dark, drinking it. The dog has stopped barking and the night is quiet again. Shona and Ruth keep up a flow of self-consciously jolly chat and Ruth feels Kate relax against her. She puts down her empty cup. 'Let's go back to bed. It's nearly three.'

'Can I sleep with you, Mum?' says Kate.

'Yes,' says Ruth, 'and when we wake up it will be light.' This seems both obvious and important to say. Ruth hears the voice of her old university tutor, Erik Anderssen, in full mesmeric lecture mode. 'Prehistoric man went to bed when it was dark and rose when it was light. It's the natural cycle of life.'

'You come with me, Louis,' says Shona. 'Isn't this an adventure?'

Ruth agrees, although, in truth, she feels that she has had enough adventures to last a lifetime.

Ruth wakes to find the room flooded with light and Kate sleeping soundly next to her. She looks at her phone: 7 a.m. The battery hasn't charged, so the electricity must still be off. She still has thirty per cent though. Not time to panic yet. Ruth gets up and goes into the sitting room. If it wasn't for the four tea cups on the table, she would have thought that she had dreamt last night's adventure. Amazing how the daylight transforms everything. In its glow, Ruth feels as if the earthquake might well have been an adventure.

There's no sound from Shona's room and there's no hot water for a shower so Ruth washes her face with cold water, does her teeth and gets dressed without waking Kate. Then she knocks on Shona's door.

'I've made you some tea,' she says. 'I thought I'd walk down to the square, see what's going on. Kate's still asleep.'

'OK.' Shona sits up in bed, rubbing her eyes. Like Kate, Louis is still fast asleep. 'Isn't Angelo coming round this morning?'

'I won't be long,' says Ruth. 'Kate's still in bed. It's not eight o'clock yet.'

'I'd better ring Phil,' says Shona. 'There might have been something on the news last night.'

Shona might say that things aren't going well with Phil, thinks Ruth, but she seems to spend a lot of time talking to him. She spent most of yesterday afternoon on the phone, chatting away in the bedroom while Ruth entertained both children. Ruth wonders if she should ring Nelson. And her dad.

'I won't be long,' she says again. 'I just want to see for myself.'

At first she thinks that Angelo must have been wrong. There can't have been an earthquake last night. The shuttered houses are quiet, but from within she can hear the sounds of children laughing, a radio playing. Surely people should be running through the streets in panic? Even Samir's house looks peaceful, and no less ramshackle than before, towels draped over the windows in place of curtains. But as Ruth rounds the corner by the square, she sees the internationally recognisable signs of an emergency: a blue van with 'Carabinieri' emblazoned upon it, a fire engine, police tape and a knot of interested spectators. Among these last she sees the familiar black shirt of Angelo. Elsa is there too, wearing what look like high-heeled trainers.

'Angelo,' says Ruth. 'What's going on?'

'Nothing much,' he says. 'Part of the church wall has come down. Don Tomaso is furious.'

On the other side of the tape, Ruth can see the priest arguing with the rescue workers, his arms flung out in protest.

'They say they have to shut the church,' says Angelo. 'Don Tomaso says churches should always be open in times of crisis.'

'He's right,' says Elsa. 'It's Sunday. People must go to church.'

'The church is unsafe,' says Angelo. 'That's what the carabinieri say.'

'Was anyone hurt?' says Ruth.

'No,' says Angelo. 'Just the wall of the church and some of the graves. That old house down there has been badly damaged too.'

Ruth looks at the house beyond the church. It certainly looks derelict, with its roof caved in and rubble everywhere, but she was pretty sure that it looked like that yesterday.

Even the damage to the church doesn't look too bad. The retaining wall has been destroyed and she can see that some roof tiles are missing, but the structure itself looks as solid and smugly classical as ever. She can't help peering beyond the wall into the graveyard. There you can see that the earth has been churned, as if some sleeping creature is trying to emerge. Tombstones tilt at strange angles and part of the ground seems to have been pushed higher, creating an odd effect, like a raked stage. Flowers and wreaths are scattered everywhere and a large bird croaks mournfully from an uprooted tree.

Ignoring the shouts of the rescue workers, Don Tomaso strides through the upturned graves to talk to them. He's wearing coveralls over his clerical clothes, the trousers torn and muddy.

'So,' he says, gesturing behind him, 'the dead are waking.'

This seems a rather macabre remark to Ruth, but Angelo laughs. 'After all, you did want it excavated.'

'It's terrible,' says Elsa, and she does sound upset, thinks Ruth. 'The dead should be left to rest in peace.'

'I will say Mass at six tonight if it kills me,' says Don Tomaso. 'We will light the candles if there's no electricity. Will you come, Ruth? There's something I'd like to show you.'

Ruth would like to say no, but she feels sorry for Don Tomaso, standing there by the battered building, and he was nice to her last night. Also, she's sure that Shona would love to attend a candlelight Mass.

'OK,' she says. 'Thank you. I should be getting back to Kate now.'

'Shall we meet by the café in half an hour?' says Angelo. Ruth stares at him. 'Why?'

Angelo looks at her as if she's mad. 'The TV company. They're filming at the site today. Remember?'

16

Cathbad is walking his dog across the salt marsh beach. He's tangentially aware that it's Sunday – the bells were ringing in Wells that morning – and he feels that he is celebrating the Sabbath in a very spiritual way, communing with nature in the company of his animal familiar. Strictly speaking, dogs aren't allowed on the beach during the summer months, but Cathbad views rules as guidance only, and guidance for other people at that. Besides, it's early, and the wide sandy beach is deserted apart from Thing, a white English bull terrier, running madly in circles. The fact that he is in charge of a dog often stigmatised by the press as a 'devil dog' does not unduly concern Cathbad. Thing, as he explains to anyone who will listen, is a good soul who is probably the reincarnation of a woman wrongly accused of witchcraft. He has no idea why this explanation doesn't always bring the comfort it should.

This beach, with its miles of sand, interspersed now by pools of eerie blue, was the place where, some eighteen years earlier, Professor Erik Anderssen unearthed a Bronze

Age henge, its wooden timbers emerging from the sand like the teeth of some great underwater monster. Cathbad and his fellow druids had wanted the henge to stay where it was, even though it would inevitably be swallowed up by the tides. But, although Erik had, at heart, agreed with them, the timbers had been taken away for preservation and now form a spectacular display in King's Lynn museum.

Cathbad stands where he thinks the sacred circle once stood and spreads out his hands to the sea and the sky. He asks them to protect his life partner, Judy, and his children, Madeleine, Michael and Miranda. Madeleine is his daughter by his first wife, Delilah, who now lives in Blackburn. The letter M, he sometimes tells people, offers significant psychic protection, but, in truth, the alliterative names are just a coincidence. Cathbad thinks of Ruth and Kate and extends the circle a little wider. Nelson's voice then sounds in his head, as it sounded when he pulled him from the quicksand the night they tried to follow the ancient path across the marshes. 'You're not dead yet, Cathbad.' Cathbad widens the circle to include Nelson and Michelle and their children.

When he opens his eyes, Thing is sitting in front of him, head on one side, a stick in his mouth. Was this twig part of the ancient timbers, a piece of prehistoric bog oak, a messenger from another world? No, it's just a stick. Cathbad throws it, sending the missile into the shallow sea that covers so many mysteries, so many bones, so many footprints. Thing hurtles after it, barking madly.

*

Nelson and Michelle are in the modern British equivalent of church: a garden centre. They follow the other couples in silent procession, occasionally adding a shrub or flowerpot to their trolley. Nelson normally loathes such places, but he is glad that Michelle is feeling well enough to be up and about at ten in the morning. She is staring rather dreamily at a flowering twig called *Gardenia jasminoides*. He hopes she isn't getting inspiration for baby names.

'All right, love?' he says.

'Fine,' says Michelle, putting the jasmine in the trolley. 'I really think that I might be over the morning sickness at last.'

'Well, that's good news at all events.'

'It is. I feel human again.' She gives him a smile and he sees that she is carefully made up (she hasn't been bothering recently) and that her hair is freshly streaked. In the hazy light of the greenhouse she suddenly looks quite dazzling.

'Why don't we have lunch in a pub?' he says. 'Laura and Bruno could join us.'

'She'll want to bring Chad.' Laura has recently acquired a boyfriend. He's less annoying that her previous beau, a public schoolboy called Andre who thought he was a hip-hop DJ, but Nelson is still at the stage of pretending that he doesn't exist.

He sighs. 'She can bring Chad,' he says, 'as long as I don't have to talk to him about teeth.' Chad is a dentistry student.

Michelle puts her arm through his. 'You're mellowing, Harry.'

'Don't let it get around,' says Nelson. 'Jo thinks I'm almost senile as it is.'

It's not so bad filming out in the open. It's not as claustrophobic, and Ruth hopes that her clothes won't matter so much. Daniella seemed to spend quite a lot of time filming their feet – Ruth's in battered Birkenstocks, Angelo's in trendily retro trainers – as they walk across the field. Then there's the dreaded walking and talking.

'Not too fast,' yells Daniella. The cameraman is walking backwards in front of them. Ricco is filming 'wide-angle shots' from the other side of the field.

Ruth slows to a crawl.

'Faster,' yells Daniella. 'You must look as if you're moving fast, but actually move slowly. Get it?'

'Yes,' says Ruth. The whole thing feels completely surreal anyway. She can't believe that she was woken in the night by an earthquake and is now walking across the sun-scorched grass talking about bones. Marta and Roberto are both at the site too. Marta says that the earthquake almost destroyed another little mountain town. 'They're still digging for survivors,' she says, crossing herself. In light of this, it's hard to worry too much about whether her bra strap is showing.

'So, Ruth,' says Angelo, once again sounding completely relaxed. 'What did you find out about Toni?' This section, Daniella explains, is being filmed in English with Italian subtitles, 'to show that the Professore speaks many languages'. As far as Ruth can see, this will only make Angelo seem even cleverer and show her up for the monoglot she is.

'Well the first thing I noticed,' says Ruth, trying hard to put one foot in front of the other in a way that is not fast and not slow, 'was that he had been buried face down. Position is always important in burials . . .'

'Say about the position first,' Daniella had told them in a hasty briefing in the back of her car. 'Play up the fact that it might mean that Toni was an outcast. Then say the stuff about shackles and tattoos. Leave the stone in the mouth till last. And say about his tongue being cut out. Viewers love a bit of . . . what's the English word, Angelo?'

'Gore,' said Angelo.

'We can't be sure that his tongue was cut out,' said Ruth. 'With no soft tissue . . .'

'Never mind that.' Daniella silenced her with a gesture. 'Just don't forget to mention the vampires.'

Now they are meant to be looking into the grave itself, both crouching on the edge of a recently cut trench.

'You found something else really disturbing, didn't you, Ruth?' says Angelo.

'Yes,' says Ruth, trying not to sway back on her heels. 'It looks as if Toni was buried with a flat stone in his mouth. It's possible that his tongue was removed. We can't be sure because there's no soft tissue left.' She looks nervously at Daniella.

'What could that mean?' says Angelo. 'A stone being placed in the mouth?'

'There have been Roman British graves with stones replacing body parts,' says Ruth, 'and I've heard of one case with a stone replacing a tongue. It was thought that this was a punishment of some sort. For treachery, perhaps.'

'Cut!' shouts Daniella. 'That's a good place to leave it. We can do some more filming at the laboratory. Viewers love the science stuff.'

'Will you need me for that?' says Ruth.

'No, we'll have Angelo speaking directly to camera.'

Ruth is rather relieved.

'That was good,' Daniella tells her. 'Viewers will love to hear you speaking English.'

Ruth can never get used to people thinking than an English accent is exotic. She would much rather be able to talk Italian.

Angelo is in high spirits. 'We'll have the filming done by the end of the week. I'm sure to get funding for the dig now. It's been a good day.'

'Except for the people killed in the earthquake,' says Marta, carefully covering the trench with a tarpaulin.

Nelson approves of the pub. It has good beer and a menu traditional enough to promise that food will be delivered on plates and not on wooden planks. Bruno is allowed in too and is even given a bowl of water. He's lying under the table now, sighing heavily but otherwise behaving well. Laura's boyfriend, Chad, seems pleasant enough, although sporting the kind of micro-beard that makes Nelson itch to hand him a razor. He's from Sheffield, which is decently northern even if it's Yorkshire and not Lancashire. He doesn't drink, because he's driving, so Nelson can't judge him on his choice of beer (it would be hard to come back from a shandy) but obviously he approves of such responsibility. One good thing about Michelle being pregnant is that she's always the one driving.

They have ordered lunch and are chatting in a desultory way when Nelson becomes aware that the TV is on in the background. He's not keen on televisions in pubs unless they're showing football, but he takes a glance in case there's a match on. Instead he sees grainy newsreel shots and the running footnote that he always associates with disasters.

Earthquake in Lazio, Italy. Many feared dead.

Ruth was right. Shona seems very keen on the candlelight Mass. 'It's the right thing to do,' she says.

'What do you mean?' Ruth isn't about to let her get away with that.

'With the earthquake and everything,' says Shona vaguely. 'Do you think we'll have to cover our hair?'

'You've been reading Margaret Atwood again,' says Ruth. 'This isn't *The Handmaid's Tale*. It's just Sunday Mass. I think wearing mantillas went out in the fifties.' She is slightly shaken because Kate, too, seems determined to go to church. She has recently started talking about First Holy Communion, an arcane induction ritual enjoyed by some of the pupils at her school which seems to involve eight-year-old girls dressed as brides. Ruth had Kate christened in a Catholic church to please Nelson, but this is going too far.

When they walk down to the church – Shona in a grey dress which has a definite nun-like vibe – they find a crowd of people on the steps. Ruth spots Marta with a woman who could only be her mother. In fact, the crowd is almost exclusively female – mothers with young children and smartly-dressed older women. There's not a mantilla to be seen.

'Why aren't we going in?' says Kate.

'I think the doors are still locked,' says Shona.

'Don Tomaso definitely said six,' says Ruth. She remembers that he also said he had something to show her. What could that be? Somehow the priest seems to think that a few confidences over the home-made wine have made them kindred spirits.

'Maybe it's not safe because of the earthquake,' says Shona. Although there is still police tape around the graveyard, the entrance to the church is clear and there's a handwritten note on the wall reading '*Massa a sei*' signed *Padre Tomaso*.

Elsa comes over to them. 'Is very strange,' she says. 'I come early to see if I can help, but I knock on door and no answer.'

'Is there another way in?'

'Round the back,' says Elsa. 'Will you come with me, Ruth?'

Ruth is not keen – she thinks that it's rather a cheek for her, a visitor, to be using the private entrance to the church – but she can hardly say no. Leaving Kate with Shona, she follows Elsa under the tape and into the graveyard. It looks stranger than ever in the late afternoon light, the graves tilted at grotesque angles and deep fissures scarring the earth. Ruth longs to look into one of the crevices – she's almost sure that she sees a gleam of bones. But Elsa hardly seems to notice. She follows the wall until she comes to a small black-painted door. She turns the handle and it opens.

'Don Tomaso?' she calls. 'Padre?'

They are in a passageway, but the church smell is over-powering: candles and incense and flower stalks. Suddenly afraid, Ruth tries to speak, to stop Elsa going any further, but the older woman has already moved through the connecting doorway. Ruth can hear her feet on the stone floor and then a sudden exclamation, half gasp, half scream.

'What is it?'

Ruth enters the church, aware of a high ceiling and a plethora of gloomy oil paintings. And there, on the high altar, is Don Tomaso. The crucified Christ looks down on him sorrowfully and Ruth knows immediately that Don Tomaso, like the saints all around him, is dead.

17

'Don't touch him,' says Ruth.

'But I must . . .' Elsa is leaning over the body, feeling for a pulse. But Ruth hears Nelson's voice, as clearly as if he is standing in the church beside her: *Don't touch the body, don't contaminate the scene.*

'We must call the police,' she says. 'The *carabinieri*? Do you know the number?'

'The police?' Elsa looks at her as if she doesn't understand. Her eyes have a glazed look and Ruth hopes that she isn't about to faint. 'I call the ambulance,' says Elsa.

'Call the police too,' says Ruth.

She thought at first that the priest must have been killed by falling masonry or something connected to the earthquake but, coming closer, Ruth sees that Don Tomaso is lying on his back with his arms spread out, echoing the figure on the cross above. And, though there are no falling beams or dislodged bricks anywhere around him, there's a telltale mark on Don Tomaso's forehead – it looks as if he has been hit with great force by a heavy object. There's something else, too. Ruth leans in, trying to see.

'I call them.' Elsa's voice seems to come from a long way away. 'The *polizia*, not the *carabinieri*.'

'You should sit down,' says Ruth. 'You've had a terrible shock.'

She guides Elsa to a pew at the front of the church. Elsa crosses herself when she sits down. Her hand is shaking. 'He was like my brother,' she says. 'I know him all my life. He was a holy man. A saint.' She starts to shiver. After a moment, Ruth puts an arm round her. Elsa continues to shake, muttering under her breath. At first, Ruth is rather alarmed, but then she realises that Elsa is praying. The prayer, something in Latin repeated over and over again, seems to have a calming effect. Elsa starts breathing normally and the shaking stops. Ruth lowers her arm and looks around her.

The church is dark and cavernous. Every inch of wall space seems to be filled with paintings of dead and dying people: crucifixions, beheadings, an arrow in St Sebastian's breast, John the Baptist's head on a plate. A frieze, white figures on a blue background, runs along the top, and even the ceiling is painted with what looks like the Last Judgement. There are statues too, in alcoves and niches, staring out from the shadows. What makes these especially disturbing is that they are clothed, some in priest's garb, some in vaguely medieval dress. It has the effect of making the figures look not more alive, but less so, like corpses in open coffins, dressed in their best clothes. Ruth thinks of Don Tomaso's words to Angelo: *Concentrate on the living.* Never, she thinks, has she been in a place more obsessed with death.

The high altar is plainer, with a simple wooden table and a modern woodcarving of the crucifixion. One heavy pewter candlestick stands on the altar. Where is its twin? wonders Ruth. Could this have been the murder weapon? She realises that, although candles abound – in tiers before every dressed-up saint and every ghoulish oil painting – none of them are lit. The electricity must have come back on. Ruth seems to remember a single, low-voltage bulb in the passageway. But the church is dark apart from a hazy, diffused light filtering in through the stained-glass windows. There is just one flickering candle, by the door, a single flame before an image of the virgin: blue cloak, white robe, eyes rolling upwards. This candle is new, tall and upright. It must have been lit fairly recently.

Elsa is still praying. She seems oblivious to Ruth's presence. Ruth gets up and walks over to the candle. She doesn't touch it but she sees an indentation on the soft wax which must harbour a fingerprint. She goes over to the main doors. They are still locked. Surely the police and ambulance will want to come in this way? Ruth pulls back the bolts and opens one of the heavy wooden doors. Sunlight rushes in, along with voices from the crowd outside. People push forward. Ruth can't understand what they are saying, but she hears the words 'Don Tomaso' repeated over and over again. She looks across the heads for Shona's red hair and beckons her forward, trying not to open the door any further.

'Something's happened,' she whispers. 'I've got to stay here for a bit. Can you take the children home?'

'What is it?' Shona's eyes are bright.

'Don Tomaso's dead.'

'No!'

The women behind Shona move closer. For a moment it looks as if they are going to barge their way into the church, but then the ambulance roars into the square and parks at the foot of the church steps. A police car follows with a squeal of tyres. The crowd parts to allow the officials through. Ruth just manages to wave at Kate in what she hopes in a reassuring way and to tell Shona that she'll see her later. Then she opens the door.

The ambulance men don't take long to ascertain that Don Tomaso is dead. They then have a long discussion with the policemen. Ruth can't understand what they're saying, but she's pretty sure that the police must be saying that they need to call in forensic teams before the body can be moved. Sure enough, the ambulance men retreat – Ruth can only wonder what the crowd outside are making of all this – and the older and more senior-looking of the two policemen approaches Ruth and Elsa.

He speaks to Ruth first. His accent seems harsher than Angelo's, and while she can sometimes get a word or two when Angelo or Elsa speaks, this is impenetrable. She looks helplessly at Elsa who, luckily, seems to be back in control. Elsa speaks to the policeman and then turns to Ruth.

'Commissario Valenti wants to speak to us both because we were here ... when the ... when we found him. The Commissario has to wait for the ... the experts ... then he will talk to us. He says he will get an interpreter for you.'

'Good,' says Ruth. She wonders how long it will all take but doesn't like to ask. The younger policeman is putting tape around the body.

'Can you tell them how we came in and what we touched?' says Ruth. 'Also, ask him to look at the candle, the one by the door. That must have been lit recently.'

Elsa looks curious, but she speaks to the older policeman. He looks a bit like a Roman emperor, thinks Ruth, with a hooked nose and a crest of grey hair. He listens, frowning, but Ruth is pleased to see that he immediately goes to look at the candle. Watching Valenti in action makes Ruth think of Nelson. She knows it's pathetic, but she can't help wishing that he was here. She remembers, too, that Angelo described the local police chief as a fascist. Is this Valenti?

The younger officer now approaches. He says something to Elsa and makes a gesture towards the door.

'He will drive us to police station,' says Elsa.

The police station is remarkably like the one in King's Lynn: a once grand house forced into public service, high corniced ceilings contrasting with stained carpets and peeling walls. The open-plan rooms are full of computers humming and people staring at screens. The best thing about the place is the air conditioning. Some of the police officers even have jumpers on.

Ruth and Elsa are shown into a small interview room. A woman police officer makes them coffee and Ruth imagines what Judy Johnson would say about this sexist allocation of roles. Ruth is actually feeling rather cold now, so the coffee is welcome. Elsa doesn't drink hers. She has relapsed into silence and Ruth doesn't know what to say to her. That's one of the problems when two people don't speak the same language. You are always having to fall back on inanities. *Isn't it hot/cold/nice/nasty. I'm happy/sad/hungry/thirsty.* Ruth's Italian certainly doesn't stretch to discussing the possible murder of a beloved priest and Elsa's English seems to have dried up. So the two women sit in silence.

After about half an hour, Valenti comes in accompanied by a woman. He introduces her as Linda Anthony. Linda smiles at Ruth and explains that she's a civilian interpreter, a university professor in art history who sometimes helps the police. She's obviously English and Ruth is ashamed at what a difference this makes. She feels as if she has an ally at last.

Valenti ushers Ruth and Linda into his office. Like Nelson's, it's a smaller space cut out of a larger room, higher than it is wide. Valenti reminds Ruth of Nelson again, in the way that he leans back in his chair, taking control of the situation.

Through Linda, Valenti asks how Ruth came to be at the church. She explains about the candlelit Mass and about how she came to accompany Elsa through the side entrance.

More gruff Italian.

'The Commissario wants to know if you're a friend of Angelo Morelli's?' says Linda.

'Not a friend, exactly.' Ruth hopes she isn't blushing. 'I'm here to advise him on an archaeological issue.'

Linda relates this and Valenti nods impatiently. Ruth describes how she found the priest's body and then she says, 'I know forensics are examining him now, but I thought I saw something odd . . .'

Both policeman and interpreter watch her.

'I thought I saw a stone in Don Tomaso's mouth.'

'A stone?' Valenti is startled into English.

'Yes, a flat stone. I couldn't be sure, because I didn't want to touch the body. But, if so, it's strange, because the body I'm examining for the dig, the Roman skeleton, it had a stone in its mouth too.'

Valenti says something to Linda, who turns to Ruth. 'How many people would have known about the stone?'

'Well, Angelo, of course. Marta and Roberto, his students. I don't know their surnames. There were others on the site yesterday. About six people. More students, I assume. Oh, and Daniella di Martile and the TV people. They were filming me talking about the bones.'

'Has this discussion been on television?' Valenti asks through Linda.

'No. They only filmed it today. I don't think it will be aired for a few months.'

'Signora Galloway' – Valenti turns to Ruth again – 'do not tell anyone else about this detail.'

'I won't,' says Ruth. 'And it's Doctor Galloway, actually.'

Valenti looks at her intently for a few moments, then scribbles some notes on his pad. Then he says, in English, 'Has Dottore Morelli told you that he fears for his life?'

Ruth is shocked, not least by the fluently phrased question. 'He has mentioned some incidents . . .'

Valenti has apparently exhausted his English because he turns to Linda again. She says, 'Do you know if Dottore Morelli suspects anyone?'

'No,' says Ruth. 'He says that maybe people are jealous . . .'

Valenti obviously understands this because he laughs.

'You stay in Pompeo's flat?' he asks Ruth.

'Pompeo? Oh, Angelo's grandfather. Yes.'

'Pompeo was a big hero to some,' says Valenti. 'But not to me. Or to Don Tomaso.'

Ruth wants to ask him what he means, but she doesn't know how to phrase the question, in any language. Valenti stands up. Clearly the interview is over.

18

In the square the next morning it's as if there's been another earthquake. People are sitting at the tables in silence, staring into their coffees. Even the fountain is still. Others are standing outside the church, staring up at the arches and the colonnade as if they might have the answer to the question on everyone's lips: how and why did Don Tomaso die? Flowers already fill the steps and, as Ruth watches, two elderly women approach and place a bouquet on the lowest stair. Then they stand there, staring, with the others.

'It's so spooky,' says Shona. 'Just standing there.'

'I suppose they're praying,' says Ruth. 'You should know.' She's a little fed up with Shona's pretence at devout Catholicism when, to her knowledge, Shona has been to church twice in their eighteen years of friendship. Shona is also apparently devastated by Don Tomaso's death. 'Such a *good* man,' she keeps saying, when she had barely exchanged two words with him. It was Ruth he had spoken to at the cultural association dinner. And it was Ruth he had invited to Mass, saying he had something to show her. What could it have been?

They are at the café because there was nothing left in the house for breakfast and because the children were showing signs of becoming stir crazy. They could really do with going to the beach again but Ruth doesn't like to ask Angelo or Graziano, not after the traumas of the last two days. At least the atmosphere in the town has had its effect on Kate and Louis. They are silent too, Louis playing on Shona's iPad and Kate staring at the church.

'Here are some more reporters,' says Shona. Cars containing television crews have been appearing regularly all morning. Now a grey Fiat comes through the archway, going far too fast. For a moment it looks as if it's going to plough through the tables outside the café, but then it comes to an abrupt halt by the church. Two men get out of the car. One is tall with greying dark hair, looking about him with obvious impatience; the other has long, grey hair in a ponytail and, to the obvious bemusement of the crowd, is wearing a purple cloak that gleams in the sunlight.

'Dad!' shouts Kate.

'Oh my God,' says Ruth.

Nelson strides over to their table. For one crazy moment, Ruth thinks that he's going to kiss her. Instead he grasps her arm, rather hard.

'Ruth! Are you all right?'

'Of course I'm all right,' says Ruth, shaking him off. 'What are you doing here?'

'I heard about the earthquake. I was worried. Your phone was turned off.'

Guiltily, Ruth remembers that she turned it off outside the church the previous day, thinking it would have been embarrassing for it to ring during the service. What with one thing and another, she must have forgotten to turn it on again.

'Dad,' says Kate reprovingly.

'Sorry, love.' Nelson goes round the table to give her a hug.

'Hi, Nelson,' says Shona, looking delighted at this fresh drama.

'Hello,' says Nelson unenthusiastically. He's not one of Shona's fans.

'You're not my dad,' says Louis suddenly.

'You're right there, son,' says Nelson. 'Your dad is currently driving me mad trying to send drones over a building site.'

Ruth looks across to where Cathbad is deep in conversation with two elderly women in black.

'Why is Cathbad here?'

'I'm not quite sure myself,' says Nelson. 'As soon as I saw the news on TV, I rang the airline and got a last-minute booking. Then I rang Judy to ask her to stand in for me for a few days. Cathbad got wind of it and said he had a friend in the area who would put me up. When I got to the airport this morning, Cathbad had booked himself on the same flight. Gave me a bit of a turn seeing that cloak, I can tell you. We've driven straight from the airport. Cathbad organised the car hire. Apparently he speaks Italian.'

They look over to where the women are showing Cathbad the church. He is speaking to them very intensely, his head bent to their level.

'How come he speaks Italian?'

'He once worked on a vineyard in Tuscany apparently. You know Cathbad, he's full of surprises.'

Cathbad leaves his new friends and comes to join them, smiling broadly.

'Ruth! I told Nelson that I didn't sense you were in danger.'

Then why did you let him come all this way, thinks Ruth. She's not sure how she feels. On one hand, she's irritated that Nelson thinks he must come running to her rescue all the time. On the other, she can't deny that it's good to see him. It's almost as if she summoned him when she thought about him in the church yesterday. It's so strange to see Nelson in Italy. He seems like a man made for cold weather (he's from the north, after all), not for blue skies and sunny piazzas. But, then again, Castello degli Angeli is now a murder scene. Perhaps it's right that Nelson is here?

'Terrible about Don Tomaso,' Cathbad is saying now, taking off his cloak. Underneath he's wearing shorts and a loose T-shirt. It's typical that he has remembered the name.

'Who?' says Nelson.

'Local priest,' says Cathbad, 'found dead in the church last night.'

'I know,' says Ruth. 'I found him.'

They all stare at her. Kate breaks the tension by saying, 'Will you take us to the beach, Dad?'

*

'That was quick,' says Michelle.

'I came as soon as you texted,' says Tim.

'All the way from Essex?' says Michelle.

Tim smiles. 'All the way from Essex.'

Michelle stands aside to let Tim into the house. Bruno, who has been lying in the hallway, sits up and barks once, loudly.

'Shh, Bruno,' says Michelle. 'He's a friend.'

'He's just protecting you,' says Tim, patting the dog. Michelle remembers him saying that his brother had a German Shepherd. She knows nothing else about Tim's family, and that thought makes her suddenly feel scared. What is she doing with a man she hardly knows? She has known Nelson since she was twenty-one.

'Come through,' she says. Tim and Bruno follow her in the sitting room, which is as tidy as ever. The morning sun streams in through the French windows; the flowers that Harry bought her at the garden centre yesterday stand proudly in their green vase. Laura is out at the pub, where she's working until the university term starts in September. And Harry is . . . Well, she can't even imagine where Harry is. Images of Italy have been chasing round in her head all night: the Leaning Tower of Pisa, the Vatican, the Colosseum, Pompeii, Venice. She can only picture him in the centre of a postcard, not in whatever squalid little town Ruth is holed up in.

'Do you want a cup of tea or coffee?' she asks Tim. Bruno's tail thumps on the wooden floor.

'No.' Tim comes over and takes her hands. 'Sit down and tell me what all this is about. You just said that Nelson had gone to Italy.'

They sit side by side on the sofa. Michelle takes a deep breath. 'He heard on the news about the earthquake. Apparently it's where Ruth and Katie are. He couldn't get Ruth on the phone, so he booked the tickets online. He never does anything like that. He hates holidays and he hates doing anything online. I always book everything.' Against her will, she can feel tears sliding down her cheeks. 'I'm sorry.'

'Don't be,' says Tim. He reaches in his pocket and comes up with a handkerchief. 'Here. It's clean.'

It is clean, and it smells of Tim's aftershave. Michelle breathes in the scent and finds herself soothed. Tim is here. He'll look after her.

'Couldn't he have waited?' says Tim. 'Ruth's phone signal may have been affected by the earthquake.'

'That's what I said. But you know Harry. He never likes to wait. He got the earliest flight this morning. I was meant to understand. Just like I've understood about everything else.' She is shocked at how bitter she sounds.

'I suppose he was worried about Kate'

'It's not Katie,' says Michelle. 'It's Ruth. It's always Ruth.'

Michelle gets up and goes to the window. This house is her pride and joy. Her refuge. Now it feels as if it could be swept away in a puff of wind. What scares her most is that she almost wants it to happen. Bruno comes to sit next to her and she plays with his ears.

'Michelle . . .' Tim is standing behind her. 'Michelle, it's OK.'

She turns and he puts his arms round her. He feels incredibly secure. Slimmer than Harry but just as solid.

'It's OK,' he says again. 'I'm here.'

She says nothing, just continues to hold him. She feels the reverberations of his voice when he speaks.

'Michelle, the baby. Could it be mine?'

She's glad that she's not looking at him

'I don't know,' she says, into his chest. 'It could be.'

Tim holds her at arms' length and looks into her eyes. 'I don't mind if it's Nelson's,' he says. 'I love you. I'll love the baby. I want to look after you both.'

Half laughing, half crying, Michelle raises her lips to his.

It's not how Nelson imagined spending the day, but there's no denying that it's rather pleasant. Ever since he saw the news broadcast in the pub, he has been haunted by images of Katie and Ruth being pulled from collapsing houses, of bloodied faces, frantic rescue workers and bodies on stretchers. Even after he had calmed down enough to check the internet, learning that the main force of the earthquake had been felt by a village twenty miles away, Nelson knew that he wouldn't be able to rest until he actually saw them. The fact that Ruth's phone was switched off didn't help either.

Michelle had been, if not understanding, at least resigned. She had been angry, Nelson knew, but didn't seem to want to confront him with the obvious question: why does Ruth mean so much to you? Laura had been the one who seemed most upset. 'Where are you going?' she'd hissed, when

Nelson stood up and announced that he was leaving the pub. 'It's the first time you've met Chad.' 'Chad can wait,' Nelson had said, but Laura looked as if this wasn't an acceptable response. She'd hardly said goodbye to him that morning. But then it had been 4 a.m. when he left the house.

What would Michelle and Laura say if they could see him now? If they could see him, the man who always complains about holidays, sitting on a private beach under an umbrella with an entirely different family. Ruth and Shona are in the water with the children, Cathbad is next to him, reading a book about ley lines. At Cathbad's suggestion they had stopped at a supermarket on the way and Nelson bought shorts, two polo shirts and some swimming trunks. He also bought a blow-up water ring for Katie. It's pink and has a unicorn's head rather incongruously attached. She's sitting in it now, like some sort of sea creature, bobbing in the shallow water. Nelson bought a water ring for Louis too (a manly thing with footballs on it), but he clearly prefers the unicorn.

'Ruth seems well,' says Cathbad.

'Yes,' says Nelson. He'd been surprised by how good Ruth looked in her swimming costume. He's noticed before that the fewer clothes Ruth wears, the thinner she looks. In the severely cut costume, she looks curvaceous rather than overweight. She's tanned, too, and her hair is longer.

'Do you think I'm mad?' says Nelson. 'Rushing off to Italy at a moment's notice.'

'All the best people are mad,' says Cathbad. 'It's a good sign that you're becoming more in touch with your emotions.'

'I'm not sure Michelle thinks it's a good sign,' says Nelson. 'I think she liked the old, buttoned-up me.'

'Now you're asking me a different question,' says Cathbad.

He's right, and to avoid any more examples of Cathbad's sixth sense, Nelson gets up to go for a swim. Rather to his surprise, Ruth says that she'll come with him. Shona says she's happy to watch the children. The bikini she has on doesn't look as if it would survive proper swimming anyway. Ruth is wearing a far more sensible costume.

The water is warmer than Nelson likes. Getting into the sea should be a test of endurance, in his book. He remembers mornings at Blackpool when the water was so cold that your arms and legs immediately went numb as all the blood rushed to keep your heart going. This is like getting into a tepid bath. Salty, too. Far saltier than the Irish sea. But as they swim out, the water becomes colder and clearer. Nelson is a strong swimmer – he was a lifeguard in his youth – but Ruth keeps pace with him. Together they swim far beyond the families and the old ladies in swimming hats. Eventually, they float on their backs for a while, not speaking. The land – the umbrellas and hotels, the men selling jewellery and sarongs – seems very far away. One of the vendors has a string of kites attached to his cart and they form a multicoloured line against the sky.

'Nelson,' says Ruth at last, 'why did you come here?'

'I told you,' says Nelson, 'I wanted to see if you and Katie were all right.'

'You can't keep doing things like that,' says Ruth. 'We're not your family.'

It's the first time that she's ever said this and he's surprised how much it hurts. Nelson looks up at the sky, which is a bright, impossible blue. Strains of pop music drift from the beach, something about fun in the sun.

'Katie is,' he says. 'She's my daughter.'

'You've got another family,' says Ruth, 'and now you're having another child.'

'Ruth,' says Nelson. 'If Michelle wasn't pregnant—'

'No,' says Ruth, so fiercely that he's silenced. 'Don't say that. You can't say that.' And she turns in the water and heads back towards the shore.

'I should go,' says Tim. He doesn't make any move to put his words into action though. Michelle raises herself on one elbow to look at him.

'Don't go.'

Tim groans, pulling Michelle down to him. 'You're a witch,' he says into her hair. 'You've bewitched me.'

Maybe she is a witch, thinks Michelle, as she kisses the wonderfully soft skin on Tim's neck. Cathbad once said that she had hidden psychic powers. On the other hand, it feels as if she is the one under a spell. Downstairs, the cuckoo clock chimes midday. Bruno whines softly from the hallway.

'I should go,' says Tim again. But his body is obviously saying otherwise.

This time Michelle is the one to pull away. 'You should go. You told them you'd be back at lunchtime.'

Tim closes his eyes for a minute and then sits up. He has the most wonderful body, thinks Michelle, looking at his naked back. It still seems amazing to her that such a beautiful man would drive nearly a hundred miles to see her, would love her, make love to her. That, as much as anything else, feels like a dream.

'All right if I have a shower?' says Tim.

'Of course,' says Michelle although it feels almost more of a betrayal to let Tim use Harry's en suite than to make love to him. She will have to change the sheets as soon as Tim has gone. But then, she thinks, Harry won't be back for two days. She might as well keep the scent of her lover close for a little longer. The thought makes her heart harden. It's not my fault, she says to the army of accusers in her head (led, disconcertingly, by her mother-in-law), he's the one who abandoned me. She starts to put her clothes on. She'll shower later.

Tim comes back into the bedroom and dresses quickly. When they go out onto the landing, Michelle avoids Bruno's eyes. She kisses Tim in the darkness of the porch and watches him walk to his car, which he has prudently left a few doors away. No neighbours about, thank goodness, though she can hear Mrs Firman's grandchildren splashing in the paddling pool. Tim raises his hand in salute and the black car moves off, solemn and anonymous, like a politician's limo. As Michelle watches, she sees a man walking slowly along the opposite side of the cul-de-sac. He's a stranger, slightly shabby looking, with glasses. The man seems to look curiously at her so she shuts the door. Michelle goes into the kitchen to give Bruno a guilt snack. When she goes back to the window, the man has gone.

19

Angelo is pleased to escape to the university. One of the problems about living with his mother is that she keeps talking, and this morning it seemed as if she would never stop. He knows she's upset about Don Tomaso and, of course, he sympathises, but even before he'd had his breakfast coffee, he'd had the whole of their childhood, how handsome the young Tomaso had been, what a surprise when he'd become a priest, how much Papa had loved him, what a good man, a living saint. Angelo had been forced to invent a meeting to get away from her. Well, now he's here he might as well look at some of the filming from yesterday. Daniella has sent the files through.

He's borrowing this room at the University of Casserta from Graziano. It's better than nothing but he misses his office in Rome, the shelves with all his books and awards, the sofa where he sometimes catches an hour of sleep and once seduced a visiting medievalist from Florence. He thinks of Ruth and their night together at the conference. He'd thought then what an interesting woman she was. She wasn't beautiful by any means, but there was something about her, an intelligence, a refusal to compromise, that he'd found very attractive. She'd been surprisingly passionate too. He wonders if there's any chance of a rematch. She's obviously not with the father of her daughter and, from what Shona said to Graziano, it seems as if there's some mystery there. Angelo ponders the possibility, drinking his third espresso and waiting for the files to upload.

He's mildly annoyed to be disturbed by a knock on the door. It's Roberto, a nice boy, not as bright as Marta, but uncomplicated, eager to please. Angelo composes his face into welcoming lines.

'Professore,' Roberto dives in, obviously greatly exercised about something, 'we've found some bones.'

'Bones? Where?' He hopes they haven't been digging at the Roman site without his permission.

'At the church. The graveyard. We went there this morning to lay flowers for Don Tomaso and Marta wanted . . .'

Angelo can guess where this is going. Marta hadn't been able to resist looking at the newly exposed earth in the graveyard. Well, he would have been the same at her age.

'We saw some bones and we thought they were modern.'

'What made you think that?'

'There was a skull and we could see a filling . . .'

Angelo thinks. No one has been buried in the graveyard at Castello degli Angeli for over a hundred years. They use the cemetery in Arpino now, and even there, bodies are routinely dug up after eight years and their bones put in the ossuary. This body must have been buried illegally. He also thinks that if Marta and Roberto have uncovered a skull, they must have been doing more than a bit of casual digging.

'The thing is . . .' Roberto is obviously uncomfortable.

'What?' says Angelo, his mind still on the churchyard.

'Marta thinks it's her great-grandfather.'

There's still a *carabinieri* van in front of the church and police tape around the graveyard, but Angelo and Roberto duck underneath and no one stops them. At the café, people are having lunch, but there's still a sombre feel about the town. Flowers now fill the wide church steps and Angelo can spot his mother's tribute, a vast cross made from lilies.

Marta is standing among the dislodged gravestones, looking guilty.

'I'm sorry, Professore,' she begins.

Angelo cuts her short. 'Show me what you've found.'

Marta leads him to a place where the earthquake has opened up a deep crevice. He can immediately see signs that some professional excavation has taken place; the lines are clean and the bones haven't been moved, just carefully exposed. But, there in the chalky soil, is what is unmistakeably a fully articulated adult skeleton, the skull grinning up at them with that telltale glint of metal in the teeth.

But Marta is pointing to the hand. One arm has been uncovered, the humerus, ulna and radius all present and correct. The hand, though, is missing the middle and ring fingers. Angelo doesn't need to ask the significance of this. He hears his grandfather's voice, from one of the long discussions they had towards the end, sitting on the balcony in his apartment, looking out over the valley.

'The boar charged Giorgio. His gun jammed and he couldn't shoot. He fought the animal with his fists and it bit two of his fingers right off. I had to shoot. I just had a second to get my aim right – one inch the wrong way and I would have killed Giorgio – but I managed it. The boar was dead and Giorgio's hand dripping with blood. I wrapped his hand in my shirt and I went to the animal and pulled out one of his teeth and gave it to Giorgio. He always wore it round his neck. For good luck, he said, and to remember I saved his life . . .'

Angelo looks at the skeleton. The clothes have rotted away but there's no sign of the lucky necklace.

'It's my great-grandfather,' says Marta.

'Yes,' says Angelo. 'I think it is.'

20

It had been a good day, thinks Ruth, as she prepares supper, listening to the sounds of *Finding Nemo* from next door. It had given her a certain pleasure to think that people on the beach probably took her and Nelson and Kate to be a proper family, though what they thought of Cathbad and Shona is anyone's guess. They had felt like a family too – swimming together, playing with Kate, eating at the café. She still thinks that Nelson shouldn't have come. He's made his choice and should stay with Michelle and their children. He hadn't liked it when she said that she wasn't his family, but it's true. He can't have it both ways, Michelle at home and Ruth at work, or during one of those dreamlike times that they have found themselves alone together, like in the snowstorm, or six weeks ago when they had climbed the stairs to her bedroom. But, all the same, it had undoubtedly been good to spend a day on the beach with Nelson. He'll be gone the day after tomorrow. Michelle has her scan soon, she knows, and Nelson will want to be back for that. Well, at least they'll have another day together before he leaves. Perhaps they can go to Monte Cassino . . .

Shona appears in the doorway, fresh from her shower. She's wearing her kimono and her hair is wet.

'I'm so sunburned,' she says. 'I used some of your aftersun. I hope that's OK.'

'Of course,' says Ruth. Shona doesn't look sunburned. In fact she looks glowing, the sort of glow that often accompanies possession of a secret. This is partly explained by Shona's next words.

'Graziano rang,' she says casually. 'He wanted to know if we wanted to go out for a drink tonight. In the café.'

'I'm a bit tired,' says Ruth. 'You go. I'll look after the children. After all, you had them yesterday while I was at the police station.'

'Yes.' For a second Shona's face clouds. 'I keep forgetting about poor Don Tomaso. It doesn't seem real, does it?'

'No,' says Ruth, although the body in the church had seemed extremely real.

'Graziano says that Angelo's discovered something in the graveyard,' says Shona. 'Some bones uncovered by the earthquake. That explains the lights we saw there just now.'

Ruth remembers the gleam of white that she'd seen when she went into the church with Elsa. She's not surprised that bones have come to the surface. They have a way of doing that. She had noticed that Angelo's car was parked by the church and she'd seen figures in the graveyard. For a moment, she wishes she was with them, excavating in the dying light, trying to do as much work as possible before nightfall. Then she reminds herself that her job at the moment is to look after the children and cook them supper. The water is boiling so she puts in the pasta.

'None for me, thanks,' says Shona. 'I ate so much at lunchtime.'

So did Ruth, but that was six hours ago. Shona wanders off to get dressed. Ruth makes a basic tomato sauce and pours herself a glass of wine. She'll try to persuade the kids to go to bed early and then she can have a lovely time reading her Ian Rankin book. She wonders why the prospect isn't as pleasing as it should be.

Nelson likes Cathbad's friend, Linda Anthony. She teaches art history and is the kind of casual yet welcoming hostess who can whip up a meal of spaghetti carbonara for five without pausing for breath. Her Italian husband, Paolo, says little, but exudes acceptance of the guests. He also uncorks some extremely good home-made wine. Sitting on Linda's terrace, eating the pasta and drinking Paolo's wine, Nelson feels himself relaxing for the first time in months, possibly years.

'How do you know Cathbad then?' asks Nelson, as Linda fills up his glass.

'We were at university together,' says Linda, smiling across the table at Cathbad. 'In Manchester.'

Linda is the sort of attractive woman who doesn't have to bother too much. Her hair is skewered into a messy bun and she is wearing a loose red dress. Even so, Nelson bets that she was one of the prettiest girls at Manchester University in the eighties.

'Linda was the only girl to have a Modigliani print in her room,' says Cathbad. 'She was effortlessly cool.'

What were you doing in her bedroom, thinks Nelson, but he doesn't voice this thought.

'We were in an experimental drama group together,' says Linda. 'Michael played a man who had been turned into a lion.'

Cathbad smiles to hear his old, pre-druid name. 'I was very proud of my man trapped in an animal's body,' he said. 'Linda was a tree.'

Linda translates this for Paolo, who says something about Apollo and Daphne.

'Delilah played Helen of Troy,' she says. 'She was so beautiful.'

Cathbad smiles and says nothing. Nelson assumes that he too thought Delilah was beautiful, seeing as he married her and they had a child together. But he understands that the thought of Delilah also brings sadness.

'I came to Florence as part of my course,' Linda tells Nelson. 'I met Paolo, who was a medical student, and, well, the rest is history.'

It wasn't a bad move, thinks Nelson. Paolo is a paediatrician, working at the local hospital, and the couple have three sons, although only one, a teenager who disappeared on a moped at the first sight of guests, is still living at home. Their house is comfortable rather than grand, but the view from the terrace, with the bougainvillea forming an undulating frame, is stunning.

'It's very kind of you to let us stay at such short notice,' he says.

'It's no problem,' says Linda. 'We've got spare rooms now and it's nice to talk English occasionally. I'm so glad that you were able to see your little girl. It must have been so worrying for you to read the news reports.'

'It was,' says Nelson. 'But Ruth and Katie are OK, thank God.'

'Ruth?' says Linda. 'Not Ruth Galloway? Doctor Ruth Galloway?'

Nelson stares. Has Ruth's fame spread this far?

'Do you know her?' he says.

'I met her yesterday,' says Linda. 'She was being questioned by the police because she had discovered a body. I was asked to translate.'

Nelson is slightly disturbed by this. Ruth hadn't spoken much about the death of the priest except to say that it almost certainly wasn't accidental. Nelson hadn't liked to ask more in front of the children, but it strikes him as ominous that violent death has followed her here, to this Italian idyll. He's now torn between professional curiosity and an almost superstitious wish to avoid the subject.

'Was that the priest?' says Cathbad. 'Everyone seems very upset about it.'

'Yes,' says Linda. 'Everyone loved Don Tomaso. He christened all three of the boys and didn't seem to mind that Paolo and I didn't really believe. The church is beautiful, too. There's a della Robbia frieze inside.' She turns to Nelson, 'I was impressed by Ruth. She seemed so cool and composed. And she stood up to Flavio Valenti, who can be a bit of a bully. Is she your . . . ?'

'She's Katie's mother,' says Nelson, not answering the implied question. 'What do the police think happened?'

'I don't think I can say,' says Linda, starting to clear away the plates. 'Confidentiality is very strict.'

'Nelson's a policeman,' says Cathbad. 'A Detective Chief Inspector.' He gives the words rather a malicious ring and Nelson remembers that Cathbad has not always been a fan of the police.

'Oh, I didn't realise,' says Linda. 'Perhaps you can talk to Commissario Valenti.'

'I don't want to get involved,' says Nelson. 'I see enough of murder at home.'

Linda and Paolo take the plates out and come back with cheese and figs and a bottle of bright yellow limoncello. Nelson normally dislikes liqueurs but this is delicious, sharp and sweet at the same time.

'I imagine it will have a big effect on the town,' says Cathbad. 'The priest dying like that.'

'They'll be devastated,' says Linda. 'And the sad thing is, they might not get another priest. The church may have to close. Don Tomaso should have retired years ago, but there aren't any new priests. In Italy, that is. The only young priests come from Africa.'

'Italy is pagan now,' says Paolo, in surprisingly good English, cutting a peach into small glistening pieces.

'Amen to that,' says Cathbad.

Ruth manages to get the children into bed by nine. Then she sits on the sofa with the balcony doors open and reads about Rebus and the grey streets of Edinburgh. But her mind keeps straying back to the church and that spread-eagled figure on the altar. Like a sacrifice, like Lindow Man lying face down in the peat bog, like the Iron Age bodies found in Denmark pegged down on the marshes in an attempt to appease the gods. Who could have killed the priest? A man who, from Ruth's short acquaintance, seemed to be the very heart of the community, loved by all. She remembers Don Tomaso's comments about the community's treatment of the refugee Samir. *Food is not love.* He hadn't been afraid to speak his mind. Was this why he had been killed? Easy to imagine the blow on the head happening in the course of a heated quarrel. Something she had once heard comes back to Ruth. *Saints cause a lot of trouble for the rest of us.* Elsa has described Don Tomaso as a saint. Had Don Tomaso been causing trouble and was that why he had been killed?

And who could have put the stone in his mouth? Ruth is pretty sure that it was there, although she will have to wait for the post-mortem to be sure. Then again, Valenti is hardly likely to share the PM results with her. But the stone seems to imply that the killer was someone who knew about the Roman body currently residing in the university laboratory. That must narrow it down a bit. She should talk to Angelo. He'll know how widely the story was known.

Stop it, she tells herself, you're not Miss Marple, this has nothing to do with you. She thinks about Angelo's sugges-tion that she investigate the attempts on his life. Could they be linked to the death of the priest? She thinks of *Stranieri andate a casa* and the skull on the doorstep. Clearly there are dark forces at work in the little town on the hill.

Ruth goes out onto the balcony, trying to clear her head. After the heat of the day, the air is pleasantly cool and smells of herbs and lemons. A full moon shines above the ruined tower. What must it have been like here during the war, with the enemy eating at the café and resistance fighters hiding in the hills? As she looks out over the dense trees, she sees a figure moving swiftly through them, carrying something that she first thinks is a stick and then, with a shock, recognises as a gun. A hunter? On an impulse, Ruth gets out her phone and takes a photograph. The flash briefly illuminates the trees then all is dark again, the only light the surreal brightness of the moon. Ruth stays watching for a while, listens as the dog barks down below and a voice is raised in greeting or exasperation. She should go to bed, she's tired after her day in the sun. She should go in and ring her father. But she stays sitting on the balcony until Shona comes home, flushed with something that looks rather more significant than sunburn.

Across the valley, in Linda's son Luca's room, which is festooned with posters of Juventus, Nelson finally gets through to Michelle. He's relieved to hear that she sounds almost conciliatory. She even asks if Ruth is all right.

'She's fine,' says Nelson. 'I'm sorry that I rushed off like that. It was just . . . all the pictures of the earthquake . . . I was worried about Katie.'

'I'm glad you put your mind at rest,' says Michelle. It's hard to tell from her voice whether she's being sarcastic or not.

'Are you all right?' says Nelson. 'Make sure you lock the doors at night.'

'I'm OK,' says Michelle. 'I've got Bruno to look after me.'

Nelson suspects that Bruno would be anyone's for a Bonio, but at least his presence gives Michelle reassurance. He asks about Laura.

'She's fine. Out with Chad.'

'Give her my love,' he says.

'I will.'

'And to you.'

'Yes,' says Michelle enigmatically. 'Goodbye. Sleep well.'

Nelson expects he'll be lying awake for hours, worrying about Ruth, Katie, Michelle, Laura and Rebecca, all his responsibilities, all his mistakes, but he falls asleep immediately and dreams of the sea.

21

Judy surveys her office with a feeling of satisfaction, feeling the tensions of the morning draining away, her shoulders relaxing, her jaw unclenching. Of course, the office isn't really hers, it's Nelson's and only on loan for a few days, but here, in the station, she feels that she can be her best self, not Michael and Miranda's Mummy, not Cathbad's life partner or her mother's daughter (she has been pushed, rather uncomfortably, back into this role during the course of her mother's visit), but DS Judy Johnson, police professional. And, one day, maybe DI Judy Johnson, with her own office. Not here – the King's Lynn force is not big enough to need another high-ranking officer – but maybe they could move, perhaps to an inner city with new challenges. Judy has lived in Norfolk all her life but she feels that this is chance, not choice. She would like to travel, move somewhere where she isn't always meeting people that she knew at school. *Weren't you in my brother's year?* No chance of lying about your age here. Cathbad's a wanderer, born in Ireland, drifted across Europe, studied in Manchester and Southampton, ending up washed ashore in North Norfolk. Cathbad wouldn't mind if they moved, as long as it's to a place with good energies, and the children are young enough to start again somewhere else.

Judy sighs and puts down her coffee cup. Nelson's desk is extremely tidy, his famous to-do list lying on top of his in tray with all the items smugly crossed off. She's probably feeling stressed because it's the holidays and Cathbad is away. She didn't mind him accompanying Nelson, Cathbad deserves a break and he knows and loves Italy, but she does wonder what's going on with Ruth and Nelson. Is their affair starting up again? Surely not with Michelle pregnant? But Ruth had definitely been odd at Clough's wedding, quiet and almost tearful at times. Judy looks up at the postcard from Clough, which is pinned to Nelson's corkboard. She can just imagine what it says: 'Having a good time. Glad you're not here. Lol.' Judy's had said 'Glad you're not her', which she took to be a spelling mistake and not something deeper. She misses Clough, which shows that she's feeling a bit down.

It's nice having her mother to stay, but she does feel that her mum, who was always happy to stay at home with her children, judges her for loving her job so much. 'I'm not going to have a job,' Michael had said the other day, 'I'm going to stay at home and make cakes.'

'Oh no,' said his grandmother, 'boys have to have jobs.'

Judy had ground her teeth. 'Childminding is a job, as I'm sure you'd agree, Mum.'

'Oh,' said her mother, taking a chocolate cake out of the oven, 'you know what I mean.' Judy did, all too well. The cake had been delicious though.

There's a knock on the door. Judy looks up to see Tanya, her fellow DS, looking resentful. It gives Judy real pleasure every time she walks past Tanya's open-plan workspace into the office, which shows that she can't be a very nice person.

'Someone to see you, Judy.'

'Who is it?' She isn't expecting anyone. In fact, the day is so quiet that she had actually considered reorganising her filing.

'She's called Marj Maccallum. Apparently she used to work here.'

'What does she want?'

'She wouldn't say. She wanted to speak to whoever's in charge.' Amazing that Tanya manages to speak at all through teeth that gritted.

'OK. Show her in.' Judy leans back in her chair and tries not to look too pleased with herself.

Judy would have known Marj for an ex-copper, or ex-forces, anywhere. It's something in her manner, calm but contained, in the way that she sits up very straight and addresses Judy in a way that is both respectful and no-non-sense. She's about sixty, with short white hair and brown skin that suggests she spends a lot of time outdoors. A dog walker, thinks Judy. She's been walking their dog, Thing, while Cathbad is away, and loves both the solitude and the camaraderie of it. She enjoys greeting another dog walkers (usually by their pet's name) and exchanging a few words without feeling bound to fall into step with them. It's the perfect human interaction and it gets her out of making breakfast.

'It's good to see a woman behind that desk,' says Marj. 'I worked here for twenty years and never made it above WPC.'

'I'm only here temporarily,' says Judy, 'I'm a DS.'

'Plenty of time,' says Marj, 'you're still young.'

Judy nods. 'How can I help you?'

Marj fixes her with a steely blue gaze. 'When I was working here we apprehended an arsonist called Micky Webb. Ever heard of him?'

'Yes, the boss has mentioned him.'

'DI Nelson put him away. A good man, Nelson. I was sorry not to see him today.'

'He's on holiday. In Italy.'

Marj looks slightly disappointed, as if she expected more from Nelson – a more macho holiday, perhaps, like trekking in the Welsh mountains or fly fishing in Scotland. 'Well, Nelson put him away and Micky swore he'd get his revenge. The usual stuff. He was a nasty piece of work, Micky. Killed his wife and kids in cold blood, whatever they said in court. Well now he's out, on licence if you please.'

'I know. I think DCI Nelson followed it up.'

'He spoke to Freddie Burnett. He was the DS on the case. I was only a PC but I was in on the arrest and you could see Micky hated that. Hated the fact that he was handcuffed to a woman. When we got to the station he leant over and whispered to me, "I'll get you for this, you c-word."'

Judy blinks, not so much at the word (one much used by the police, though not ever by Nelson) but at the way Marj can't quite bring herself to say it.

'Well, now Micky's out and I've seen him.'

'Seen him? Where?'

'Outside my house. I live in Bungay now. Got a nice little house there. Anyway, one day I'm walking my dog . . .'

Bingo, thinks Judy.

'. . . and I see him, standing there, on the street corner, watching me. I say, "Hello, Micky. Long time no see," and he turns and walks away without a word. Well, the next day, my dog was poisoned.'

Judy sits up straighter. 'What?'

'Mabel was poisoned. As soon as I saw her vomiting in the garden I knew immediately what had happened and got her to the vet in time. She's going to be all right, thank God. But I found what she'd been eating – a steak, lovely piece of meat – and took it to the lab. I've still got friends there. The results came back today. It had been poisoned with antifreeze.'

'And you think it was Micky Webb?'

'Stands to reason,' says Marj. 'He saw me with Mabel and he knew how to get at me. He thought, that dog's all she's got now. Actually I've got a fuller life than ever now I'm retired. The grandkids come to stay all the time. But Micky wasn't to know that. He poisoned that steak and threw it into my garden. How else would it have got there? Mabel's greedy, like all Westies, she'd eaten almost all of it by the time I got to her.'

Judy looks at Marj. She believes her completely, but could Micky really be bent on revenge? The DCI had followed it up and didn't seem worried. Judy thinks of Thing and feels her blood pressure rising. Anyone who could attack an animal like that doesn't deserve to be at large. It was a cowardly crime too. Micky wouldn't dare confront Nelson to his face, but he would come after a solitary woman and her dog.

'I'll pay Micky a visit,' she says.

'Good,' says Marj, with a sudden grin. 'He'll hate that.'

As arranged, Nelson is at the café in Castello degli Angeli bright and early the next morning. He is pleased to see that Shona, Ruth and the children are already there. They are sitting with a bearded man who seems on very good terms with Shona.

'This is Graziano,' says Ruth. 'He's a friend of Angelo's, the archaeologist I'm working with.'

Nelson has heard rather a lot about this Angelo. He imagines him as a weedy, academic figure with horn-rimmed spectacles, or as an Italian version of Phil, prancing about in shorts, pretending he's Indiana Jones.

'Graziano's offered to take me and the kids to the swimming pool,' says Shona, 'so you and Ruth can spend the day together.' She smirks in a way that he finds irritating, but there's no denying that a day with Ruth on her own sounds pretty good.

'I'm taking Rainbow,' says Katie.

'Rainbow?'

'My blow-up unicorn. I'm going to let Louis share it. Sometimes,' she adds darkly, looking at Louis, who has discovered the chocolate centre of his pastry and is occupied by smearing it over his face.

'Share nicely,' says Nelson. 'Are there lifeguards at the pool?' he asks, cutting into a giggly conversation between Shona and Graziano, carried out half in Italian, half in English.

'Yes,' says Graziano, 'and I am a trained lifeguard too. I used to spend my summers in Formia.'

'Nelson's a policeman,' says Shona, as if this needs explaining. Graziano looks shocked, as people often do.

'Where do you want to go?' Nelson asks Ruth, who has been looking at him rather sardonically.

'I'd like to see Monte Cassino,' she says. 'The abbey, you know.'

'I've seen the film,' says Nelson. 'Fine by me. I've got the car. Cathbad and Linda have gone to Rome by train. There are about a million pictures they want to look at.'

'Linda?' says Ruth.

'Linda Anthony,' says Nelson. 'Apparently she knows you.'

'Yes,' says Ruth. 'She translated when . . .' She looks towards the church then gives an exclamation. 'Angelo!'

A man is walking quickly towards them. He is dressed in jeans and a black shirt and is about ten years younger and a foot taller than Nelson's imaginary Angelo.

'Ruth!' Angelo doesn't bother to greet anyone else. 'Something terrible has happened. They've arrested Samir.'

The name doesn't mean anything to Nelson, but Shona and Ruth exchange glances.

'Samir?' says Ruth. 'You mean the refugee who lives in the ruined house?'

'Yes,' says Angelo. 'Apparently he was seen leaving the church that afternoon. That's all the evidence they have. Valenti's such a fascist. He'll do anything to pin it on a refugee.' He stops, seemingly aware of Nelson for the first time.

'This is Harry Nelson,' says Ruth, 'a friend of mine.'

Graziano says something in Italian to Angelo and Nelson thinks he catches the word '*poliziotto*'.

'Good,' says Angelo, 'we need a policeman on our side. Ruth, you must help me. You saw the body. My mother says it was horrible. Samir would never do anything like that. He was devoted to Don Tomaso.'

But people often kill those that they are devoted to, thinks Nelson. He's pretty sure that Ruth is thinking the same thing.

'Is that all the evidence they have?' she asks. 'That he was seen leaving the church?'

'Apparently there's DNA evidence too,' says Angelo. 'I've got a contact in the lab.'

Nelson disapproves of leaks, but if Valenti can get DNA evidence in twenty-four hours, he's either a miracle worker or a dictator.

'This Samir,' says Nelson, 'what does he say? Has he denied it?'

'Yes,' says Angelo, 'but he doesn't speak very good Italian. They've sent for an Arabic translator from Rome. We've got to help him.'

'I'm sorry,' says Ruth. 'I don't know what I can do.'

Angelo sighs and sits down next to them. The waitress brings him coffee without being asked. He drains it in one gulp.

'Angelo,' says Ruth. 'I heard that you've found some bones in the graveyard.'

Nelson groans inwardly. If Ruth gets into a bone conversation, they'll never get away. Angelo smiles slightly, as if recognising and acknowledging archaeological curiosity. 'Yes,' he says. 'The earthquake exposed some bones. We think they're quite modern. In fact' – he lowers his voice, although nobody appears to be listening – 'we think they might be the remains of Marta's great-grandfather, Giorgio.'

This means nothing to Nelson, but Ruth seems fascinated. 'The one who was a friend of your grandfather's?'

'Yes. Giorgio was killed by the Nazis but no one ever found his body. Until now, that is.'

'Could I look at the excavation?'

'Of course,' says Angelo. 'It's not an official excavation, though, and perhaps it never will be. But I could show you now if you like?'

Ruth looks at Nelson. 'Perhaps another time,' she says.

Judy is at the house in Spalding bright and early. She wants to catch Micky Webb on the hop, getting ready for work perhaps, stressed and off guard. But when she knocks at the door of The Nook, she is met by a woman wearing an actual apron. 'The Boss' it reads, over a picture of Marlon Brando as the Godfather. Ruth wouldn't approve. To her, The Boss will only ever be Bruce Springsteen.

Judy shows her warrant card. 'Is Micky in?'

'Yes.' The woman's welcoming smile falters. 'What's this about?'

'I'd rather explain to Micky,' says Judy. 'Can I come in?' She is, in fact, already over the threshold, but it never hurts to be polite.

Micky is sitting at a table in the sitting room, obviously waiting for the full English to be served. There are mats on the table, HP and tomato sauce, even a little vase of flowers. Cathbad always cooks breakfast for Judy and the children but even he draws the line at flowers and, being a vegetarian, bacon is off the menu. Judy can smell it frying now and her stomach rumbles. Doing without bacon is the only bad thing about living with Cathbad.

'Hi, Micky,' says Judy, sitting down. 'I'm DS Judy Johnson from the King's Lynn police. I'd like to ask about your whereabouts on Sunday afternoon.'

'What's this about?' says Micky, echoing his wife. He's an insignificant looking man, balding, bespectacled. But Judy isn't fooled. Often the most inoffensive looking people are the most deadly, because they go through life unnoticed.

'Were you in Bungay at 4 p.m. on Sunday the twenty-fourth of August?'

'I . . .' Micky looks at his wife, who is standing in the doorway.

'Just answer the question, Micky,' says Judy, remembering that Micky supposedly doesn't like women who are in authority. Why then did he marry a woman who wears an apron saying 'The Boss', even while cooking his breakfast?

'I might have been,' says Micky at last. 'I like it there. I like the church, St Mary's.'

'Isn't that where the devil is supposed to have appeared in the form of a black dog?' says Judy, remembering the legend from school.

'The devil is all around us,' says the wife, in a pleasant, chatty voice.

Judy ignores this. 'What were you doing in Bungay on Sunday, Micky?'

'I just went there for a walk.'

'Rather a long way for a walk, isn't it?'

'I like Bungay,' says Micky, 'and I like driving.'

'So you drove there to have a walk. And, while you were there, did you see a woman called Marj Maccallum?'

Micky is silent. They both jump when the smoke alarm goes off, caused, no doubt, by burning toast. The Boss retreats into the kitchen.

'Because,' says Judy, 'Marj says that she saw you.'

'It's a programme,' says Micky in a rush. 'You're supposed to seek out people you've wronged and apologise to them. I went to see DCI Nelson but was scared to knock on his door. It was the same with WPC Maccallum. When she spoke to me my nerve failed and I ran away.'

'Did you go back the next day and poison her dog?'

'No!' Now Micky looks really shocked. His wife comes back into the room and puts her hand on his shoulder.

Comfort or a warning? 'No,' says Micky again. 'I wouldn't . . . I couldn't . . . I love dogs. I'd never do anything like that.'

Judy has been looking through the files. There was a cat in residence in the Webb house at the time of the fire. It had been luckier than the human occupants and had been found, alive and well, in a neighbour's garden a few days later. No dog though.

'You can't just come in here and make accusations like that,' said Mrs Webb.

Judy knows this, too, so she deliberately softens her voice. 'Micky, I'm here to warn you that if you approach any other member or ex-member of the King's Lynn force, you'll be in breach of your licence. Do you understand?'

Micky nods. 'Yes.'

'DCI Nelson is keeping a close eye on you.'

'He's . . .' says Micky suddenly, then stops.

'He's what?'

'He's a good man.'

Marj had said that too, and Judy believes that, by and large, it's true. Nelson doesn't always make the right decisions though. Had Micky been about to say that Nelson was away? If so, how did he know? Something in the home set-up didn't seem right either. The couple were either hiding something or they were afraid. All the same, it is hard to refuse when Louise Webb offers her a bacon sandwich. She manages it though.

Ruth enjoys the drive to Monte Cassino, although Nelson's driving seems even more terrifying than usual as they ascend the mountain and he steers the left-hand-drive car through a series of hairpin bends.

'Be careful,' she says. 'I don't want to die just yet.'

'We're all dying,' says Nelson, but he slows down slightly. 'This is some climb.'

'It's a natural vantage point,' says Ruth. 'It was bombed by the Allies in the war. Did you know that?'

'Yes,' says Nelson. 'I used to read Sven Hassel books when I was a boy. There was one about Monte Cassino.'

'I've never read Sven Hassel,' says Ruth.

'So I've read something you haven't,' says Nelson. 'Wonders never cease.'

'The Allies thought that the Germans were in the monastery,' says Ruth, 'but they weren't. Only civilians and monks.'

'I don't think it's ever been proved whether the Germans were camped there or not,' says Nelson, 'but they were certainly in the area.'

Ruth doesn't think it's worth getting into a discussion about Allied war crimes. She's noticed before that Nelson often gets defensive when he thinks she's attacking Britain.

'It's terrible when historical monuments are destroyed,' she says, 'like in Iraq and Syria today.'

'It's worse when people die,' says Nelson. He takes the final corner too fast and veers over to the wrong side of the road.

The words have a sobering effect. They are silent as they drive up to the car park. There, at the foot of the slope leading up to the monastery, is a new impediment: the guard refuses to let Ruth enter because she has bare arms.

'You need to cover,' he says, gesturing.

'This is ridiculous,' says Ruth. 'It's like something from the Middle Ages. I bet men don't have to cover up.'

Nelson points to a sign indicating, in crude picture form, that no bare arms or shorts are allowed for either sex.

'I've got a long-sleeved shirt in the car,' he says. 'It's the one I was wearing yesterday. Why don't you put that on?'

Ruth almost refuses, but she wants to see the monastery and, though she doesn't want to admit this to herself, she quite wants to wear Nelson's shirt. It's dark blue denim and smells of him. The guard smiles thinly and lets them pass. As they walk away, they can hear him telling some German tourists that their shorts are too short.

The newly built monastery looks as impressive as a Greek temple, its walls rising white against the sky. They walk through cloisters and archways into a stone courtyard with a well in the middle. The view is breathtaking, the whole of the Liri Valley spread out below them, each hill seemingly crowned by a particularly scenic castle or crenellated town. Italians do seem keen on building in the most inaccessible places, thinks Ruth. Even their fields look impossible, almost vertical on the sides of mountains, yet they are neatly cultivated, terrace after terrace, rows of vines and sunflowers, tiny farm vehicles moving between them.

'St Benedict founded a hospital here,' says Ruth. 'The oldest hospital in Europe. The oldest medical school in the world was nearby, in Salerno.'

Nelson does not seem interested in the Benedictine rule.

'Tell me about this Angelo person,' he says. 'How come he asked you to help him?'

'I suppose he'd heard of my work,' says Ruth, still looking at the view and not at Nelson. She doesn't want to tell him about the one-night stand in Trastevere. Not because she's embarrassed, she tells herself, just because it would complicate things.

'Yes,' says Nelson. 'Phil said that you were getting quite an international reputation.'

'He did?' Ruth can't supress a feeling of satisfaction. 'He's probably just jealous.'

'He'd be even more jealous if he could see Shona with her beardy admirer.'

'Graziano? Do you think there's something going on between them?'

'Don't ask me,' says Nelson. 'I'm hardly an expert on relationships.'

There's a short silence, and then Ruth says, 'I came here because I wanted to get away from Norfolk for a while. To get used to the idea that you and Michelle are having a baby.'

'Believe me,' says Nelson, 'I took some time to get used to it too.'

'But you are now?'

There's another silence. Nelson leans on the balustrade, looking away from her. He seems to be choosing his words very carefully. 'She's my wife, Ruth. I can't leave her when she's pregnant. Maybe after the baby is born . . .'

Ruth wonders what Nelson would say if she repeated the conversation she had with Tim, that day at her cottage. Does Nelson ever suspect that Michelle's baby might be

Tim's? Well, he will know soon enough if it is. But she has got to stop him before he goes any further. It was the same yesterday in the sea. If he says that he wants to be with her, she doesn't think she will be able to stand it.

'You can't say that,' she says. 'I don't want you to. You've chosen to stay with Michelle and I accept that.'

'In June,' says Nelson, 'after we slept together that time, I was going to leave her for you. But then she said she was pregnant.'

'I know,' says Ruth. 'Everything changed.' The day she had slept with Nelson was the day that her mother had died. Sometimes it feels as if her whole world has been reshaped.

'Yes,' says Nelson. 'I'm sorry.'

'It's not your fault.'

They are silent for a moment longer and then, as if by mutual agreement, they walk on, through the arched passageway ahead of them. At the door of the church, Ruth's phone rings. It's Angelo. She answers, risking stares of disapproval from a passing flock of nuns.

'Ruth,' says Angelo, 'Valenti says that Samir's DNA was found on Don Tomaso's fingertips. They found his fingerprints on a candle in the church too. They're charging him with murder.'

Ruth is touched that Angelo is so incensed on Samir's behalf. She remembers him speaking to Samir at the cultural association dinner, offering him food. Angelo may not have seen eye to eye with Don Tomaso, but it seems that they shared some of the same values. She remembers what Angelo said about being an outsider in his own town. Maybe this is why he identifies so strongly with the refugee. But she really doesn't see what she can do.

'I'm sorry,' she says.

'He didn't do it,' says Angelo. 'You need to tell Valenti. Or get your policeman friend to talk to him. He won't listen to me.'

'He won't listen to us either,' says Ruth. 'And if he's got DNA evidence . . .'

Angelo rings off. Ruth turns to Nelson. 'Samir's DNA was found on Don Tomaso's fingertips,' she says. 'That sounds as if he tried to fight him off, doesn't it?'

Nelson is silent. He's looking into the church, where Mass appears to be starting. There's a chanted prayer, either in Latin or Italian – Ruth's not sure which – a call and response that probably hasn't changed since St Benedict built his first abbey.

Nelson turns to Ruth. 'Was Samir a Catholic?'

'I don't know,' says Ruth. 'Why?'

'He could have gone to Don Tomaso for communion,' says Nelson. 'If he was an old-style Catholic he would have taken the host in his mouth. That would account for his saliva being on the priest's fingers.'

'We'd better tell Angelo,' says Ruth.

22

Angelo insists on them going to see Commissario Valenti. He meets them outside the police station in Arpino.

'I've told Valenti that an important British policeman is here,' he tells them.

'I bet he loved that,' says Nelson.

'It's professional courtesy,' says Angelo. 'I'd want to know if a famous archaeologist, like Ruth, was in the area.'

Ruth senses Nelson looking at her quizzically. He says, 'I'm not exactly Sherlock Holmes, you know.'

'But you are well known,' says Angelo. 'I've googled you. The Lucy Downey case, those murders at Walsingham. Besides, Sherlock Holmes wasn't a policeman.'

Ruth is impressed by Angelo's literary knowledge, though she guesses it will have less of an effect on Nelson. But he doesn't raise any more objections and they enter the building, to be told that Commissario Valenti will see them in a few minutes.

The same woman police officer shows them into Valenti's office and asks them if they want coffee.

'Bloody hell,' says Nelson. 'Judy would have me up in court if I asked her to make tea.'

'Quite right, too,' says Ruth.

Valenti rises to meet them. He greets Angelo by name and the two men shake hands. There's a distinct restraint between them though. Ruth remembers that Angelo had described the police chief as a fascist and Valenti certainly seemed less than enthusiastic about Angelo yesterday.

'DCI Nelson has a theory on the case,' Angelo begins.

'Yes?' says Valenti, politely but not exactly encouragingly.

Angelo launches into Italian and Ruth recognises the words '*comunione*' and '*testimone*'. Valenti surveys them narrowly, tapping his fingers together. He says something to Angelo and Ruth notices that his Italian is rougher and more guttural. Perhaps Valenti has a regional accent and Angelo speaks with a posh Roman voice.

Angelo turns to them. 'This fits with Samir's story. He says that he came to the church at five o'clock. He goes every day, apparently. He's a devout Catholic but he doesn't like attending the public Masses. He says he entered the church at five o'clock, said his confession, took communion, lit a candle by the statue of the Virgin Mary and then left by half past. Federica from the café saw him leave. Marta too.'

'Marta?' says Ruth.

'Yes, she was in the square with her mother, waiting for the church to open.'

'I saw them there at six,' says Ruth. 'But they must have got there pretty early to be in the square at half five.'

'Marta is rather religious,' says Angelo. 'Strange, because

she's very intelligent in other ways. She probably wanted to get to church early to pray.' He says this like it is an outlandish and esoteric activity. Which perhaps it is, thinks Ruth.

'So does this mean that Samir has an alibi?' says Ruth.

'Flavio – Commissario Valenti – is going to interview him again. The interpreter is here now. This could mean that he gets out on bail, at least.'

Valenti has been watching them intently. Now he says something to Angelo. It sounds like an order.

Angelo turns to Nelson. 'The Commissario wants to speak to you in private. We'll wait outside.'

Nelson has formed rather a good impression of Flavio Valenti. He seems a no-nonsense policeman. His desk is ordered and Nelson is almost sure that he spots a to-do list with items neatly crossed out. From the attitude of the woman police officer who showed them in, Nelson can tell that Valenti has the respect of his team, coffee-making requests aside. All the same, he isn't sure how they can have a conversation when Valenti doesn't appear to speak any English.

So he is surprised in more ways than one when Valenti leans forward and says, 'I want to talk to you police officer to police officer.'

'You speak English,' says Nelson.

'I speak a little,' says Valenti. 'Not good enough for witness statements but good enough for this chat. Yes?'

'Yes,' says Nelson, although he has no idea what's coming next.

'When Morelli tells me your name, I google you. You come from King's Lynn?'

'Yes, it's a town in Norfolk, a county on the east of England. It's very . . .'

His voice dies away. He's never sure how to describe Norfolk, and he's still not sure how he ended up there, washed up on the very edge of the country.

'Much crime in Norfolk?' Valenti gives it two distinct syllables. Nor–Folk.

'Yes,' says Nelson. 'You'd be surprised.'

'There is not much crime here. This, the death of a priest, is a very serious crime. The worst. There is . . . how do you say? Weight on me to solve it.'

'Pressure,' says Nelson. 'Pressure on you to solve it. I can understand that.'

'Have you many refugees in Norfolk?'

'Yes,' says Nelson, 'as a matter of fact we have. Lots of refugees and asylum seekers. Immigrants workers, too, mainly in agriculture.'

'So do we in Italy. And when there is a crime, there is always . . . pressure to blame the refugee.'

'It's the same in England,' says Nelson. 'With some people.'

'But I do not blame Samir for this reason. He was seen in church and there was DNA evidence. Is enough reason to hold him, yes?'

'Yes,' says Nelson. 'I would have done the same.'

'But I will interview him with interpreter. If he is innocent, I will let him go. But then, I have a problem. Who killed this good old priest?'

'Was anyone else seen leaving the church?'

'No, the church is closed because of earthquake. Only way in is through back entrance. That is good. Much mud, many trees and bushes.'

'Plenty of places to get evidence,' says Nelson, understanding immediately. It's the only thing he likes about plants: clothes can get caught on them, people can get scratched by thorns and leave their footprints in the mud. A well-placed bramble bush can be a treasure trove of evidence.

'Yes. Witnesses see Samir leave church at half past five. The doctors say Don Tomaso killed between four and six.'

'But other people could have come in and out unnoticed.'

'Yes. Café was closed and only a few people in the square. Federica, who work at café, was clearing up after the earthquake. Some chairs and tables damaged. Marta Bianchi and her mother are waiting for the church to open. They see Samir. He is very visible because he is wearing Juventus top.'

'Black and white stripes,' says Nelson. 'Like Newcastle.'

'*Di preciso.*'

'Did this Samir look to be in a hurry?' asks Nelson. 'Furtive?'

'No, he is walking slowly but people do behave ... strange ... sometimes after a murder.'

Nelson knows this is true. Sometimes killers carry on completely as normal, as if convincing themselves that the crime never happened.

'What did Samir say when you arrested him?'

'He says he does not do it. He loves Don Tomaso, who has been good to him. He calls on the Virgin Mary and the saints.'

Valenti smiles thinly. Nelson guesses that he is not a religious man.

'Commissario Nelson,' says Valenti. Nelson rather likes the sound of this. 'How well do you know Angelo Morelli?'

'Hardly at all,' says Nelson. 'I'm a friend of Doctor Galloway's.' He's aware how weak this description is, but how could he begin to describe their true relationship? Ruth had introduced him as her friend earlier, and that will have to do.

'Dottore Morelli,' says Valenti, 'believes someone is trying to kill him.'

'He does?'

'Yes, he believes someone is jealous of his work. Recently there was graffiti outside his house and an animal's skull left on his doorstep.'

Nelson is alarmed. Ruth and Katie could be in danger.

'What are you doing about it?' he says, aware that he sounds accusing.

'I do nothing,' says Valenti. 'I just wait.'

Nelson does not think that this sounds like a satisfactory plan of action.

'I wait,' says Valenti, 'because I do not think it is true. I think it is a story, like the story he tells about his grandfather, the hero.'

'I've never heard the story about his grandfather.'

'Apparently he was a hero in the resistance. These days,

everyone's grandfather was in the resistance. But me, I'm proud to say that my father was a fascist.'

'You are?' Nelson is not sure that he's heard this right. And Valenti's *father*? Surely he's too young to have had a father who was alive in the war?

'He was chief of police during the war and an admirer of Mussolini. I grew up with Il Duce's picture on my wall. I don't share his views, you understand. I am social democrat. But I understand them.'

'They were different times, I suppose.' This is the best that Nelson can manage.

'*Di preciso*,' says Valenti, as if Nelson has said something very profound. 'Don Tomaso, he understood too. He often tells me that my father was a fine man and did his best. But Pompeo, Angelo's grandfather, he live in that house like a recluse. He tells its secrets to no one. Are you a father, Commissario Nelson?'

'Yes, I have three daughters.'

'You are a lucky man. I have one son. He's studying medicine at the university. But, when he's graduated, I'm sure he'll go to live in Rome.'

He says this like he will lose his son to the other side of the world, but Rome is only an hour away. Still, Nelson understands the sentiment.

'My two oldest daughters moved away from home,' he says, 'but one has just come back. She's training to be a teacher.'

'A fine profession,' says Valenti. 'So you see, we have this beautiful town but it is full of old people. The young have left us. Castello degli Angeli is dying.'

We're all dying. That's what Nelson had said earlier. But he has the sense that his fellow policeman is saying something else entirely. That he's trying to give him some sort of hint.

'When's Dad coming back?' says Laura, who is busy concocting her breakfast smoothie. The smell of overripe berries is making Michelle feel nauseous.

'I'm not sure,' she says. 'I think he just got a one-way ticket because it was such a rush. He says he'll try to get back for the scan on Thursday.'

When she had spoken to Nelson last night he'd sounded rather sheepish. Yes, he had seen Ruth and Katie. Their town wasn't badly affected by the earthquake. He was staying with some friends of Cathbad's, very nice people. He would be back in a couple of days. Michelle had responded in kind. Inwardly, she was thinking she would ring Tim and see if he could come over. Tim has taken some leave and is staying at a B&B in King's Lynn for a few days. Michelle refuses to let herself feel guilty. That will come later, she knows.

'What time are you working today?' she says to her daughter's back.

'Twelve until two,' says Laura, 'but I might meet Chad afterwards.'

'Why not?' says Michelle. 'It looks like it'll be a nice day.'

Laura sits down at the table with her witchily purple drink. 'Will you be OK on your own? I could come back if you like. We could watch a film together. Or old episodes of *Grey's Anatomy*.'

Tears come into Michelle's eyes. 'No, you go out with Chad. I'll be fine. I'm feeling much better these days.'

'If Dad's not back by Thursday, I'll come to the scan with you,' says Laura. 'I'd like to. I'll be the first to see the baby. Apart from you and Dad, of course. That way it'll like me better than Rebecca.'

'The baby will love both of you,' says Michelle. 'It's lucky to have such lovely big sisters.'

'Are you going to find out the sex?' says Laura. 'It feels odd saying "it".'

'I don't know,' says Michelle. 'We didn't want to know with you two. Just having a healthy baby was enough.'

'If it's a boy, Dad will want to call it Jimmy after that football player he likes.'

'Over my dead body,' says Michelle.

Angelo has to go back to the university. 'But I will come round to the apartment later, if I may?' Ruth can hardly refuse, even though Nelson is looking at her rather oddly.

Ruth and Nelson have lunch in Arpino, in the beautiful square with the statue of Cicero looking down on them. Ruth thinks of the morning that she spent in Elsa's apartment. Some of the windows overlooking the piazza must be hers. She wishes she'd thought to ask after Elsa. She must still be in shock, Ruth thinks. Hadn't Elsa said that Don Tomaso was like a brother to her?

It's all very odd. She came to Italy to escape, and here she is talking murder with Nelson. But, all the same, there is something magical about spending this time with him, like tourists, like a couple. They eat spaghetti with clams and drink cold red wine, slightly fizzy. They talk about the case, about Italy, about Monte Cassino, about Cathbad's proficiency in Italian, about Kate and Louis, about whether Shona is having an affair with Graziano. Things they do not discuss: Michelle, pregnancy, when Nelson is going home.

Kate is due back from the swimming pool at three, so Nelson drives Ruth back to Castello degli Angeli, where she walks up to the apartment alone. She's getting used to the heat, she thinks, she can climb the hill in one go without stopping for breath. When she gets to the green door, she is surprised to see Marta letting herself in with a key.

'My mother lives upstairs,' Marta explains. 'I'm staying with her.'

Ruth had known that there were other apartments in the castle, it's just rather a surprise to think that Angelo's student is living a few feet away from them. She recalls that it was Marta who saw Samir leaving the church yesterday. She mentions this as they climb the stairs. Marta looks troubled.

'I felt terrible when I heard that they'd arrested Samir. I'm sure he didn't do it. Samir revered Don Tomaso. God rest his soul.' She nods her head piously.

'You didn't see anyone else leaving the church?' Ruth realises that the murder must have been committed in the brief time between Samir's departure and her own arrival.

'The police asked me this,' says Marta. 'I didn't see anyone leaving, but I wasn't really looking. People started arriving for the service and we were all chatting on the steps . . .' She looks embarrassed, as though this behaviour was unseemly in some way.

Ruth decides to change the subject. 'Angelo was telling me about the bones that were uncovered in the graveyard.'

'Yes,' says Marta. 'Did he tell you that I think they are the remains of my great-grandfather?'

'He did say that, yes.'

'It is a great relief,' says Marta. 'We will be able to give him a proper burial at last. My mother is very happy.'

This reminds Ruth of something. 'Do you know anything about Don Tomaso's funeral?' she says. She thinks that she should probably go.

'In Italy it's traditional to have the funeral very quickly,' says Marta. 'In the twenty-four hours after death, if possible. But we don't know when the police will release his body. We all want the funeral here, in Don Tomaso's church, but apparently the bishop wants it at the cathedral.'

This rings a faint bell in Ruth's mind, but she doesn't know why. They have reached Ruth's landing now.

'I should be going in,' she says. 'Shona and the children will be back soon.'

'Have they gone to the swimming pool with Graziano?' says Marta.

'Yes. Do you know Graziano?'

'He was my tutor at university,' says Marta. 'But I don't know him well. I know his wife better. *Ciao*.' And she takes the rest of the stairs at a run.

*

The children get back at four, overexcited and fractious. Shona looks hot and stressed and immediately disappears to lie down. Ruth feels guilty, thinking of her lovely, adult day with Nelson, even if it had been interrupted by a visit to a police station. She puts on a DVD of *Despicable Me* and wonders if she should start preparing supper.

She is staring at a chicken and wondering how to turn it into a child-friendly meal when the doorbell rings. It's Angelo. Ruth had forgotten that he'd said he would call round. She always finds it rather stressful when he's in the apartment, imagining him looking for marks on the marble floor or stains on the leather sofas. Louis broke another glass that morning.

She offers coffee but, to her surprise, Angelo says, 'Have you got anything stronger? That's what they used to say in New York. I feel like a scotch on the rocks.'

'I haven't got any whisky,' says Ruth, 'But I've got some wine. We bought it at the supermarket. Would you like a glass?'

'I certainly would,' says Angelo, sitting at the table. Ruth pours herself a glass too, just to be polite.

'Do you think the police will release Samir?' she says.

'I don't know. The communion story does explain the DNA, and they've got no other evidence. Valenti's a stubborn bastard though.'

'Nelson liked him,' says Ruth. 'He thought he was a proper old-fashioned copper.' She says this in rather a good Blackpool accent, which is wasted on Angelo. He is looking at her very intently. He's a great one for staring. One of his TV fans has probably told him that he has mesmeric eyes.

'DCI Nelson,' he says, 'is he an old friend?'

'You could say that,' says Ruth. She swallows some wine, rather quickly.

'Is he Kate's father?'

Ruth hesitates but, sooner or later, Angelo will probably hear Kate calling Nelson 'Dad'.

'Yes,' she says, 'but we're not together. He's married to someone else.'

'That must be hard,' says Angelo.

'It is sometimes,' says Ruth. She wants Angelo to drop the subject but doesn't know how to do this without seeming rude. Maybe Angelo is thinking of his own daughter, all those miles away in America.

But Angelo seems to realise that she doesn't want to talk about Nelson. He says, 'I have some news on the skull.'

'The skull?' For a moment, Ruth thinks he means Don Tomaso's skull. But then she remembers: the animal skull on the doorstep.

'My colleague at the university thinks it belongs to a wolf.'

This sounds an odd way of putting it. As if the wolf is about to turn up at lost property to claim it back.

'It was a wolf's skull?'

'Yes,' says Angelo, 'not hard to find in these parts.'

'But why would it be left on my doorstep – your doorstep?'

Angelo shrugs. 'Wolves are traditionally linked with Rome. You know the story of Romulus and Remus being suckled by a wolf? Maybe it's to do with the Roman site.'

'You said when we first met that some people didn't approve of excavating Roman sites.'

'That's right,' says Angelo. 'Some people still see the Romans as invaders.'

Is that still possible, after nearly three thousand years? thinks Ruth. When did the Roman Empire start? She thinks it was about 700 BCE. Can the folk memory really be that strong?

'Do you still think that someone is trying to kill you?' she asks. She remembers Valenti's snort of laughter at the idea.

'I think someone still wants to sabotage the dig,' says Angelo, 'but now that the TV people are involved again, I think I'm certain to get more funding. And that's thanks to you, Ruth.' He raises his glass to her.

'I didn't do much,' says Ruth. 'Just a few observations on the bones.'

'But the presence of a foreign expert made all the difference,' says Angelo. 'Daniella loved you on camera.'

'She did?' This seems unlikely.

'Yes, you were so natural and unaffected.'

People said this about Ruth's previous TV appearances too. She knows it's meant to be a compliment, but she always thinks that 'natural' is a synonym for 'overweight and sweaty'.

'I'm glad you think I helped,' she says. Angelo doesn't answer; he is staring at something behind her. Ruth follows his gaze and sees that he's looking at the picture that fell down during the earthquake. Ruth cleared all the glass away from the children's bedroom, and the framed canvas is now propped against the kitchen wall, a strange blur of shapes and colours.

Ruth explains what happened. 'Do you want me to move it out of the sunlight? In case it gets damaged?'

Angelo seems to come back to earth. 'You couldn't damage a picture that bad,' he says.

No sooner has Angelo left and Ruth shoved the chicken in the oven than there's another buzz on the intercom. This time it's Cathbad, looking tanned and unusually conventional in a white shirt and chinos, accompanied by Linda Anthony.

'I've brought presents from Rome,' says Cathbad. 'And Linda wanted to say hello.'

'Hi,' says Linda. 'Just hoping that you're all right after yesterday.'

Was it only yesterday? It seems years since Ruth stood in the dark church and saw the body on the altar.

'I'm OK,' says Ruth. 'It's good to see you again. Would you like some wine?'

'That would be lovely,' says Linda. 'I'm exhausted. I think Cathbad wanted to see every picture in the Vatican Museums.'

From the shrieks of delight next door it seems that the children are pleased with their presents. Ruth hopes that Shona hasn't been woken up. Cathbad comes back into the kitchen and presents Ruth with a snow globe of the Vatican and a book about the excavations in Pompeii. Ruth agitates the glass ball and the synthetic flakes fall on the dome, the pillars and the obelisk. She remembers telling Cathbad that she had loved snow globes as a child. She's touched that he has remembered.

Ruth tells Cathbad and Linda about Nelson's visit to the police station.

'DCI Nelson on the case again,' says Cathbad.

'I'm glad he is on the case,' says Linda. 'I never thought that poor Syrian man did it.'

'I wonder who did,' says Cathbad. 'Somewhere like this, people living in the same place for generations, there must be so many resentments simmering under the surface.'

He says it almost with relish, but Ruth shivers. It feels too close to home, sitting in Angelo's grandfather's apartment, with the bones of his friend lying in the churchyard only a few hundred metres away.

'I know,' she says. 'Don Tomaso talked about the war as if it was yesterday. Angelo talks about the Romans as if they've only just left. Angelo's grandfather was a resistance hero; so was Marta's great-grandfather. Angelo implied that Commissario Valenti was a fascist.'

'Flavio Valenti's father was the police chief here during the war,' says Linda. 'People say that he collaborated with the Germans, but it must have been a difficult situation for him. He probably wanted to keep the town safe – the Nazis carried out terrible reprisals in places where there were resistance uprisings. Valenti once told me that his father had admired Mussolini but so did a lot of people, Churchill included. And he was in power, after all. To listen to people here now, you would think that everyone was in the resistance.'

'History is written by the victors,' says Cathbad.

'It's especially important to Commissario Valenti,' says

Linda, 'because it's all only a generation away. His father was fifty when he was born.'

'It's true about people living here for generations,' says Ruth. 'These apartments seem to have been handed down through families. I've only just realised that Marta lives upstairs. Her great-grandfather must have lived in the apartment once.'

'It's Marta's mother, Anna, who lives upstairs,' says Linda. 'I think Marta's just staying there for the dig. I know Marta Bianchi, and Roberto Esposito too. He's a nice boy. One of my sons knew him at school. He was mad about archaeology and about wildlife. The problem is that there are no jobs here for young people. My two oldest sons have gone to work in Rome and I'm sure Massimo will follow them.'

'How long have you lived here?' says Ruth.

'About thirty years,' says Linda. 'I'm a newcomer, really. But that's why I called. I'd like to invite you to dinner. All of you, Shona and the children too. Tomorrow night. Will you come?'

'That's very kind,' says Ruth. 'I'd love to.'

My last night with Nelson, she thinks.

23

When Ruth goes down to the shop the next morning to buy bread, she finds out that Don Tomaso's funeral is to be held later that day. The police must have released his body. The church doors are open and the flowers have been pushed to the side to form a pathway. Between the flowers a red carpet is being laid down.

'It's at two o'clock,' says the woman in the *panetteria*. 'The whole town will be there. The bishop himself is going to say Mass.'

Ruth thinks she should attend the funeral. After all, she discovered the priest's body. She is involved, whether she likes it or not. The trouble is, Shona will want to go too. She'll say it's out of respect, but really she'll be drawn to the drama of the occasion. And if Shona comes, who will look after the children? Perhaps they could bring them? But she can't imagine Louis sitting still for hours of Latin chanting and incense waving.

Predictably, Shona says that it's her duty to go. 'It would be wrong not to,' she says. 'He was so good to us.'

Ruth had liked Don Tomaso, but she doesn't see that he was so very good to them. He gave them a glass of his home-made wine, that was all. But he hadn't been judgemental about Ruth being an unmarried mother. He was a kind man, she thinks, and she'd like to go to his funeral for that reason alone. She rings Cathbad.

'Of course I'll babysit,' he says. 'I can send positive thoughts at the same time. Prepare libations. Strew some herbs.'

Ruth laughs rather nervously. She's not quite sure if he's joking or not. 'Just bung on a Disney DVD,' she says, 'and they'll be fine.'

'We'll have fun,' says Cathbad. 'Leave it to me. Linda's preparing a feast for tonight.'

'I'll look forward to it. Cathbad?'

'Yes?'

'Do you know when Nelson's going home?'

'I think he's going to try to book tickets for an early flight tomorrow. I know he wants to get back for the scan.'

Cathbad's voice is understanding. He knows about Kate's parentage, but Ruth is never sure how much else he knows about her and Nelson.

'Thanks for babysitting,' she says. 'I'll see you at one thirty.'

Shona is pleased at the outcome. It turns out that she and Louis are spending the morning with Graziano. He is going to show them his grandparents' house in the moun-tains. Ruth wonders if she should tell Shona that Graziano is married. But maybe she knows already? And it might not necessarily put her off. Phil was married when she first met him. Besides, Ruth is longing to have some time alone with Kate.

Shona goes off in high spirits, wearing white jeans and rope-soled sandals that don't look ideal for rough terrain. Kate immediately settles down happily with her felt tips and draws a succession of pictures of Italy. 'It's a fresco,' she says. 'Cathbad told me about them.' Ruth watches her daughter, lying on the floor in a circle of sunshine (the way Flint does at home), absorbed in her work. She loves reading and drawing and hasn't had enough time to do either this holiday; Louis is always interrupting or breaking something. Still, the two have got on very well, considering.

Ruth should phone her father; she should get out one of her archaeology books and start preparing for the new term; she should look up periosteal infections in bones. But, instead, she sits in Angelo's uncomfortable leather chair, watching Kate. The sun is streaming in from the balcony, she can hear voices from the fields below, the whine of a cultivator. Ruth's eyes start to close.

She's woken by the intercom buzzing. Who can it be? Shona, coming back for something she's forgotten? Angelo? She presses the speaker. 'Hello?'

'Hello, Mrs Galloway,' says an unknown voice. 'This is Samir Ahmadi.'

'Oh,' says Ruth. 'You'd better come up.'

The man on the doorstep doesn't resemble the furtive figure seen lurking on the edges of the cultural association dinner. Samir is now smartly dressed in a white shirt and dark trousers, and his hair is held back by the sort of hair-band beloved by footballers. He's also younger than she first thought, late thirties at the most. He is carrying a bunch of carnations, which he presents to her with a slight bow.

'For you.'

'Thank you,' says Ruth. 'But why?'

'Commissario Valenti said you believed that I did not kill Don Tomaso. He said that you helped prove my story.'

'That was Nelson, really,' says Ruth. 'He's a policeman back in England and he spoke to Commissario Valenti. And it was Angelo, Angelo Morelli, who was first convinced you were innocent.'

'I know Signor Morelli,' says Samir. 'He is a good man. I must thank him. And his mother, too, she often brings me food and clothes.'

'Would you like a cold drink?' says Ruth. 'Coffee?'

'Just tap water, please.'

Ruth leads the way into the kitchen. Samir sits at the table and Ruth runs the water to get rid of the sulphuric taste. While Ruth's back is turned, Kate wanders in and starts showing Samir her pictures. She is sometimes like this, reserved with well-meaning people like teachers and elderly relatives, outgoing with complete strangers.

'This one is the church,' she is saying. 'It's got dead people in it.'

'You are an artist,' says Samir. 'These are very fine.'

'I want to be an actress,' says Kate, getting comfortable on the chair opposite.

'Kate,' says Ruth, 'why don't you go and watch a DVD?

You know how to turn it on. You can take these grapes with you.' She puts some grapes in a bowl and holds them out in a way that she hopes isn't too obviously placatory.

Kate takes the bowl and leaves the room very slowly.

'You have a beautiful and clever daughter,' says Samir.

'Yes,' says Ruth. 'Thank you.'

'I left two daughters in Syria,' says Samir. 'I hope I will see them again.' And, without warning, his eyes fill with tears.

Ruth turns off the tap and pours Samir a glass of wine. While drinking it and eating the rest of the grapes, he tells his story. He was a journalist in Syria, reporting on economics and on the human rights struggles in the south of the country. It wasn't long before he fell foul of President Assad's forces and, after reporting on the Damascus protests in 2011, Samir realised he was being followed by the secret police. He knew that he had to flee the country, and managed to get in touch with an underground movement that smuggled refugees into Jordan. He left in 2012, after arranging for his wife and children to follow him. That was the last he heard of them for nearly three years until, last year, he received a message that his family had sailed from Libya to Italy. Samir travelled through Jordan and Egypt to Libya, where he managed to get on a boat bound for Sicily. 'The crossing was hell,' he says, 'hours clinging to the sides of this little fishing boat in the baking sun, no food or drink, hundreds of us, men, women and children. Thank God the Italian coastguard saw us and saved us.' In Sicily he heard that his family had gone north, to Rome, but there the trail went cold. None of the refugee charities in Rome had heard of his family. 'I fear they are dead,' he says, 'drowned in the Mediterranean, the sea of souls.'

'How did you end up in Castello degli Angeli?' says Ruth.

'I got in touch with a Catholic charity in Rome,' he says. 'Pope Francis, he really cares for refugees and his charities are very good. Catholics are a minority in Syria, though we are one of the oldest Christian communities in the world. Did not Christ appear to St Paul on the way to Damascus?'

'That's what he said,' says Ruth, who is no fan of St Paul. 'Are Catholics persecuted in Syria?'

'Yes,' says Samir. 'We are in constant danger from jihadi extremists. In areas under jihadi control, Catholics have been ordered to convert to Islam or pay *jizya* – a heavy tax – or face death. Thousands of Catholics have been forced from their homes. Catholic clerics have been killed and, in Hasaka, hundreds of Catholics were kidnapped by the militia. It was another reason why we had to leave. I contacted a Catholic group because I thought they might have heard of my family. They had no news but they sent me to Don Tomaso. He found me a place to live and looked after me. My faith was all I had left.' He bows his head.

'So Don Tomaso helped you,' says Ruth.

'Yes,' says Samir, 'and every day, at around five, I'd go to the church for communion. It was all I lived for. That, and the possibility of hearing news of my family. I went into the church on Tuesday, took communion and prayed for a while. I left Don Tomaso praying at the altar steps. I didn't kill him, I promise you.'

'I believe you,' says Ruth.

'I know,' says Samir, raising his head. 'God bless you.'

'Have the police released you?' says Ruth.

'I am released on bail,' says Samir, 'but my lawyer thinks they might drop the charges. He is a good man. He came from Rome and brought me these clothes' – he touches his shirt – 'so that I look respectable. And Commissario Valenti says that he will help look for my family.'

'That's good,' says Ruth, feeling inadequate. 'I do hope you find them.'

'Pray for me,' says Samir, seizing her hand.

And Ruth finds herself promising to do just that.

Judy is not quite sure what she is doing here, standing outside the Nelsons' house. Although her meeting with Micky Webb had left her feeling unsettled, she doesn't think that he would really be a danger to Nelson's family. But something has made her drop by this lunchtime. She had thought that Michelle might be at work, but her car is in the drive. Judy rings the bell and waits. She has only been to this house a few times. Nelson and Michelle invited her for Sunday lunch once, something they have done for all the team. She remembers that the food had been good and plentiful, but the formality of the occasion – best china, two sorts of wine, lots of cutlery and different shaped glasses – had made her feel rather uncomfortable. She was used to seeing Nelson at work, brisk and uncompromising, barking orders. It had been a shock to see him pouring wine and getting things from the kitchen, carving the meat, making jokes about the gravy. Michelle, she remembers, had been pleasant but slightly reserved. She'd looked fantastic though and had only eaten two potatoes. Judy had had eight and two mini Yorkshire puddings as well.

Where is Michelle? She hasn't taken the dog for a walk, because Judy can see him through the frosted glass, wagging his tail, obviously realising that she is a friend. Judy stands back and looks up at the windows. All the blinds are drawn. This cul-de-sac is a sought-after location, Judy knows, and the houses are all large and detached with big gardens and double garages. Even so, Judy prefers her tiny cottage on the coast at Wells. This place reminds her of the semi-detached where she had lived with Darren during their short marriage. Everything neat and tidy, everything the same. She's just debating whether to ring again when the door opens.

'Judy!' Michelle says, very loudly. She sounds surprised and not entirely welcoming.

'Hi, Michelle. Can I come in for a minute?'

'Is it Harry? Has something happened to him?'

'No. Nothing like that. I just wanted to have a word about something else.'

Michelle stands back and lets her into the house. 'Let's go into the lounge,' she says. 'Do you want anything to drink? Tea? Coffee?'

'No thanks. I'll only stay a minute.'

The sitting room looks very tidy to Judy, but Michelle whisks around, clearing away jackets and papers. When she sits down, Judy thinks that she looks tired, but that's probably the pregnancy. Judy felt exhausted in the first few months with both Michael and Miranda. Michelle is also dressed unusually casually in leggings and a loose sweat-shirt. Her feet are bare. Judy wonders if she was lying down upstairs and feels guilty for disturbing her.

'It's probably nothing,' says Judy, 'but has Nelson mentioned a man called Micky Webb to you?'

Michelle frowns. 'Was he the man who burned down his house and killed his children? Harry said that they'd let him go. It's not right, in my opinion. He should have got life.'

Michelle sounds a bit like someone on a radio phone-in but Judy doesn't necessarily disagree.

'Yes, he's out on licence. The thing is, before he went inside, Micky vowed to get even with Nelson. I know DCI Nelson's been to see Micky, and I have too. He claims to be a changed man, got religion and all that. I just wanted you to be on your guard, that's all. I'll send a PC round to your house now and again. I don't think you're in any danger. It's just to be on the safe side.'

There's a sound upstairs and Michelle jumps. Judy feels guilty again. She has obviously spooked her. The boss will be furious with her for upsetting his pregnant wife.

'I'm sure it's nothing to worry about,' she says. 'And you've got Bruno to look after you.'

Bruno wags his tail on the wooden floor.

'I'll keep an eye out,' says Michelle. 'I'd better get dressed now. Bruno needs his walk.'

The church is packed for Don Tomaso's funeral. Ruth and Shona squeeze into a pew at the back, where their view is partly obscured by an ornate pillar. 'It's so difficult to know what to wear,' Shona had said earlier. 'My only black dress is rather formal.' But she has worn the dress anyway (it's not formal as much as tight and short), and very gorgeous she looks too, with her red hair piled up on top of her head. Ruth has had to settle for black trousers and a grey top. The church is a sea of deepest black. There's none of this 'no black, please, we're here to celebrate life'. This congregation have come here to mourn, and they are mourning in black to the sound of Latin chanting from the choir above. Ruth sees Elsa near the front, sitting next to Angelo, who usually wears black anyway. This time he's in a dark suit, as are most of the men, even though the temperature is steadily rising. Ruth spots Graziano, Marta, Roberto and many others that she knows by sight: the old men from the café, the woman at the *panetteria*, the lifeguard at the swimming pool. Among the group of men standing by the doors, she sees Samir in his white shirt. It was brave of him to come, she thinks, given that yesterday he was in custody, charged with Don Tomaso's murder. There seems something almost ominous about the way the whole town has gathered together, like actors in the last scene of an Agatha Christie play. The last time the community was assembled like this it was for the cultural association dinner with food and dancing and lights in the trees. This is something else entirely.

When Don Tomaso's coffin is borne into the church, a sigh runs through the congregation, almost a moan. Behind the coffin comes an elderly figure in purple robes carrying a staff, presumably the bishop, and what looks like a whole shoal of priests, six of them, followed by altar servers carrying candles and incense. The high altar is soon full of men. No women, of course. Ruth's friend Hilary, a woman priest in the Anglican church, would have something to say about that, but to Ruth the whole ceremony seems so alien that this gender imbalance hardly matters. The clothed saints watch from the alcoves, the air is full of smoke and, when the Mass starts, the chanted words seem neither Latin nor Italian but another language altogether.

Ruth thinks of the church three days ago, the dark space lit only by a single candle, the dead body on the altar. The whole town had known that Don Tomaso was in the church, preparing for Mass. Who had entered the church, presumably through the graveyard, and killed the priest? Samir had left the church at five thirty; Ruth and Elsa had entered at about six fifteen. Who had taken advantage of those forty-five minutes to commit murder? As Marta had said, the churchgoers had all been gathered on the steps, chatting. It would have been easy for someone to arrive – and leave – without being noticed.

More chanting, more singing, the smoke rising upwards. Ruth begins to feel very hot indeed. Maybe she's having a hot flush? She's about the age for them, after all. Or maybe it's just because the church now resembles a cauldron. She fans herself with the order of service.

'Are you all right?' whispers Shona.

'How long have we got to go?' Ruth whispers back.

'I think we're about halfway through. This is the Eucharistic prayer.'

Suddenly Ruth knows that she has to get some air or she

will faint. She mutters an excuse to Shona and slides out of the pew. She sees Samir looking but no one else seems to notice when she opens the small hatch within the double doors and edges out.

Outside, the air is not noticeably cooler. Ruth sits in the shade of the porch for a bit but her head is still pounding. The square is completely silent, the café and the shops are all closed, their shutters down. A black cat walks slowly across the cobbles, pausing to wash itself by the fountain. It's like *High Noon*, Ruth thinks. *Do not forsake me, oh my darlin'*. She feels quite desperate for a glass of water. Soon, this need overpowers everything else. She knows she will have to go back to the apartment, open the fridge and take out that glorious green bottle of San Pellegrino.

The walk up the hill seems longer than ever. Will she be back in time for the end of the service? Shona won't panic if she doesn't reappear – she'll gravitate to Graziano and weep a few picturesque tears in his arms. Thank God, here's the green door. Ruth can almost taste the water, imagines it filling her dry mouth, running down her throat. She lets herself in and climbs the stairs. Then she stops. A woman is letting herself out of Ruth's apartment, a middle-aged woman smartly dressed in black. The woman pauses on the landing for a moment and then continues up the stairs without noticing Ruth in the darkness of the stairwell. Ruth doesn't recognise her, but there's something familiar about the woman's face. She's willing to bet that her mysterious visitor is Marta's mother, Anna.

24

Ruth doesn't go back to the church. She lets herself into the apartment, goes to the kitchen and drinks the mineral water straight from the bottle. It's only when her thirst is quenched that she thinks about the woman in the hallway. Why was Marta's mother coming out of her, or Angelo's, flat? She must have known that Ruth, in common with everyone else in the town, would have been at the church. Why wasn't Anna there too? She had been planning to go to Mass on Sunday, after all, so she must be fairly devout. Marta had been with her mother when she saw Samir leaving the church. Ruth walks around the apartment. She doesn't think anything has been moved, but the place is in rather a mess, so it's hard to tell. She recognises signs of Cathbad's play style, the chairs pushed together to form a den, the books spread across the floor, the felt-tipped pictures depicting unicorns and dragons.

She is just starting to tidy up when Cathbad himself appears, accompanied by Kate and Louis, all bearing branches from olive trees.

'We're having a funeral rite,' says Kate. 'We're waving leaves and Cathbad has poured some wine on the ground.'

This doesn't really seem any stranger than the ceremony in the church.

'You didn't pull those branches down from the trees, did you?' says Ruth.

'They were already on the ground,' says Cathbad. 'One of the farm workers said we could have them.'

'We're doing a funeral for Don Thingummy,' says Kate.

'Don Tomaso,' says Ruth.

'Yes, him. We're remembering him because he's dead.'

'We've poured wine on the earth as a libation,' says Cathbad, 'and we're raising a cairn to Don Tomaso, to mark his transition to the Otherworld.'

'A cairn is a pile of stones,' Kate explains.

Ruth is not sure that she can cope with any more funeral rites. She wonders if she should object to Cathbad teaching Kate about the Otherworld. She had always intended to tell Kate, calmly and quietly, that death is the end, there's no heaven or hell and we only live on in the memories of our families and friends. The trouble with this is that, when faced with an actual death, it seems a shocking and unbearable proposition. Ruth found herself telling Kate that Granddad believed that Grandma was in heaven, without adding her own total disbelief in this cosmology.

'How long were you outside for?' she asks Cathbad.

'About ten minutes,' says Cathbad, 'not long.'

Anna must have been waiting for her chance then, maybe

listening from above as the children clattered downstairs. Why had she been in the apartment?

'Is the funeral over?' says Cathbad.

'No, but it was too hot. I came back for a glass of water.'

'It's nearly three now.' Cathbad doesn't wear a watch, but always mysteriously knows the time. 'It's not worth going back now. Shall I make us a cup of tea?'

'That would be lovely,' says Ruth.

Nelson has been trying to book tickets home. His daughters always say that he's not computer literate, and it's true that in the office he leaves anything complicated to Leah, his PA. But he booked his flight out to Italy so he thinks he can manage to book seats for himself and Cathbad on the way back. But he had reckoned without several crashing websites, a fluctuating internet connection and a baggage controllers' strike at Fiumicino. Eventually it becomes obvious that he can't get a flight home tomorrow. He will have to stay in Italy another day and go back on Friday. He won't be there for the scan. What the hell will Michelle say?

He's been working on the laptop in Luca's room, and he gets up now and stretches. He needs some air. The house is quiet; Paolo is at work and Linda is in the kitchen preparing food for tonight. Massimo, the youngest son, is out somewhere on his moped. Cathbad is babysitting and Ruth will be at the funeral. Nelson wonders what she will think of a long church service in another language. He knows that Ruth's tolerance for organised religion is pretty low, thanks to her evangelical parents. But he understands why

Ruth will feel that she has to go – she was the one who discovered the body. He can't help wondering what is going on at the police station. Will Valenti have released Samir on bail? Has he any other suspects? And what is Angelo's role in all this? Valenti seemed to be implying that Angelo had invented a plot to kill him. Why would he do that? Nelson hadn't greatly taken to Angelo – he still can't forgive him for being relatively young and good-looking – but the man had seemed quite rational to him. Ruth seems to rate him as an archaeologist. Why would he make up stories about a murder attempt?

On his way to the front door, he passes the kitchen. Linda is making pasta using a small machine like a mangle. Nelson wonders why she bothers when the shops are full of the stuff, every shape and colour that you can imagine, but he's touched that she's making so much effort for their farewell meal.

Linda looks up when he passes, pushing her hair back with a floury hand. 'Any luck?'

'No. The internet kept crashing and there's a baggage controllers' strike at the airport tomorrow.'

'Oh, I'm sorry. The reception is bad here in the hills. Will you be able to get tickets for Friday?'

'I think so. The only thing is I'll miss my wife's scan. You know, I told you she was expecting a baby.'

'Yes, so exciting for you. I would have loved to try for a fourth, a girl perhaps, but Paolo wasn't keen. He thinks the world's overpopulated. Has your wife got someone else who can go to the hospital with her?'

'Yes, our daughter Laura's at home. She'll go with her.'

'That's all right then,' says Linda comfortably.

Is it all right? wonders Nelson. He goes out onto the terrace and stares moodily over the valley. Will Michelle forgive him for not getting back in time? And what will happen when the baby is born? He implied to Ruth that maybe, at some point in time, they could be together. Is he imagining a scenario where the baby isn't his, but Tim's? But he can't believe that. Michelle would never betray him like that, whatever he has done to her. He must have mistaken the expression on Tim's face at Cloughie's wedding. The baby is his and he must go home and play happy families. At this moment, the thought brings him no pleasure at all.

Ruth is trying to get ready to go to Linda's, whilst keeping an eye on both children. Shona has shut herself in her room 'to talk to Phil'. Ruth wonders what she is saying. Shona had come back from the funeral in the company of Graziano, both of them looking very cheerful in the circumstances. Shona hadn't minded Ruth disappearing. 'It was very hot,' she said. 'I thought I was going to faint at one point. I'm glad I stayed though. I took communion, the first time in ages. I think I might start going to church again.' She had shaken down her red-gold mane, Graziano staring at her admiringly.

Shona will no doubt have the perfect outfit for dinner at Linda's but Ruth feels quite unequal to the challenge. She looks at the garments hanging in the corner of the cavernous wardrobe in something like despair. She'd like to look mysteriously glamorous, but she hasn't exactly brought the clothes for it. She will have to settle for cotton trousers and a white shirt. Maybe she could borrow a scarf from Shona, but she never really knows what to do with scarves. How can women like Shona and Michelle keep them draped all day? Ruth's scarves either fall in her coffee or try to strangle her.

Kate and Louis run in, halfway through a game of chase. They haven't had enough exercise today and are both rather giddy. Even so, Ruth doesn't think that chase is a good idea in a rented apartment. She manages to persuade them to sit down and watch yet another DVD. It is the holidays, she tells herself, they can't be doing creative stuff all the time. And they did have that craft/folklore/witchcraft session with Cathbad earlier.

But no sooner has the comforting Disney castle appeared on the screen than there's a buzz from the intercom. Ruth freezes. Who can it be? Angelo? Marta's mother again? She's surprised to find herself feeling rather scared. It's just because she might have to talk Italian, she tells herself.

She picks up the receiver. '*Ciao*?' That's the wrong thing to say on the phone but she can't remember what the phrase-book recommended.

'Hello, Ruth,' says a woman's voice, in accented but clear English. 'It's Elsa Morelli. Can I come up?'

Why is Elsa here? Ruth thought that she'd still be at the reception after the funeral, which is being held in the church hall. Ruth presses the button to open the door. What can Angelo's mother want with her?

Elsa looks as smart as ever, in a slim back dress and a silver scarf (here is a woman who knows how to do scarves), but when Ruth switches on the hall light, she sees that Elsa's eyes are bloodshot and her face looks more lined than it did before. The elegant high cheekbones look almost skull-like.

'I'm looking for my son,' says Elsa. 'Is he here?'

'No,' says Ruth, surprised. 'Wasn't he with you? I saw him at the church.'

'He left the reception early. I thought he might be here. He's not answering phone.' Elsa holds out her own mobile – an iPhone in a sparkly case – as if to prove that she has been calling her son.

From the sitting room come the strains of 'Some Day My Prince Will Come'.

'Ah, *Snow White*,' says Elsa. 'One of my favourites.'

'My daughter loves it,' says Ruth, 'even though it's so old.' And a feminist nightmare, she adds in her head. 'Would you like a cup of tea or coffee?' she says, when Elsa shows no sign of leaving.

'Tea, please. If it's not too much trouble.'

'Not at all,' says Ruth. 'We're going out for dinner, but not for an hour yet.'

In the kitchen, Ruth puts on the kettle and Elsa sits at the chrome and glass table. 'This kitchen is so beautiful. Angelo does it very well. He gets rid of all my parents' old furniture.'

'Did he?' Ruth has often wondered about this.

'Yes, so we can rent place out. It's comfortable, yes?'

'Very,' says Ruth, though this is not exactly the word she would have chosen to describe the apartment.

'It's easier,' says Elsa. 'I can hardly imagine my father here. He had a very old-fashioned . . . what's the word? Cook stove. But he did all his own cooking and cleaning, right to the end.'

'Angelo said that he lived to . . . to a good age,' says Ruth. She hates this phrase, but she can't think of another. Her mother had died at the age of seventy-seven, which some people would describe as a 'good innings'. It didn't feel like that to Ruth. It felt far too soon.

'Yes, ninety-six. Angelo was very close to him. This death – Don Tomaso – it brought it all back. It's so terrible. You were there, Ruth. You know.' Tears fill her eyes.

'Yes,' says Ruth. 'It was terrible. I know you were close to Don Tomaso.'

Elsa wipes her eyes on a tiny lace handkerchief. What sort of woman uses actual hankies any more? 'We were brought up together,' she says. 'We had the same nanny. The same English nanny.'

'But you're so much younger,' says Ruth, without thinking.

Elsa smiles. 'Thank you. I am seventy-nine, Tomaso was eighty-three. There's not much difference. He was like big brother. His family were rich, and I think they felt sorry for my parents because they were young and poor. So they let us share Elizabeth, the nanny.'

Seventy-nine. Ruth had taken Elsa for at least a decade younger. The English nanny explains the oddly dated phrases used by both Elsa and the priest. *Tea for two. A penny for them.*

'Don Tomaso must have known Pompeo, your father, then,' says Ruth.

'Yes, Papa was a hero to all the younger boys,' says Elsa. 'Papa and Giorgio. It was a dangerous time, but to boys like Tomaso and my brother, Franco, it all was all a big adventure, skulking around, hiding in the hills, carrying messages. They didn't realise it was life or death.'

Ruth makes tea, thinking how strange it is that they are sitting in Pompeo Morelli's kitchen, talking about a time when a casual word in the wrong place could mean death. What did it say on the posters they had in England? Ruth has seen it on tea towels. *Careless talk costs lives.*

There's a sudden howl from the sitting room – Kate, mid-yell: 'Give that back! I hate you!'

'Excuse me.' Ruth hurries out. Louis has taken the remote control and is in the process of hitting Kate with it. Ruth takes the device and puts it on a high shelf. She feels furious with Louis for hitting Kate, but there's no doubt that Kate can be very bossy and was probably enjoying her despotic command of their viewing.

'Just watch the film quietly,' she tells them. 'I'll get the remote down when we have to leave.'

When she gets back to the kitchen, Elsa is kneeling down, looking into a cupboard.

'I don't know where anything is any more,' she says. 'I was looking for sugar.'

It's not until much later that Ruth remembers what Elsa told her, the day the TV people filmed at her apartment: *I never take sugar. I have to watch my figure.*

25

After the emotion of the funeral and the strangeness of the visit from Elsa (not to mention Marta's mother breaking into the apartment), it's a relief to be at Linda's. They sit on the terrace as the sky darkens over the valley. There are lights in the trees and the cicadas are singing. For Ruth, it feels almost magical to be sitting at a long candlelit table with Kate on one side and Nelson on the other. She can't think of another time when they've all eaten like this together. Linda's husband, Paolo, a darkly handsome doctor, pours wine and speaks Italian to Cathbad. Linda and Shona talk about art and Louis is asleep across three chairs. Kate sits very upright, proud that she's still awake at ten o'clock at night. For Ruth it's as if the horrors of the last few months have never happened: her mother dying, Michelle's pregnancy, this strange holiday and Don Tomaso's death. If she shuts her eyes she can only smell the lemon-scented evening and the hear the clink of glasses and the sound of mingled Italian and English.

Pero ... sempre ... Michelangelo ... the Sistine Chapel ...
allora ... Valpolicella ...

'What are you thinking, Ruth?' says Nelson.

'I was thinking how surreal this all is,' says Ruth. 'You wouldn't know that there had been a murder a few days ago.'

'I know,' says Nelson. 'I kept thinking about it today. It feels odd not being part of the investigation.'

'They've released Samir,' says Ruth. 'He came to see me today.'

'Did he? Why?'

'He wanted to thank me. Valenti told him that the English people thought he was innocent.'

'Do you think he's innocent?'

'Yes. He told me his story. It's so tragic. He doesn't know if his wife and children are alive or dead. Don Tomaso had been kind to him. I can't imagine Samir hurting him. His religion is almost all he has left.'

'But if he didn't kill him,' says Nelson, his face dark in the candlelight. 'Who did?'

'Ruth,' Shona calls across the table, 'are you talking about the murder?'

The word has its usual effect. In the silence that follows, Ruth can hear Louis breathing and a dog barking in the valley. Is it the same dog that she hears at night?

'It's so terrible,' says Linda. 'Why would anyone kill an old man like Don Tomaso?'

'The old are not always innocent,' says Cathbad, holding a peach up to the light and admiring its sheeny glow.

'Jesus, Cathbad,' says Nelson. 'Is that from your book of a hundred meaningless phrases?'

'It's not meaningless,' says Cathbad, 'just because you don't understand it.'

Ruth wonders why Cathbad seems to be needling Nelson. She knows that, in the past, Cathbad held a deep grudge against the police, resulting from what he felt was the death of an innocent man. But she had thought that his subsequent friendship with Nelson, and his belief in his integrity, had softened the edges of this. Maybe, but some of the resentment is clearly still there.

Paolo says something in Italian. He talks for a long time and sounds very serious. Ruth wonders if he's telling them about some event involving his own work with children, perhaps a case where the police got things terribly, tragically wrong.

But, when Linda translates, it transpires that Paolo is simply offering them some limoncello.

Linda offers to drive Ruth and Shona home. 'I don't drink much,' she says. 'I'm always expecting to have to collect one of the boys.'

'You're very kind,' says Ruth. And she suddenly feels an affection towards this woman who has, so readily and happily, taken them under her wing. And they will probably never see her again. To her horror, she feels as if she's about to cry. It must be the wine.

'Bye, Nelson,' she says, her arm round a sleepy Kate. 'Safe journey home.'

'Oh, I'm not going back until Friday,' says Nelson. 'I couldn't get a flight tomorrow.'

So he won't be back for Michelle's scan, thinks Ruth. Trying for a light tone, she says, 'Well, I'm sure we'll see you around then.'

Nelson stoops to kiss Kate. 'Yes,' he says. 'I'll see you tomorrow.'

Ruth does not want to cry any more. She helps Shona carry the still-sleeping Louis into Linda's car and then puts Kate's seatbelt on. There are no child seats but it's a short drive and the roads will surely be clear. Ruth gets into the front passenger seat, leaving Shona between the two children in the back.

The roads are pitch black, the moon appearing fitfully from behind clouds, but Linda drives confidently and competently, her headlights sweeping this way and that as they climb up the mountain. She stops once because a porcupine, like a small armoured car, is crossing the road.

'Hills everywhere in Italy,' says Linda, starting up again. 'It's hell on the clutch.'

Everyone in the back is asleep. Ruth tries to stay awake to keep Linda company, but finds her head nodding. Her remarks are starting to feel a bit random. 'Do you like it here?' she asks, for what seems the tenth time.

'I love it,' says Linda, 'it's so . . .'

But they never find out what it is because a car suddenly appears round a bend and comes hurtling towards them on the wrong side of the road. At first it seems that there must be a head-on collision but Linda swerves to the left and the car bumps along the grass verge, narrowly missing a tree and coming to the rest on what feels like the very edge of a precipice. Linda and Ruth stare at each other and, in the back, the children wake and start to cry.

26

Nelson and Cathbad have a final limoncello with Paolo on the terrace and then repair to their rooms. Nelson is getting quite fond of the pictures of Juventus, but when he gets under the black and white striped duvet he finds he can't sleep. It's too hot under the covers so he throws them off. Then he gets up and goes to the window and opens the heavy wooden shutters. He leans out of the open window, breathing in the night, which has a particularly foreign smell, he thinks, herbs and lemons and something else, something dark and peaty, like Paolo's home-made wine. He's pretty sure that he's getting bitten to death by mosquitos, but it's worth it for the air.

Something's worrying him and it's not the usual worries, although they don't exactly help: Michelle, Ruth, his daughters, what's happening back at the station. It's something about this case, the death of the priest. Was it something Ruth said or was it something that happened at the police station? Nelson tries to cast his mind back. He remembers bloody Tim talking about something he called a memory house. Apparently you have to go in and search through the rooms until you find the hidden memory. Can Nelson find the key to his memory house? *House.* That's it. *Pompeo, Angelo's grandfather, he live in that house like a recluse. He tells its secrets to no one.* There must be some mystery about the house where Ruth and Katie are staying. He wishes they weren't staying there; he wishes they were coming home with him tomorrow. But he can just hear Ruth's voice if he were to suggest this. *I'm here to work, Nelson, it's not a holiday.* Except today, at Monte Cassino and in Arpino, it had felt like a holiday. Though the murder of Don Tomaso has somewhat soured the atmosphere. He is roused out of his slight reverie by a voice calling from the hall. It's Paolo, but he's never heard the genial doctor sounding so urgent and upset.

'Harry! Cathbad! Quickly! Linda has had an accident'.

Ruth and Linda stare at each other for a full minute. Then Linda reaches out a shaking hand and turns the ignition off. Ruth twists round in her seat. 'It's OK,' she says to the children, 'we just came off the road. Everything's fine.'

'Jesus,' says Shona. 'What happened? That car was driving straight at us.'

'Let's see if we can get out,' says Linda. 'No one move until I say.' She opens the car door and swings her legs round.

'Turn the car headlights on,' says Ruth. 'Then you can see how close we are to the edge.'

'Good idea.' Linda turns the key and the headlights shine out into the darkness. There seems to be nothing in front of them. Ruth can hear the wind rustling through the trees and the sharp cry of a night bird. 'Be careful,' she says.

When Linda gets out, the car rocks and Shona suppresses a scream.

'It's OK,' says Ruth, though she doesn't know why anyone would believe her.

Linda looks in through the open door. 'We're quite close to the edge on this side, but I think it's OK. Everyone get out Ruth's side and I'll ring Paolo to come and get us.'

Ruth gets out and opens the back door. She undoes Kate's seatbelt and scoops her up, feeling, for a moment, that selfish mother's love that doesn't care if the rest of them plunge to their deaths on the rocks below. Linda comes round and takes Kate's hand.

'Come on, Kate. Let's go and stand by the side of the road.'

Ruth reaches in and takes Louis, who now seems dumb with fear. Linda and the two children climb up the bank that leads to the road. Shona scrambles out of the car and briefly collapses into Ruth's arms. 'God,' she says, half laughing and half crying. 'First the earthquake, then a funeral and now this. What a holiday.'

'Don't say I never take you anywhere,' says Ruth.

They leave the car and climb the bank to stand next to Linda and the children. Linda goes back to the car to collect the warning triangle which is apparently mandatory in Italy. She puts it in the road. 'That should stop people driving into us.' She has also collected blankets. Ruth and Kate wrap themselves in one, Shona and Louis in the other. They smell of wood smoke and security.

'What about you?' says Ruth to Linda.

'I'm all right. I've got my pashmina.' Linda cuts an incongruously glamorous sight, standing by the roadside in her hot pink pashmina. Next to her, Ruth feels like a tramp. Kate, her equilibrium restored, is humming to herself inside the folds of the blanket.

'Was that driver drunk, do you think?' says Ruth.

'Maybe,' says Linda. 'Did you see what sort of car it was?'

'Small,' says Ruth. 'A little Fiat or a Renault. Black or grey. It looked dark anyway.'

'It looked dark because its headlights were off,' says Linda.

Ruth hardly has time to digest this before they hear cars approaching. A few seconds later Paolo's Alfa and Nelson's rented Fiat are pulling up beside them.

'Ruth.' Nelson bounds over to her and briefly puts his arms round her. 'Are you OK?'

'I'm fine,' says Ruth. 'A car pushed us off the road.'

'We nearly went over the cliff,' says Kate brightly from under the blanket.

Nelson picks her up. 'You're fine now, love. Daddy's here.'

That's not why they're fine, thinks Ruth, but she's willing to let it pass for now. She sees Cathbad getting out of the car, his hair gleaming white in the moonlight. He waves to Ruth and the three men go down to look at Linda's car. When they emerge, Nelson is looking grim and Paolo worried. Only Cathbad seems serene and untroubled, as if a trip to a lonely country road in the middle of the night is just what the nature spirits ordered.

'Needs a tow truck,' says Nelson.

'Si,' says Paolo, dusting his hands on his cream chinos. 'I call in the morning.'

'What happened?' says Nelson, coming to stand beside Ruth.

'A car forced us off the road,' says Ruth. 'I think it was deliberate.'

Linda is speaking in Italian to Paolo while Cathbad plays hopscotch with the children to distract them. It's a surreal sight: Cathbad, his grey ponytail bouncing up and down, skipping along the deserted country road, followed by two children, laughing hysterically, excited now by the night-time adventure.

Nelson looks at Ruth. 'Who knew we were at Linda's tonight?'

'Surely you can't think they meant to push us off the road,' says Linda.

'I always think the worst,' says Nelson. 'It's being a policeman. But driving in the dark without headlights looks pretty suspicious to me.'

Cathbad skips up to them. 'I think we should get Ruth and Shona and the children home,' he says, 'and worry about the rest in the morning.'

'You're right,' says Nelson. 'You're quite sensible for a nutter. Come on, Ruth. I'll drive you home.'

As Ruth gets into the car, she reflects that she never thought she'd be in a situation where being driven by Nelson proved to be the safer option. But, as Cathbad gets in the front and she and Shona squeeze into the back with the children, there's no doubt that Nelson's bulky silhouette in the driving seat is very comforting indeed.

27

Morning finds Ruth and Nelson back in Valenti's office. Linda is with them, acting as an interpreter, although Valenti again seems prepared to speak in English.

'You say this car push you off the road?'

'Yes,' says Nelson. 'And it had its headlights off. Seems deliberate to me.'

'Did you recognise the car, Dottore Galloway?' Valenti turns to Ruth.

'No,' she says, 'but it was small and dark, maybe a Fiat or a little Citroën.'

'I will find out if any cars were stolen last night,' says Valenti, 'and double-check with the *carabinieri*. But that road is dark, there are no cameras. It seems unlikely we will find the driver.'

'Someone tried to kill Ruth and the children,' says Nelson – rather aggressively, Ruth thinks.

'And me,' says Linda.

'I am taking it seriously, Commissario Nelson,' says Valenti, 'but in the absence of any evidence . . .'

'This must be linked to the murder of the priest,' says Nelson. 'Ruth finds a dead body and then someone tries to kill her. That's a coincidence, and as a policeman, I don't like coincidences.'

Valenti smiles, rather humourlessly. 'I too do not believe in coincidence.'

'Have you had any more leads on the case? I gather you let the Syrian go?'

'Samir Ahmadi is free on bail,' says Valenti. 'I cannot discuss the case further.'

This seems to be a dismissal. They stand outside in the street, sweltering after the arctic police station, and discuss their next move.

'You should come home, Ruth,' says Nelson. 'It's not safe here.'

Linda bristles, perhaps at the slur on her adopted country. 'This is a lovely place. I can't see that Ruth is in any danger.'

'Someone tried to kill you last night!' Nelson's voice echoes around the square, and several people shopping at the food market turn to look at them. 'I'm sorry,' says Nelson, 'but you said yourself that it looked deliberate.'

'I just can't think why anyone would want to hurt us,' says Linda. 'I think it was just some teenage joyrider, maybe drunk or on drugs.'

'Maybe,' says Ruth. She doesn't want to give Nelson the chance to boss her around, but she is feeling rather less sanguine than Linda. She remembers the odd, highly charged atmosphere at the funeral; Anna letting herself out of the flat; Elsa's strange behaviour last night.

'I'm going back next Wednesday,' she says. 'That's not long. I'm sure we'll be all right.'

Alanine, arginine, asparagine . . . what comes next? It's only three years since uni, but six years since A level biology, a lifetime ago. But Laura has always listed the amino acids when she wants to calm herself down. The trouble is, forgetting them makes her feel stressed. Aspartic acid, cysteine, glutamine . . .

'What's taking them so long?' says her mother. 'It must be my turn soon.'

They are sitting in the waiting area – pink walls, seascapes, plastic flowers – waiting for Michelle's scan. Ever other woman seems to have a husband or partner in attendance and Laura feels very conscious of being out of place. She's both too old and too young for this place. Then again, maybe people think she's the one having the scan. Mum doesn't look very pregnant yet, and she's forty-six, Laura's twenty-four, lots of women have babies at her age. Unconsciously Laura pats her concave stomach in the gap between crop top and jeans. She can't imagine ever being pregnant. Going to the gym again has made her more body-conscious; every time she eats something she imagines it magnified inside her, waiting to be zapped by more exercise. Her parents have no idea about those years when every mouthful was a cosmic battle between good and evil. 'You're too skinny,' her dad always says, but he says it in a rather proud way. She knows he'd be more concerned if she was overweight. Like Ruth. Don't think about Ruth. Glutamine, glutamic acid, glycine . . .

'I think you're next,' she says to her mother. 'After the woman with red hair.'

'You will come in with me, won't you?' says Michelle.

'Of course,' says Laura. 'I'm looking forward it.'

That's her line and she's sticking with it. 'We've got to support Mum,' she'd said to Rebecca during their regular FaceTime chat last night. 'She's got support,' Rebecca had said, lounging on her bed in Brighton, 'she's got Dad.' Laura had reminded her that he was still in Italy, told her that he'd been caught up in a murder investigation. Rebecca had laughed – 'good old Dad' – and taken a swig of coke. Laura wanted to tell her what the drink was doing to her insides, much less her calorie count, but she knew this would not be a good idea. Rebecca has none of her body issues – no issues of any kind it seems, sails through life doing the minimal amount of work, making friends and forgetting them, getting angry about the small stuff but letting the big terrors (the ice caps melting, their parents' marriage) wash over her.

She doesn't know why she's so worried about her parents. She had a terrible suspicion a few months ago when Dad turned up with Ruth's daughter Kate, saying that he was looking after her for the afternoon. There was something about the way Dad had been with the little girl, something solicitous and protective, that had sent her synapses buzzing. Kate was gorgeous, dark like Rebecca, funny and cheeky. Could she be Dad's daughter? He's always working with this Ruth woman. But then, Laura's met Ruth, and surely no one who was married to Mum would look twice at someone so overweight and untidy. Laura has always been so proud of her elegant mother, a woman much admired by all her friends. And now Mum's having a baby and Dad seems pleased about it, although worrying all the time like he usually does. It's just . . . why did Dad disappear to Italy like that? He was worried about Ruth, Mum said, but doesn't Ruth have her own friends and family to worry about her? 'I look after my own,' Dad always says, and they tease him for sounding like the Godfather. But now he seems to be looking after Ruth and Kate and he's not coming home for the scan. Histidine, isoleucine, leucine . . .

A nurse appears with a clipboard. 'Michelle Nelson.'

'We're on, Mum.'

Linda says that she wants to shop at the market, so Nelson and Ruth go to a café for coffee and *cornetti* (an Italian form of croissant). Ruth feels rather awkward with Nelson today. She had steeled herself to say goodbye last night, but now here they are again, back in their usual positions: Nelson protective and bossy, Ruth defensive and stubborn. She also knows that Nelson will be thinking about Michelle and the scan. She knows it's not fair, but she feels slightly resentful that Nelson was not present for any of her antenatal visits. He wasn't even there for the birth. Cathbad had been with her. She still remembers the midwives staring at his robes – he had come from a Halloween party.

'So you're going back tomorrow,' she says.

'Yes,' says Nelson. 'I managed to book the flights first thing this morning.'

'That's good.'

'Yes.'

There's a silence. Ruth watches Linda making her way through the market, chatting with people, bargaining with the stallholders. What must it be like to move to another country? Would you always feel an outsider, as Samir obviously does? Linda seems completely at home, but then she has an Italian husband and Italian children.

'I'll come round today and say goodbye to Katie,' says Nelson, and she can hear from his voice that he's trying to be conciliatory. Responding in kind, she doesn't correct him about the name.

'Why don't you come for supper?' says Ruth. 'I'll make some pasta. It won't be as good as Linda's though. I'd better ask her too, hadn't I?'

But when Linda returns with a basket full of mysterious food, she says that she and Paolo have plans tonight. Ruth can't help feeling slightly relieved.

Michelle has been feeling tense all morning. She knows that the scan won't tell her who the father is, but she can't help imagining that someone – the radiographer, or Laura – will know that there's some sort of complication. In addition, she is worried that there will be a real, i.e. medical, problem. She is old to be having a baby. They've had the screening for Down's but there are lots of other conditions that she has discovered through long nights googling 'geriatric pregnancy'. *As long as it's healthy* – that's the mantra she has been repeating to herself all morning. Laura keeps saying that everything will be OK, but she's only a child herself, really, what does she know? She has been wonderful though. Michelle takes her daughter's hand as they walk towards the radiography room.

'It'll be fine,' she tells her.

'Of course it will,' says Laura.

As long as they both believe that they are reassuring each other, everything will be OK.

The radiographer rubs some gel on Michelle's stomach and apologises for her cold hands.

'Cold hands, warm heart,' says Michelle.

'So they say,' says the radiographer, going back to her machine.

Michelle twists her head and half smiles, half grimaces at Laura. Laura smiles back but she's looking very nervous. The last time Michelle saw that look was when she was driving Laura into school to collect her A level results. But they had been fine; Laura is a clever girl. This will be fine too. She arranges her face into a cheerful shape.

'Here we go.' The radiographer is moving her stethoscope thing over Michelle's stomach. The screen fills with cloudy white shapes, the darkness between them pulsating in an odd, animal way. Michelle props herself up to look. She's trying to remember from her other pregnancies, but this looks good. There's the heart. Is that an arm or a leg?

'There's your baby,' says the radiographer. 'A healthy size.'

Michelle breathes again. Laura squeezes her hand.

'There's the heart,' says the radiography, pointing. 'And

an arm, leg, a bit of the head. Ah, now there's a good angle. Do you want to know the sex?'

Michelle opens her mouth to say, 'No, all we want is a healthy baby,' but instead says, very loudly and decisively, 'Yes please.'

The radiographer laughs. 'Well, it's early days but there's not much doubt. It's a boy.'

Michelle leans back on her paper pillows. She finds that she's crying. A boy. Harry will be pleased. She knows that he secretly wants a son. But so does Tim. What a mess.

'A boy, Mum,' Laura is saying. 'It'll be fun to have a boy. God, I bet he'll be just like Dad.'

The radiographer passes Michelle a box of Kleenex which is conveniently to hand. She doesn't like to think of other occasions when women have cried in this room.

'The baby's fine,' says Laura, stroking her mother's hair. 'That's the main thing.'

'Yes,' says Michelle. 'Yes, it is.'

28

The first person Ruth sees when she gets back to Castello degli Angeli is Angelo. He is standing looking over the half-demolished wall of the church. Marta is with him. Don Tomaso has not been buried in the graveyard. Perhaps the ground isn't consecrated any more. His body has been taken to the cemetery in Arpino and the funeral flowers have all gone with him. The square is now almost as it was when Ruth first saw it, apart from the broken wall and the police tape around the graveyard.

'Have you got any news on the investigation?' says Angelo, dispensing with the usual niceties – rather, thinks Ruth, as Nelson often fails to say goodbye or thank you. 'Is Valenti making any attempt to solve the murder?'

'Samir has been released,' says Ruth.

'I know,' says Angelo. 'That's good news. I saw him at the funeral. Were you there?'

'Yes,' says Ruth, feeling slightly guilty. 'But I left a bit early.'

'I don't blame you,' says Angelo. 'All that mumbo jumbo. "I am the resurrection and the life." It sticks in my throat.'

'Some of us believe it,' says Marta. Ruth admires her for standing up to her professor, even if she doesn't share her faith.

'I know,' says Angelo. He doesn't apologise though.

'Your mother was looking for you yesterday,' says Ruth. 'Did she find you?'

'She's always looking for me,' says Angelo. 'Yes, she caught up with me. She's very upset about all this. She and Don Tomaso were old friends, like brother and sister.'

'She told me,' said Ruth. She hesitates, wondering if she can ask more about Elsa and her slightly strange behaviour yesterday. As she stands there, irresolute, she hears a car driving across the cobbles behind her.

'It's Roberto,' says Marta. 'I must go. Will you keep me informed about the bones, Professore?'

'Of course,' says Angelo. 'Have fun.'

Marta colours but does not reply. She nods at Ruth and sprints across the square. Ruth watches her getting into Roberto's Fiat.

'I think they're dating,' says Angelo. 'That's a very American word. Dating.'

'It's catching on in England too,' says Ruth. 'I think it means something different from "going out".'

'Yes,' says Angelo, 'friendship with benefits. There's a lot to be said for it.'

He's smiling at her. Ruth prays that she's not going red. 'Can I see the bones?' she says, in what she hopes is a businesslike way. 'Do you think you'll be able to excavate?'

'I don't know,' says Angelo. 'This is a murder scene now.

The scene of the crime people were here all day yesterday. Even during the funeral.'

Ruth sees that a white tent has been erected over the back door of the church. She knows only too well how important this is. This is the way the murderer must have walked. The police will have combed every millimetre looking for clues.

Angelo, though, has ducked under the tape and is holding it up for her.

'Do you think it's all right?' she says.

'Sure,' says Angelo. 'No police here today.' Which isn't quite what she is asking.

You can almost see the complete skeleton now, the earth showing through the ribcage. Ruth can see that it has been professionally exposed and can imagine how frustrating it is for Angelo not to be able to excavate the bones, one by one, number them, chart them and take them to the lab.

'Do you still think that this is Marta's great-grandfather?'

'Giorgio? Yes, I'm almost certain. He was missing the two fingers of one hand, you see. A boar bit them off. He kept the boar's tooth as a souvenir, wore it round his neck. My grandfather always used to tell that story.'

Ruth can see the bones quite clearly, almost as if the hand has been positioned to show the missing digits.

'It must be emotional for Marta,' she says. 'She was saying that her mother wants to give her great-grandfather, her mother's grandfather, a proper funeral.'

'Yes,' says Angelo. 'I think that's important to Anna.'

'Angelo,' says Ruth, 'is there any reason why Anna would have a key to your grandfather's apartment?'

Angelo, who has been squatting down, looking into the grave, straightens up and looks at her. 'I don't know. Why?'

'When I came back early from the funeral I saw her letting herself out of the apartment. At least, I think it was her. She looked very like Marta.'

Angelo shrugs. 'I suppose Nonno must have given her a key. They were neighbours, after all.' But Ruth thinks that he looks troubled, all the same.

Laura drives them home. She is conscious of going very carefully, signalling miles in advance, as if she's taking her driving test again, leaving acres of space between her car and the one in front. *Only a fool breaks the two-second rule.* This is more like the half-hour rule. It's as if the new sibling is already backseat driving. Typical man. After her tears in the hospital, Mum is now almost hysterically happy, babbling on painting the baby's room blue and taking it to football matches. Steady on, Mum, Laura wants to say. Just because it's a boy, it doesn't mean it's going to be Wayne Rooney. He might be gay or bi or non-binary, or he might simply prefer dolls to footballs. Laura had been rather keen on football herself in primary school in Blackpool, but when she got to the girls' school in Lynn, the only sports on offer were netball and hockey. What if the boy grows up and decides that he wants to transition to be a girl? She can't imagine either of her parents coping well with such a situation. Mum has lots of gay friends, but in terms of gender politics, she's stuck in the Dark Ages. And as for Dad . . .

'What about names?' she says, cutting into a rambling lecture about the Boy Scouts and the benefits of getting muddy. 'Have you thought of boys' names? Please don't let it be Jimmy.'

'I like Lucas,' says Michelle, 'or Scott.'

'They sound like Radio 2 DJs,' says Laura. 'Rebecca and I have got really traditional names. What about James or Henry? William? George? Timothy?'

'Timothy is nice,' says Michelle. She has gone quiet again, staring out of the window. Laura takes a wide, slow turn into the cul-de-sac. It's a nice day and there are children playing in some of the front gardens; old Mr Bates is mowing his lawn. She parks carefully in the drive. Bruno is barking inside the house. That might be because he's just heard them arrive, but there's something hoarse and urgent about the sound that makes Laura think that he's been barking a long time.

'We'll have to take him for a walk,' says Michelle.

'I'll do it,' says Laura.

But when she puts Bruno's lead on, he doesn't pull to get to the park and the open country – he drags her round to the back garden and sniffs all along the boundaries, tail down, serious, like the police dog he almost was.

'Come on, Bruno,' says Laura. 'Walkies.'

But Bruno stays staring at the wall at the bottom of the garden, head to one side. As if he's thinking.

Back in the apartment, Ruth assembles the food she has bought for tonight. It will be a version of spaghetti bolognese, even though Linda told her than Italians only use tagliatelle with bolognese sauce. Shona and Graziano have taken the children to the swimming pool, leaving Ruth to get on with preparing supper. It's all in the preparation, according to Linda. Instead, Ruth gets out her phone and calls her father.

He takes a long time to come to the phone, during which time Ruth has lived through many scenarios (he has had a stroke and is lying helpless on the floor, he's dead in bed beside the picture of her mum, he's fast asleep watching *Cash in the Attic*). It turns out, though, that Arthur was in his garden, a jealously guarded strip of south London grass with flower beds at the sides and a greenhouse at the bottom.

'I've got such a crop of tomatoes this year,' he says.

'That's nice, Dad. Don't do too much though.'

'I just potter. Ade from the church comes to mow the lawn.'

Much as she recoils from the beliefs of her parents' evangelical church, Ruth has to admit that fellow worshippers have been very good to her father since her mother's death. They help with shopping and gardening; they cook him Sunday lunch. And the fact that many of them, including Adedayo, are black does much to stifle her father's *Daily Mail*-esque views.

'When am I going to see you, Ruth?' he says now, not plaintive, just enquiring. 'Simon, Cathy and the boys are coming over on Saturday. We're going to the carvery for lunch.'

When's Saturday? Ruth has rather lost track of the days. She looks at the recycling calendar. Today is Thursday, it seems.

'Soon, Dad,' she says. 'Remember, Kate and I are in Italy at the moment.' Please don't let him be losing his memory.

'I remember,' says Arthur. 'You're on your holidays. With Shona and her little lad. How is she?'

'Fine. Getting on well with the locals.'

'What about you? Have you been to the beach?' Arthur is a south London boy. For him, holidays are symbolised by 'going to the beach'. In his case, Southend or Brighton.

'Yes, we have,' says Ruth. 'There are lovely beaches here. Very clean. And I'm doing consultancy work too. We'll be back next week.'

'How does Katie find the food?'

'Fine, Dad. She loves pasta and pizza, as you know. She's having a great time.'

'Be careful,' says Arthur. 'It's not the same as home.'

That's very true, thinks Ruth, saying goodbye after more promises to visit Eltham soon. Castello degli Angeli does feel very foreign, in a way that she has never experienced before. She was an enthusiastic traveller as a student, backpacking around Europe several times, and she always felt that, by and large, people were the same everywhere. But now she is conscious of undercurrents that she can't understand, resentments and hostilities flowing just below the surface like an underground stream. Why do people in twenty-first century Italy still resent the Romans? Why did Don Tomaso warn of the dangers of waking the dead? And who could have killed the saintly parish priest? Cathbad had thought it very interesting, 'people living in the same place for generations', but Ruth wonders if it is actually rather dangerous.

Angelo's grandfather was a resistance hero, Valenti's father was a fascist and Marta's great-grandfather lies dead in the churchyard. So many different generations, yet their descendants are still living in the same stone-walled town.

She has been pacing the rooms while she reflects and now finds herself in the children's bedroom. Mindlessly, she straightens their beds and starts putting clothes away in drawers. As she does so, she sees the picture, the one that fell during the earthquake, which she has put back on the wall, minus its glass. Not that Angelo seemed to care very much about it. Ruth looks at the interlocking geometric shapes. Kate thought they depicted elephants in a sandstorm and Louis ships at sea, but, the more she looks, the more Ruth thinks that the picture shows two men walking away into the distance. There is something about the background, the jagged shapes, the blur of green and gold and silver in the foreground, that reminds Ruth of something. She takes the picture and carries it into the sitting room, where she can see the view from the balcony. Yes, there's the valley, that outcrop of rock, the lone tower, the river snaking its way through the olive groves. The picture shows the Liri Valley. Ruth looks at the back to see if there's a title and sees, on the wood of the frame, the name of the artist: Giorgio Bianchi.

Nelson gets the call when he returns to Linda's house after dropping Ruth back at Castello degli Angeli. He sees the name 'Michelle' and says to Linda, 'I've got to take this.'

'Of course,' says Linda, taking her basket from the back seat. 'I'll see you in the house.'

'Hello, love.'

'It's a boy,' says Michelle. Her voice sounds odd, as if she's trying not to cry.

'A boy? Are you sure?'

'The scan was very clear, apparently.'

Nelson doesn't remind her that they had decided not to ask the sex. He has forfeited all rights to that. His mind is crowded with images: his father, a quiet man at home, yelling encouragement from the touchline; himself as a boy in a houseful of women; his daughters; Tim at Clough's wedding, the expression of longing on his face.

'How are you?' he says. 'Is everything OK?'

'I'm fine,' says Michelle. 'The baby's fine. *He's* fine. Laura came with me. She was so sweet. She's walking Bruno now.'

'I love you,' says Nelson helplessly.

'I love you too,' says Michelle.

'I'll see you tomorrow,' says Nelson.

'Good,' says Michelle. 'Bruno misses you. He's been behaving really oddly today.'

When Michelle has rung off, Nelson sits for a moment in the car, staring at his screen saver, which shows Rebecca, Laura and Michelle, arms around each other, bronzed and beautiful on a long-forgotten holiday.

29

'It's a boy,' says Michelle. It's the first thing she says to Tim as he rises from the park bench to greet her. It's risky meeting in the open, but the house isn't safe either, not after Judy came calling yesterday. Michelle has visited the B&B once. Three-quarter bed, slippery counterpane, soap container fixed to the wall. Never again.

Tim takes her hands. 'A boy? Are you sure?'

'They were pretty sure,' says Michelle. She knows that she should be feeling guilty, conveying the same news to her husband and her lover, but she suddenly feels light-hearted and rather carefree. It's a sunny afternoon and they are in The Walks, a beautiful open space near the station.

'How do you feel?' asks Tim.

'Good,' says Michelle. 'It makes a difference, seeing the baby on the screen. And knowing the sex. You can say "he" inside your head, rather than "it".'

'How is he feeling?' says Tim with a smile.

'He's fine,' says Michelle. 'I think I felt him moving last night.'

'That's early, isn't it?'

'He's advanced for his age.'

Tim laughs, and Michelle wonders if he will say anything about the possibility that the baby is his. So far Tim has been treating the baby as if it (he) is an entity in his own right and not anything to do with him or Nelson. They walk along the flower-lined pathways, going in no particular direction. Michelle knows that it's dangerous, meeting so close to the police station. What if they saw Judy or Tanya? They are careful not to touch or stand too close, but Michelle thinks that if anyone saw them together, they would know.

'Have you thought of any names?' says Tim.

'Laura suggested Timothy,' says Michelle, looking at him sideways.

Tim laughs but she thinks he sounds embarrassed. She seldom mentions the girls to him. 'I hated the name when I was growing up,' he says. 'My brothers called me Tiny Tim. Think it must be the only Dickensian character they'd ever heard of. Not that they knew it was Dickens. They got it from *The Muppet Christmas Carol*.'

As Tim is well over six foot, the joke must have worn thin after a while, thinks Michelle. Whenever Tim mentions his family, she has a sense of him coming from an entirely different world. He has a sister called Blessing, which sounds foreign and exotic. Tim's mother is Religious (she thinks of it with a capital letter). Harry's mother is too, of course. Michelle has lost track of the number of strange Catholic ceremonies she has attended with Maureen: baptisms and communions, confirmations, something called Benediction which involves a golden cup shaped like the sun. Michelle has always been willing to attend church with her mother-in-law, which is one reason why she's such a favourite with her. But Maureen Nelson is also fundamentally a creature of this world – an organiser, a pragmatist, a woman who rules her family with a rod of iron. Don't think about Maureen, Michelle tells herself. If anyone possesses second sight, it's not Cathbad, it's Maureen.

'What are we going to do?' she says now. 'When Harry comes back? When the baby's born?' She means when they know who the father is. She realises that she has stopped walking.

'I don't know,' says Tim. 'Let's take it one day at a time.' He sings suddenly, in a surprisingly high, sweet voice: *'One day at a time, sweet Jesus.'*

Michelle looks at him enquiringly. Tim laughs. 'It's a favourite hymn of my mum's.'

One day at a time. It sounds good to Michelle. She risks squeezing Tim's arm.

'Let's go and get an ice cream,' she says. 'I've got a craving for ice cream.'

She didn't have cravings with the girls, but this boy is obviously different. He's clearly determined to make his presence felt.

After speaking to her father, Ruth prowls the apartment, thinking that she should really start tidying up. Kate and Louis have spread everywhere: toys in both bathrooms, Lego in the kitchen, colouring pens all over the sitting room, swimming stuff drying on the balcony. Ruth keeps picking things up and putting them down again. They're in the apartment for another five days. They'll only get it untidy again. The thought of staying on after Nelson has left makes her feel depressed somehow. She wants to go home too. She doesn't want to spend another five days at the beach or the water park; she wants to be back in her cottage with Flint. Get a grip, she tells herself. You're having a holiday in a beautiful part of Italy, you should be enjoying every second of it. But maybe that's it: she has slipped into the trap of thinking that she's on holiday, and so has fallen prey to second-week-of-the-holiday blues. She's primarily here to work. She will see if she can go to the laboratory tomorrow and have a look at the bones again.

Ruth goes into the kitchen and starts chopping onions. She thinks of the night of the cultural association dinner and the men serving food on the church steps. *Food is not love.* That's what Don Tomaso had said, but, sometimes, food does stand in for love, or at least for care. Ruth is not a great cook, but she loves it when Kate enjoys something she's made. Linda said that when her sons come home she cooks them all their favourite foods, to remind them no one cooks like Mamma. She thinks about Angelo and Elsa. They seem on excellent terms but what was it that Angelo said? 'She's always looking for me.' Maybe all that devotion can be a bit oppressive.

Ruth thinks about Samir and his story, the primal narrative of refugees everywhere: the flight from oppression, the sea crossing, the rejection in the promised land. She cannot believe that Samir, the man who sat crying for his family, could have murdered Don Tomaso. But if he didn't do it, who did? Ruth remembers the crowd of women on the steps of the church. But, like Marta and her mother, they were probably talking among themselves. It would have been fairly easy for someone to sneak into the church by the rear entrance, although they would have to have moved quickly. There was what Nelson would call a 'narrow window of opportunity' for the crime to have been committed.

Ruth remembers the figure that she had seen hunting in the olive groves at night. Was that Samir? She doesn't blame him if it was. When you've got no food, you're entitled to go hunting, but it would present him in a rather different light. She picks up her phone and starts clicking through the pictures. There's Kate and Louis at Heathrow, with their animal-shaped travel pillows. There are the first pictures of the house, the gleaming marble floors, the views from the balcony. There's Toni, Angelo's skeleton, the picture jarringly out of place amid the blue skies and laughing children. There's the swimming pool and the beach. There's Nelson with Kate. She is holding her inflatable unicorn and he is grinning, shielding his eyes from the sun.

Nelson will know about the scan by now. Will they know whether the baby is a boy or a girl? Ruth doesn't really like to think about it. If it's a boy, she knows that she'll be jealous because Nelson will be so happy, so pleased with Michelle for bearing him a son (the biblical language seems to suit the situation somehow). But, at least, if it's a boy, Kate will retain her position as youngest daughter. Ruth pushes the thought away and goes back to her pictures. There it is. The figure seen from the balcony, moving through the trees and carrying a gun. Ruth enlarges the image with her fingers. It's hard to tell, but the figure, in a dark top and trousers, looks too slight to be Samir. In fact, looking at it now, Ruth is almost certain that it's a woman.

Nelson spends the afternoon packing. Not that he's got much to pack: the few clothes he brought with him, the shirts and shorts he bought for the beach, some presents that he's picked up for Michelle and the girls. It all fits into his sports bag. Thank God for that, because he hates waiting for baggage, hates waiting for anything, really. Cathbad just brought hand luggage too, he remembers, probably a bag containing his spare robe and some incense. He'd been rather disapproving of Cathbad's funeral rites yesterday.

It's been an odd few days, he thinks. It's been time out in a way, spending these days with Ruth and Katie, eating together, going to the beach together. It's a snapshot of what life would be like if he were married to Ruth. There would probably be more rows than he has with Michelle, but there would definitely be compensations. But he mustn't think like that. He's grateful now that Ruth wouldn't let him finish that fatal sentence: 'Maybe after the baby is born . . .' He can't do anything until the baby (his son!) is here and then, at least, he'll know whether his suspicions about Tim are correct. 'You stand out,' Tim used to say, 'as a black policeman in Norfolk. It's a real disadvantage.' Maybe, thinks Nelson, but it will certainly help to make the baby's parentage clear. What will he do then? Will he leave Michelle if it's clear that the baby isn't his? Will he try to make a life with Ruth? It seems to him that, whichever way he looks, there's no easy solution. He half wishes that he could stay here for ever, spending the days with Ruth and Katie, Michelle and the girls safely at home. But he has to get back. There's his job, for one thing. He's itching to get back to work.

Cathbad appears in the doorway. He's wearing shorts and a pink shirt and looks brown and healthy. Bloody Cathbad, thinks Nelson, not without affection, always manages to come up smelling of roses.

'I've printed out our tickets,' he says.

'That's good,' says Cathbad. 'I'm looking forward to seeing Judy. I don't think she's really enjoyed her mother's visit. Their auras aren't aligned at the moment.'

'She's coping fine at work,' says Nelson. 'Good practice for her. She should really take the inspector's exam soon.'

'Have you spoken to her?' says Cathbad.

'Only exchanged emails,' says Nelson. 'Why?'

'Did she mention a man called Micky Webb?' says Cathbad.

'Yes,' says Nelson. 'She went to see him. Not really necessary. I'd already dealt with it.'

'I have a dark feeling about him,' says Cathbad. 'Be on your guard.'

'I always am,' says Nelson.

'Yes, you are,' says Cathbad, 'but are you looking in the right direction?'

One of Cathbad's irritatingly enigmatic remarks, thinks Nelson. But, as he sits on the terrace later with Linda and Paolo, watching the shadows lengthen in the valley, Cathbad's words keep coming back to him. *Are you looking in the right direction?*

30

Ruth has been rather dreading the final meal – the Last Supper, as Cathbad insists on calling it – but it's actually a rather jolly occasion. This is partly because of Cathbad himself, who is on his best form, keeping the children entertained with stories about statues coming to life, joking with Nelson about his driving, asking Shona about Roman themes in Shakespeare's plays. While Shona is describing the plot of *Coriolanus*, Nelson says to Ruth, 'Michelle's had the scan. It's a boy.'

'That's great,' says Ruth, hearing her voice echoing tinnily in her own head. 'And everything's OK?'

'Yes, it seems so.'

'I'm glad.'

'Why are you glad?' says Kate. Ruth didn't know that she had been listening.

'I'm glad because I'm with you, sweetheart,' says Nelson, jumping in.

But tomorrow you'll be with your other family, thinks Ruth. She gets up. 'Anyone want more pasta?'

'Oh, I couldn't,' says Shona, who has eaten a minuscule amount, 'I must have put on a stone while I've been in Italy.'

'The food's good,' says Nelson. 'I'll say that for Italy.'

'Even though there aren't any chips?' says Cathbad.

'I'm middle class now,' says Nelson. 'Sometimes I even eat vegetables.'

Both Cathbad and Nelson have seconds of pasta, which pleases Ruth. It didn't taste bad, she thinks, just mysteriously unlike Italian food. After pudding, the children go to watch a DVD and the adults drink limoncello, a gift from Paolo.

'It's been wonderful to be back in Italy,' says Cathbad. 'This is a beautiful town, even if it is grieving at the moment.'

'Everyone's devastated about Don Tomaso,' says Shona, looking suspiciously dewy-eyed. 'The funeral was just so sad. Grown men breaking down in tears.'

Ruth wonders which grown men these were. She'd thought that the atmosphere at the funeral had been charged with something other than grief. Fear, perhaps.

'I wonder if we'll ever know what happened,' says Nelson. 'I hate leaving a case unsolved.'

'I'm sure Angelo will keep in touch,' says Ruth. 'And maybe your friend the Commissario will let you know.'

'We'll never really know,' says Cathbad. 'Towns like this keep their own secrets.'

It's said lightly, but something like a shiver runs around the room. Ruth looks towards the doorway into the hall. For a moment she thought that someone was waiting there in the shadows. Someone she didn't know, but who was, nonetheless, curiously familiar.

Laura is surprised, but pleased, that her mother wants to go to the gym that evening.

'Nothing strenuous,' says Michelle, 'just swimming. I feel as if I haven't had any exercise for weeks.'

'I'll drive you,' says Laura. 'I'd like to have a workout.' This is an understatement. Laura is *desperate* for exercise, her entire body craving it. She likes to work with weights because then you're really competing against yourself; it's not showy, like pounding away on the running machine, but there's such an intense satisfaction when you push yourself just a little further every time, each muscle pair working in its own way, stretching and contracting. She flexes a bicep, anticipating.

'I hope I can still fit into my swimming costume,' says Michelle.

She takes ages getting ready, during which time Laura starts to worry that the costume doesn't fit, that her mother is feeling sick or has lost her nerve. But then Michelle appears in black tracksuit trousers and a pink top, her hair tied back in a ponytail.

'I'm ready.'

'Great.' Laura has her bag ready by the door. She almost sprints to the car. Bruno starts to whine as soon as he sees the gym bags, and by the time they are backing out of the drive, he is working himself up to full banshee.

'He'll upset the neighbours,' says Michelle.

'He'll go to sleep as soon as we're out of sight,' says Laura.

The gym is full of the after-work crowd, but Laura finds herself a mat by the full-length windows. She can see the pool and her mother swimming up and down, doing a racing turn at each end. Both her parents are good swimmers; Dad used to be a lifeguard and Michelle did synchronised swimming. Laura remembers swimming in the freezing Blackpool sea with Dad, her hands and feet going numb. Mum had stayed on the beach on those occasions – she doesn't like swimming in the open water. Laura watches her mother affectionately, almost protectively, and then focuses her attention on the weights.

Afterwards, she feels brilliant. She has a shower and meets Mum in the lobby. Michelle looks happy too, her hair wet, finishing a KitKat.

'I bought one for you too,' she says.

'You're eating for two,' says Laura, putting the chocolate bar in her bag. She'll find a way of getting rid of it later.

'I think that's a myth,' says Michelle.

They stop at Waitrose for some healthy food and then drive home, the radio playing the kind of soppy songs Michelle likes. Laura even forgives her for singing along to Take That. She's just relieved that her mother is happy again. And tomorrow Dad will be home. Back for good, as Gary Barlow would say.

'Bruno *has* gone to sleep,' says Michelle as they get out of the car.

'I told you he was putting it on,' says Laura, opening the boot to get out the shopping. She refuses to let her mother help with the bags, so Michelle opens the front door.

'Bruno!' she shouts. 'We're home.'

But there's no answering bark or clattering of toenails as Bruno comes hurtling along the hall. There's only silence. Laura puts down the shopping and runs up the stairs. Sometimes Bruno sneaks in and sleeps on one of the beds. But every bed is neatly made, with duvet and matching counterpane – even Rebecca's, because Michelle can't stand to see unmade beds. There's no sign of the dog anywhere. Laura hears her mother searching downstairs and the back door opening.

Laura runs down and joins Michelle in the garden.

'How can he have got out?' she says.

'The back door was open,' says Michelle. 'Wide open.'

'It was locked,' says Laura. 'I checked.'

'So did I,' says Michelle.

They look at each other as the silence grows around them.

Ruth only gets a few moments alone with Nelson. The children have said goodbye, Kate gripping Nelson with a bear hug that involves arms and legs, and Shona is supervising them getting into bed. Cathbad, in a moment of pure tact, leaves first because he 'wants to see the fountain in the moonlight'. Ruth and Nelson are left on the landing. An in-between place, thinks Ruth, one of the liminal zones so beloved of her ex-tutor Erik. The wood between the worlds.

'Bye then, Ruth,' says Nelson.

'Bye,' says Ruth. 'Safe journey.'

He hesitates, and then he kisses her. A proper kiss, which takes her by surprise. For a moment, she kisses him back, and then she backs away. She raises her hand as if they are already several feet apart.

'Goodbye,' she says again. 'See you soon.'

She lets herself back into the flat. At least she didn't cry, she tells herself.

Laura rings the RSPCA and the vet. 'He's microchipped,' she says, 'and he's very home-loving, He wouldn't go far.' She hears her voice wobbling and says goodbye very quickly.

Michelle is sitting on the sofa in her gym gear, twisting a strand of hair between her fingers. Rebecca does that too when she's worried.

'Harry will never forgive me if anything happens to his dog,' says Michelle.

'I'm sure he's OK,' says Laura. 'He's probably just wandered off somewhere.' She longs for her father to come back. She's sick of being the adult. She wants to lie on the sofa and cry. She wants to hear her Dad summoning forces from King's Lynn CID to search for Bruno. She thinks of Judy and Clough (Uncle Dave to her and Rebecca) coming to the rescue with their professionalism and calm.

'Shall we ring the station?' she says. 'Maybe Uncle Dave will be there.'

'He's on his honeymoon,' says Michelle. Twist, twist, twist.

'Judy, then.'

'Let's wait for a bit. Like you said, he's probably just wandered off.'

What about the open back door, thinks Laura. But she says nothing and they both sit on the sofa, their ears straining for the familiar bark.

By nightfall they are starting to panic. Laura rings the RSPCA again and is told that no one has found a stray German Shepherd. Eventually, she does ring the King's Lynn police, but it's a desk sergeant she doesn't know and, though he's perfectly nice and sympathetic, she doesn't quite have the nerve to ask to be passed to CID.

She goes out in the car, leaving Michelle at home in case Bruno comes back. It's dark now and the residential streets are quiet, but she stops at every alleyway or open patch of grass. 'Bruno! Bruno!' Once she hears a dog bark and her heart jumps, but it's only an elderly Great Dane on a lead, coming back from his evening walk and letting the neighbourhood cats know of his presence. She drives past the allotments, the trees heavy with fruit. It must be nearly autumn, she thinks. How can they face a winter without Bruno? Last Christmas, she and Rebecca had bought him a stocking full of dog treats. They've only had Bruno a year, but already he's one of the creatures she loves most on earth. In fact, she loves him second only to Mum, Dad and Rebecca (in joint first place). More than Chad? Definitely more than Chad. She's crying now and she wipes away the tears with the back of her hand. She can't afford to go to pieces. She has to stay strong for Mum.

Back home she finds her mother in the garden, rattling a fork against Bruno's dish. Normally this sound has him slavering at their side in seconds but now there is nothing, just the birds singing in the twilight. Michelle is shivering, so Laura makes her come back inside. She makes tea, thinking that this is a very British thing to do. Why do they think that pouring water on some dried leaves will make them feel better? It does though, momentarily.

Neither of them feel like supper. They sit down and watch a programme about past *X Factor* winners. The new series is set to start on Saturday. Rebecca FaceTimes halfway through. She loves the show and likes to feel as if they're watching as a family.

'Don't tell her about Bruno,' Michelle whispers. 'I don't want her to worry.' So Laura has to carry on a fake-cheerful conversation about boy bands versus girl bands and whether JLS should have beaten Alexandra Burke. Rebecca also wants to talk about the baby. 'Maybe he'll be a pop star.'

'Mum's into gender stereotyping,' says Laura, 'he's only allowed to play football.'

'That's not true,' says Michelle, twisting her hair.

'We'll make him a modern man,' says Rebecca, as if she is offering to knit him one for Christmas, 'he'll be the perfect boyfriend by the time we've finished with him.'

Chad is the perfect boyfriend, thinks Laura, when the programme and the FaceTime chat have both finished. How come she doesn't feel even tempted to ring him?

'What do you want to watch now?' she says to Michelle.

'I don't know,' says her mother. 'Shall we ring the RSPCA again?'

*

'Let's have an early night,' says Shona, and Ruth readily agrees. But, alone in her bedroom, she finds that she can't sleep. Determinedly, she turns off the light and closes her eyes, but words and images keep floating behind her eyelids, as though she is watching a TV channel that can't be switched off. She sees herself kissing Nelson on the landing; Don Tomaso's body being carried into the church; a skeletal hand with a missing finger; a cat walking across an empty square.

Why all this talk of the dead?

There must be so many resentments simmering under the surface.

Being a hero doesn't make you popular. Not in Italy anyway.

They believed that it would prevent the bodies returning to haunt the earth.

He was a holy man. A saint.

Towns like this keep their own secrets.

It's no good. Ruth gets up and walks into the sitting room. There are no curtains at the balcony window and she can see the valley below, silver and black in the moonlight. She thinks of the picture painted by Giorgio. What had Pompeo thought when he looked at it? It seems strange that, having treasured it all these years, it should have been relegated to what is obviously a spare bedroom.

Ruth goes to the door of the children's room. They are both sleeping peacefully. There's no sound from Shona either, no telltale buzz of a telephone conversation. In fact, the apartment is completely silent; there's no ticking clock, no comforting creaking of the furniture. The modern tables and chairs give nothing away and the marble floors are as silent as tombstones. A light shines suddenly from a small table.

It's a phone – Nelson's phone. Ruth recognises it immediately because he doesn't have a case and the phone always looks battered, the screen slightly cracked. Nelson must have put it down when Kate hugged him and forgotten to pick it up. Maybe he'd been more upset at saying goodbye than she had realised. Ruth picks up the phone. It's password protected, but she sees there is a missed call from Michelle. Probably just more heart-warming baby news. Ruth is quite glad that she doesn't know the password. She'll text Cathbad and tell him that the phone is here. Nelson can pick it up on his way to the airport tomorrow morning.

She pads into the kitchen. She will make herself a cup of tea and take it back to her room. Then she'll text Cathbad. It's only when she switches on the electric kettle that she realises that there must have been another power cut. She tries the light switch. Nothing. She considers getting her phone and using the torch app to look in the cupboard, but she remembers Angelo saying that the electricity often goes off unexpectedly in the mountain villages. She'll just have a cup of tea and wait. Now where did Shona put that old kettle, the one they used on the night of the earthquake? She spots it up on the top shelf, and climbs on a chair to retrieve it. As she climbs down, she hears something rattling inside the old kettle. Perhaps its innards are coming loose? She prises off the lid and looks inside.

There's something there. Something small and metallic. Shona can't have noticed it when she used the kettle before – understandable in the circumstances. Ruth picks up the object between finger and thumb and puts it on the kitchen table.

Moonlight is shining in through the high, barred window. Ruth sees immediately that she is looking at an animal tooth, mounted with silver on one end as though intended to be worn on a chain. She hears Angelo's voice: *He kept the boar's tooth as a souvenir, wore it round his neck. My grandfather always used to tell that story.* This must be the talisman that Giorgio took from the animal that tried to kill him – rather as prehistoric people painted the animals they hunted, hoping that this would give them power over their prey. Ruth picks it up; the tooth is sharp and cold. It feels odd, holding such a totemic object in her hand. Why had Pompeo kept it and why had it been hidden away in an old kettle?.

'Ah, you find it,' says a conversational voice.

It's Elsa, standing in the doorway. She's as beautifully dressed as ever and she is smiling warmly. It takes Ruth a few minutes to register the fact that Elsa has appeared in their flat in the middle of the night. And the fact that she's holding a gun.

Laura and Michelle both jump at the knock on the door.

'They've found him!' says Michelle.

'Thank God.' Laura leaps up and almost runs to the door. Poor Bruno, he must be tired and hungry by now. He'll be so pleased to see them, the sweet puppy. She opens the door, smiling, arms outstretched.

There's a man there. A smallish man wearing glasses. He doesn't have Bruno with him, nor does he look particularly threatening.

Except for the gun in his hand.

31

'What are you doing here?' says Ruth. Her voice is shaking. Why oh why did she leave her phone in her room? Why doesn't Shona wake up? The children are sleeping only a few metres away and Ruth is trapped in the kitchen facing a woman with a lethal weapon.

'I have key,' says Elsa, as if this explains everything. The gun is a heavy, old-fashioned thing. Ruth thinks that it might be a hunting rifle. It can't possibly be loaded, can it? Elsa gestures with it now, the muzzle pointing at the boar's tooth, still in Ruth's hand.

'That was Giorgio's. I knew it must be here. Where did you find it?'

'In the old kettle,' says Ruth.

Elsa laughs. The sound is almost like her usual laugh, but the note is slightly wrong. 'The kettle. Trust the English-woman to look in the kettle.'

'But . . .' Ruth is trying to figure out what on earth is going on, though she can hardly focus on anything except the gun in Elsa's hand. 'Why is it here?'

'Papa killed Giorgio,' says Elsa. 'I did not know at the time, but Papa told me, in his last days. Giorgio was traitor, passing secrets to the Nazis. It broke Papa's heart but he had to kill him.'

Ruth slowly places the tooth on the table, where it glints in the moonlight. Why did Pompeo keep it? As a reminder of the friend he had killed? Is that why he also kept Giorgio's painting on the wall? Why Elsa kept his photograph in her house?

'I didn't know where he buried him,' says Elsa, 'but I suspected the old graveyard. That's why I asked Angelo to stop excavation there.'

'Why?' says Ruth. 'No one would know, after all these years.'

'Someone did know,' says Elsa.

'Don Tomaso,' says Ruth.

'Sì. Don Tomaso. He knew. I think Papa confess to him.'

And suddenly Ruth remembers what had bothered her when Marta was talking about the priest's funeral. *We all want the funeral here, in Don Tomaso's church, but apparently the bishop wants it at the cathedral.* It was the echo of her conversation with Angelo, that first night, sitting in the square. Angelo had been talking about his hero grandfather. *He had a state funeral, at the church in Cassino.* Why was Pompeo's funeral in Cassino and not at San Michele e Santi Angeli, the church in the town where he had lived all his life? Was it because the parish priest knew that he was a murderer?

'But Don Tomaso wouldn't say,' says Ruth. 'He was a priest.' Can she overpower Elsa, who is seventy-nine, after all? But the gun might be loaded. It could go off and kill or injure Ruth, and then Elsa would be free to go on a killing spree in the flat. She tries to send a thought message to Shona: *Wake up. Call the police.*

'People get careless when they get old,' says Elsa. 'After Giorgio's body was found, I could take no risks. Already Marta was suspicious.'

She certainly was, thinks Ruth. Her mother, too. Was that why Anna had been in the flat on the day of the funeral? To look for the boar's tooth as proof of . . . what? Proof that her grandfather had been murdered? Ruth had thought that it might have been Marta or Roberto, both of whom drive little Fiats, who had forced them off the road that night, but it could easily have been Elsa. Didn't she tell Ruth that she drove a small car?

'What does it matter?' says Ruth, trying to sound soothing. 'It was all so long ago.'

'How can you say that?' says Elsa. 'And you an archaeologist! It matters because I want people to remember Papa as hero.'

'He was a hero,' says Ruth, thinking that heroism very much depends which side you are on. Was it heroic to bomb the monastery at Monte Cassino? Maybe some people think so.

'Yes,' says Elsa, 'and soon anyone who says otherwise will be dead.'

She levels the gun at Ruth.

*

Judy is driving home when she gets the message from control. 'Missing dog,' says the operator.

'What's that got to do with me?' says Judy. She wants to get home in time to see Michael before he goes to sleep. Miranda will already be in bed. 'She's ever so good with me,' her mother said smugly yesterday. 'I just read her a story and she closes her little eyes. "Goodnight," I say. "Don't let the bedbugs bite." "Goodnight, Nanny," she says.'

She closes her little eyes with me too, thinks Judy, but then she opens them again and demands another story. But Michael will be waiting for her, she knows. He always tries to stay awake to say goodnight to her.

'Nothing,' says the operator, sounding rather offended. 'It's just that it's DCI Nelson's dog.'

'Bruno? Are you sure?'

'Yes. I double-checked the address. His daughter rang it in. She sounded very upset.'

'Thanks for telling me,' says Judy.

She pulls in at the side of the road. It's only a dog, she tells herself, dogs go missing all the time. Thing is always burrowing under their fence to try to scrounge food from the old lady next door. But Nelson is away and she knows that both his daughters adore the dog. And Michelle is pregnant and might be stressed. Besides, there had been something odd about Michelle when Judy had called in on her the other day. She'd seemed on edge, almost as if she were scared.

Judy sighs and starts to perform a U-turn.

*

'Get into the house,' says the man. 'Unless you want to go the way your dog did.'

'What have you done with Bruno?' says Laura. She's surprised to find that, for a moment, she isn't even scared, just murderously angry.

'Get into the house.' The man gestures with the gun.

Run, Mum. Laura tries to send a thought message but it can't have worked because Michelle appears in the hallway. 'Who is it?'

Laura sees her mother's face go pale when she sees the gun, but her voice, when it comes out, is harder and stronger than she has ever heard it.

'Get out of my house!'

'Not until I've paid your precious husband back for what he did to me,' says the man. 'I lost ten years of my life because of him. Now I'm going to get even.'

'I've already called the police,' says Michelle. 'They'll be here any moment.'

Laura knows she's lying – for one thing, she can see Michelle's phone on the hall table – but she's proud of her mother for putting up a fight, and it stiffens her own resolve. She picks up Michelle's phone and, with quick digital native's fingers, types 'Help man with gun' and sends it to the last two people on Michelle's Messages list.

'Put that down!' the man shouts, and Laura obeys. 'Get into the lounge.'

He knows where the rooms are, thinks Laura, he's been spying on the house. She follows her mother into the sitting room. Michelle takes her hand. 'It'll be all right,' she whispers. Laura doesn't see how it can be, but she's grateful that her mother is taking charge again.

'Sit down,' says the man. Maybe he's not going to kill us if he's telling us to sit down, thinks Laura. She thinks of all the things she wants to do: become a teacher, get married, have children, swim with dolphins, go skydiving in Australia. What if this is it and she never has a chance to do anything else? She clings to her mother's hand. At least she'll die next to someone she loves.

'You're that man,' says Michelle. 'Micky something. The man who burned down his house.'

'I didn't burn down my house,' says the man, sounding petulant, as if he's a child being wrongly accused of breaking a plate. 'I was miles away at the time.'

'You still killed your wife and children,' says Michelle. 'You're a coward.'

Laura can't believe that her mother is talking back to him like this, and she's not convinced that it's a good idea. She squeezes Michelle's hand. 'Mum, please.'

This proves to be a mistake, because it focuses the man's attention onto her. He moves the gun a few centimetres so that it's pointing at Laura's head.

'No,' says Michelle. 'Not my daughter. Kill me instead.'

'No!' shouts Laura, as the gun moves slowly back.

Elsa gestures for Ruth to sit down, and she does so. Elsa takes a seat opposite her and places the gun carefully on the table. It's like a queasy replay of the time that Ruth visited Elsa in her flat. She remembers the older woman plying her with food and drink, like a scene from *Alice in Wonderland*. Eat me. Drink me. The mad hatter's tea party. Now there's a potentially lethal weapon between them. Ruth only has to stretch out her hand to grab it. She starts to slide her fingers across the glass table.

'I remember Giorgio so well,' Elsa is saying. 'I was only small when he died, but I remember. He was always with Papa, always laughing, joking with him. Papa protected him, like when the boar attacked him. Giorgio was charming but weak. He liked drawing and painting.' She says this like it is a fatal flaw. 'Papa was man of action. He liked hunting and shooting. I hunt, too – at night, when no one can see.'

'I saw you,' says Ruth. 'I saw you from my balcony. You were walking through the olive groves with a gun. I took a photograph.' Elsa must have been carrying the gun that is on the table now. Is it Pompeo's old rifle? If Elsa was hunting with it, then the gun still works. She edges her hand closer. She can almost touch the barrel.

'Angelo thinks I'm safely tucked up in bed,' says Elsa, employing another of her Mary Poppins phrases, 'but really I'm out hunting. Like Papa.'

As soon as Elsa leaves, Ruth will be on the phone to Angelo, telling him about his mother's late-night adventures.

'Tell me about Pompeo and Giorgio,' says Ruth, thinking that she must keep Elsa talking. Surely Shona will hear voices and wake up? She can hear Nelson's phone buzzing in the sitting room. It's almost as if it knows that Ruth desperately wants to contact its owner. 'They were both in the resistance, weren't they?'

'Yes,' says Elsa. 'It was terrible time, frightening time. The Germans were here, in Castello. We see them here every day, swaggering around the streets, eating at the café. Papa and the partisans were hiding in the hills. We would leave food at the crossroads for them. Then, one night, Papa appears. I see his face at the window and I remember Mamma screaming because he looks so wild. He says that Giorgio is killed by collaborators and that he has to bury his body in secret. He is sitting at the table, crying, his head in his hands. I remember he has Giorgio's boar's tooth necklace with him. That's how I knew it wasn't buried with the body. Why I knew it was here.'

'Did Don Tomaso know Giorgio?'

'Of course. He knew them all. He was older than me and he used to run errands for the partisans. All the boys did. He saw some terrible things, too. Men shot, women raped. He saw the Nazis round up partisans in one town near here and shoot them like dogs. Tomaso once told me that was why he became a priest. I never thought he would. He was such a handsome boy . . .'

She lapses into silence. Ruth remembers Elsa sobbing in the church. *He was like my brother. I know him all my life. He was a holy man. A saint.* It seems impossible, but someone killed the priest and, if it wasn't Samir, then it was someone else who knew the church well. Could it be . . . ? No, surely not. Elsa isn't capable of murder. But then, Ruth thinks, she hadn't thought her capable of threatening her at gunpoint

either. Maybe Elsa had killed Don Tomaso and then deliberately insisted that Ruth accompany her into the church so
that they could discover the body together, so that attention
would be diverted away from her. Ruth remembers Samir
saying that Elsa used to give him clothes. Did she give him
the distinctive black and white striped Juventus top that
allowed him to be spotted from a distance?

'Elsa,' she begins hesitantly, still moving her fingers forward, 'about Don Tomaso . . .'

'Don Tomaso knew,' she says. 'And when Giorgio's body
was found, he thought we should tell Marta. He was going
to tell Angelo. To get him to talk to Marta. Angelo adored
his grandfather . . .' Suddenly she puts her hands over her
face and sobs. Ruth grabs the gun. She stands up, pushing
her chair back.

'Ruth?' says a voice. 'What's going on?' It's Shona,
standing there in her shorty pyjamas, taking in the scene:
Ruth standing in the kitchen holding a gun, the chair on
the floor, Elsa sitting at the table sobbing.

'It's OK,' says Ruth. 'Elsa's just a bit upset.' She wishes she
knew how to check if the gun is loaded.

Shona opens her mouth to speak but shuts it when there's
a buzz at the door.

'Open it,' says Ruth. For a crazy moment she thinks that
it must be the police – and she's almost right.

'Hi, Ruth.' Nelson now appears in the doorway. 'I think
I left my phone here. What are you doing with that rifle?'

*

'Get up,' says the man to Laura.

'No!' Michelle leans across her, protecting her.

'I'll shoot both of you then,' says the man. 'That's fair. I lost all my children, after all. Thanks to DI Nelson.' He wipes his eyes with his free hand. Is it possible that he'll start crying and they'll be able to overpower him? Laura has read of such things. But how? They would be killed as soon as they moved. She prays Mum won't remind the man that it's his own fault, not Dad's, that his children died. Michelle is half lying across her now, and Laura whispers, hardly more than a breath, 'I sent a message.'

'Get up! Get up!' Suddenly the man is shouting, completely out of control. They stand, Michelle still in front of Laura, shielding her. He raises the gun.

Then several things happen at the same time. When Laura retells the events later, she puts them in some sort of order, shaping, rationalising, but at the time they are a blur, moving so fast that the room seems to spin, colours merging into each other like the Wall of Death at the fair, and so slowly that sound is stretched out in an endless, distorted scream.

The man levels his gun. Someone bursts into the room and throws himself at the armed man. At the same time the patio doors shatter as an animal – half wolf, half human, it seems to Laura – hurls itself into the fray. The gun goes off and there's a smell of burning. Michelle screams – 'Tim!' – and carries on screaming. Bruno is standing over the prostrate body of a man, growling, the man's arm flopping in his mouth. Michelle is cradling another man in her arms, sobbing and screaming.

Laura feels as if she's moving underwater. For a moment, no one is taking any notice of her and she wonders if she's even there. Then she hears sirens and voices outside. Mum is holding the man in her arms. He's a stranger, youngish, black, good-looking. There's a stain of red on his chest that's getting bigger all the time.

'Tim,' Michelle is sobbing, 'don't die, please don't die.'

The man opens his eyes and half smiles. 'I love you,' he mouths. Then his eyes close and, as clear as day, Laura watches his spirit leaving his body, a multi-coloured bird that flies out through the shattered glass doors and vanishes into the night. And, at the centre of everything – the sirens, the sobbing, the noise of the armed police entering the room, Bruno growling – there is an immense, immeasurable silence.

32

Nelson takes the gun from Ruth and cracks it open.

'It's not loaded,' he says. 'What's the hell's going on?'

'Elsa came to see me,' says Ruth, 'with the gun. I think she may have killed Don Tomaso.'

Elsa is still sitting at the table. She has stopped crying and now seems almost in a trance.

'We need to call Valenti,' says Nelson.

'Your phone's in the other room,' says Ruth. 'It's been buzzing all night.'

At that moment the lights come on, leaving them all staring at each other: Shona in her pink-checked shorts, Nelson still holding the gun, Ruth steadying herself against the stove, Elsa at the table.

'I'll go and call,' says Nelson. He leaves the room, taking the gun with him. Nobody in the kitchen speaks. It's as if they are waiting for their cue. Seconds later, Nelson is back. His face, thinks Ruth, has completely changed. It's as if the real Nelson has been replaced by an actor. He's on the phone, listening to a message. They all watch as he stabs in a number. 'Judy? What's happened? . . . Jesus Christ . . . Are they all right? . . . My God . . . How did he . . . ? Can I talk to her? . . . OK . . . You do that . . . Call me later.'

He clicks off the phone. Ruth and Shona are staring at him. Even Elsa looks round. Ruth has only once before seen that look on Nelson's face. She had hoped never to see it again.

'What is it?' she says, suddenly scared.

'Someone tried to kill Michelle and Laura. Someone with a grudge against me.'

'Oh my God,' says Ruth. 'What happened? Are they all right?'

'They're in hospital, but apparently they're not hurt. Tim saved them. Laura managed to send a message to Tim . . . and to me. Tim rushed in just as the man was preparing to shoot. He got in the way of the bullet.'

'Is he OK?' says Ruth.

'He's dead,' says Nelson, and turns away from them, covering his face.

Laura doesn't recognise Judy at first. She is just another person in dark clothes with a shocked expression. It's only when Judy squats down on the floor next to her that her face seems to come into focus.

'Laura. It's me, Judy. Are you OK? Are you hurt?'

'No,' says Laura. 'The man. The one who came to save us. I think he's dead.'

Judy's face quivers as if she is about to cry, but when she speaks again, it is in the same calm voice.

'I'm afraid he is.'

I know, Laura wants to say, I saw his soul leave his body. But she doesn't want Judy to think that the whole experience has deranged her.

'Do you know who he was?' she says.

'His name was Tim,' says Judy. 'And he was a policeman. He used to work with your Dad.'

Mum, who has been silent as the paramedics fuss around her, suddenly starts to cry, really sobbing, bending over with her head almost on her knees. Laura gets up and puts her arm round her.

'Don't, Mum. Please.'

But Mum continues to sob as the body of the man – Tim – is lifted onto a stretcher. One of the paramedics pulls the sheet over his face in a gesture that seems both matter-of-fact and tender. Laura sees Judy watching, wiping her eyes.

Something wet pushes itself into her hand. It's Bruno, tail wagging as if the whole thing is a tremendous game. Laura hugs him. 'Bruno! Are you all right?'

She can't see any glass in his coat or any marks on him anywhere. She buries his face in his thick, glossy fur.

'Laura.' It's Judy again. 'We need to get you and your mum to hospital. I'll call Jan – she's one of our dog handlers – to come and look after Bruno. And I'll get a glazier to mend the windows.'

The paramedics are helping Mum to her feet. She is still crying, but more quietly now. The room seems to be full of people – talking on their phones, checking the garden, running upstairs. The man with the gun has disappeared. They must have taken him out when Laura was still in a trance. Laura turns to Judy. 'Are you coming with us?'

'I'll meet you at the hospital,' said Judy. 'I've got to sort a few things out here. I only came because I got the message that Bruno was missing.'

'He was lost,' said Laura, 'but he found us. He saved us.'

'Yes,' says Judy. 'He was a hero. Look, I've been talking to your dad. He sends his love and says he'll be home tomorrow. Can you call him? He's out of his mind with worry, as you can imagine.' She hands Laura her phone. It looks like an object from another life.

Ruth calls Valenti on her phone. Nelson seems incapable of doing anything. He just sits on the sofa with his head in his hands. After a while his phone rings. 'Laura? Hello, love. No, it's OK. I'll be home tomorrow . . .' He goes out into the hall. There's so much tenderness in his voice that Ruth finds herself wanting to cry. Again.

Shona bustles around, making them all cups of tea. A typical Englishwoman, Elsa would say. Elsa herself is still sitting at the kitchen table. Ruth puts two sugars in her tea and urges her to drink it. She doesn't want the woman to collapse, after all. Incredibly, the children stay asleep.

Nelson comes back into the room. He goes to the window and looks out into the darkness. Ruth wants to talk to him, but she doesn't know what to say. She can hardly believe that Tim is dead. Tim, the handsome, troubled man who had sat in her front garden talking about Michelle. *I'm sorry, Ruth, but I feel like I'm going mad here.* Now he has died saving Michelle's life. Laura's too. Ruth can only imagine what Nelson is feeling: guilt, sorrow, jealousy. She goes to him and puts her hand on his arm. At least he doesn't shake it off.

Valenti appears about thirty minutes later, accompanied by the woman police officer. He speaks in Italian to Elsa and gently helps her to her feet.

'I'll need a statement from you tomorrow, Dottore Galloway,' he says.

'Of course,' says Ruth.

'And you, Commissario Nelson.'

'I'll be in England,' says Nelson. 'I didn't see or hear anything anyway.'

He sounds as if he will fight anyone who disagrees with him. Valenti, at any rate, does not argue. The police officers leave the flat, Elsa walking between them.

'I'd better go,' says Nelson. 'My flight is first thing in the morning.'

'Be careful, Nelson,' says Ruth. She doesn't know quite what she means by this. Be careful driving back to Linda's? Be careful that the plane doesn't crash? Be careful when you get home and your marriage is in smithereens?

Nelson smiles at her but it's as if he's already far away. She listens to his feet descending the stairs. She turns to Shona, who is standing in the hallway, looking rather helpless.

'It feels as if I'll never see him again.'

Laura is alone in the A & E cubicle. A woman called a forensic nurse practitioner was with her but she's been called away.

She's not sure where her mother is. Michelle had become hysterical again in the ambulance, shaking and shivering, crying uncontrollably. Laura was really worried about her. 'She's pregnant,' she told the paramedics. 'Look after her.' At the hospital, Michelle had been ushered away, a nurse on each side. Laura was left with the police officers, clasping a silver foil cape like she had just run a marathon. And she feels as tired as if she has just run twenty-six miles. It seems incredible, but the thing she most wants to do now is curl up on the floor of the cubicle and go to sleep.

But she can't sleep. Her mother might need her. Her mother, who had been prepared to die for her. Alanine, arginine, asparagine . . .

Someone knocks on the flimsy side of the cubicle. 'Laura?' It's Judy, who is now wearing a fluorescent police jacket. She comes in and puts her arms round her. 'It's all right,' she says. 'You were really brave, but you're safe now.'

Laura struggles to control herself. Judy passes her a tissue and a cone-shaped paper cup of water. 'Take a sip and try to breathe,' she says. Laura does so. Aspartic acid, cysteine, glutamine . . .

'What happened to the man?' she says at last. 'The one who wanted to shoot us?'

'Micky Webb?' says Judy. 'He's in custody, charged with attempted murder. He won't see the light of day again, I promise you.'

'Where did that other man, Tim, come from? It was like he appeared out of nowhere. Like Bruno.'

'I don't know,' says Judy. 'He must have got wind that

something was up. I don't know how. As I say, he doesn't work in Lynn any more.'

'Where's Mum?'

'A nurse is with her now. She's a bit shaken but she's not hurt. You've spoken to your dad?'

'Yes, he's coming home as soon as he can.'

'Good,' says Judy. 'It doesn't feel right without him, does it?'

'No,' says Laura, 'it doesn't.' She takes another sip of water and tries breathe properly. Glutamine, glutamic acid, glycine, histidine, isoleucine, leucine, lysine . . .

'When you're up to it,' says Judy, 'we need to ask you some questions, but I'll be with you all the time. We'll take it very gently.'

'Who was that man?' says Laura. 'What did you call him? Micky something?'

'Micky Webb,' says Judy. 'You dad put him in prison years ago and he held a grudge. He got out recently and . . .' Her voice changes suddenly. 'Oh Laura,' she says. 'It was my fault. I should have known. Webb went after someone else involved in the case. He poisoned her dog. I thought he might come after you. I came to warn your mum but I should have done more.'

Laura thinks she understands only about one word of this. 'You said you thought he'd poisoned Bruno.'

'Yes. He broke into the house and took Bruno. It looks as if he fed him poisoned meat and shut him in a shed in the allotments at the end of your road. But Bruno being such a big, strong dog, he threw up the poison and broke out. Then he came home.'

Bruno had been nearby when they had been calling him and rattling the fork on his plate. Had he heard them? He'd certainly picked up their distress somehow. And he'd come to save them.

'He came flying in through the French windows,' she says. 'I thought he was a werewolf at first.'

Judy smiles, although a moment ago she had looked as if she was crying. 'He was like an avenging angel. Nelson will be so proud of him.'

'He wasn't even hurt,' says Laura. 'Not a scratch on him.'

'He's a miracle dog.'

'What about Mum?' says Laura. 'Is she OK? You know she's pregnant?'

'Yes,' says Judy. 'I had a word with the nurse just now. They're bringing a midwife to check her over but they think she's fine. In shock though. As you must be too.'

'She seemed to know the man,' says Laura. 'She kept saying his name.' He said he loved her, she wants to say, they were the last words he ever spoke. But how can she ever say this to anyone? Perhaps she imagined it, like she imagined the bird flying out into the night.

'Poor Mum,' she says instead. 'She was crying and crying in the ambulance.' She realises now that Tim's must have been one of the contacts in her mother's Messages list. Tim and Dad.

Judy gives her a little hug, more like a mate than a police officer. 'It'll be very hard for your mum. You'll have to look after her for a bit.'

'I know,' says Laura. 'I always do.'

'I know,' says Judy. 'Nelson will be proud of you.'

Michelle lies on the bed. 'Stay still,' they told her. 'Think of the baby.' She dutifully folds her hands on her stomach, but she's thinking of her other baby, her eldest baby. Laura. She had been quite prepared to die for Laura. She's surprised how brave she had felt, how clear-cut her reasoning. She had felt ten feet tall when she had faced that low-life with a gun. She'd seen him raise the weapon and thought, well, this is it, perhaps it's for the best, Harry and the girls will be fine without me. But then Tim had burst in and restored her life and her future. Except that he won't be in it. Beautiful, brave, gallant Tim. He had died for her. How can she go on, knowing that? How can she not?

She feels the tears falling into her hair. Maybe it's all a nightmare and she'll wake up to find herself sitting on the sofa with Laura watching the *X Factor*, Rebecca commenting sarcastically from the phone. Rebecca! She doesn't even know what's happened. She's in Brighton, drinking wine with her flatmates, perhaps demolishing a takeaway, thinking of her parents with their dull, conventional life in King's Lynn. Michelle doesn't want to ring her and destroy this illusion. 'Laura and I were held at gunpoint. A man died saving us.' *A man.* They'll never know what Tim was to her, and she can never say. Even Harry will never know. She must be kind to Harry. He'll be riven with guilt when he hears the news. He'll think it's his fault. He put Micky Whatsit in prison and, when he came to get his revenge,

Harry had been hundreds of miles away. With Ruth. But Michelle isn't even angry about that any more. It seems that all her emotions died when the gun went off and she saw Tim fall to the floor.

The nurse is back with another woman, someone vaguely familiar.

'I've brought a midwife to have a look at you,' she says. 'Just to be on the safe side.'

The safe side. Michelle has lived her life on the safe side and look where it's got her.

'The police are waiting to talk to you,' says the nurse, patting her shoulder, 'but this is more important.'

'Yes,' says Michelle, 'the baby is the most important thing.'

One day at a time, she thinks. One day at a time.

33

Ruth calls Cathbad and tells him what has happened. She wants him to be prepared for Nelson's return.

'Don't worry,' says Cathbad. 'I'll look after him.'

'It's so awful,' says Ruth. 'Poor Tim.' She doesn't tell him about Elsa and her late-night visit. One problem at a time.

'Maybe this is what Tim was meant to do,' says Cathbad. 'We can't know all the patterns of the great web. We can just hope that it will make sense one day.'

'Please,' says Ruth, 'promise me that you won't mention the great web to Nelson.'

All the same, she thinks when she put her phone down, she's glad that Nelson has Cathbad, if only for the journey home. She can't imagine Nelson's meeting with Michelle, knowing that another man died saving her. She knows that Nelson will always feel guilty for leaving his phone with Ruth, will almost feel that, in that moment, he had chosen Ruth and Kate over his lawful family. But this isn't true, Ruth thinks. These last few days have been time stolen out of reality. By tomorrow, Nelson will have been swallowed by real life.

She sleeps late and is surprised, when she makes her way into the kitchen, to find Marta sitting at the table with Shona and the children. Ruth can hardly look at that table without shuddering. At least Valenti took the gun with him.

Kate comes to hug her. 'We're having Nutella pancakes.'

Shona smiles. 'I thought we deserved a treat. Are you all right?'

'Yes. You?'

'OK. Last night feels like a dream doesn't it?'

'Ruth,' says Marta. 'Can I have a word?'

'I think I need to be at the police station at ten.' Ruth looks at her watch.

'I'll drive you. There's something I want to say first.'

They go into the sitting room and sit on the sofa, facing the balcony windows. It's another beautiful morning, with just a slight mist clinging to the valley, a faint whiff of autumn.

'I want to apologise,' says Marta.

'What for?'

'It was me who wrote the graffiti outside the house, who put the wolf's head on your doorstep.'

'You? Why?'

'I wanted to stop the Roman dig. Too much time and money is spent on the Romans. What is so special about the Romans? Yes, they were good at engineering, but so are all fascists. Mussolini drained the Pontine Marshes, everyone will tell you that, and built new cities. The Romans were warriors and builders but there are many more interesting Italic peoples. You know I am writing a thesis on the Volsci?'

'I think someone might have told me that.'

'There was a Vosci warrior called Camilla in Virgil's *Aeneid*. Virgil said she could outrun the wind and run over crops so lightly that she never even bent them. She could walk on the waves without getting wet.'

Marta's eyes are shining. It doesn't take a psychologist to see that she thinks of herself as a modern-day Camilla.

'That's a great story,' says Ruth.

'The Volsci were highly sophisticated people,' says Marta. 'And they rebelled against their oppressors. Like my great-grandfather in the war.'

'Yes,' says Ruth. Elsa had said that Giorgio was a traitor, a collaborator, but she is not about to mention this to his great-granddaughter.

'I wanted to stop the Roman dig. All Professore Morelli cared about was getting the TV people interested. That's why he got you involved. You're a famous foreign archaeologist. I thought, if I could scare you off, the dig would be over. I got the wolf's skull from Roberto, he works at the sanctuary. I thought that, if you went home, we could concentrate on the excavations in the graveyard. I was almost sure that my great-grandfather was there. My mother always said that he had been buried there, in the heart of the town.'

The heart of the town in more ways than one, thinks Ruth.

'The attempts on Angelo's life?' she says. 'The messages on his phone, the brakes on his car, the mobile phone in the trench. Was that you?'

'I left the messages,' says Marta, 'and I did the trick with the mobile phone.' She smiles suddenly. 'That was me. I'm good with technology. Remember I told you that Graziano was my tutor at university? I used to study computer science.'

'Why did you do it?'

'To teach him a lesson. To make him look stupid. He's so pleased with himself.'

Ruth can hardly deny this. Angelo is rather self-satisfied, but she's not sure that he deserved having his dig disturbed, to say nothing of sending him photographs of skeletons. She's beginning to see the serious, devout Marta in a different light.

'What about cutting the brakes on his car?'

Marta looks shocked. 'Oh, I wouldn't do that. I didn't want to kill him, just jolt him a bit. Maybe it was an animal? Roberto says animals sometimes sleep under cars and they can chew through the brakes.'

This is what the mechanic had said, Ruth remembers. Even so, she thinks that Marta still has some explaining to do.

'I saw your mother letting herself out of this apartment on the day of the funeral,' she says. 'Do you know what she was doing?'

Marta sighs. 'She was looking for the boar's tooth. The one my *bisnonno* used to wear round his neck. It wasn't with his skeleton and she thought it might be in this house. She has a . . . what is the word? Obsession.'

'Wait there,' says Ruth. She goes into the kitchen and takes the tooth from the shelf where Shona has put it for safekeeping. She puts the talisman into Marta's hand, thinking that at least something from the past has been restored. A break in the great web has been mended.

Marta drives to the police station where Valenti is waiting for her. Linda Anthony is there, too.

'I ask Linda to translate,' says Valenti. 'I think this might be complicated.'

You can say that again, thinks Ruth.

Through Linda, she tells Valenti about Elsa's visit. She hopes to skate over the gun, but Valenti seems particularly interested in this detail.

'The Commissario wants to know if you want to press charges for attempted murder,' says Linda.

'Oh no,' says Ruth. 'I don't think she ever planned to kill me.' Even as she says this, she remembers imagining Elsa going on a rampage around the apartment. At the time, she had not been so sure that the older woman didn't have murder on her mind.

She tells Valenti what Elsa said about Don Tomaso, about him wanting her to tell Marta the truth about her great-grandfather's death. Valenti asks a series of sharp questions. Did Elsa confess to killing Don Tomaso? If not, did she know who did kill him? What had she said about the priest's death?

'She didn't exactly confess,' says Ruth. 'And she became upset when I asked her directly.'

Valenti says something to Linda, sounding rather regretful.

'He says that Elsa is too confused to interview at the moment,' says Linda. 'A doctor has said that she's in a state of nervous collapse. She's in hospital.'

'Has Angelo seen her?'

'Yes, he's with her now, apparently.'

Valenti says something which Linda does not translate. Ruth remembers that he is not one of Angelo's fans. Valenti asks Ruth to complete and sign a witness statement and then she is free to go. In the street outside, Ruth manages a few words with Linda.

'How was Nelson when he left this morning?'

'Quiet,' says Linda. 'Stunned. I think it's hit him very hard. He must be so worried about his wife and daughter. Especially as his wife is pregnant.'

'Yes,' says Ruth. 'It's such an awful thing to happen. I knew the policeman who died. He was a nice man, quite young. I keep thinking about his family.'

'Your holiday hasn't been very peaceful, has it?' says Linda. 'You must be longing to get home.'

'Yes,' says Ruth. 'Shona's trying to change our tickets now.'

When she gets back to the apartment, she finds a note from Shona. She has managed to get them flights home tomorrow. She and Graziano have taken the children for a last visit to the swimming pool. Thank God, thinks Ruth. We can go home. Suddenly she longs to see Flint again, to sink her face into his orange fur, which always smells faintly of circuses.

She sets about tidying the flat. She sweeps and washes the marble floors, wipes down every surface, sorts the recycling into its multiple categories and leaves it in bags by the front door. She also wraps yet another broken glass in newspaper and hides it at the very bottom of the 'mixed materials' bin. For some reason, it feels imperative that they leave not a trace of their occupancy. From a forensics point of view, she knows this is impossible. 'We always leave something of ourselves behind' – that's what Mike Halloran, one of Nelson's crime scene investigators, says. But Angelo is hardly going to be swabbing the floors for traces of saliva, or looking for fibres in the bath plug.

She had secretly hoped that she could leave without seeing Angelo, but she had sent him an email say that she was leaving tomorrow ('for personal reasons'), so she is not entirely surprised when the intercom buzzes and Angelo's voice says, 'Ruth. Can I come in?'

His first words are, 'I'm sorry about last night. About my mother visiting.'

'Visiting' is not quite how Ruth would describe Elsa breaking into the apartment and threatening her with a gun, but she says, 'That's OK. She was . . . confused.'

'Exactly,' says Angelo, starting to stride around the flat, slipping slightly on the newly washed floors. 'That's what Valenti can't see. The doctors say that she's had a complete breakdown. She's under sedation.'

Ruth makes appropriately sympathetic noises.

Angelo is now looking into the children's bedroom. Ruth is slightly irritated by this. She hasn't started tidying in there yet, because the Kate and Louis will only untidy it again. She'll strip their beds in the morning. Then she sees that Angelo is looking at Giorgio's picture, which she has hung back on the wall. The subject matter is now so obvious to Ruth that she can't believe she ever considered the painting an abstract.

Angelo stares at it for so long that Ruth almost asks him if he's all right. Then he turns back to her. 'Did Mamma say anything about Don Tomaso?'

'Yes,' says Ruth carefully. 'She said that Don Tomaso knew that your grandfather killed Giorgio. She said that he wanted to tell Marta.'

Angelo is still standing very still. Ruth sees that this news is not a surprise to him.

'Nonno told me something of the sort in his last illness,' he says. 'Giorgio was passing resistance secrets onto the Nazis. My grandfather shot him. It broke his heart. Giorgio was his dearest friend. That's why he held on to this terrible picture. He made me promise not to sell it.'

'Did you know that Giorgio was buried in the church graveyard?' says Ruth.

'Yes,' says Angelo. 'I think it was as close as my grandfather could get to consecrated ground. That's why I didn't want to do the excavation there.'

'Don Tomaso told me that he had something to show me,' says Ruth. 'Do you think it was Giorgio's body?'

'Maybe,' says Angelo. 'Who knows?'

Ruth says tentatively. 'Do you think that your mother quarrelled with Don Tomaso?'

'What are you trying to say?' says Angelo. 'That an old woman, barely weighing one hundred and twenty pounds,

hit her oldest, dearest friend over the head with a candlestick and killed him? It's preposterous.'

'I wasn't implying anything,' says Ruth. There's a silence
and then she says, 'Do you want me to post the keys through
your letterbox tomorrow?'

The ugly look fades from Angelo's face. 'I'm sorry, Ruth.
That would be fine. Do you want a lift to the airport?'

'It's OK,' says Ruth. 'Marta's taking us.'

When Angelo has gone, Ruth gets out her phone to call
Commissario Valenti. She sees now that it was Angelo who
killed Don Tomaso. Otherwise how would he know that
a candlestick was the murder weapon? She should have
known really as soon as she saw the stone in the priest's
mouth. It's as if she had looked down at Angelo's feet and
seen, instead of handmade Italian loafers, cloven hooves.
She remembers what Angelo had said, with his Mephis-
tophelean smile, that first evening, at the café. *All priests are
charlatans*, he'd said then. *Being a hero doesn't make you popular.*
She imagines that Angelo confronted Don Tomaso about
his wish to tell the truth about Giorgio's death. The murder
would have been committed in the heat of the moment but
it was still a murder. Angelo killed Don Tomaso and may
even have tried to kill Ruth and Kate by forcing their car off
the road. Because he would have known that Ruth would
make the link with the stone. The stone put in the mouth
as a punishment for treachery. Why hadn't she done so
earlier? Because Angelo was a colleague, an ally, her friend
in a strange land. Well, all she can do is pass her suspicions

on to Valenti and hope that Angelo, lapsed Catholic that he is, will still retain the impulse towards the confessional. It's a strong compulsion, as Ruth herself knows. Hadn't she too been tempted by it, that evening at the table with Don Tomaso?

But Angelo had maintained a shred of decency. He hadn't wanted Samir to be blamed for the murder that he alone knew he hadn't committed. Ruth hopes that this counts in his favour. In the earthly courts of justice, at least.

As she dials Valenti's number she thinks she really should have known.

Angelo. The dark angel.

34

The next morning, Marta drives Ruth, Shona and the children to the airport. It's a tight squeeze in the Fiat 500 but Ruth is grateful not to have to face Angelo or Graziano. She doesn't know if Valenti has taken Angelo into custody. She only knows that the policeman was not surprised to hear her story. He too must have suspected as soon as he saw the stone, which is why he asked Ruth not to mention it to anyone.

What will Marta say if her professor is charged with murder? Marta says that she is going to switch back to computing anyway. 'You know where you are with computers,' she says. Roberto is changing to zoology. It turns out that Marta and Roberto are dating, to use Angelo's phrase. That must have been why Roberto seemed to have been following them home that time. He had actually been on his way to see Marta, perhaps to sing at her window like a troubadour. Marta explains earnestly to Ruth that she believes in pre-marital chastity for both sexes. Good luck with that one, thinks Ruth.

Kate and Louis wave goodbye to the square and the fountain. Federica is setting up the tables outside the café, ready for breakfast. The church is still closed. The angels on the roof are white sentinels against the sky as Ruth looks back to get her last glimpse of Castello degli Angeli. Will the church ever open again? Despite herself, Ruth hopes that it will. *We always leave part of ourselves behind.* What has she left behind in Italy? Part of her heart, perhaps. She has fallen in love with the Liri Valley and the little terracotta town on the hill. She will never forget swimming in the sea with Nelson and, best of all, the day that had spent alone together. If it's the only day they ever spend as a couple, at least it was a good one. She's left some of her professional vanity behind, too, because she is sure that Marta was right: Angelo only asked her to advise on the bones in order to tempt the TV company back to the Roman dig and deflect attention away from the body in the churchyard. Possibly he had asked her because she hadn't said no to him in the past. What was it that Angelo said? *The presence of a foreign expert made all the difference.*

They are on the motorway now, Marta following signs for Fiumicino airport, manoeuvring the little car through the maze of traffic. 'Did Angelo ever borrow your car?' she asks Marta. 'All the time,' says Marta, 'it's easier to drive on the mountain roads.' Ruth had once thought that it was Elsa, driving her little car, who had tried to drive them off the side of the mountain that night? But it must have been Angelo, driving Marta's Fiat. Had he been prepared to silence her, to kill Linda, Shona and the children too? Ruth will never know for sure.

Marta parks so near to the departures hall that they are almost at the check-in desk. 'Goodbye,' says Ruth, giving her a hug, 'Keep in touch. Good luck with the computers.' Marta has bought farewell presents for the children – two fluffy wolf cubs – and these enliven the endless queues inside the terminal as the children make the little creatures talk and howl.

'You should call them Romulus and Remus,' says Ruth.

Kate looks as her as if she is mad. 'We're calling them Ant and Dec.'

They check in their bags and prepare for the security ordeal. Shona has all her make-up in a see-through container, but Ruth invariably has a bottle of water or some hand gel buried at the bottom of her travel bag. The official motions Kate through the scanner first, and Ruth hates to see her go alone, through the sinister, empty door frame that looks like the portal to the other world in *Prince Caspian*. But Kate skips through quite happily. It is Ruth who is stopped and searched, though why, exactly, she never discovers. Perhaps it's the interesting flint in her pocket; it's certainly not a preponderance of metal jewellery. Shona makes a great fuss about removing her earrings, bracelets and necklace, but she passes through the portal without a sound.

Then they are on the other side and waiting for their gate to be called. It's a strange in-between place, thinks Ruth, neither Italy nor England, neither earth nor air. Like the landing at the apartment, like the wood between the worlds, like the liminal zone between life and death. Travellers wander up and down carrying duty-free bags as the dead are meant to carry coins to take them to the Underworld. Overhead screens carry messages from distant lands: Paris, Hamburg, New York, Amsterdam, Tokyo. So many places, so many destinations.

'Will you keep in touch with Graziano?' Ruth asks Shona while the children are busy making the wolves present a talent show.

Shona sighs and passes a hand through her bright hair. There are a few strands of grey near the parting, Ruth notices. No doubt Shona will deal with this abomination as soon as she gets back to her hairdresser, but the sight of them lifts Ruth's spirits slightly.

'I don't think so,' says Shona. 'I liked Graziano, but it was just a holiday fling. No, my life is with Phil now. Phil and Louis.'

She doesn't say it sadly or happily. She says it as if it is a fact of life, which of course it is. Soon Ruth will have to pick up her bag and pass through the gate, back to her own life. She sits patiently, watching the ever-changing screen in front of her.

EPILOGUE

It's a full policeman's funeral. The streets are closed and uniformed officers form a guard of honour as the hearse bearing Tim's coffin makes its journey from the police station to the church. Tim's mother opted to have the funeral here, in King's Lynn, rather than at home in Essex. 'He loved it here,' she tells Nelson, 'he loved being part of the team. He always spoke so fondly of you, DCI Nelson. He said you taught him a lot.' Nelson bears this as another nail in the crucifix of guilt he's been carrying around for the last few weeks. Meeting Tim's mother had been torture. Not that Edina Heathfield had been angry or accusatory. She was a sweet-faced, middle-aged woman in black, who held his hands and talked about Tim being with the angels now.

After Castello degli Angeli, Nelson thinks that he's had enough of angels for a lifetime. But he's glad that Tim's mother has this belief; she's going to need it in the days to come.

'He admired you very much,' said Edina. 'The boss. That's what he always called you.'

'He was a first-class police officer,' said Nelson. 'And he died a hero.'

Both these things are true, but Nelson notices that they don't stop him being intermittently angry with Tim. He had been having an affair with Nelson's wife, after all. Michelle admitted as much to Nelson as soon as he returned from Italy. She said it like it didn't matter much any more and, in the relief of knowing that Michelle and Laura were unharmed, adultery seemed almost an insignificant detail. That day, all Nelson had wanted to do was hold his wife and daughter close. Rebecca was home by midday on Friday and, that first evening, they had all sat in a huddle on the sofa, facing the mended French windows, as if they couldn't bear to be separated. At one point, Bruno had felt left out and heaved himself onto their joint laps. No one told him to get down. It is the considered opinion of the Nelson household that nothing is too good for Bruno.

It was in the long nights afterwards that the other feelings came back to Nelson: anger, loss, jealousy and, especially, guilt. The guilt of knowing it was his actions that had sent Micky Webb to his front door with a gun; that he had ignored warnings – from Jo, from Freddie, even from Cathbad – and left his family to go swanning off to Italy; the guilt of knowing that Laura had sent the same message to him and to Tim (the last two contacts on Michelle's phone) and that it was Tim who had come to the rescue while Nelson had been eating with Ruth, kissing her, driving off and leaving his phone bleeping its SOS to the empty air. In these moments, Nelson grits his teeth and curses the day

Tim ever arrived at Lynn police station. It all started there, he thinks, ignoring the fact that it started long before. It started the day that he walked into the University of North Norfolk looking for an archaeology expert.

Now he watches as Tim's coffin is taken from the hearse and borne on the shoulders of six uniformed officers. Edina walks behind, brave in an enormous hat, supported by a son on each side. Tim's sisters follow; one of them (Blessing?) is quite young and weeping copiously. Nelson never heard Tim mention a father and no paternal figure is in evidence today. Jo comes next. Jo never met Tim, but she is the superintendent and it's up to her to lead the troops, a responsibility that she takes very seriously. Superintendent Gerry Whitcliffe, Nelson's former nemesis, will also be at the church. Whitcliffe had at least known Tim, who had been one of his protégés. Even so, Nelson bets that Jo will insist on reading the lesson.

Jo is in uniform, which came as quite a shock to Nelson. It makes her look rather formidable, although he is sure she's had the jacket fitted to be more flattering. Judy walks with Jo, her eyes downcast. She has been deeply shaken by Tim's death. Judy was fond of Tim, they worked closely together for a while, and she too feels guilty. She had followed up Marj Maccallum's allegation but had, like Nelson, dismissed Micky Webb as weak and ineffectual. And that may have been true: Micky would never have dared confront Nelson to his face, but he was brave enough to come after his wife and children with a gun.

Nelson and Clough are next in line. Clough has come back

early from his honeymoon, looking incongruously tanned and well. When Clough first appeared at the station, bearing duty-free gifts because, even in an emergency, he couldn't see why people should be denied chocolate, Nelson had been so pleased to see him that he had wanted to cry. He'd compromised by giving Clough a half hug, half handshake. 'Good to see you, boss,' Clough had said. 'Bloody Tim, eh? Always wanting to be centre of attention.' There had been tears in his eyes at the time, but Nelson had welcomed the black humour as much as he welcomed Clough's solid presence. Now, Clough is walking slowly beside him, unusually smart in a black suit and tie. 'Tim was a proper copper,' he had said to Nelson last night, when they had toasted Tim with duty-free whisky, Nelson's office door bolted against outsiders. 'There aren't many of them about.'

There's one less today, thinks Nelson, as he follows the coffin, now draped with the union flag, into the church. Among the police dignitaries, he had been touched to see Sandy Macleod, his old colleague from Blackpool CID, who had also once worked with Tim. He nods at Sandy as he makes his way to the front of the church. Michelle, Laura and Rebecca come to sit with him, Michelle wearing a black shift dress that conceals her pregnancy. Michelle had insisted on seeing Tim's mother in private. Nelson doesn't know what passed between them, but now Edina turns round and takes Michelle's hand. 'God bless you, darling.' Did Michelle tell Tim's mother that she might be carrying his child? That is something that Nelson and Michelle have never discussed. The new baby is the one bright spot in their lives, and Nelson doesn't want to spoil things by the slightest suggestion that all is not as it should be. They have settled on the name George and not a day passes without Laura and Rebecca speculating on 'Baby Georgie', the best and brightest baby in the history of childbirth.

He looks along the pew at Laura. She's pale but she looks composed, though she's holding tightly onto Rebecca's hand. The sisters, whose relationship has always improved with distance, have really supported each other in the last few weeks. Laura's boyfriend Chad also seemed very supportive, but Laura told Nelson yesterday that they have split up. 'I realised that I preferred Bruno,' she said, enigmatically. Still, Nelson can relate to that: he prefers Bruno to most humans too.

He allows himself one sweep of the church to look for Ruth. He hasn't seen her since Italy but, according to Judy, she is planning to come to the funeral, accompanied by Cathbad. The church is too full, though; he can't see a purple cloak anywhere. Perhaps Cathbad too has succumbed to the anonymity of a black suit.

Nelson has kept in touch with Valenti, who told him that Angelo Morelli has been charged with Don Tomaso's murder. Nelson had been shocked. He would never have considered Angelo, whom he had filed away, despite the height and the good looks, under the heading 'academic'. But he had confessed, according to Valenti. 'Sing like a canary,' he said, obviously in high good spirits. 'Isn't that what you say in England?' Nelson wonders what Ruth thinks about this development. She had seemed very friendly with Morelli. In fact, Nelson had sometimes wondered if it was more than just friendship – not that he has any right to speculate in this way. Valenti has also managed to locate Samir's wife and children and the family have now been reunited. 'Samir send his thanks to you and Dottore Galloway,' said Valenti. 'He is very grateful for all that you did for him.' Nelson thinks that he did very little, but any amount of goodwill is welcome now; any suggestion that he's not a thoroughly terrible person. He wonders how the hell he is going to get through the hours, days, weeks and months ahead.

Laura stares at the flower arrangements on the altar, at the satin flowers on Tim's mother's hat, at the shoulders of his two brothers, massive in black. She mustn't cry, she tells herself. Not when Tim's family are being so brave. The youngest sister is crying though, proper tears, her body bent forward as if she's in pain. She's only young, still at school, Laura thinks. What can it feel like to lose your brother when you're so young? Laura squeezes Rebecca's hand, as if this will keep her sister safe. And they've got a brother too, now. Dear Baby Georgie. He will never know how much he has helped over the last two weeks, how he has managed to restore his family's sanity.

That was why she had finished with Chad, really. He was nice enough, but he could never mean as much to her as her family, including the canine member. Surely the whole point of a boyfriend is that they could, at some point, become the most important person in your life. A lot of things had become clear to Laura in those stretched-out seconds when Micky Webb had pointed the gun at her. She realised that she loved her family and that they loved her. She realised that motherhood can make you as brave as a lion and that nothing stands in the way of a German Shepherd who is determined to protect his family. And, for now, she'd rather be on her own than trying to assemble a pale imitation of that devotion. She will go back to university, become a teacher and hope to meet someone as nice as her dog. Dad keeps saying that she should think it over, go back to counselling and all that. Funny, Dad has never liked any of her boyfriends, and now he seems to think that Laura breaking up with Chad is a sign that she's cracking up. But it all makes perfect sense to her.

She has been seeing a post-traumatic stress counsellor called Pippa and she's been quite helpful, has taught her a few breathing exercises (though she still prefers her amino acids routine) and got her to visualise her feelings and all the rest of it. Judy has been great, too. She has kept Laura and Michelle up to date with the case against Micky Webb. They will both have to testify in court which, in her present state of mind, Laura quite welcomes. 'You might be able to give evidence via video link,' said Judy. But Laura is looking forward to staring him in the face. *You tried to kill me, but you didn't succeed.*

Her only problem is sleeping. She's tired all day, but when she goes to bed, the whole sequence starts again in her brain: the knock on the door, the gun levelled at them, the dog breaking through the window, her mother screaming with Tim in her arms. The only thing that banishes these images is putting on her headphones and watching old episodes of *Parks and Recreation*. She's on series seven now.

Walking the dog helps, too. Dad doesn't like her going out on her own, but more and more these days she is conscious of two entirely contradictory emotions: the desire never to let her family out of her sight and the desire to be alone. Walking Bruno seems to be the only way to achieve both these things. Last week she took him to Holt Country Park where, walking through the pine trees, she'd seen Cathbad, Dad's druid friend, walking his bull terrier. She hadn't recognised him at first because he wasn't wearing his cloak. In fact, in jeans and a T-shirt with chemical symbols on it, he had looked like any other ageing hippie, like half the science lecturers at uni. It was the T-shirt she had noticed first, because it showed the chemical structure for Valine, one of her favourite amino acids. She'd slowed to look at it and the man had said, 'Laura?'

She'd only met Cathbad a few times before that, and he'd once given her a dream catcher for her birthday, but it had seemed quite natural to walk with him for a while. When Cathbad had said, 'How are you feeling after last week?' she found that she didn't mind talking to him about it. In fact, she told him lots of things she had never told anyone before, including the fact that she had seen Tim's spirit leave his body in the form of a bird. Cathbad had taken this quite seriously. 'Many people believe that the soul leaves the body at the moment of death or just afterwards,' he said. 'That's why nurses in hospices will often leave the window open in a room where someone has died.'

'Our windows were broken,' said Laura, 'it could just fly straight through.'

'Bruno cleared a path for Tim,' said Cathbad. 'It's often the way.'

'Do you think I really did see it?' said Laura. 'I've been wondering if I'm going mad.'

'Never think that,' said Cathbad. 'Madness is just a word people use when they suppress their spiritual energies. You saw Tim's spirit and that should be a great comfort to you. He has flown to the other realm, where he will watch over you all.' He'd looked to the sky when he had said that and smiled. The memory of his smile is a comfort now.

Next to her, Rebecca mouths 'OK?' Laura nods. She looks up at the altar, imagining that she can see a great bird spreading its wings, as brightly coloured as the flowers below it.

Ruth and Cathbad are sitting near the back of the church. Seats are by invitation only, and the service is being relayed to the crowd outside over loudspeakers. Ruth and Cathbad are there only because of Judy, who secured them two spaces reserved for the police. They have to sit very close together and Ruth is feeling hot in her black dress. She thinks of Don Tomaso's funeral and that unbearable sense of oppression, as if the tensions in the church might snap at any minute. This is different. The overwhelming feeling in this church is simply one of sadness. Cathbad is wearing black too and, as usual when out of druid costume, he looks worryingly normal, a grey-haired man in a suit and tie, his face serious as he watches the coffin, with its patriotic covering, being carried to the front of the church. '**HERO PC DIES SAVING WOMAN**' was the headline in the *Daily Express*. Of course, Tim wasn't a PC, he was a DS, and strictly off duty at the time, but the truth never got in the way of a good headline. '**POLICE OFFICER DIES IN HOUSE SHOOTING**' – that was the more sober offering from *The Times*. All the papers were agreed though: Tim was a hero and Micky Webb was an out-and-out villain. 'The callous child killer free to walk the streets,' in the *Mail*'s words. None of the papers have guessed at the relationship between Michelle and Tim, though Nelson came in for some between-the-lines sniping: 'while her husband DCI Harry Nelson was enjoying a solo holiday in Italy . . .'

Ruth hasn't seen Nelson since she's been back, and she doesn't expect to. She has thrown herself into preparing for the new terms, her own and Kate's. Phil has been surprisingly fair and her new timetable isn't as bad as it could have been. Shona, too, is preparing for teaching, and the two of them spent a blissful day buying books in Norwich. Summer is over; it's September, the time of endings and beginnings. Ruth has visited her father, helped him in the garden and even accompanied him to church. Kate had loved going to the children's service and dressing up as John the Baptist. Ruth hopes that this was for the theatrical potential of the role alone.

Now Kate is back at school and adoring year two. 'We read proper books with chapters,' she told Ruth at the end of the first day. 'I'm on the top reading table.' Ruth is grateful for Kate's resilience and for her relentless competitiveness. Both will stand her in good stead in life.

Ruth peers at the front of the church, trying to see Nelson. She really needs glasses for distances now. All she can see is the stained-glass window, showing the Holy Spirit in the form of a dove appearing over the heads of the apostles. Below it are the trestles bearing Tim's coffin. She thinks of Don Tomaso dying on the steps of his own altar. *Saints cause a lot of trouble for the rest of us.* Don Tomaso had kept Pompeo's secret all those years; Ruth finds it hard to think that he would ever have broken the seal of the confessional, yet Angelo had killed the priest to silence him. Now, the grandmothers of Castello degli Angeli will remember Don Tomaso and bring flowers to his church. And, according to Marta, the town will soon have a new priest, a Somalian refugee. There's a symmetry there somewhere.

The other night, when she couldn't sleep, Ruth had watched Angelo's television programme, *I Segreti del Passato,* on YouTube. There were no subtitles, so she could only understand about one word in a hundred, but Angelo had smiled out of the screen at her, handsome and slightly raffish in his black shirt, extolling the wonders of the Roman Empire. *Yes, they were good at engineering, but so are all fascists.* She should have known that it was a bad sign, in Italy, to wear a black shirt. But Angelo hadn't been a fascist; his grandfather had been a partisan, one of the good guys. Even so, Pompeo Morelli had killed a man and his grandson had followed in his footsteps. Angelo has confessed, according to Valenti, and the police found the missing candlestick from the church, hidden in the well at the Roman site. Ruth remembers Angelo telling Shona that wells had a ritual as well as practical significance to the Romans. It makes sense that this is where he would conceal the murder weapon.

Elsa had known, Ruth is sure. That's why she had wept when she said that Angelo had loved Don Tomaso – not out of guilt but out of sorrow – and the knowledge had almost driven her mad. According to Marta, Elsa is still in hospital.

Ruth thinks again of Micky Webb, whom she has never met; the man responsible for the church full of police officers stifling their tears behind a collective stiff upper lip. He also had an angelic name, Michael. San Michele e Santi Angeli. But, of course, the devil was once an angel too. She thinks of her mother's gravestone in Eltham Cemetery: *At rest with the angels.*

Cathbad, who is also really called Michael, turns to her and says, 'Are you all right?'

'Yes,' says Ruth. 'It's just . . . this is so sad, isn't it? Such a waste.'

'Who knows what happens in the hereafter?' says Cathbad. 'Perhaps we will all meet again some day.'

It's a nice thought, thinks Ruth. She just wishes she could believe it – a cosmic dinner party with Tim, her mother, Erik. All the outcast dead eating and drinking together. Would it be rather a sticky affair? What if her mother were sitting next to Marilyn Monroe or a Renaissance Pope, someone of whom she would be sure to disapprove? Still, she's pretty sure that her mother would have approved of Tim, and Erik, of course, could charm anyone. Perhaps they are all up there, having a merry time, looking down on the living with benevolent pity. She tried to sell a secular version of this idea to Kate last night. 'Tim lives on because we remember him,' she had said, 'just like Grandma lives on because we remember things she said and did.'

'Grandma said I was a sunbeam once,' said Kate, who was trying to stand on her head.

'There you are then,' said Ruth, 'we'll remember her whenever we see a sunbeam.' Which is not that often, to be honest, in Norfolk.

Cathbad takes her hand. 'Courage, Ruth.' She is about to reply when the gospel choir, from Tim's mother's church, bursts into glorious life above them.

The words are written on the order of service, which has a picture of Tim in uniform on the cover. Timothy Aloysius Heathfield, 1981–2015.

> Just a closer walk with Thee
> Grant it, Jesus, is my plea
> Daily walking close to Thee
> Let it be, dear Lord, let it be.

It's a wonderful sound, full-throated and confident, the voices of people who are all convinced that, one day, they will see the face of God.

'Tim was a good man,' Cathbad had said earlier. 'A peaceful soul.'

But Ruth isn't sure whether Tim really was all that peaceful. She remembers him firing a gun once, and now he has flung himself in front of a bullet to save the woman he loved. She thinks of him more as an errant knight, a gallant figure unsuited to the modern world. What had Tennyson's Galahad said? 'My strength is as the strength of ten, Because my heart is pure.'

The choir is building up to a climax. Next to Ruth, Cathbad is singing lustily.

> When my feeble life is o'er
> Time for me will be no more
> Guide me gently, safely o'er
> To Thy kingdom's shore, to Thy shore.

Then the singers take their seats and the vicar begins with more traditional words of mourning and regret: '"I am the resurrection and the life," saith the lord.'

'What is death,' Cathbad had said once, 'but a dispersal of matter?'

Tim's body has been placed in a wooden coffin, which will soon lie in the earth, marked by a stone cross. 'The burial is a journey,' Erik used to say, 'from flesh to wood to stone.' But flesh and wood will decay; even stone will crumble. They will change, but they won't disappear. Everything changes, but nothing is destroyed.

Ruth stands and sits with the rest of the congregation, listening to Jo read the lesson in a voice which falls just on the right side of theatricality, hearing Tim's brothers recall him with heartbreaking inarticulacy: 'He was the clever one . . . We used to say he was Mum's favourite . . . He always wanted to do good in the world.' Then, finally, the choir are singing – 'When the Saints Go Marching In' – and the coffin makes its way out of the church. People applaud when it goes past, a surprising, triumphant sound in the ancient church, and one which makes Ruth want to cry all over again. She sees Tim's mother going by, smiling and wiping her eyes, the brothers, both heavyset with tattoos peeking out from the necks of their formal shirts, weeping like babies. The sisters, more composed, clasping bunches of roses. Jo, in uniform, head held high. Judy, giving Cathbad the ghost of a smile. Then Nelson and Michelle. He is grim-faced, his Italian tan only making him look more saturnine than ever, not looking left or right. Michelle is pale, dressed in loose-fitting black, her hand on Nelson's arm. How must she be feeling today? Sorrowful at the death of her lover? Happy that she has her husband by her side? How many hours has Ruth spent speculating on Michelle's emotions? But the woman is an enigma, as ever. Nelson's daughters are next, arms linked like Jane Austen sisters. Ruth has forgotten how pretty they are: Laura wearing a black dress, her blonde hair tied back in a plait; Rebecca, her dark hair loose, wearing a trouser suit. Laura catches Ruth's eye as she passes – a cool, calculating stare, as if she knows everything and forgives nothing.

Outside the church, they watch as the hearse moves away to the private burial. Onlookers throw flowers in its wake. Nelson and his family get into one of the long, black cars and are driven away. Ruth watches from the steps, enjoying the cool breeze and the sun on her face. She's glad that she's not going to the interment. It's probably a tasteless thought to have, but she's glad that she's alive.

'Come on, Ruthie,' says Cathbad. 'Let's get back to Hecate. We'll build a bonfire in the garden. Prepare some libations. Concentrate on the living.'

It's an echo of Don Tomaso, the man whom Cathbad surely would have seen as a kindred spirit. In the face of so much sadness, Ruth is grateful for Cathbad's presence, for his indomitable optimism; so much so that she decides to forgive him for 'Ruthie' and 'Hecate'. She follows him to the car park, switching on her phone, which she had muted for the service. She has one new message.

'Hi, Ruth. It's Frank. I'm back in England.'

ACKNOWLEDGEMENTS

The Liri Valley, Arpino and, of course, Monte Cassino are all real places, beautiful and rich in history. However Castello degli Angeli and its inhabitants are completely fictional. Fregellae also existed and I'm grateful to Michael Whitehead and Andrew Maxted for taking a research trip to the Archaeological Museum at Ceprano where many relics are held. There was no earthquake in Lazio in 2015 but earthquakes are, sadly, not uncommon in the region.

Thanks to Dr Linzi Harvey for the information on bones and periosteal infection. As usual, I have adapted this advice to suit the plot and so any subsequent mistakes are mine alone. Thanks also to Luisa Petruccione for checking my Italian phrases. Again, any mistakes are mine.

Every year I auction a character name to raise money for CLIC Sargent, the charity that helps teenage cancer sufferers. This year the auction was won by Linda Anthony and she features as Cathbad's old university friend. Many thanks to Linda for bidding and I need hardly say that her fictional namesake is completely imaginary – although she is married to the handsome Paolo. Thanks to Marj Maccallum and Jan Adams for taking part too.

Thanks, as ever, to my wonderful editor, Jane Wood. It's hard to believe that this is the tenth Ruth book and Jane has edited all of them, improving them greatly in the process! I'm so grateful to Jane and everyone at Quercus for their unfailing support. Thanks also to my fantastic agent, Rebecca Carter, and all at Janklow and Nesbit. I feel very lucky to work with these incredible people. Many thanks to my American agent, Kirby Kim, everyone at Houghton Mifflin Harcourt and all the publishers around the world who produce these books with such love and care.

I'd also like to thank all the readers who have enjoyed the books. I love corresponding with you on Facebook, Twitter and Instagram. You don't know how much I appreciate you, especially on days when the book seems to be going backwards. Special thanks to Clair and Anne Everitt for their support and friendship. Thanks also to all my crime-writing friends, especially the other members of the Crime Quartet: William Shaw, Lesley Thomson and Susan Wilkins. Special thanks to Lesley for Chapter 3.

Love and thanks always to my husband, Andrew, and our children, Alex and Juliet. This book is for Andy.

Elly Griffiths

2018

Read an excerpt from

THE STONE CIRCLE

A RUTH GALLOWAY MYSTERY

1

12 February 2016

DCI Nelson,

Well, here we are again. Truly our end is our beginning. That corpse you buried in your garden, has it begun to sprout? Will it bloom this year? You must have wondered whether I, too, was buried deep in the earth. Oh man of little faith. You must have known that I would rise again.

You have grown older, Harry. There is grey in your hair and you have known sadness. Joy too but that also can bring anguish. The dark nights of the soul. You could not save Scarlet but you could save the innocent who lies within the stone circle. Believe me, Harry, I want to help.

The year is turning. The shoots rise from the grass. Imbolc is here and we dance under the stars.

Go to the stone circle.

In peace.

DCI Harry Nelson pushes the letter away from him and lets out something that sounds like a groan. The other people in the briefing room – Superintendent Jo Archer, DS Dave Clough, DS Judy Johnson and DS Tanya Fuller – look at him with expressions ranging from concern to ill-concealed excitement.

'He's back,' says Clough.

'Bollocks,' says Nelson. 'He's dead.'

'Excuse me,' says Jo Archer, Super Jo to her admirers. 'Would someone mind putting me in the picture?' Jo Archer has only been at King's Lynn for a year, taking over from smooth, perma-tanned Gerald Whitcliffe. At first she seemed the embodiment of all Nelson's worst nightmares – holding meetings where everyone is supposed to talk about their feelings, instigating something unspeakable called a 'group huddle' – but recently he has come to view her with a grudging respect. But he doesn't relish the prospect of explaining the significance of the letter to his boss. She'll be far too interested, for one thing.

But no one else seems prepared to speak so Nelson says, in his flattest and most unemotional voice, 'It must have been twenty years ago now. A child went missing. Lucy Downey. And I started to get letters like this. Full of stuff about Gods and the seasons and mystical crap. Then, ten years on, we found a child's bones on the Saltmarsh. I wasn't sure how old they were so I asked Ruth – Dr Ruth Galloway – to examine them. Those bones were nothing to do with the case, they were Iron Age or something, but I got Ruth to look at the letters. She thought they might be from someone with archaeological knowledge. Anyway, as you know, we found Lucy but another child died. The killer was drowned on the marshes. The letter writer was a Norwegian professor called Erik Anderssen. He died that night too. And this,' he points at the letter on the table, 'reads like one of his.'

'It sounds like someone who knows you,' says Judy.

'Because it goes on about me being grey and sad?' says Nelson. 'Thanks a lot.'

No one says anything. The joys and sorrows of the last few years are imprinted on all of them, even Jo.

After a few seconds, Jo says, 'What's this about a stone circle?'

'God knows,' says Nelson. 'I've never heard of anything like that. There was that henge thing they found years ago but that was made of wood.'

'Wasn't the henge thing where you found the murdered child last time?' says Jo, revealing slightly more knowledge than she has hitherto admitted to.

'Yes,' says Nelson. 'It was on the beach near the Saltmarsh. Nothing's left of it now. All the timbers and suchlike are in the museum.'

'Cathbad says they should have been left where they were,' says Judy.

Judy's partner, Cathbad, is a druid who first came to the attention of the police when he protested about the removal of the henge timbers. Everyone in the room knows Cathbad so no one thinks this is worth commenting on, although Clough mutters 'of course he does'.

'This is probably nothing,' says Jo, gesturing at the letter which still lies, becalmed, in the centre of the table. 'But we should check up the stone circle thing. Nelson, can you ask Ruth if she knows anything about it?'

Once again everyone avoids Nelson's eye as he takes the letter and puts it in his pocket.

'I'll give her ring later,' he says.

'How did you know about the stone circle?' says Ruth.

Nelson is taken aback. He has retreated into his office and shut the door for this phone call and now he stands up and starts to pace the room.

'What do you mean?'

'A team from UCL were digging at the original henge site just before Christmas. They think they've found a second circle.'

'Is this one made of stone?'

'No,' says Ruth and he hears her switching into a cautious, academic tone. 'This is wood too. Bog oak like the other one. But they're calling it the stone circle because a stone cist was found in the centre.'

'What's a cist when it's at home?'

'A grave, a coffin.'

Nelson stops pacing. 'A coffin? What was inside?'

'Human skeletal matter,' says Ruth. 'Bones. We're waiting for carbon-14 results.'

Nelson knows that carbon-14 results, which tests the level of carbon left in human remains, are useful for dating but are only accurate within a range of about a hundred years.

He doesn't want to give Ruth the chance to explain this again.

'Why this sudden interest in the Bronze Age?' says Ruth.

'I've had a letter,' says Nelson.

There's a silence. Then Ruth says, her voice changing again, 'What sort of letter?'

'A bit like the ones I had before. About Lucy and Scarlet. It had some of the same stuff in it.'

'What do you mean "the same stuff"?'

'About corpses sprouting, shoots rising from the earth. Imbolc. The sort of stuff that was in Erik's letters.'

'But . . .' Nelson can hear the same reactions he witnessed in his colleagues earlier: disbelief, anger, fear. 'Erik's dead.'

'He certainly looked dead to me when we hauled him out of the water.'

'I went to his funeral. They burnt his ashes on a Viking boat.'

'So it can't be him,' says Nelson. 'It's some nutter. What worries me is that it's a nutter who knows a bit about me. The letter mentions a stone circle. That's why I rang.'

'It can't be this circle. I mean, no one knows about it.'

'Except your archaeologist pals.'

'Actually, they've got funding for a new dig,' says Ruth. 'It's starting on Monday. I was planning to drop in for a few hours in the morning.'

It's Friday now. Nelson should be getting ready to go home for the weekend. He says, 'I might drop by myself if I'm not too busy. And I'd like to show you the letter because, well, you saw the others.'

There's another tiny sliver of silence and Ruth says, 'Isn't the baby due any day now?'

'Yes,' says Nelson. 'That might change my plans.'

'Give Michelle my best,' says Ruth.

'I will,' says Nelson. He wants to say more but Ruth has gone.

2

———

Ruth reruns this conversation on a loop as she drives to collect her daughter from Sandra, her childminder. She has deliberately been keeping her interactions with Nelson to the minimum. She sees him every other Saturday when he takes Kate out for the morning but she manages to keep their conversation general and upbeat; they sound like two breakfast TV presenters handing over to the weather forecast. 'How are you?' 'Fine. Getting sick of this weather.' 'Yes, when's the sun going to come out?' But this latest development takes her back to a time that still feels dangerous and disturbing: her first meeting with Nelson, the discovery of the bones on the marsh, the hunt for the missing children, her last encounter with Erik. Over the last ten years she has, by and large, dealt with these memories by ignoring them but the discovery of the new henge in December, and now Nelson's mention of the letter, has brought everything back. She can still feel the wind on her face as she ran across the uncertain ground, half-land half-sea, knowing that a murderer was on her trail. She can hear Lucy's voice calling from deep underground. She can see the police helicopter, like a great misshapen bird, stirring the waters of the tidal pool that had taken a man's life.

Corpses sprouting, shoots rising from the earth. That's what Nelson had said, the words sounding strange in his careful policeman's voice, the vowels still recognisably Lancastrian even after twenty years down south. It had to be a coincidence and yet Ruth does not trust coincidences. One of the few opinions that she shares with Nelson.

Kate, her seven-year-old daughter, is drawing at Sandra's kitchen table and acknowledges Ruth with a friendly, yet dismissive, wave.

'I'm doing a Valentine's card,' she says.

Ruth's heart sinks. She has managed to forget that it is Valentine's Day on Sunday (VD she calls it in her head). In her opinion, the whole thing is an abomination: the explosion of bleeding hearts in the shops, the sentimental songs on the radio, the suggestion that, if you are not in possession of a single red rose by midnight, you will die alone and be eaten by your pet cat. Ruth has had her share of Valentines in the past but this doesn't lessen her distaste for the whole business. She's never had a card from Nelson; their relationship is too complicated and clandestine. *Roses are red, violets are blue. You've had my baby but I can't be with you.* She tries not to think about Nelson presenting his heavily pregnant wife with a vast bouquet (he will go for something obvious from a florist, red roses tied in ribbon and encased in cellophane). She wonders who is the intended recipient of Kate's artwork.

Ruth doesn't ask though and Kate doesn't tell her. She puts the card, which seems to show a large cat on a wall, in her school bag and goes to put her coat on. Ruth thanks Sandra and has the obligatory chat about 'thank goodness it's Friday, let's hope the rain holds off'. Then she is driving off with her daughter, away from the suburbs towards the coast.

It's dark by the time that they get home. When they get out of the car they can hear the sea breaking against the sandbar and the air smells brackish which means that the tide is coming in. Ruth's cottage is one of three at the very edge of the marshes. Her only neighbours are an itinerant Indigenous Australian poet and a London family who only visit for the occasional weekend. The road is often flooded in winter and, when it snows, you can be cut off for days. The Saltmarsh is a bird sanctuary and, in the autumn, you can see great flocks of geese coming in to hibernate, their wings pink in the sunlight as they wheel and turn. Now, in February, it's a grey place even in daylight, grey-green marshes merging with grey sky and greyer sea. But there are signs that spring is coming, snowdrops growing along the footpaths and the occasional glimpse of bright yellow marsh marigolds. Ruth has lived here for twenty years and still loves it, despite the house's increasing inconvenience for a single parent with a child whose social life now requires a separate diary.

It was on the beach at the edge of the marshes that the henge was first discovered. Ruth remembers Erik's cry of joy as he knelt on the sand before the first sunken post, the sign that they had found the sacred circle itself. She remembers the frenzied days of excavation, working desperately to remove the timbers before the sea reclaimed them. She remembers the druids protesting, the bonfires, the burning brands. It was during one of the protests that she first met Cathbad, now one of her dearest friends. And now they have found a second circle. Ruth worked on the dig in December and performed the first examination on the bones found in the stone cist. Now, during this second excavation, a lithics expert will look more closely at the stones and archaeologists will try to date the wooden posts. Ruth is looking forward to visiting the site again. It will never be the same as that first discovery though, that day, almost twenty years ago now, when the henge seemed to rise from the sea.

'Hurry up, Mum,' says Kate, becoming bored by her mother staring out to sea. 'Flint will be waiting for us.'

And, when Ruth opens the door, her large ginger cat is indeed waiting for them, managing to convey the impression that he has been doing this all day.

'He's hungry,' says Kate, picking the cat up. There was a time when he seemed almost bigger than her, even now on his hind legs he reaches up to her waist.

'There's food in his bowl,' says Ruth. But, nevertheless, she removes the perfectly edible cat food and replaces it with a fresh offering. Flint sniffs at it once and then walks away. He isn't really hungry – he has just consumed a tasty vole – but he does like to keep his human minders on their toes.

Kate switches on the television, a habit that never ceases

to annoy Ruth but she doesn't say anything. She starts to cook macaroni cheese for supper, one of her stock of boring but acceptable dishes. She tries to read the *Guardian* at the same time, propped up behind the pots which should contain tea and coffee but are actually full of mysterious objects like old raffle tickets and tiny toolkits from Christmas crackers.

She has left her phone in her bag by the front door but Kate calls to tell her it is ringing. She manages to catch the call in time. Frank.

'Hi,' he says. 'How was your day?'

'OK. Phil is more monomaniacal than ever. I'm expecting him to make his horse a senator at any minute.' Phil is Ruth's boss at the University of North Norfolk. He adores publicity and is very jealous of the fact that Ruth occasionally appears on television.

'Same here.' Frank is teaching at Cambridge. 'Geoff now continually refers to himself in the third person. "Geoff is disappointed with student outcomes" "Geoff has some important news about funding".'

Ruth laughs and takes the phone into the kitchen.

'Frank was wondering if you wanted to go out for dinner tomorrow.'

'Ruth doesn't know if she can get a babysitter. Shall we stop this now?'

'I think we should. I could come over and cook?' Frank, a single father for many years, has his own small store of recipes but at least they are different from Ruth's.

'That would be nice.' Please don't let him mention VD.

'I'll come to you for seven-ish. Is that OK?'

'Great. Kate would like to see you before she goes to bed.' Which, on a Saturday, is becoming later and later. Ruth will have to bribe her with an audio book.

'See you then.' Frank rings off but seconds later she receives a text:

Are you pleased I didn't mention Valentine's?

Ruth doesn't know whether to be pleased or slightly irritated.

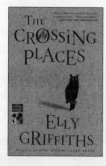

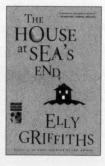

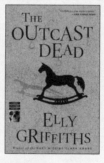